CANDLELIT REGENCY CHRISTMAS

A CANDLELIT REGENCY CHRISTMAS

LOUISE ALLEN

First Published in Great Britain 2017
By Mills & Boon, an imprint of HarperCollins*Publishers*
1 London Bridge Street, London, SE1 9GF

A CANDLELIT REGENCY CHRISTMAS © 2017 Harlequin Books S.A.

His Housekeeper's Christmas Wish © 2015 Melanie Hilton
His Christmas Countess © 2014 Melanie Hilton

ISBN: 978-0-263-93171-6

9-1117

MIX
Paper from
responsible sources
FSC® C007454

Printed and bound in Great Britain
by CPI Group (UK) Ltd, Croydon, CR0 4YY

HIS HOUSEKEEPER'S CHRISTMAS WISH

LOUISE ALLEN

For the Hartland Quay-istas –
Linda, Jenny, Lesley, Catherine and Janet –
with love

Louise Allen loves immersing herself in history. She finds landscapes and places evoke the past powerfully. Venice, Burgundy and the Greek islands are favourite destinations. Louise lives on the Norfolk coast and spends her spare time gardening, researching family history or travelling in search of inspiration. Visit her at louiseallenregency.co.uk, @LouiseRegency and janeaustenslondon.com

Chapter One

Alex Tempest did not normally trample nuns underfoot, nor anyone else, come to that. Alexander James Vernon Tempest, Viscount Weybourn, prized control, elegance, grace and athleticism—under all normal circumstances.

Skidding round corners on the ice-slick cobblestones of Ghent, however, was not normal, not in the gloomy light of the late-November afternoon with his mind occupied by thoughts of warm fires, good friends and rum punch.

The convent wall was high and unyielding when he cannoned into it. Alex found himself rebounding off the wall and into a nun, dressed all in black and grey, and blending perfectly with the cobbles. *She* was certainly yielding as she gave a small shriek of alarm and went flying, her black portmanteau bouncing away to land on the threshold of the convent's closed gates.

Alex got his feet under control. *'Ma soeur, je suis désolé. Permettez-moi.'* He held out his hand as she levered herself into a sitting position with one black mitten–covered hand. Her bonnet, plain dark grey with a black ribbon, had tipped forward over her nose, and she pushed it back to look up at him.

'I am not—'

'Hurt? Excellent.' He could only make out the oval of her face in the shadow of the bonnet's brim. She seemed to be young by her voice. 'But you are English?' He extended the other hand. Presumably there were English nuns.

'Yes. But—'

'Let's get you up off that cold ground, Sister.' Her cloak, which seemed none too thick given the weather, was black. Under it there was the hem of a dark grey robe and the toes of sensible black boots. 'Take my hands.' Probably nuns were not supposed to touch men, but he could hardly get excommunicated for adding that small sin to the far greater offence of flattening her to the ground.

With what sounded like a sigh of resignation she put her hands in his and allowed him to pull her upright. 'Ow!' She hopped on one foot, swayed dangerously and the next moment she was cradled in his arms. After all, one did not allow a lady to fall, even if she was a nun. 'Oh!'

Alex braced his feet well apart on the slippery cobbles and looked down at as much as he could see of his armful, which wasn't a great deal, what with her billowing cloak and ferocious hat brim. But even if he couldn't see any detail, there was plenty for his body to read. She *was* young. And slender. And curved. He dipped his head and inhaled the scent of her. Plain soap, wet wool and warm, rapidly chilling, woman. Rapidly chilling *nun. Pull yourself together, man. Nuns are most definitely on the forbidden list. Pity...*

'I'll ring the bell, shall I?' he offered with a jerk of his head towards the rusty iron chain hanging by the door. It looked like the sort of thing desperate criminals clung to when claiming sanctuary, although, judging by the small barred peephole set into the massive planks, the sanctuary on offer might be rather less welcoming than a prison cell. 'It seems as though you have twisted your ankle.'

Mentioning parts of the anatomy was probably another sin, but she made no attempt to smite him with a rosary, although the body that was already stiff in his arms became rigid. 'No. Absolutely not. Thank—'

'I really think I should get someone to come out.'

'—you. I am due down at the canal basin. Sister Clare is expecting me.' Crisp, polite and obviously furious with him, but constrained through charity or good manners from saying so, he concluded. An educated, refined voice masking some strain or perhaps sadness. He was used to listening to voices, hearing what was behind the actual words; anyone was who did much negotiating. *What are you hiding, little nun?*

But the polite irritation was what was on the surface. That was fair enough. He'd knocked her down; the least he could do was to take her where she wanted to go and not to where, from the way her body arched away from the door, she did not want to be. 'But you should see a doctor. What if there is a bone broken?' Alex bent, juggled his armful of cross woman as best he could, caught the handles of the portmanteau in his fingers and straightened up. 'Which canal, Sister?'

'I am going to Ostend early tomorrow morning. Sister Clare runs a small hostel for travellers down at the port here and I will spend the night with her. But I am not—'

'This way, then.' Alex began to walk downhill. 'It just so happens I can take you to a doctor on the way.'

'I do not wish to be any trouble, but—'

'You cannot walk and all the cabs have vanished as they always do when one most needs one. It is not out of my way.'

And they were not actually going to see a *doctor*, although Grant had virtually completed his medical education at Edinburgh when he'd been forced to give it up.

'Yes, but I—'

'Have no money?' Nuns were supposed to be penniless, he seemed to recall. 'Don't concern yourself about that, it is my fault you were injured and he's a friend. What is your name? I'm Viscount Weybourn.' He didn't normally lead with his rank, but he supposed a title might reassure her.

Her body shifted in his arms as she gave the sort of sigh that needed a lungful of air. She was probably mortified at being carried by a man, but if she wouldn't go back into the convent then there wasn't much option. He made another valiant, and unfamiliar, effort not to notice the feminine curves pressed against his body. He wasn't used to getting this close to women unless they both intended to take things considerably further.

'Teresa—'

'Sister Teresa.' Of course, nuns were named for saints, weren't they? 'Excellent. Here we are.' The lights of Les Quatre Éléments glowed though the gathering dusk and he headed for them like a mariner spying a safe, familiar harbour.

'An *inn*? Lord Wey—'

'A very respectable inn,' Alex assured her as he shouldered through the front door into the light and heat and bustle of a well-run hostelry. 'Gaston!'

'Milord Weybourn.' The innkeeper came hurrying out of the back. 'How good to see you again, milord. The other gentlemen are in your usual private parlour.'

'Thank you, Gaston.' Alex headed for the door on the

right. 'And some tea? Coffee? What would you like, Sister Teresa?'

'*Gentlemen? Private* parlour? Lord Weybourn, put me down this—'

'Tea,' he ordered for her. Tea was soothing, wasn't it? His little nun needed soothing; she was beginning to wriggle in agitation like a ruffled hen and, *hell*, if she didn't stop she wasn't the only one who'd need it. Soothing, that was, not tea. He really needed a woman. How long had it been? A month? That was far too long.

Alex kicked the door closed behind him and leaned back against it for a moment while he sought for his usual composure. Nuns apparently did not wear corsets. The discovery was seriously unsettling. The soft weight of a small breast against his forearm was *damnably* unsettling. He was reacting like a green youth and he didn't like the feeling.

'My dear Alex, why the drama?' Crispin de Feaux lowered the document he was studying, stood up and regarded the scene in the doorway with cool detachment. Possibly if he had erupted into the room pursued by sword-wielding soldiery Cris might have revealed some emotion, but Alex rather doubted it. 'Have you taken to abducting nuns?'

'Nuns? Surely not?' Over by the fireplace Grant Rivers swung his boots down from the fender and stood, too, dragging one hand through his hair. Characteristically he looked responsible and concerned.

'What do you bet?' Gabriel Stone dropped a handful of dice with a clatter and lounged to his feet. 'Although it hardly seems Alex's style. High-fliers, now…'

Alex narrowed his eyes, daring him to continue

stripping her with that insolent gaze. Gabe grinned and slumped back into his chair.

'I slipped on the ice and knocked Sister Teresa to the ground, injuring her ankle in the process.' Alex pushed away from the door and carried his burden over to the settle by the fire. 'I thought you should check it for her, Grant.'

'There you are, Sister Teresa, you're in safe hands now and tea is on the way.' The infuriating creature deposited Tess on the settee opposite the handsome brown-haired man and sketched a bow. 'This is Grantham Rivers, a very handy man with a sprained ankle.' She caught the grin Lord Weybourn sent the doctor and the doctor's eye roll in return as his friend turned on his heel and sauntered over to the other two men.

'I am not—'

'A nun. I know.' The doctor sat down. He was polite, but didn't seem too happy. 'Unlike Alex, I know that nuns wear wimples and do not trot around the streets alone.'

'Do none of you allow a woman to finish a sentence?' Tess demanded. She had gone beyond miserable since her interview with Mother Superior a week ago had knocked all her certainties into utter chaos. She'd forced herself into the same state of stoical, unhappy acceptance that had kept her sane, somehow, all those years ago when Mama and Papa had died. Now the shock of being hurled off her feet had sent her into an unfamiliar mood of irritation.

Or possibly this was the effect men had on women all the time. As her association with the creatures since the age of thirteen had been limited to the priest, an aged gardener and occasional encounters with tradesmen, this could well be the case. For the first time in her life celibacy began to sound appealing. But now she was alone with four of them, although they *seemed* safe enough, sober and respectful.

'Normally, yes, we have much better manners. Alex is doubtless disconcerted at his very unusual clumsiness in felling you to the ground, but I have no excuse. How should I address you, ma'am?'

'Miss Ellery. Tess Ellery, Doctor.'

'Not doctor. Plain Mr Grantham Rivers. But I almost completed my medical training at Edinburgh, so I am quite safe to be let loose on minor injuries, Miss Ellery.' He regarded her as she sat there looking, she had no doubt, like a somewhat battered crow. 'May I take your cloak and bonnet? I will need you to remove your shoe and stocking so I can examine your ankle. Shall I send for a maid to attend you?'

He looked serious and respectable. Considering that she had not shed so much as a glove in male company for years, Tess wondered why she was not more flustered. Perhaps being knocked to the ground and then carried by a tall, strong, over-masterful aristocrat might have reduced her capacity for flusterment. Was that a word? More likely the fact that her world was so out of kilter accounted for it.

'Miss Ellery?' Mr Rivers was waiting patiently. She searched for normal courtesy and some poise, found a smile and felt it freeze on her lips as she met his eyes. He had the saddest eyes she had ever seen. It was like gazing into the hell of someone's private grief, and staring felt as intrusive and unmannerly as gawping at mourners at a funeral.

'No, no maid. I can manage, thank you.' Tess made a

business of her bonnet ribbon and cloak clasp and murmured her thanks. He laid the garments at the end of the settle, then went to stand with his back to her, shielding her from the room as she managed her laces and untied her garter to roll down her stocking. 'I cannot get my boot off.'

'The ankle is swelling.' Mr Rivers came and knelt down in front of her. 'Let me see if I can remove it without cutting the leather.'

'Please.' They were her only pair of boots.

'Have you any other injuries?' He bent over her foot, working the boot off with gentle wiggles. 'You didn't bang your head, or put out your hand and hurt your wrist?'

'No, only my ankle. It turned over as I fell.' Removing the boot hurt, despite his care, so Tess looked over his head at the other three men for distraction. Such a strange quartet. Mr Rivers with his tragic eyes, gentle hands and handsome profile. Her rescuer, Lord Weybourn, tall, elegant and relaxed. Deceptively relaxed, given the ease with which he had lifted and carried her. The blond icicle who looked like a cross between an archangel and a hanging judge and the lounging dice player who seemed more suited to a hedge tavern frequented by footpads than a respectable inn in the company of gentlemen.

Yes, an unlikely combination of friends and yet they were so easy together. Like brothers, she supposed. *Family*.

Lord Weybourn met her gaze and lifted one slanting eyebrow.

'Ah, that made you jump, sorry.' Mr Rivers's fingers were probing and flexing. 'Tell me where it hurts. Here? When I do this? Can you wriggle your toes? Excellent. And point your foot? No, stop if it is painful.'

He certainly seemed to know what he was doing. He

would bind it up for her and Lord Weybourn must find her some conveyance, given that the collision was all his fault and she wouldn't be able to get her boot laced again over a bandage. None of these men were behaving in a way that made her uneasy. There were no leers or winks, no suggestive remarks. Tess relaxed a little more and decided she could trust her judgement that she was safe here.

His lordship was half sitting on the edge of the table, laughing at something the dice player had said. Now he had shed his hat and greatcoat she could see that the impression of elegance could be applied to his clothing as much as to his manner. Ten years in a nunnery did not do much for her appreciation of male fashion, but even she could see that what he wore had been crafted from expensive fabrics by a master who could sculpt fabric around broad shoulders and long, muscular legs, and that whoever looked after his linen was a perfectionist.

Unlike his friends, the viscount wasn't conventionally good looking, Tess thought critically as Mr Rivers rested her foot on a stool and stood up, murmuring about cold compresses and bandages. Mr Rivers was the image of the perfect English gentleman: strong bones, straight nose, thick, glossy dark brown hair and those tragic, beautiful green eyes. The blond icicle belonged in a church's stained-glass window, giving impressionable girls in the congregation palpitations of mixed desire and terror at the thought of his blue eyes turning on them or that sculpted mouth opening on some killing rebuke. Even the dice player with his shock of black hair, insolent gypsy-dark eyes and broad shoulders had the attractiveness of a male animal in its prime.

But Lord Weybourn was different. Very masculine, of

course... Oh, yes. She gave a little shiver as she recalled how easily he had lifted and carried her. And he had a touch of something dangerously other-worldly about him. His hair was dark blond, his nose was thin, his cheekbones pronounced. His eyes, under winging dark brows, were, she guessed, hazel and his chin was firm.

It was his mouth, she decided, focusing on that feature. It was mobile and kept drifting upwards into a half smile as though his thoughts were pleasant, but mysterious and, in some way, dangerous. In fact, she decided, he looked like a particularly well-dressed supernatural creature, if such things ever reached a good six feet in height with shoulders in proportion—one who ruled over forests where the shadows were dark and wolves lurked...

He glanced across at her again and stood up, which snapped her out of musings that probably had something to do with Sister Moira's *frisson*-inducing tales of Gothic terror, told at recreation time when Mother Superior was not listening. Only Sister Moira's fantasy beings never provoked feelings of...

'Is Rivers hurting you?' Lord Weybourn came over and hitched himself onto the table opposite. His boots were beautiful, she thought, watching one swinging idly to and fro. It was safer than meeting his gaze. 'I haven't managed to break your ankle, have I?'

'No, you haven't, fortunately.' Mr Rivers came back and hunkered down by her feet. 'This will be cold,' he warned as he draped a dripping cloth over her ankle. 'I'll bandage it up after you've had your tea and a rest.'

'This seems a very pleasant inn,' she said for want of a neutral topic. Conversation with men was a novelty. 'Do you use this place frequently?'

'From a long way back,' Lord Weybourn said. 'Even

when the war was on some of us would slip in and out in various guises. Very handy, Les Quatre Éléments.' He grinned. 'We called ourselves the Four Elementals as our names fit so well.'

'Elementals? I know the four elements—air, water, fire and earth. So which are you?'

'Alex Tempest—air.'

'So you are water, Mr Rivers? That works well with your soothing medical skills.'

He gave a half bow in acknowledgement. 'Cris is de Feaux, hence the French *feu* for fire.'

'Of course.' She could easily imagine the blond icicle as an archangel with a burning sword. 'And earth?'

'Gabriel Stone is nothing if not earthy.' Lord Weybourn titled his head towards the dice player, who was playing left hand against right hand, dark brows lowered in a scowl of concentration.

Mr Rivers changed the cold cloth on her ankle again. Tess smiled her thanks, then forgot both injury and elements as a maid deposited a laden tray on the settle beside her. Tea, she had expected, but not pastries dripping with honey, little cakes and dainty iced biscuits. Lord Weybourn stole a biscuit and went back to the others.

'I should—'

'Eat up. Sorry,' Grant Rivers said. 'Interrupting you again.'

'I fear I will not know when to stop.' Vegetable soup and wholemeal bread had made a warming midday meal, but they had tasted, as always, of practical, frugal worthiness and sat lumpily on a stomach fluttering with nerves. There was nothing worthy about the plate beside her. Mr Rivers simply nodded and strolled off to join his friends, leaving her to sip her tea—with sugar!—while she contemplated the temptation. Perhaps just one of each? To leave them untouched would be discourteous.

Half an hour later Tess licked her fingers, feeling slightly, deliciously queasy as she contemplated a plate empty of all but crumbs and a smear of cream.

Mr Rivers strolled back and shifted the tray without so much as a smirk or a frown for her greed. 'I'll strap up your ankle now. Let's put this blanket over your knees and you can take a nap when I'm done. You were chilled and a little bit shocked, I suspect. A rest will do no harm.'

He was almost a doctor, he knew what he was talking about and she supposed there was no great hurry, provided she was with Sister Clare for the evening meal. And this was…interesting. Watching men, relaxed and friendly together, was interesting. Being warm and full of delicious sweets was indulgent. A mild sensation of naughtiness, of playing truant, was definitely intriguing. She knew she shouldn't be here, but they all seemed so… harmless? Wrong word. Perhaps it was her innocence deceiving her…

Tess blinked, on the verge of a yawn. Last night had been cold and her head too full of churning thoughts, hopes and worries for her to sleep much. Mr Rivers was right—a little nap would set her up for an evening of doling out stew to humble travellers who would otherwise be huddled in their cloaks on benches for the night. Then she would have to try to sleep on a hard bed in a chilly cell alongside Sister Clare's notorious snores before an even chillier dawn start. Sister Moira always said those snores counted as a penance in themselves, so they would be enough to pay for the consumption of a plate of pastries, Tess decided, as she snugged down in the corner of the settle and let the men's voices and laughter wash over her. Just a little nap.

'Mmm?' *Citrus cologne, starched linen...* She was being lifted again by Lord Weybourn. It seemed natural to turn her head into his shoulder, inhale the interesting masculine scent of him.

'You will get a crick in your neck in that corner, little nun. And we're becoming noisy. There's a nice quiet room just here, you can rest.'

That sounded so good. 'Sister Clare...'

'I remember. Sister Clare, down at the canal dock. Boat to Ostend in the morning.'

What is all this nonsense the sisters tell us about men? Anyone would think they were all ravening beasts... These four are kind and reliable and safe. And the mattress was soft when he laid her down and the covers so warm and light. 'Thank you,' Tess murmured as she drifted off again.

'My pleasure, little nun.' Then the door closed and all was quiet.

Chapter Two

Tess swum up out of sleep, deliciously warm and with a definite need for the chamber pot. *Too much tea.* 'Ouch!' Her ankle gave a stab of pain as she hopped across to the screen in the corner, made herself comfortable and then hopped back. It was still light, so she could not have slept long. In fact, it was *very* light. She pulled aside the curtain and stared out at a corner of the inn yard with a maid bustling past with a basket of laundry and a stable boy lugging a bucket of water. It was unmistakably morning.

She hobbled to the door, flung it open. The four men were still around the table. The dice player and the blond icicle were playing cards with the air of gamblers who could continue for another twelve hours if necessary. Mr Rivers was pouring ale into a tankard with one hand while holding a bread roll bulging with ham in the other. And Lord Weybourn, who she now realised was the most unreliable, infuriating man—regardless of her pulse quickening simply at the sight of him—was fast asleep, his chair tipped on its back legs against a pillar, his booted feet on the table amidst a litter of playing cards.

The fact that he was managing to sleep without snoring, with his mouth mostly closed and his clothing unrumpled, only added fuel to the fire.

'Lord Weybourn!'

'Humph?' He jerked awake and Tess winced at the thump his head made against the pillar. 'Ouch.'

The other men stood up. 'Miss Ellery. Good morning. Did you sleep well?' Mr Rivers asked.

'I told him. I told him I had to be down at the canal port. I told him the boat left very early this morning.' She jerked her head towards Lord Weybourn, too cross to look at him.

'It *is* early morning.' He got to his feet and she could not help but notice that he did not look as though he had slept in his clothes. He was as sleek and self-possessed as a panther. What *she* looked like she shuddered to think.

Tess batted an errant lock of hair out of her eyes. 'What time is it?'

The blond icicle glanced at the mantelshelf clock. 'Just past nine.'

'That isn't *early*, that is almost half the morning gone.' Tess hopped to the nearest chair and sat down. 'I have missed the boat.'

'You can buy a ticket on the next one. They are frequent enough,' the viscount said, stealing Mr Rivers's unguarded tankard. The ale slid down in a long swallow, making his Adam's apple move. His neck was strapped with muscle.

'I do not have any money,' Tess said through gritted teeth, averting her eyes from so much blatant masculinity. If she knew any swear words this would be an excellent opportunity to use them. But she did not. Strange that she had never felt the lack before. 'I have a ticket for the boat that left at four o'clock. It arrives in Ostend with just enough time to catch the ship across the Channel. The ship that I have another ticket for. I have tickets, useless tickets. I have no money and I cannot go back to the convent and ask for more. I cannot afford to repay it,' she added bleakly.

'Ah. No money?' Lord Weybourn said with that faint, infuriating smile. 'I understand your agitation.'

'I am not *agitated*.' Agitation was not permitted in the convent. 'I am annoyed. *You* knocked me down, my lord. *You* brought me here and let me sleep. *You* promised to wake me in time for the boat. Therefore this is now your problem to resolve.' She folded her hands in her lap, straightened her back and gave him the look that Mother Superior employed to extract the admission of sins, major and minor. Words were usually not necessary.

She should have known he would have an answer. 'Simple. Grant and I are going to Ostend by carriage later today. You come with us and I will buy you a boat ticket when we get there.'

This was what Sister Luke would describe as the Primrose Path leading directly to Temptation. With a capital *T*. And probably Sin. Capital *S*. No wonder they said it was a straight and easy road. Being carried by a strong and attractive man, eating delicious pastries, sleeping— next door to four men—on a blissfully soft bed. All undoubtedly wicked.

After that, how could travelling in a carriage with two gentlemen for a day make things any worse? She wasn't sure she trusted Lord Weybourn's slanting smile, but Mr Rivers seemed eminently reliable.

'Thank you, my lord. That will be very satisfactory.' It was certain to be a very comfortable carriage, for none of these men, even the rumpled dice player, looked as though they stinted on their personal comfort. She found she was smiling, then stopped when no one leaped to their feet and started to bustle around making preparations. 'When do we start and how long will it take us?'

'Seven and a half, eight hours.' *Finally*, Lord Weybourn got to his feet.

'But we will arrive after dark. I do not think the ships sail in the dark, do they?'

'We are not jolting over muddy roads all day and then getting straight on board, whether a ship is sailing or not.' The viscount strolled across to one of the other doors, opened it and shouted, 'Gaston!'

'They do sail at night and I am taking one to Leith at nine this evening,' Mr Rivers remarked. 'But I am in haste, you'll do better to take the opportunity to rest, Miss Ellery.'

'I am also in haste,' she stated.

Lord Weybourn turned from the door. 'Do nuns hurry?'

'Certainly. And you know perfectly well that I am not a nun, my lord.' The maddening creature refused to be chastened by her reproofs, which showed either arrogance, levity or the hide of an ox. Probably all three. 'I am expected at the London house of the Order.'

'The Channel crossing is notoriously uncertain for weather and timing. They will not be expecting you for a day or so either way. Unless someone is at death's door?' He raised an interrogative brow. Tess shook her head. 'There, then. Arrive rested and, hopefully, not hobbling. Always a good thing to be at one's best when making an entrance. Breakfast is on its way.'

He sauntered out, lean, elegant, assured. Tess's fingers itched with a sinful inclination to violence.

'You might as well contemplate swatting a fly, Miss Ellery,' the blond icicle remarked. Apparently her face betrayed her feelings graphically. He inclined his head in a graceful almost bow. 'Crispin de Feaux, Marquess of Avenmore, at your service. Rivers you know.' He gestured towards the third man. 'This, improbable as it might seem, is not the local highwayman, but Gabriel Stone, Earl of Edenbridge.'

Lord Edenbridge stood, swept her an extravagant courtesy, then collapsed back into his chair. 'Enchanted, Miss Ellery.' His cards appeared to enchant him more.

'I'll send for some hot water for you.' Mr Rivers held the bedchamber door open. 'You will feel much better after a wash and some breakfast, believe me, Miss Ellery.'

Tess thanked him, curtsied as best she could to all three men and sat down on the bed to await the water. It wasn't their fault. She knew just who to blame, but because she was a lady—or, rather, had been raised to have the manners of one—she would bite her tongue and do her best to act with grace. Somehow. As for breakfast at this hour—why, it was going to be almost noon by the time it was finished at this rate.

As she had suspected, the carriage proved to be very comfortable. 'I keep this and my own horses over here,' Lord Weybourn explained when Tess exclaimed in pleasure at the soft seats and the padded interior. 'Job horses and hired vehicles are unreliable.'

'You come to the Continent frequently, my lord?' Tess settled snugly into one corner and submitted to Mr Rivers arranging her legs along the seat and covering them with a rug. A hot brick wrapped in flannel was tucked in, too. Such luxury. She would enjoy what good things this journey had to offer, especially as the future seemed unlikely to hold much in the way of elegant coach travel.

'We all do.' Lord Weybourn folded his length into an opposite corner while Mr Rivers took the other. They had given her the best, forward-facing position, she noted. 'Cris—Lord Avenmore—is a diplomat and spends half his time at the Congress and half doing mysterious things about the place. Gabe enjoys both travelling and fleecing any gamester foolish enough to cut cards with him and Grant here buys horses.'

'I have a stud,' Mr Rivers explained. 'I import some of the more unusual Continental breeds from time to time.'

'And you, my lord?'

'Alex.' He gave her that slanting, wicked smile. 'I will feel that you have not forgiven me if you *my lord* me from here to London.'

It seemed wrong, but perhaps that degree of informality was commonplace amongst aristocrats. 'Very well, although Alex Tempest sounds more like a pirate than a viscount.'

Mr Rivers snorted. 'That's what he is. He scours the Continent in search of loot and buried treasure.'

'Art and antiquities, my dear Grant.' Alex grinned. 'Certainly nothing buried. Can you imagine me with a shovel?'

Tess noted the flex of muscles under the form-fitting tailoring of his coat. Perhaps it was not achieved by digging holes, but the viscount was keeping exceptionally fit somehow. *No*, she thought, *not a shovel, but I can imagine you with a sword.*

'I am a connoisseur, a truffle hound through the wilderness of a Continent after a great war.'

'Poseur,' Mr Rivers said.

'Of course.' Alex's ready agreement was disarmingly frank. 'I do have my reputation to maintain.'

'But forgive me,' Tess ventured, 'is that not business? I thought it was not acceptable for aristocrats to engage in trade.' And perhaps it was not acceptable to mention it at all.

'Social death,' Grant Rivers agreed. 'So those of us who cannot rely upon family money maintain a polite fiction. I keep a stud for my own amusement and profit and sell to acquaintances as a favour when they beg to share in a winning bloodline. Alex here is approached by those with more money than taste. Gentlemen are so very grateful when he puts them in the way of acquiring beautiful, rare objects from his collection to enhance their status or their newly grand houses. Naturally he cannot be out of pocket in these acts of mercy. Gabe is a gambler, which is perfectly *au fait*. It is strange that he rarely loses, which is the norm, but you can't hold that against a man unless you catch him cheating.'

'And does he?'

'He has the devil's own luck, the brain of a mathematician and the willpower to know when to fold. And he would kill anyone who suggested he fuzzes the cards,' Alex explained. 'And before you ask, Cris is the only one of us who has come into his title. The rest of us are merely heirs in waiting. He's a genuine marquess.

'And you, little nun? Given that we are being so frank between friends.'

He knew perfectly well that she was not a nun, but perhaps if she ignored the teasing he would stop it. 'I, on the contrary, have not a guinea to my name, save what Mother Superior gave me for food and the stagecoach fare in England.' Tess managed a bright smile, as though this was merely amusing. It had been quite irrelevant until Mother Superior's *little discussion* a week ago.

Dear Teresa had been with them for ten years, five since the death of her aunt, Sister Boniface. She had steadfastly declined to convert from her childhood Anglicanism, so, naturally, she had no future with the convent as a nun. Equally obviously, she could not go to her, er...*connections* in England. And then Mother Superior had explained why.

Teresa was twenty-three now, so what did she intend to do with her life? she had asked while Tess's understanding of who and what she was tumbled around her ears.

I must have looked completely witless, Tess thought as she gazed out of the carriage window at the sodden countryside. She had been teaching the little ones, the orphans like herself, but that apparently had been merely a stop-gap until she was an adult. And, she suspected now she had a chance to think about it, until Mother Superior was convinced no conversion was likely.

But it was all right; even if there was no money left from the funds Papa had sent to her aunt, she would manage, somehow. The dream of a family in England, people who might forgive and forget what Mama and Papa had done, had evaporated. She would not repine and she would try not to think about it. She could work hard and, goodness knew, she wasn't used to luxury.

Heavy clouds rolled across the sky, making it dark enough outside for Tess to glimpse her own reflection in the glass. *What a dismal Dora! This bonnet doesn't help*. She sat up straighter, fixed a look of bright interest on her face and tried to think positive thoughts.

What was wrong with the little nun? Alex watched her from beneath half-closed lids. Beside him Grant had dropped off to sleep, and he was weary himself after a hard night of cards, brandy and talk, but something about the woman opposite kept him awake. If she was not a nun, what was she doing going to a convent, dressed like a wet Sunday morning in November? Her accent was well bred. Her manners—when she was not ripping up at him—were correct and she was obviously a lady.

A mystery, in fact. As a rule Alex enjoyed mysteries, especially mysterious ladies, but this one was not happy and that put a damper on enjoyable speculation. There was more to it than her sprained ankle and irritation over missed boats, he was certain. Tess was putting a brave face on things whenever she remembered to. No coward, his little nun.

Alex grinned at the thought of *his* nun. The *nunneries* he was acquainted with were very different establishments. She raised one slim, arching dark brow.

'Comfortable, Miss Ellery?'

'Exceedingly, thank you, my lord…Alex.' Yes, that smile was definitely brave, but assumed.

'Ankle hurting?'

'No, Mr Rivers has worked wonders and there is no pain unless I put weight on it. I am sure it is only a mild sprain.' She lapsed into silence again, apparently not finding that awkward. No doubt chatter was discouraged in a nunnery.

'So what will you be doing in London? Making your come-out?'

She had taken her bonnet off and he remembered how that soft, dark brown hair had felt against his cheek when he had lifted her to carry her to her bed. It was severely braided and pinned up now, just as it had been last night, and he wondered what it would look like down. The thought made him shift uncomfortably in his seat and he wrenched his mind away from long lashes against a pale cheek flushed with rose and the impact of a pair of dark blue eyes.

His... No, *Miss Ellery* laughed, the first sound of amusement he had heard from her, albeit with an edge to it. Her hand shot up to cover her mouth, which was a pity because it was a pretty mouth and it was prettier still when curved.

'My come-out? Hardly. No, I will stay at the London house until the Mother Superior there finds me position as a governess or a companion.'

'With a Roman Catholic family?' That might take a while, there were not that many, not of the class to be employing well-bred young females of her type. Rich merchants were a possibility, he supposed.

'No. Not only am I not a nun, I am also an Anglican.'

'Then, what the bl—? What on earth are you doing in a nunnery?'

'It is a long story.' She folded her hands neatly in her lap and seemed to feel that ended the discussion.

'It is a long journey,' he countered. 'Entertain me with your tale, please, Miss Ellery.'

'Very well.' She did not look enthusiastic. 'I will make it as concise as possible. My father's elder sister, Beatrice, converted to Catholicism against the violent disapproval of her parents and ran away to Belgium to join an order of nuns.

'But Papa, after he came of age, started writing to her. My parents enjoyed travelling, even though there was a war on, and besides, it was often cheaper to live on the Continent.' She bit her lip and her gaze slid away from his. *A prevarication?* 'So just after my thirteenth birthday we were in Belgium and Papa decided to visit my aunt.'

'And that was when?' *How old is she? Twenty?* Alex tried to recall what was happening seven years past.

'Ten years ago. I am twenty-three,' Tess admitted with a frankness no other unmarried lady of his acquaintance would have employed.

'1809.' Alex delved back in his memory. He had been seventeen, half tempted by the army, finally deciding against it for the very good reason his father would probably have had a stroke with the shock of his son and heir doing something his parent approved of for the first time in his life. 'Most of the action was towards the east at that time, I seem to recall.'

'I think so.' Tess bit her lower lip in thought and Alex crossed his legs again. Damn it, the girl—woman—was a drab little peahen for all the rainwater-washed complexion and the pretty eyes. What was the matter with him? 'Anyway, it was considered safe enough. We arrived in Ghent and Papa visited the convent and was allowed to see my aunt, who was Sister Boniface by then. But there was an epidemic of cholera in the city and both Mama and Papa… They both died.'

She became so still and silent Alex wondered if she had finished, but eventually, with a little movement, as though shaking raindrops off her shoulders, she gathered herself. 'When Papa realised how serious it was he sent me to my aunt with all the money he had. I have lived there ever since, but now I do not want to become a nun and the money has run out, paying for my keep, so I am ready to make my own way in the world.'

'But your grandparents, your aunts and uncles—surely you have living relatives? Cousins?'

'There is no one I could go to.'

There had to be, surely? Her gaze slid away from his again and Tess stared out of the window. There was some story here, something she wasn't telling him, and she was too honest to lie. Alex bit his tongue on the questions. It was no concern of his. 'And the convent was not for you?'

Tess shook her head. 'I always knew I was not cut out to be a nun.' She managed a very creditable smile.

There must be relatives somewhere, Alex thought, forcing back the query. Perhaps the runaway aunt had caused the rift, which was hard on Tess. He understood what it was like to be rejected, but he was a man with money and independence, and these days, power of his own. He knew how to hit back and he'd spent more than ten years doing just that. This was a sheltered, penniless young woman.

'Now I know you better I can tell that you're not suitable for the cloister,' he drawled, intent on teasing her out of introspection. 'Too much of a temper, for one thing.'

Tess blushed, but did not deny the accusation. 'It is something I try to overcome. You did provoke me excessively, you must admit, although I should not make excuses.'

'Go on, blame me, I have a broad enough back.' Alex smiled at her and noticed how that made her drop her gaze. *Not at all used to men. A total innocent with no idea how to flirt. Behave yourself, Tempest.* But she was a charming novelty.

'I will spend December and perhaps January at the

London convent, I expect. I do not imagine anyone will be looking to employ a governess or a companion just now.' She fiddled with the fringe on the edge of the rug. 'A pity, because it would be wonderful to spend Christmas with a family. But still, it is always a happy season wherever one is.'

'Is it?' Alex tried to recall the last Christmas he had spent with his family. He had been almost eighteen. His parents had not been speaking to each other, his batty great-aunt had managed to set the breakfast room on fire, his younger siblings had argued incessantly and at dinner on Christmas Day his father had finally, unforgivably, lost his temper with Alex.

There are some things that a mature man might laugh off or shrug aside as the frustrated outpourings of a short-tempered parent. But they are usually not things that a sensitive seventeen-year-old can accept with any grace or humour. Or forgive. Not when they led to tragedy.

Alex had left the table, packed his bags, gone straight back to Oxford and stayed there, taking care to extract every penny of his allowance from the bank before his father thought to stop it. When the news had reached him of just what his father's outburst had unleashed he'd settled down, with care and much thought, to convince his father that he was exactly what he had accused him of being, while at the same time living his life the way he wanted to.

'You will be going home for Christmas, surely?' Tess asked.

Alex realised he must have been silent for quite some time. 'I am going back to my own home, certainly. But not to the family house and most certainly not for Christmas.'

'I am sorry,' she said with every sign of distress on his behalf.

Beside him Grant gave an inelegant snort and woke up. 'Christmas? Never say you're going back to Tempeston, Alex?'

'Lord, no.' Alex shuddered. 'I will do what I always do and hole up in great comfort with good wine, excellent food, brandy, a pile of books and a roaring fire until the rest of humanity finishes with its annual bout of plum pudding–fuelled sentimentality and returns to normal. What about you?'

'I promised to call on Whittaker. I was with his brother when he died in Salzburg, if you recall. He lives just outside Edinburgh and I said I'd go and see him as soon as I was back in Britain.' Grant shifted his long legs into a more comfortable position. 'Can't stay too long, though, I'll go straight from there to my grandfather in Northumberland.'

'How is he?' Grant was the old man's heir and he'd be a viscount in his own right when he went, given that his father had died years ago.

'He's frail.' Grant was curt. He was fond of his grandfather, Alex thought with an unwelcome twinge of envy.

'He will be helped by your company at Christmas,' Tess said warmly.

'He'd be glad to see Grant at any time.' Alex managed not to snap the words. 'What is it about Christmas that produces this nonsense anyway?'

It was meant as a rhetorical question, but Tess stared at him as though he had declared that it rained upwards. 'You are funning, surely?' When he shook his head she announced, 'Then I will remind you, although I cannot truly believe you are really such a cynic.' She paused, as though to collect her thoughts, then opened her mouth. 'Well, first of all there is…'

Please, no, Alex thought despairingly. If there was anything as bad as Christmas it was someone who was an enthusiast about it.

'Evergreens…' the confounded chit began. 'Cutting them and…'

Alex glowered.

Chapter Three

'And it is so cold, but that is part of the fun, everyone wrapped up and the snow crunching underfoot, and that gorgeous smell of pines.' Tess closed her eyes, the better to recall it. Memories of those wonderful English Christmases from many years ago, before Papa had said they must go abroad. There hadn't been much money and it had been a different village each year.

She had never asked why they kept moving; she had simply taken it for granted, as children do. Now, from an adult perspective, she realised they had probably been keeping one step ahead of recognition and scandal and that was why they'd left the country—the Continent was cheaper and there would be less gossip.

But we were happy, she thought, recalling snowball fights at Christmas and unconditional love all the year round. When she opened her eyes again Alex Tempest's mouth was pursed as though he had bitten a wasp. *Grumpy man.*

She pressed on, ignoring him, all the precious memories bubbling up, unstoppable. 'And planning what presents you can give your friends and finding them or making them. That's almost better than receiving gifts. There's all the fun of hiding them away and wrapping them up and watching the other person's face when they try to guess what's in the parcel.'

Mr Rivers was smiling, even though his eyes were still sad. Tess smiled back. 'And all the food to prepare. And church on Christmas Eve and the bells ringing out and being too excited to sleep afterwards and yet, somehow, you do.'

Lord Weybourn, *Alex*, looked as though he was in pain now. What was the matter with the man?

'Have you done your Christmas shopping already, Miss Ellery?' Mr Rivers asked. 'You seem to be someone who would plan ahead.'

'I had to leave my gifts with the nuns to give out. I sewed most of them and my stitchery is not of the neatest.' She wished she believed the cliché about it being the thought that counts, but she could imagine Sister Monica's expression when she saw the lumpy seams on her pen wiper. There was never any danger of Tess being asked to join the group who embroidered fine linen for sale, or made vestments for Ghent's churches.

'But next year I will have wages and I will be able to send gifts I have purchased.' There, another positive thing about this frightening new life that lay ahead of her. She had been saving them up and had almost reached ten. *Living with a family. A family.* The word felt warm and round, like the taste of plum pudding or the scent of roses on an August afternoon.

Tess left the thought reluctantly and pressed on with her mental list. *A room of my own. Being able to wear colours. Interesting food. Warmth. London to explore on my afternoons off. Wages. Control of my own destiny.*

She suspected that the last of those might prove illusionary. How much freedom would a governess's or companion's wage buy her? She glanced at Alex, but his eyes were closed and he was doing a very creditable imitation of a man asleep. He really did not enjoy Christmas, it seemed. How strange.

Mr Rivers continued to make polite conversation and she responded as the light drew in and the wintery dusk fell. Finally, when her stomach was growling, the carriage clattered into an inn yard and, as the groom opened the door, she caught a salty tang on the cold breeze.

'Ostend. Wake up, Alex. You sleep like a cat, you idle devil.' Grant Rivers prodded his friend in the ribs. 'May I take the carriage on down to the docks? You'll be staying here the night, I'm guessing, and I'll send it right back.'

Alex opened one eye. 'Yes, certainly have it. Higgs, unload my luggage and Miss Ellery's, then take Mr Rivers to find his ship.' He uncurled his long body from the seat and held out his hand to Tess. 'If you can shuffle along to the end of the seat, I will lift you down.'

She was in his arms before she thought to protest. 'But I must find a ship, my lord.'

'Tomorrow. We will both take a ship tomorrow. Now you need dinner, a hot bath and a comfortable room for the night. Now, don't wriggle or I'll drop you.'

'But—'

'Goodbye, Miss Ellery.' Grant Rivers was climbing back into the carriage and men were carrying a pile of beautiful leather luggage, topped with her scuffed black portmanteau, towards the open inn door. 'Safe voyage and I hope you soon find a congenial employer in London.' He pulled the door shut and leaned out of the window. 'Take care, Alex.'

'And you.' Alex freed one hand and clasped his friend's. 'Give Charlie a hug from me.'

'Who is Charlie?' Tess asked as he carried her into the inn. It was seductively pleasurable, being carried by a man. For a moment she indulged the fantasy that this was her lover, sweeping her away…

'His son.' Alex's terse answer jerked her out of the dream.

'Mr Rivers is married?' Somehow he had not looked married, whatever that looked like.

'Widowed.' Alex's tone gave no encouragement for further questions.

Perhaps that was why Grant Rivers's eyes were so sad. She closed her lips on questions that were sure to be intrusive as the landlord came out to greet them.

'LeGrice, I need an extra room.' Alex was obviously known and expected. 'A comfortable, quiet chamber for the lady, a maid to attend her, hot baths for both of us and then the best supper you can lay on in my private parlour.'

'Milord.' Known, expected and not to be denied, obviously. The innkeeper was bustling about as though the Prince Regent had descended on his establishment. Perhaps she would see the Prince Regent when she was in London. Tess was distracted enough by this interesting thought not to protest when she was carried upstairs and into a bedchamber.

The sight of the big bed was enough to jerk her out of fantasies of state coaches and bewigged royalty, let alone thoughts of romance. 'Please put me down.'

It must have come out more sharply than she intended. Alex stopped dead. 'That was my intention.'

'Here. Just inside the door. This is a bedchamber.'

'I know. The clue lies in the fact that there's a bed in it.' He was amused by her vapours, she could hear it in his voice, a deep rumble that held a laugh hidden inside it.

Her ear was pressed against his chest. Tess jerked her head upright. 'Then, please put me down. You should not be in my bedchamber.'

'I was last night when I put you to bed.'

'Two wrongs do not make a right,' she said and winced at how smug she sounded.

'Nanny used to say that, did she?' Alex walked across to the hearthside and deposited her on a chair.

'Sister Benedicta,' Tess confessed. 'I sounded just like her, how mortifying.'

'Why mortifying?' He leaned one shoulder against the high mantelshelf and lounged, as pleasing to the eye as a carefully placed piece of statuary, the lamplight teasing gilt highlights out of what she had thought was simply dark blond hair. She wondered how much of that lazy perfection was deliberately cultivated.

'Because it was a commonplace thing to say and I have no intention of being commonplace.'

That faint smile curled Alex's mouth again and Tess found herself staring at his lower lip and puzzling over why, when he smiled, which stretched his lips, the centre of the lower one seemed somehow fuller.

'That is an uncharitable insult to Sister Benedicta,' she said hastily. 'Only sometimes, when she managed to string an entire conversation together consisting of nothing but clichés, I had to bite my lip to stop myself screaming in sheer boredom.' *Biting lips...why on earth should that image...? Stop it!*

'I will remove my dangerous male presence from your bedchamber and leave you to bathe in comfort.'

He straightened up and strolled to the door. 'Supper in an hour, do you think?'

'Yes. Perfect. This is lovely, thank you. A fire and a hot bath and a maid,' Tess gabbled, as a pretty girl, all apple cheeks and blond braids, ducked under Alex's arm as he held the door open. He simply grinned at her and went out.

This was indeed the Primrose Path to Perdition. Luxury, warmth, leisure, being waited on. And all because she hadn't had the willpower to stay awake last night and insist she be taken down to Sister Clare to do her duty. It was not fair, she had thought she had conquered all those silly yearnings and *what-ifs* and *if-onlys*. Now she was having a taste of things she had dreamed about, all served up by an attractive man, and it would make her new life that much harder to adjust to. *My dangerous male presence. Oh, yes, indeed.*

It's a hair shirt, that's what it is, she thought wildly as a serving man lugged in a tin bath, set it in front of the fire and another brought buckets of steaming water to fill it. She was being given a hint of the life she might have had if Mama and Papa had not died, if she'd had a few pounds to her name. If she'd had a family.

If...if. If wishes were horses, beggars would ride. And there's another cliché. The maid said something and Tess grabbed her handkerchief, blew her nose inelegantly and made herself concentrate. *'Dank u,'* she said and submitted to having her cloak unfastened and her gown unlaced. *'Wat is uw naam?'*

Damnation. Tess was crying, or on the edge of it, he could hear it in her voice. He was not used to feminine tears unless they were accompanied by a tantrum and demands for expensive trinkets. Alex pushed himself away from the wall outside her door and negotiated the ill-lit landing towards his own room. Her ankle probably hurt, she was tired, she was cross, cold and hungry and she wasn't used to men. He shouldn't tease her. In fact, he should probably find some respectable Flemish maid of at least forty summers and employ her to travel with Tess to London while he took another ship.

On the other hand, *he* knew he wouldn't do anything out of line, she would probably feel fine in the morning once she was rested and he was enjoying her company. She was refreshingly different, was Tess. He was used to simpering young ladies who had been schooled in the arts of husband catching until they all appeared to have been pressed from the same gingerbread mould, or to experienced women of the world who would flirt and employ their charms on him, just as he amused himself in return.

Tess was as straightforward as a schoolroom chit, but with maturity and intelligence to go with it. Perhaps she was what all those little butterflies flitting around Almack's in their pastel gowns would have been like if they hadn't been spoiled. Anyway, he enjoyed her company, when she wasn't prosing on about Christmas and families, so he would award himself the gift of escorting her. After all, she would be safer with him than just a maidservant if there were men up to mischief on the way. He knew all about men up to mischief, none better.

And the indulgence of observing innocence at close quarters was made safe by the fact of who she was. No one was going to descend like the wrath of God announcing that he'd compromised the chit and must now marry her. Marriage was not in his plans, and wouldn't have been, even if he had every intention of infuriating his family. A wife, he had long ago decided, would mean a loss of freedom for no discernible gain, given that mistresses combined sexual expertise with no limitations whatsoever on his lifestyle. One day, perhaps…but not yet, not for a long while.

He grinned at himself for finding virtue in doing what he wanted, sobered at the memory of her wide eyes and almost trembling lip and peered at the next door in search of his chamber. The room numbers were hard to make out in the gloom. Where the devil was his? *Ah, next one.* His foot made contact with something soft, there was a muffled sound somewhere between a mew and a squeak and a weight attached itself to the toe of his right boot.

Alex lifted his foot, hopped to the door, opened it and in the light from several branches of candles examined the small ball of orange fluff attached to the immaculate leather of his Hessian. 'Let go.' No effect. The dratted creature obviously only spoke Flemish. Ignoring the hastily muffled laughter of the maid who was laying out towels on the bed, he hopped to the chair, bent down and attempted to prise off the kitten without leaving scratches that would give his valet hysterics.

'You, I suppose, are a punishment for sending Byfleet on ahead with the heavy luggage.' He held it up by its scruff while it stared cross-eyed at him and mewed pitifully. 'He doubtless has a particular tool for removing kittens from footwear.' He turned to hand the kitten to the maid, but she had gone, the sound of her giggles fading down the corridor. Alex put the animal on the floor and it gazed up at him, tail tip twitching, its pink tongue protruding a fraction beneath its whiskers.

'I suppose you think you are endearing?'

The kitten mewed, then made a leap for the dangling tassel of his Hessian.

'No!' Alex caught it in midair. 'You are a menace. On the other hand, females like cats and they dote on babies of all varieties. I suppose she might take to you. You'll make her smile at any rate.' The maid had left the basket she had brought the towels in. Alex upended it over the kitten, which squeaked piteously. 'Humbug. You are obviously a loss to the acting profession. Here.' He screwed up a scrap of paper, pushed it under the basket and then began to undress to the sounds of shredding and fierce miniature growls.

Tess straightened her back and lifted her chin with the vague feeling that perfect deportment might compensate for wallowing in wicked luxury. A hot bath instead of a chilly sponge-down, soft towels, fine-milled soap, a fire. Bliss. Even having to put on her drab grey gown again could not entirely suppress the fantasy that she was now a glamorous woman, perfumed, exquisitely gowned and coiffed, an exotic creature that any man would put on a pedestal and worship from afar.

At least *afar* would be safe. Tess knew perfectly well from observation and whispered gossip what men got up to in close quarters given any encouragement, and her fantasy did not quite dare explore that. Although when she contemplated a certain gentleman's shoulders—

The door opened and Alex walked in, carrying, for some reason, a small wicker basket. 'You are very pink,' he remarked after one glance at her face. 'Bath too hot?'

'Er, no, I am sitting too close to the fire, I expect.' *And blushing like a rose, fool that I am.* Apparently it would take more than one luxurious bath to turn her into a lady capable of stealing a man's breath. 'What is in the basket?'

'A very early Christmas present for you.' He placed it on her lap. 'I thought you needed cheering up.'

He had bought her a hat! Or perhaps a muff, or a pretty shawl. A lady could not accept articles of apparel from a man, she knew that. Tess used to sneak into the back of the room when Mrs Bond had given the lectures in deportment that were intended to prepare the young ladies who had been sent to the convent to finish their education. Tess should not have been there because, obviously, she was not going to be launched into society or have a Season, so she had no need to know all about attracting eligible gentlemen in a ladylike manner. But it had been a pleasant daydream.

Those rules did not apply to her, she decided as her fingers curled around the sharp corners of the basket. *I am not a lady. I am an impoverished...orphan. A bonnet is not going to compromise me.*

The basket seemed to move as she opened it, and then a small ginger ball of fluff scrambled out and latched on to her wrist. Needle claws dug into her skin. 'Ouch! You have given me a *cat*?' Not a hat. Was he drunk?

'A kitten.' Alex came to his knees in front of her, tossed aside the basket and tried to prise the ferocious little beast from her arm. 'Ow! Now she has bitten me.'

Good. '*He* has bitten you. Marmalade cats are usually male.'

'Really?' All she could see of Alex was the top of his head as he bent over her and wrestled with the kitten. The top of his head and those broad shoulders... What was it about that part of a man? Or was it only his? Tess had not reached the age of three and twenty without having admired some good-looking men from afar, and being closeted in a convent did nothing to suppress perfectly natural yearnings, however sinful those might be.

His big hands were gentle, both on her wrist and with the kitten, who was becoming more and more entangled in Tess's cuffs. 'Little wretch,' Alex was muttering. 'Infernal imp. If you were a bit bigger, I'd skin you for glove linings, I swear.' But she could hear the laughter in his voice as he did battle with his minuscule opponent. 'I wonder if tickling will work.'

Abruptly the needles were withdrawn from her wrist, there was a scuffle under her elbow and the marmalade kitten shot out, skidded across the polished boards and perched on the cross-rail of the table.

Alex lost his balance, pitched forward and for an intense, endless, moment her arms were full of his solid torso, his mouth was pressed into the angle of her shoulder and her face was buried in his hair.

He smelt of soap and clean linen, the now familiar citrus cologne and something…simply male? Or simply Alex? His hair was thick and tickled her nose, and when she shifted to support his weight her fingertips found the nape of his neck, bare and curiously vulnerable. His lips moved against her skin, she felt his hot breath and the tension in his body, then he was pushing back, rocking on to his heels, his eyes dark and his expression unreadable.

'Hell's teeth—' Alex huffed out a breath and smiled. It seemed a trifle strained. 'Sorry, I do not mean to swear at you and I certainly did not mean to flatten you. I seem to be making a habit of it.' Whatever he had felt in her arms it was not excitement, delight or any of the other things her fantasies had conjured up with a dream lover. *Naturally.*

'Why did you give me a kitten?' Tess asked, more tartly than she intended.

Alex shrugged and stood up. He had the sense not to carry on apologising, she noted. 'You are miserable. I thought it would cheer you up. Ladies seem to like small baby creatures to coo over.'

'I cannot speak for the *ladies* in your life, my lord, but I do not *coo*. And do they not prefer diamonds?'

'I am surprised at you, Miss Ellery. What do you know about ladies who prefer diamonds?'

'Why, nothing.' Tess widened her eyes at him innocently. 'But surely your mother or sisters—or your wife, of course—would prefer a gift of jewellery to kittens?' She knew all about kept women from the whispered conversations when she joined the boarders after lights out. They all had brothers or cousins who were sowing their wild oats in London and they exchanged confidences about who were considered the worst rakes, the most exciting but dangerous young men.

'Hmm.' Alex shot her a quizzical look, but she dropped her gaze to her scratched wrist and began to wrap her handkerchief around it. 'I do not buy my sisters or my mother presents, and I am not married.'

'No, I suppose I should have deduced that you were not.' Tess tied a neat knot in the handkerchief and looked up.

'Indeed?' His eyes narrowed and she discovered that relaxed, amiable Lord Weybourn could look very formidable indeed. 'And how did you arrive at that conclusion?'

Chapter Four

'How did I deduce that you were not married?' Tess swallowed. She had strayed into dangerous personal territory and she could only hope he did not think she had been fishing...that she had any ulterior motive. She fought the blush and managed a bright smile. 'It was easy from what you said about Christmas. If you were married, your wife would not allow you to spend it cosily beside the fire with your brandy and books. You would be out visiting your in-laws.'

'So you imagine that if I were to be married I would live under the cat's foot, do you?' The relaxed, rather quizzical smile was back again.

'Not at all. But visits to relatives are what happens in families.'

'I wouldn't know. I am out of practice with them.'

'That is a shame.' She dreamed about being part of a family, a real family, even if there would be bickering about whose turn it was to entertain the awkward relatives for the holiday season. It was a long time since she had experienced a Christmas like the ones she had enthused about in the carriage. A long time since she had known a family, and this man had that gift and was apparently happy to throw it away.

'A shame? Not at all.' Alex moved away as the landlord, followed by a maid, started to bring in their dinner. 'It is freedom.'

They said no more until they were alone again. Tess ladled soup into bowls while Alex shredded roast chicken into a saucer and put it down for the kitten. 'There you are. Now leave my boots alone. What are you going to call him?'

So I'm going to have to keep him, am I? Trust Alex to give me a kitten, not a bonnet. 'Noel,' she decided, adding a saucer of milk beside the chicken. 'Because he is a Christmas present.'

'You really are an exceedingly sentimental young woman.' Alex passed her the bread rolls. 'Butter?'

'Thank you. And I am not sentimental, it is you who are cynical.'

'Why, yes, I cry guilty to that. But what is wrong with a little healthy cynicism?'

'Isn't it lonely?' Tess ventured. It was ridiculous, this instinct to hug a large, confident male. Perhaps that was how lust seized you, creeping up, pretending to be some sort of misguided, and unwanted, compassion.

'What, forgoing gloomy evergreen swags, tuneless carol singers, bickering relatives and enforced jollity? I will enjoy a period of quiet tranquillity and then my friends return to town eager for company.'

Tess set her empty soup bowl to one side and waited in silence while Alex carved the capon. There was something very wrong within his family, obviously, if he did not give his mother and sisters presents and he preferred solitude in London to a festive reunion. She bit her lip and told herself not to probe. The atmosphere of plain speaking between the nuns that prevailed in the convent was not, she suspected, good training for polite conversation in society.

Alex passed her a plate of meat and she reciprocated with the vegetables, racking her brains for what might be suitable small talk. 'I do not remember London at all well.' *Or at all.* 'Is your house in Mayfair?' That was the most fashionable area, she knew.

'Yes, in Half Moon Street, off Piccadilly. Just a small place because I travel so much.'

That appeared to have exhausted that topic. 'Your valet does not travel with you?'

'I sent him on ahead, along with my secretary and several carriages full of artworks. It was a most successful trip this time.'

Tess thought she detected a modest air of self-congratulation. Was that simply the pleasure at a successful chase or was Alex reliant on the income from his dealing? It seemed a precarious existence for a viscount. Maybe he could not afford lavish celebrations and entertainment at Christmas, she pondered, in which case she had been unforgivably tactless to have pressed him about it. Although he certainly seemed to spend money on his comforts without sign of stinting. Perhaps that was an essential facade, or he ran up large debts.

'Have I dropped gravy on my neckcloth?' he enquired, making her jump. 'Only you have been staring at it for quite a while.'

'I was thinking that your linen is immaculately kept,' Tess admitted. 'Your neckcloths and your shirts.'

Alex choked on a mouthful of wine. 'Do you always say what you think?'

'Certainly not. Should I not have mentioned it?' *But it had been a compliment...*

'Perhaps not comments about gentleman's clothing?' Alex suggested.

'Goodness, yes, of course. The outside world is such a maze, full of pitfalls.'

'Are you nervous of what you will find in London?' He put the question in such a straightforward way, without any show of sympathy, yet she sensed he understood just how frightening this was. Mother Superior had certainly shown no such insight, only the expectation that Tess would obediently accept her lot in life despite the blow she had delivered.

'Terrified,' she admitted baldly. 'But there is no point in giving way to it—that will only make it worse. I will soon find my way around my new world. I did with convent life after all.'

Alex watched her over the rim of his goblet, his hazel eyes intelligent, and not, for a change, mocking. 'It must have been a shock to find yourself there. Wine? This is very good.' He refilled his own glass from the decanter.

'Thank you, but, no. I've hardly ever had it before and I do not think I should start now.' Tess scrutinised her conscience and admitted, 'You are offering me too much temptation as it is.'

The air went still, as though someone had taken a deep breath and not let it out. 'Temptation?' Alex said with care, as he set down his knife and fork.

'Food, servants, luxury,' she explained.

'Ah. The temptations of comfort, you mean.' He picked up his glass again and turned it slowly between long fingers. The heavy signet ring on his left hand caught red highlights from the claret. 'This is not luxury, although it is very civilised. You are tempted by luxury?'

'I do not know. I obviously have no concept of it if this is merely *comfort.*'

'What are your expectations of your new employment then?'

'Simplicity, I have no doubt. After all, I will be somewhere between a poor relation and an upper servant in the scheme of things. Mother Superior explained that very clearly.' *Along with everything else.* 'But I will be in a home and that is the important thing.'

'It is? I would have thought that salary and security would be the highest priority for someone in, forgive me, your position.'

'No, not for me. Being able to earn my own living and to have some security is essential, obviously. But being within a family is what is most important. If I am caring for children that is assured, but an elderly lady or an invalid will have family, too, people who care for them.'

There was movement around her skirts and Noel climbed up, claws pricking her thigh, before he settled down into a small, warm ball on her lap. Tess cupped one hand over him, felt his little belly tight as a drum with chicken and milk. The vibration of his purrs was soothing. 'Warmth. I want warmth.'

The maid came in with an apple tart and cleared the used dishes. Alex watched in silence while Tess served them both, then took the cream with a murmur of thanks. 'You will miss that from the convent, I suppose. The close community.'

She stared at him, almost confused that he could understand so little. How to explain? Impossible. 'No.

I will not miss it.' *Ever. That cool, detached, ruthless honesty that seems not to care how it hurt. 'You are a bastard, Teresa. That is the fact of the matter and you must adjust your expectations accordingly.' Horrid old woman...*

Tess felt stupid with weariness and carefully suppressed worry. The tart was delicious, but it was an effort to eat now. She pushed back her chair and stood, the kitten nestled in one hand. 'I must take Noel out into the yard or we will be dealing with an accident.'

'Give him to me.' Alex stood as she did. 'You can hardly hop out there with your bad ankle and your hands full of kitten.'

'What are you going to do with him?' Tess asked, suspicious. Perhaps he was regretting his impulse to saddle them with a demanding baby animal. She steadied herself with her free hand on the table.

'I will take him out to investigate a nice patch of earth, then I will put down yesterday's news-sheets near the hearth, add a saucer of milk and upend the basket over the top. Will that do?'

'Very well. I hope he will not miss his mother.' She worried as she tipped the kitten into Alex's waiting palm where it snuggled down, obviously feeling safe in the cage of his fingers. *Who could blame it?*

'If he cries I will take him into my bed, give him one of my best silk stockings to play with and ring down to the kitchen for some lightly poached salmon,' Alex assured her, his expression serious.

'I wouldn't want to put you to so much trouble. Perhaps I should have him in my room—' Then she saw the crease at the corner of his mouth and the wicked look in his eyes. Tess drew herself up to her full five feet five inches. 'You, my lord, are unkind to make a jest of me. Thank you for a delightful supper.'

She took a step to sweep past him in a dignified manner, forgot her sore ankle and twisted sideways with a yelp of pain.

'Definitely best not to drink the wine. You are quite unsteady enough as it is.' Alex caught her one-handed.

Her hip was against the table, her nose was buried in the V of his waistcoat and her hands, she discovered, were clenched around his upper arms. All she had to do was let go and straighten up, use the table as a support to make her way to the door. *Let go.* He felt so good, so warm and solid and…expensive. Fine broadcloth coat against her cheek, silk waistcoat against her chin, fine linen under her nose. Tess wanted to burrow into the luxurious softness with all that masculine hardness beneath it. His chest, those biceps, that big hand pressed against her back, the tantalisingly faint edge of musk.

'Tess?' His mouth was close to her ear—he must have bent down. His breath tickled, his lips were so near.

'Yes.' *Whatever the question is—yes.*

From the region of her diaphragm there was an outraged yowl, a wriggle and a small paw reached up and fastened onto the front of Alex's waistcoat.

'You little devil, that's Jermyn Street's best.' He stepped back, the kitten hooked to the fabric.

'I will leave you to deal with your kind present, my lord.' It was not easy to exit with dignity, not hobbling, pink in the face and with ginger hairs clinging to her drab grey skirts, but at least Alex had the more difficult task of extricating tiny claws from intricate, hideously expensive embroidery. 'Goodnight.'

Tess closed the door behind her, then cracked it open

again at the sound of muttered curses. She'd wished she knew some swear words: now she did.

'Did you sleep well?' Alex enquired. His little nun was decidedly wan as they stood at the foot of the gangplank of the *Ramsgate Rose*. Come to think of it, he was feeling a trifle wan himself, what with kitten herding and a night spent fighting inappropriate arousal and an unfamiliar guilty conscience. Although quite what he was feeling guilty about he was not certain. He might be feeling an unexpected physical attraction to an innocent young lady, but he was perfectly well able to resist it. He'd come across enough of them in the past and simply diverted any physical needs to the mistress of the moment. It was just that he had never spent so much time with one of the innocents before.

'Thank you, yes.' Tess was tight-lipped, her knuckles showing white on the handle of the wicker basket. They had eaten in their own rooms that morning and this was the first good look that he'd had of her in broad daylight.

'Nervous?' Alex ventured. A sharp shake of the head. 'Do you get seasick?' *Oh, well done, Tempest, now she's gone green*. If not green, then certainly an unhealthy shade of mushroom.

'I was when we came over to the Continent, but that was years ago. I am sure I will be fine. It is simply a matter of willpower, is it not?'

Not in Alex's experience, not after seeing any number of strong-willed friends casting up their accounts over a ship's rail. 'Not so much strength of will, more a question of tactics,' he offered, taking her elbow to guide her up the steep planks. 'We stay on deck as much as possible, eat dry bread, drink plenty of mild ale.

'And don't try to read,' he added. Even with his own cast-iron stomach the recollection of trying to study the *Racing Chronicle* in a crowded, overheated cabin brought back unpleasant memories. Grant's appropriately named filly Stormy Waters—by Millpond out of Gale Force—had romped home by a head without any of Alex's guineas on it that week at Newmarket.

Most of the passengers were making for the companionway down to the first- and second-class saloons. Alex steered Tess to a slatted bench under the mainmast and settled her on it with the cat basket, her portmanteau and his boat cloak. 'I'll go and see to my luggage, you set the kitten on anyone who tries to take my seat.'

At least that produced a smile, he thought, intercepting an icy glare from a beak-nosed matron as he made his way to the rail to watch his luggage being swung on board. Obviously she didn't like the look of his face. He shrugged mentally. He hadn't liked hers much, either.

At first it was easy to keep Tess's mind off her stomach. The harbour was full of things to look at, the kitten needed tending to and, even when they cast off, the view was entertaining enough, the water sufficiently sheltered. Alex was rewarded with smiles and the colour in her cheeks and found himself experiencing a warm glow of satisfaction.

The chit would have him as sentimental as she was, he thought with an inward grimace, but if thinking avuncular thoughts was sufficient to stop him recalling that she was a grown woman only a few years younger than he was, then so be it. Tess Ellery was an innocent and he was not, which left him back exactly where he started—as an escort to a respectable lady.

She had fallen silent while he brooded. Alex glanced

sideways and saw that the greenish tinge was back, the roses had gone and, from the set of her mouth, the smiles with them. 'It is quite rough, isn't it?' Tess ventured.

Not as rough as it is going to get was the honest answer. 'A little lively, yes,' Alex agreed. 'Tell me about your ideal employment. A cosy old lady or a pair of charming children?' Some must be charming, not that he had ever encountered any for any length of time, other than his own younger siblings. He and Matthew had scrapped and bickered, and his sisters had been, by definition, girls, which meant they were as irritating and mystifying to a youth as females could be. He supposed he'd felt affection for them, he just didn't feel he knew them.

'I do not mind.' Tess showed some signs of animation. 'Just so long as it is a family.'

'Otherwise you will miss the convent life too much?' he suggested as he shook out his boat cloak and put it around her shoulders. Spray was beginning to blow back from the prow. It might be unusual to find himself acting responsibly, but at least he wasn't being treated to the kind of spoiled tantrums his most recent mistress would have thrown under these circumstances. Which, come to think of it, was why she was no longer in his keeping.

'Thank you.' Tess snuggled into the heavy wool with a wriggle that reminded him of that dratted kitten making itself comfortable. 'Miss the convent? Oh, no. It is worse being lonely in a crowd than by yourself, don't you think?'

Alex tried to remember when, if, he had ever felt lonely. Alone, yes, but he was comfortable in his own company and always had been. When he wanted human contact he had a wide social circle; when he needed close friends he had them, the other three members of what the dean of his Oxford college had referred to bitterly as the Four Disgraces.

'I suppose so,' he agreed. 'But in the convent, all those Sisters must have been like sisters, as it were.'

Tess gave a little shrug as though the cloak had developed uncomfortable creases. 'Friendships are not encouraged. The sisters treat everyone the same and the boarders go home for holidays and they make friends within their own group. They all come from very good families.'

'And you do not?'

'I am an...orphan with no connections. But everyone was very kind,' she added brightly.

Alex was conscious of a sudden and startling urge to box the ears of the unknown Mother Superior. He had no trouble translating *very kind* into *impersonal, remote, efficient, cool*. Tess had been fed, clothed, educated, kept healthy and respectable. Her body and her morals had been cared for; her heart and her happiness, it seemed, could look after themselves if she did not choose to become a nun. Although that was not so very different from a child's upbringing in any aristocratic family. He was sure his mother had loved him, but it had never occurred to her to play with him, let alone talk to him outside the hour before she changed for dinner.

'I'm sure they were kind.' And now she was heading for a life of respectable drudgery, neither a member of a family nor an upper servant. But she seemed to realise already what her position was, even if she had had rose-coloured ideas about the joys of family life. It would be no kindness to tell her that and, he supposed, a miracle might happen and she would find herself in the household of her dreams. He looked at the cloudy sky, then fished out his watch. 'Have some bread and ale, best to eat a little, often.'

'Thank you. In a minute.' Tess got up and folded his cloak one-handed, clutching at the mast with the other. 'I need…I mean, I assume that the…'

'Ladies' retiring room?' Alex suggested. 'Yes, that will be down below.' He stood and gave her his arm as far as the entrance to the companionway. 'Can you manage the stairs with your ankle? Sure? Hold on tight as you go.'

The smell hit Tess halfway down the steps. Hot, crowded humanity, food, alcohol, an unpleasantness that she guessed was the ship's bilges and a clear intimation that several people had already been unwell.

Only urgent personal need made her fight her way through the crowded first-class cabin and whisper in the ear of an amiable-looking lady.

'Over there, my dear. Wait a moment.' She dug in her reticule and handed a small object to Tess. 'Take my smelling salts.'

Five minutes later Tess hobbled back, returning the bottle with sincere thanks and a mental resolution to hang on, however long the rest of the voyage proved to be.

She picked her way back to the stairs and encountered a frigid stare from a middle-aged matron in a large bonnet. She looked vaguely familiar. *She probably thinks I am an intruder from second class*, Tess thought, avoiding her eyes. She certainly would have been if it were not for Alex's insistence.

How easily things can change, she thought as she stumbled with the motion and caught hold of a handrail. *If Alex hadn't been in a hurry on icy cobbles I would have caught a boat yesterday, I wouldn't have a sore ankle,*

I'd have been packed into the second-class cabin feeling ill, I wouldn't own a ginger kitten and my life wouldn't be complicated by proximity to a large, infuriating—and devastatingly attractive—male.

On the whole, even with the ankle, she rather thought she preferred things this way, an adventure before life became worthy and serious again.

Chapter Five

The infuriating male in question was waiting for her when she emerged into the fresh air on deck. 'Hellish down there, isn't it? Come on back to our roost and be thankful it isn't raining.' Alex sounded quite unconcerned about the effect of salt spray on his expensive greatcoat or the disorder of his wind-ruffled hair now he had abandoned the fight to keep his hat on his head.

'What is it?' he asked once he had her settled again. 'I'm delighted to see that green tinge has gone, but I did not expect to see a smile.'

'You dress so elegantly, but look at you now.' She cocked her head to one side to study him in the waning light. It would be dusk soon. 'You are not the slightest bit concerned about your clothes or your hair. I believe you are a fraud, my lord.'

'I think not. I take my appearance very seriously. One has a reputation to uphold,' Alex drawled, but there was an edge to his voice as he said it and the mischievous tilt to his lips had been replaced by a thin smile.

You are not what you seem, Lord Weybourn, Tess thought as she snuggled back into the embrace of the boat cloak. The problem was, he did not seem to be the same person from one hour to the next. He appeared the indolent man of fashion, yet was close friends with a trio of gentlemen who looked as though they could hold their own in a back-alley fight, and his body was hard as nails under that expensive tailoring. He sneered at her enthusiasm for Christmas, called her sentimental, threatened Noel with a future as glove linings—and yet he was kind to her, had given her a kitten and was infinitely patient with the creature's attacks on his person.

He was also very—sinfully—attractive. She had no business acknowledging that, she knew perfectly well. She was a convent-reared young woman about to begin earning her living. Her antecedents were handicap enough, but any smudge on her reputation would mean an end to her prospects for decent employment, and the sooner she resigned herself to frugal, upright spinsterhood, the better.

'What was that great sigh for?' Alex enquired. 'Hungry?'

'No, I'm just…' *Wishing for the moon. Wishing I had never set eyes on you so my foolish imagination had nothing to work with. The angle of your jaw, the scent of your skin, the way your hair curls at the ends with the damp wind... The impossibility of a man like you in my life.* 'Cold.'

'Me, too.' He began to unbutton his greatcoat. 'Let's get rid of that coal scuttle of a bonnet and do something about it.' Before she could protest the thing was off her head and jammed behind her portmanteau and she was on Alex's knee, the flaps of his coat around her, the hood of the cloak over her head.

'Alex! My lord, this is—'

'Outrageous, I know. Stop squeaking, you sound like Noel.' His voice by her ear was definitely amused. 'This is shocking, but practical. The choices are go below and be warm but nauseous, sit up here in chilly isolation or share body heat.' She felt his legs move, a most disconcerting effect. 'There, the kitten's basket is under the cloak, too. Happy?'

'Ecstatic,' she muttered. Alex's snort of amusement was warm on her neck. 'I suppose the sea crossing isn't this bad in the summer.' She did her best not to think about the grey sea under the darkening, slate sky, the tossing white wave crests, the icy water.

'It can be delightful in the summer,' Alex confirmed. 'Go to sleep.'

'Huh.' It was her turn to snort. She might as well try to fly.

Tess woke cramped, warm and confused in a snug cave, huddled against something that moved in a steady rhythm. It took her a while to sort through the sensations. Someone else's skin, a fresh cologne, salt, a seat that shifted slightly beneath her, a world that rocked and heaved. *A ship. A ship and Alex.*

She sat still for a moment, inhaling the essence of warm, sleepy man. Somehow she had got between the flaps of his coat as well as his greatcoat and her cheek rested on skin-warm linen. *Dangerous.* Tess struggled upright on his knees, batting the edges of his greatcoat apart so she could see out.

'Good morning.' Alex pushed her to her feet, keeping one hand on her arm as she staggered. 'There's the English coast ahead.'

'Thank heavens.' She felt sticky and thirsty, but there

was land, the sun was struggling out of the clouds low on the horizon and the long night was over.

'Have some ale.' Alex was on his knees beside the luggage. He passed her an open bottle and then scooped a protesting kitten out of its basket. 'Yes, I know. We are cruel and horrible and you want your breakfast. You can share mine.' He poured a little milk into his cupped palm from a stoppered jar and Noel lapped, purring furiously while Alex extracted cold bacon one-handed.

'Do you want to eat or shall we wait until we can find a decent inn?'

'Wait,' Tess said with decision. She felt all right now, but there was no point in tempting fate, especially when she had to venture below decks again. That couldn't wait, but she lingered a moment, hand braced against the mast, looking down on Alex's tousled head as he bent over the kitten. Such a kind man.

'I'll just…' She waved a hand towards the companionway. 'I won't be long.'

It was much worse below decks now after a rough, crowded night. Even the smartest passengers looked haggard and unkempt. The first-class saloon was crowded and difficult to negotiate and, when Tess emerged from the room assigned to ladies, she turned to see if she could make her way forward and up through a different hatch.

She skirted the second-class cabin, an even more unpleasant sight than the first class, and tried a narrow passageway with a glimmer of what looked like daylight at its end. It opened out into a small area at the foot of another set of stairs so she gathered her skirts in one hand, took the handrail with the other and started to climb, one step at a time.

'What we got 'ere, then? You're trespassing into the

crews' quarters, sweetheart. Lost, are you? Or looking for some company?'

A sailor, big and burly, was descending the steps towards her. Tess retreated backwards, away from the smell of tar and unwashed man, the big hands, the snaggle-toothed smirk.

'I want to get back on deck. Kindly let me pass.'

'Kindly let me pass.' He mimicked her accent and kept coming. 'I don't take orders from passengers.' His eyes, bright blue in his weather-beaten face, ran over her from head to foot and a sneer appeared on his face as he took in her plain, cheap gown. 'I can show you a good time.' He put out a hand and gave her a push towards a door that was hooked open. Inside she could glimpse a bunk bed.

Tess turned, clumsy with her painful ankle, and he caught her by the shoulder. 'Not so fast, you stuck-up little madam. What the—?'

He broke off as one elegantly gloved hand gripped his shoulder. 'You're in the way, *friend*,' Alex drawled, his tone suggesting they were anything but friends. His gaze swept over Tess and she stopped struggling.

'And something tells me this lady does not welcome your attentions.' His voice was low, almost conversational, his half smile amiable. 'I suggest you remove your hand from the lady.' Alex was as tall as the sailor, but looked about half his weight. The man shifted his stance to face him, his posture becoming subtly more threatening as he dropped his hand from Tess's shoulder.

Tess looked at the great meaty hands and the knife in his belt and swallowed. Then she began to pull off her gloves. If he attacked Alex, her only weapons were her nails and her feet. 'This brute—'

'This little *lady* came looking for some company.' He leered at Tess. 'Then the silly mort got all uppity on me.'

'And you are?' Alex sounded almost comatose with boredom as he drew off his right glove and tossed it to Tess.

'I'm the second mate of this 'ere ship and I don't take any nonsense, not from bits of skirt what don't know their place and not from passengers, neither.'

'Hmm. I wasn't intending nonsense,' Alex remarked, the last word almost a growl. He bunched his fist and hit the man square on the jaw. The sailor went down like a felled tree, hitting his head on the handrail as he went.

'Damn.' Alex shook his hand. 'I hope I haven't killed him. It means such a fuss with the magistrates.' He sounded like himself again.

He gave the unconscious man a nudge in the ribs with one booted foot. 'No. He's breathing.' Alex stepped over the sprawled figure and frowned down at Tess. 'Are you all right? Did he do more than touch your shoulder? Because if he did he's going to wake up minus his wedding tackle.'

'No.' She blinked at him, trying to square the carefree figure in front of her with the dangerous-sounding man who had delivered that sledgehammer of a blow. 'You hit him very hard.'

Alex shrugged. 'He deserved it and if you give a lout like that a tap, all you do is make him angry and more dangerous. Now, where can we stow him?'

'In there.' She pointed at the open door.

Alex dragged the unconscious man inside, then hunkered down, felt the sailor's head, rolled back an eyelid and pushed him onto his side. 'He'll do.'

Tess sat down on the bottom step. It felt safer down

there, less as though the deck was going to come up and hit her. She wasn't used to violence, and facing that leering creature had made her stomach heave, but Alex... Alex had been wonderful.

She should have been appalled and frightened by the violence, but it had been thrilling, that explosive, focused power. Tess looked at Alex. Most of the time he was so kind and carefree, but she now knew he was capable of behaving like a storybook hero. She had forgotten those muscles.

'Let that be a lesson to you,' said her hero flatly as he pulled on his glove and shut the cabin door. 'Do not go wandering off, do not speak to strange men.'

Tess felt her warm storybook glow vanishing. 'I didn't *wander off.* And I did not speak to him. He accosted me.'

'You are far too trusting—as bad as that blasted kitten. You let yourself be carried about Ghent by a strange man, you spend the night with four of them...'

'That is totally unfair! You knocked me down, you assured me I'd be safe!'

'Not so much trusting as gullible,' Alex snapped. The image of Sir Galahad wavered and vanished altogether. There were shouts on deck; the motion of the ship changed. 'We're coming into harbour.' Alex climbed up the companionway and looked round. 'We'd better get on deck before someone removes our baggage.'

Tess stalked after him with as much dignity as she could manage with a limp. As they made their way past sailors hauling down sails and securing ropes she saw that the harbour was getting closer by the second. *England. Home? It will be in time*, she reassured herself, trying not to glare resentfully at Alex's back.

He reached their place under the mast and turned,

flexing his hand as though reliving that blow. 'I'm sorry, I should not have snapped at you. I was concerned when you did not come back.' When she did not speak, he shrugged. 'Look, I wanted to tear his head off and I couldn't, not once he was unconscious. I was…frustrated.'

'That's a very primitive reaction.' *And an exciting one, I fear.* When Alex simply grunted Tess smothered her smile and picked up Noel's basket. 'There's a good boy. Did you miss your uncle Alex, then?' There was a yowl and a ginger paw shot out of a gap in the weave and fastened on Tess's sleeve. 'Poor little chap, you want to get on dry land, don't you?'

'I have not made any promises about that hellcat,' Alex said. 'Any more nauseating baby talk and *Uncle Alex* will start thinking about glove linings again.'

Tess slanted a look at him that said she knew perfectly well he was bluffing. *Minx.* She seemed to be all right after that unpleasant scene. No vapours, no wilting into his arms at the most inconvenient moment. In fact, he had a strong suspicion that she would have had a go at the man herself, given half a chance. He managed to suppress a grin and checked their bags. 'Don't try to carry the cat basket. Wait there and I'll get someone to fetch the lot.'

He walked to the rail and waited while the ship bumped against the quayside and the gangplank was let down, then he hailed a porter and made his way back across the now-crowded deck to Tess. She was sitting patiently where he had left her, looking around with intelligent interest. Drab, neat, brave little nun, he thought. She looked serious, a little anxious. Then she saw him and her face lit up in a smile that held nothing but pleasure at his return and something inside him went *thud.*

To have a woman smile at him was no novelty. The respectable ones were always glad to welcome him to their homes and their social events; the unrespectable ones greeted his interest with attention that flattered his title and his pocketbook, if nothing else. But Tess's warmth, her lack of artifice, were like an embrace. He was going to miss the chit when he handed her over, and he never thought he'd feel that about a respectable female. Or a lightskirt, come to that.

'Those bags there.' He pointed them out to the porter, who reached for the cat's basket, as well.

'Oh, be careful!' Tess caught it by the handle.

'I'll carry it.' Alex picked it up, gave Tess his other arm and offered up a silent prayer of thanks that no one he knew was likely to be around to view one of the *ton*'s most stylish gentlemen in a travel-stained condition and escorting a nun and a ginger kitten off a cross-Channel ferry.

'Thank you.' She was still limping a little and he tucked his arm close, trapping her hand against his side to make sure she was safely supported. She was just the right height for him. 'You *are* kind, Alex.'

'No, I am not.' He steadied her down the gangplank, then directed the porter to follow them to the Red Lion. 'I'm too selfish to be kind.'

'Nonsense.' She gave his arm a little shake.

'I am. And too indolent to make the effort to be unkind,' he added.

'I don't believe that, either. Perhaps you don't care enough,' Tess murmured, just loud enough for him to hear.

'Care? Of course I care.'

'What about?' She tipped her head to one side to look up at him. 'Other than your *comfort*?'

'My friends.' He'd die for them if he had to, not that he'd ever say so. A man didn't need to; friends just knew. 'Hunting down art and antiquities.' *My honour.* That was something else you didn't talk about, but it was why he lived as he did now.

'Your family?'

Damn it, she was as persistent as that little cat once she had her claws into something. 'No.' Tess gave a little gasp and it stuck him that he might have been tactless. She had lost her own family and she probably did not need telling about someone who would mourn his mother and his sisters if anything happened to them, but who would be quite happy never to set eyes on his father and brother again.

'Here we are.' The open door of the Red Lion was a welcome sight and a distraction from uncomfortable thoughts. Alex dealt with the landlord, checked that the chaise was waiting, ordered hot water and a meal and paid the porter.

'There's your chamber over there.' He gestured towards the door out of the private parlour as they found themselves alone. 'They'll bring some hot water in a moment.'

Tess ignored the gesture and suggestion. 'I'm so sorry.' She stood in front of him, her face a picture of concern.

'Why? What for?'

'I'm sorry that you are estranged from your family and that I raised the subject. It must be so difficult.'

'Don't be sorry.' He shrugged. 'Certainly it isn't difficult. I just ignore them, they ignore me. They say you choose your friends but not your family, but you can choose how much you see of any of them.' Had home ever really felt like a good place to be? It must have done once, before his father had decided that he was so utterly unsuitable to be his heir, such a disappointment to him.

'But what if something happens to them?'

'It won't.' He took her by the shoulders, turned her around and walked her to her chamber door. 'My father's like an ox.' *Certainly has the sensitivity of one.* 'Now freshen up, then we'll eat and be on our way.'

Chapter Six

'Goodbye and thank you so much for your assistance, my lord. For looking after me and for Noel.' Tess stood outside the gates of the convent, her bag and the cat's basket at her feet. Would a curtsy be appropriate? He was an earl… On the other hand she would probably fall flat on her face, and what she wanted to do was certainly not to make a formal gesture. Not at all. She wanted to wrap her arms around his neck and kiss him on that wicked, mobile, mocking mouth.

She managed her best smile instead. *Chin up, back straight. Fairy-tale adventure over.*

'You'll be all right now?' Alex frowned at the metal-studded black oak of the door. 'This doesn't look like the most hospitable of places.'

'Convents don't, from the outside.' *Or the inside, in my experience.* 'And I will be perfectly fine. Thank you again.' She put out her hand, brisk and impersonal, and when he took it and gave it a quick squeeze she tried not to think about how his arms had felt around her.

Alex pulled the iron chain beside the door. Somewhere far away a bell clanged. 'I'll wait in the carriage until you are safe inside. Goodbye, little nun.' He stooped, dropped a quick kiss on her cheek and strode back to the chaise.

'Yes?' enquired a disembodied voice from behind the darkened grille while Tess was still fighting with a blush.

If she had only moved her head a fraction that brief kiss would have fallen on her lips. It would have been her first kiss. 'Teresa Ellery. Mother Superior is expecting me.'

The door swung open and she stepped inside. It banged closed behind her and she heard the sound of hooves on the cobbles as the chaise moved off. *The prison gates slammed behind the doomed woman... Stop it!* The effect on the imagination of reading Minerva Press novels, smuggled in by the boarders, was exceedingly unwelcome just at the moment.

She limped after the silent nun down a dark, tiled passageway to a door. The sister knocked and opened it, urged Tess in with a gesture, then closed it behind her.

Offices in convents must be all created from the same pattern book. Dark walls, small fireplace, solid, plain desk placed uncompromisingly in the centre of the room with the chair turned with its back to the window and any possibility of a distracting view. It was all safely, depressingly, familiar.

'Miss Ellery. I confess I am most surprised to see you.' From behind the desk Mother Superior studied her, unsmiling. She was thin and pale and Tess thought she looked unwell.

'Good evening, Mother.' She bobbed an awkward curtsy, hampered by her sore ankle. 'I was delayed on my journey—'

'So I understand.' The nun glanced to one side and Tess realised they were not alone. Seated against the wall was a middle-aged woman who looked vaguely familiar. '*Delayed* hardly seems adequate to cover your... activities. Mrs Wolsey was on the same boat as you from Ostend.'

Of course, this is the disapproving matron who glared at me.

'Mrs Wolsey has a niece boarding at the convent. She recognised the clothing of the Ghent house orphans and then she recalled seeing you there.'

It began to dawn on Tess that all was far from well. 'I missed the canal boat. I had a fall and hurt my ankle and—'

'And took up with some rake. Yes, that much is obvious. Your disgraceful behaviour was observed. Embracing in public, sleeping in his arms, going into an inn with him. I am both deeply shocked and exceedingly disappointed, as will be my Sister in Ghent when I write to inform her of this.'

'I can explain, Mother—' Tess began, only to be cut off by a slicing hand gesture from the nun.

'Enough. I have no wish to hear you make things worse by lying to me. I most certainly cannot have a woman of your character in this house. Your antecedents are bad enough, but this behaviour is the limit. You will leave at once.'

'My character? But I have not done anything wrong. I can explain everything that occurred. It was all perfectly innocent. And what about my employment?' The room swam with shifting shadows, flickering candlelight, waves of disapproval. It was unreal; she was bone-weary. Tess wondered vaguely if she was going to faint. Perhaps they would put her to bed if she did and she would wake up in the morning and this would all be a dream.

'You think that I could recommend you to any decent

household? There is only one kind of employment for fallen women, my girl, and I suggest you go and seek it forthwith.'

Not a dream. Fight back. 'I did not *do* anything. I am not Lord Weybourn's lover.' Tess tried to stand up straight, find some authority in her voice. 'I had an accident, hurt my ankle. He helped me, just as I said.' *And I do not want to be here, with you, you judgemental old witch*, she thought as a spark of anger burned through the confused fog of misery. *My antecedents, you horrible woman? Two parents who loved each other, who loved me? I am illegitimate—how is that my fault?*

'Lord Weybourn? Hah!' Mrs Wolsey said. 'One knows all about the likes of him. A society rakehell, I have no doubt.'

'How does *one* know this?' Tess enquired. How dare this woman judge Alex? 'I hardly think you would move in the same circles as he does, ma'am.' The tail end of her temper was almost out of her grasp now.

'You insolent girl,' Mother Superior snapped. 'You will leave at once.'

'To cast a sinner out into the night is hardly a very Christian act.' Tess abandoned the effort to be civil, hobbled to the door and, with her hands full of the portmanteau and cat basket, somehow got it open. 'But I would not stay here now if you begged me. Good evening to you both.'

Behind her she heard a small bell ringing violently and the sound of Mrs Wolsey's voice. She seemed to be gibbering with anger. Tess reached the front door before Sister Porteress caught up with her, flung back the bolts, stepped over the threshold and left the door swinging on its hinges. Moments later it slammed behind her with emphatic finality.

'And I hope your righteous indignation keeps you warm at night,' Tess muttered. In front of her was Golden Square, a white-stone statue at its centre glimmering faintly in the light from the lamps set outside the houses. Men muffled up against the dank mist hurried past, a cab rattled over the cobbles on the far side. A clock, quite close, struck nine.

Tess put down her luggage to pull her cuffs over her knuckles. Her mittens felt as though they had been knitted out of thin cotton, not wool, and her toes were already numb.

A woman walked slowly down the side of the square, so Tess picked up her things again and limped across to her. 'Excuse me, can you tell me if there is anywhere near here where I can get lodgings? Only—'

'Get off my patch,' the woman hissed, thrusting her face close to Tess's. She smelt of spirits and strong perfume. 'Unless you want your pretty face marked.'

'No, no, I don't.' Tess backed away and the woman stalked past with a swish of petticoats, only to slow to a hip-swinging saunter before she reached the corner.

'Evening, my dear.' A male voice behind her made her jump. 'Feeling friendly, are you?'

'No, I am not.' Tess whirled round. 'Go away or I'll… set my cat on you.' There was a feline shriek of indignation from the swaying basket and the man stepped aside and walked off hastily.

'Sorry, Noel,' she murmured. 'We can't stay here, it isn't safe.'

Perhaps if she found a hackney carriage the cab driver would take her to a respectable lodging house. There didn't seem to be much alternative. If she stayed on the streets she would either be assaulted, taken by some brothel keeper or she would freeze to death.

Tess slipped her hand though the slit in the side of her skirt seam and touched the reassurance of her purse. Thanks to Alex she still had the stagecoach fare from Margate to London in her pocket and some guilders that she could probably change at a bank in the morning. They were all that stood between her and penury, so she just had to pray that lodgings were cheap.

'What do we have here?' A man's voice, so close behind her, had her spinning round. There were two of them.

'Good evening.' She tried for a confident tone. 'Could you direct me to a cab rank, please?'

'We can direct you, missy, that's for sure.' There was a chuckle as one of them moved round behind her. 'Right down our street.'

On a cold, dank evening there was nothing quite like the simple pleasure of one's own chair, by one's own fireside with a bottle of best cognac to hand. Alex stretched out stockinged feet to the blaze and swirled the glass under his nose. He had the rest of the evening before him to digest a good meal, catch up on his correspondence, read a book…*worry about Tess in that bleak convent.*

No wide hearth with unlimited coals for her. Certainly no brandy to keep her warm after a plain dinner. He shifted, searching for a comfortable position in a chair that had always been perfect before. She was used to convent life. Just because he'd hate it didn't mean that she wouldn't be feeling as though she was home again.

And surely they'd find her a good position soon, one where she wouldn't be run ragged by some acid-tongued old woman or harassed by her charges' older brothers. Who did he know who might be able to employ her? The problem was, he didn't know any respectable matrons well enough to ask them to employ an unknown young woman without them leaping to conclusions based on his reputation, not Tess's. One look at that oval face with the expressive blue eyes, that soft, vulnerable mouth...

She was none of his business. Alex gave himself a mental shake, sat up and reached for the pile of letters his secretary, William Bland, had produced when he'd gotten home.

'The financial matters are all docketed and on your desk, my lord. There is nothing of pressing importance. There are a few invitations despite the fact that your return date was uncertain.' He'd handed over a stack of gilt-edged cards. 'And these items appear to be of a personal nature and have not been opened.'

By *personal*, William meant he had separated out all those with fancy-coloured wafer seals and any that had a whiff of perfume about them. They could wait, too, Alex decided, dropping them back on to the table beside his glass and picking up the invitations again. *No, no, possibly, definitely, no...*

There was the sound of the knocker. Curious. No one, surely, knew he was home yet? Alex squared off the pile of pasteboard rectangles and listened to the murmur of voices from the hall. Because he was away from home so often he did not trouble to employ a butler, and Mac-Donald, the younger of the two footmen, was on duty tonight.

The caller was still talking. Alex swung his feet down off the fender and pushed them into his shoes. Damn it, MacDonald was inexperienced, but even he should be able to get rid of unwanted visitors in less time than this. Alex stood up as the door of the study opened.

'A Miss Ellery has called, my lord.' MacDonald, who had a fine set of freckles to go with his red hair, was blushing painfully. 'I have told her that you are not at home, my lord, but she says she will sit on the front step until you are. So I have seated her in the front room because she does seem to be a lady, my lord. Only—'

Hell, what had gone wrong with the confounded female now? Alex told himself he was exasperated, not pleased. Not anxious. Certainly *not* pleased. 'Show her in, MacDonald.'

'Miss Ellery, my lord.' MacDonald opened the door.

There wasn't a female member of staff living in, either, Alex recalled. The scullery maid and Hannah Semple, his cook/housekeeper, came in by the day. Damn, this got stickier the more he thought about—

'Hell's teeth, Tess, what's happened to you?'

She stood there on the threshold swaying slightly, the basket in one hand, her bag clutched in the other. Her hair was half-down and a great bruise was coming up on her left cheek. Tess set down her luggage as he started towards her. 'I'm so sorry to disturb you at this hour, my lord. Only...'

Her eyes rolled up and her legs gave way as he reached her. Alex caught her now-familiar weight in his arms, laid her down on the chaise longue against the wall and bit down hard on the stream of oaths that fought for escape. 'MacDonald, send Byfleet down with the medical kit, tell Phipps to go for Dr Holt and you get round to Mrs Semple's lodgings and tell her I need her back here to spend the night. *Go!*'

Then he sat back on his heels and took a deep breath.

His hands, he was shocked to see, were clenched, ready for violence, and he glared at them until they relaxed. She had been walking unsupported, he told himself; she had been able to argue with MacDonald. She couldn't be seriously hurt. He still wanted to punch whoever had done this to her.

'My lord?' Byfleet came in and set down a tray of gauze pads, small bottles and jars on a side table, the familiar kit for when Alex had overdone things in the sparring ring.

'This is Miss Ellery, a young lady I escorted over from Ghent. She should be in a convent in Golden Square, which is where I left her. I have no idea how she got here, nor what happened, but you can see her face.'

The valet, who specialised in never being flustered, bent over the couch. 'A nasty bruise. I would hazard the guess that she has come into violent contact with a brick wall. I suggest we remove her outer clothing, my lord, and that I clean the area before she wakes, in case the skin is broken.'

Between them they got Tess out of her bonnet and cloak, took off her boots, one of them unlaced already over the bandaged ankle.

'No gloves, my lord,' Byfleet observed, and held out Tess's right hand for Alex to see. There was a dark red stain under the nails. 'One concludes that she scratched her assailant.'

'Excellent,' Alex muttered and held the bowl for Byfleet as he began to clean her cheek. 'Is that going to scar?' Bad enough that they'd hurt her, worse if she had to look in the mirror at the results for the rest of her life.

'I doubt it, my lord.' Byfleet took a fresh piece of gauze, covered it in ointment and laid it over the bruise.

'She is young and seems healthy, and the skin is not broken.' He probed with his fingertips. 'Nor is the cheekbone.'

Tess regained consciousness suddenly and woke fighting. One moment she was limp under Byfleet's hands, the next she had lashed out for his face. Alex caught her wrists before she could make contact. 'Hush. Lie still, you are safe with me. This is Byfleet, my valet. He is helping you.'

'Alex.' She let him push her back against the cushions. 'I'm sorry.' She began to smile at Byfleet, then stopped with a hiss of pain.

'The doctor and my housekeeper are on their way. Are you hurt anywhere other than your face?'

She lay still, obviously thinking about it. 'My ankle— I had to run. And my shoulder. They grabbed me and I swung round and hit a wall.'

There had been more than one of them, and she's a slip of a girl, defenceless. The instinct to punch something became a desire to get his hands around throats and not let go.

Byfleet moved to the foot of the chaise and began to unbandage her ankle. 'The doctor will need to look at this, my lord. It is very swollen.'

'Who was it?' Alex asked, trying to keep the fury out of his voice.

Tess shrugged, winced. 'Goodness knows, just two men who thought they'd found easy prey in the dark.'

'How did you get away?'

'I kneed one of them in the groin and then hit the other round the ear with my bag. Then I ran and there was a hackney. He'd just put down a fare, so I scrambled in.'

'Yes. Of course you did,' Alex said faintly. *A defenceless slip of a girl? Perhaps not.* 'After you had hit one bully, emasculated another and run on a sprained ankle. Why the blazes aren't you tucked up in bed at the convent?' he demanded.

Tess grimaced at his tone. 'Because I am a fallen woman, undoubtedly your mistress and unfit for decent company.'

'What?'

'Someone who knows Mother Superior was on the boat, she recognised me, saw us together on deck. I was asleep on your lap, if you recall.' Tess closed her eyes.

Weariness, pain—or shame? How dare they make her ashamed. She was innocent. He was the one who had been fighting lascivious thoughts for two days and nights...

'Mother Superior threw me out and I was looking for lodgings when this happened. I'm sorry to have bothered you, but afterwards, I didn't think I could manage to find anywhere to stay...' Her voice trailed away. Alex closed his right hand around her wrist and she rallied, opened her eyes. 'I'm sorry to be a nuisance. Tomorrow, when it's light, I'll find somewhere.'

A bustle in the hallway announced the arrival of Dr Holt and Hannah Semple. Alex stayed where he was beside Tess and explained the situation to both of them. It was an effort to keep the fury out of his voice as he described what had happened.

His housekeeper cast her bonnet and cloak into MacDonald's hands. 'Poor young lady! I'll stay with the doctor.' She flapped her hands at Alex and Byfleet as though they were a couple of stray small boys underfoot.

Alex made himself get up and walk away, out into the hall. It was ridiculous to feel concerned. Tess was in good hands and he obviously couldn't stay in the room while the doctor checked her over. But still it felt wrong to be doing nothing and the only things that occurred to him—descending on the convent and giving the Mother Superior a piece of his mind and then scouring the Soho area for a couple of men with scratched faces—were obviously equally unlikely to prove effective.

Besides, she was not his responsibility. He had delivered her safe and sound. *Oh, for heaven's sake! Of course she's my responsibility. If I hadn't decided it would be amusing to have the company of an innocent for a while, she'd never have been in this fix.*

'I will rouse the kitchen staff to produce some soup, my lord.' Byfleet vanished through the service door. Trust his valet to come up with a helpful suggestion when all he could do was contemplate violence. Alex resisted the urge to kick the hall hatstand and went into the drawing room to wait with what patience he could muster.

Chapter Seven

To Alex's relief Dr Holt emerged after only ten minutes. He accepted a glass of brandy and the offer of a chair by the fire. 'An alarming assault on the young lady, but she is more shaken than hurt. There was no…er…interference with her person, if you understand me.

'The bruised area will heal without a mark, although it will be temporarily painful and disfiguring, I have no doubt. Miss Ellery's ankle appears to have been healing well after a slight sprain, from what she tells me, but the sudden strain has wrenched it again. She must put no weight on it for several days until the swelling subsides. I have left instructions with your housekeeper.'

Alex made a conscious effort and pulled himself together. 'That's a relief. Poor Cousin Teresa.'

'A cousin, is she?' The doctor rolled the brandy glass between his palms, then inhaled the vapours and leaned back with a sigh. 'Excellent cognac, this. I didn't like to encourage her to speak. It will be painful.'

And thank heavens for small mercies. 'She came up to London to visit an old friend on an impulse, I gather, hoping for an introduction as a governess,' Alex improvised. 'Found her away from home, became confused, ended up in the wrong place at definitely the wrong time. I'm a distant connection, but this was the only address she could recall in her distress.' He leaned across to top up the other man's drink. 'I'll send her home in my carriage as soon as she's up to it.'

'Awkward that, you being a bachelor and so on,' Dr Holt remarked. 'Still, who's to know, eh? And you've an excellent housekeeper in Mrs Semple.'

Did he believe that piece of invention about Tess being a cousin? Not that it made much difference whether he did or not, considering that the presence of even a first cousin in the house would be considered shocking when there were only servants to chaperon her.

'Damned awkward,' Alex agreed. He made himself lean back casually, crossed his legs to appear relaxed. 'Still, not much to be done about it at this time of night. Glad I could find you at home and didn't have to call out someone upon whose discretion I cannot rely.' The hint was as much of a threat as he needed to make. No society doctor was going to risk the wrath of a titled patient, especially when the young lady in question was some drably clad poor relation and not a source of fascinating speculation.

There was a tap on the door and Hannah Semple came in and bobbed a curtsy. 'I've made up a bed in the Blue Chamber, my lord. Shall I get MacDonald to carry the young lady up?'

'I'll be with you in a moment, Mrs Semple.' Alex shook hands with the doctor and saw him out, then went back to the study. Tess was lying back against the chaise longue cushions, her face pale, the bruise on her swollen cheek coming out in red-and-purple patches already.

'I'll take you to your room. You'll feel more yourself in the morning.'

'I'm sorry to be such a nuisance,' Tess murmured again.

'Stop talking and stop apologising.' Alex bent and gathered her up. She was too thin, he thought as he went up the stairs, careful not to knock her foot against the wall. Didn't they feed them in those blasted nunneries? No more than a wisp of a thing, for all her height and those distracting curves. He'd knocked her for six in Ghent, injured her, then two louts had set about her, and in between she'd had a tiring sea voyage with another attempted assault and a nasty shock when she reached what should have been a safe haven. Any other female of his acquaintance would be distraught by now.

What the devil am I going to do with you, little nun? he thought, looking down at the tangled mass of hair that obscured her face from him. Tess was safe for tonight, but by this time tomorrow he had to have a plan—and her out of the house.

'Here we are.' The door to the Blue Chamber was ajar and he shouldered his way in to find that a fire was burning cheerfully in the grate and the covers were turned back. Hannah Semple had even thought to provide a stool to go over Tess's ankle to keep off the weight of the blankets.

'What about Noel?' Tess tipped her face up so she could look at him. 'Poor thing, he was so upset with all the banging about.'

'I'll look after Noel,' Alex promised, staring into the deep blue eyes fixed so earnestly on his. For some reason his breathing was all over the place. *Must be out of condition. I'd better get along to Jackson's for some exercise.*

'Oh, thank you.' Her arm tightened around his neck and, before he could react, Tess's soft mouth was pressed to his.

Heaven. Hell. Alex struggled against temptation and felt it slip under his guard like an opponent's rapier entering his side. The smell of Tess was familiar, but the taste of her was like a new drug, a draught of best champagne, a mouthful of summer berries. He ran his tongue along the join of her lips and felt her surprise, swallowed the little gasp as she opened to him. There was innocence in that reaction, but this was no girl, this was a grown woman in his arms, a sensual woman, who was exploring her natural instincts, and the effect, after so many assured and experienced women, was deeply erotic.

His hands tightened on the soft, slender body as he took one long stride towards the bed, his mouth still on hers. Her tumbled hair brushed over the knuckles of his right hand, the one around her shoulders, and it was every bit as soft and tactile as he had imagined. When it was all down it would reach her waist, would brush over his naked chest—

His foot hit the bedpost and jarred him back to the reality of what he was doing, with whom he was doing it. Alex snapped back his head, laid Tess against the pillows and stepped away as though a chain had jerked him.

'I'm sorry. I did not mean to do that.' As an apology that was wrong in so many different ways he couldn't begin to count them. What the devil was the matter with him? He wasn't usually this clumsy.

'It was my fault.' Tess was trembling, her face flushed, her eyes wide. On her cheek the ugly bruise was deepening. 'I meant to say thank you and I didn't think... I meant to kiss your cheek.'

Of course she had. After the day she'd had now he had taken her innocent gesture and turned it into another assault and she was blaming herself. 'Tess—'

'Thank you, my lord.' Hannah came in, brisk and efficient and smiling, her words a clear dismissal. She had known him since they had both been children and, it was quite clear, she was going to take no nonsense from him now. 'You can leave Miss Ellery to my care.'

'Goodnight, Miss Ellery,' Alex said formally. 'Mrs Semple will look after you excellently, you may be sure.'

'I'll be sleeping in the dressing room, my lord.' Hannah nodded towards the corner of the room. 'With the door open. Then if Miss Ellery becomes alarmed in the night I am close at hand.'

With a poker at the ready for randy males was the unspoken part of that declaration. Alex managed a smile for her and took himself off. He needed brandy. No, he needed to strip off and stand under the stable yard pump, but he was going to have to settle for brandy.

Back in the study he flung himself into his chair and reached for his glass, raised it to his lips as an indignant voice began to yowl from inside the wicker basket by the fireside.

'You took the words right out of my mouth, Noel,' Alex said as he set down his glass untouched and went to open the basket. Somehow, in a matter of moments, he had acquired a cat, a nun, and his well-ordered, pleasantly selfish life was upside down.

Had the housekeeper seen them? Tess fought against the instinct to simply close her eyes and pretend that kiss had never happened. But that would be rude. She met the other woman's gaze and read nothing but concern there.

'I've got a nightgown for you,' Mrs Semple said. 'Mac-Donald had the sense to tell me why I was being called for, so I thought I had best bring some things, just in case. Let's get you undressed and into bed, shall we, Miss Ellery?'

The other woman was not much older than she was, Tess thought as she did her best to help with the undressing. It seemed young to be a housekeeper. 'Is Mr Semple the butler here?' she asked with a vague notion of making polite conversation under extraordinary circumstances.

'I'm a widow, Miss Ellery. I don't live in as a rule, not with an all-male household, you understand.'

'But you're so young. Oh, I'm sorry, that was tactless, I'm not thinking very straight.'

'And no wonder. My husband was killed at Waterloo. He was one of his old lordship's grooms, but he was set on the army.' She tucked Tess in with a brisk pat at the sheets, then stepped back to survey the room. From her nod she was satisfied with what she saw. 'Now, what can I fetch you to eat, Miss Ellery? A nice little omelette with some bread and butter and a cup of tea?'

'That sounds perfect, thank you.' Tess closed her eyes and leaned back into the comfort of piled pillows. She wondered vaguely if she would be able to stay awake to eat it and drifted off to sleep.

'She's asleep.' Hannah Semple closed the study door behind her and came to take the chair opposite Alex. 'And what have you got there?'

Alex stroked his palm over the kitten's body and

smiled as the rumbling purr vibrated through his hand. 'This is Noel. I set out to cross the Channel and come home alone with a pile of artworks, yet ended up with one kitten and a nun who isn't.'

Hannah kicked off her shoes and curled up in the armchair. 'And what, Alex my lad, are you going to do with them?'

'I was hoping you'd be some help with that, Hannah.' He looked at her with affection, his childhood playmate, the daughter of their estate manager at Tempeston. He'd watched her march off to follow Willie Semple to war when both he and Hannah were just seventeen, and she'd written to him five years later when she returned to England, a widow in search of a place. In front of the other staff she was meticulously formal; alone with him they were simply old friends.

'The kitten goes with Tess—but what the blazes am I to do with her?'

'Take her to bed by the looks of things,' Hannah observed.

Alex winced. 'You saw that? She meant to kiss me goodnight on the cheek. Things slipped. She's an innocent, Hannah, not the kind of girl to take to bed.'

'And you'd know. But I'd agree with that. She's as green as spring grass, you've only to look at her.' That was definitely a verbal cuff round the ear, he thought. 'What's she doing in London?'

Alex recounted the tale. 'I need to find her decent employment,' he concluded. There was no way he could wash his hands of her now.

'You need to get her out of this house,' Hannah countered. 'She can come back with me tomorrow, if she's up to it. I've a spare room in my apartment, nothing fancy, but she'll be safe, comfortable and respectable. *Then* we can find her employment.'

The relief of it caught him by surprise, but not as much as the pang of regret that Tess would be leaving. 'I'll pay for her lodging, of course, and whatever you need to furnish her room. And she'll need kitting out with some respectable clothes. I don't know what that nunnery thought it was doing, sending her out at this time of year in those thin things.'

'I'll see to it. You're used to setting up birds of paradise in bijou little houses, not respectable young women in decent lodgings.' Hannah sorted through the items on the end of her chatelaine and came up with a set of tablets and a pencil. 'Now, what are your plans? Where are you going for Christmas?'

'I'm staying here, as well you know. Will you join me for Christmas dinner, Hannah?'

'I will not, but thank you. I'll be off to my in-laws like every year.' She sighed. 'I wish you'd go home, you stubborn man.'

'I *am* home, and in the absence of a warm invitation to the ancestral mansion, this is exactly where I am staying.' And there'd be the sound of trotters on the roof tiles as the flying pigs landed before that particular invitation arrived.

'It is ten years past, Alex.' Hannah looked into the fire, not meeting his eyes. 'Surely it is time to forgive?'

'When I forget, then I'll forgive.' Surely she knew it was not just for him? A young man had died that bitter Christmas because of his father's blind prejudice and need to hit out at his elder son.

'You'll have to go back one day. You are the heir.'

'Over his dead body or mine. If it's the latter, then

I suppose they'll let me have my shelf in the ancestral vault.' He smiled at her to show that this was something he did not care about, that it no longer hurt.

Hannah simply shook her head. 'You're as pig-headed as the earl is—you know that, don't you?' She cocked her head on one side and regarded him beadily. 'Why not take a wife and produce an heir? That's a revenge for you, Lord Moreland knowing that his precious lump of a younger son won't inherit.'

'And shatter all his fondly held beliefs about me? How unkind that would be. And what if I turn out to be as bad at marriage and fatherhood as he has?'

'Impossible.' Hannah grinned at him, suddenly finding her humour again. 'No one could be that bad. I'm off to bed. I just hope that nice lass doesn't have nightmares, bless her.'

When the door closed behind her with a soft click Alex sat on, stroking the kitten, his unfocused gaze on the sinking embers. Tess would doubtless tell him that Christmas, on top of everything else, was the perfect time for reconciliation and forgiveness. It was a good thing she was leaving. Just for a moment he believed that she might even convince him it was true.

'I ought to say goodbye to Lord Weybourn,' Tess said as Mrs Semple fastened the strap on Noel's basket. 'I must say thank you.'

'You can send him a note.' The housekeeper nodded to MacDonald, who opened the door and carried Tess's bag down to the waiting hackney. 'We need to get you to your new lodgings and work out what shopping you require.'

'I haven't much money,' Tess ventured. She had very definitely been removed from the house, she thought, finding herself wedged into her seat with the cat basket deposited on her lap. *Mrs Semple doesn't approve of me. She saw that kiss and she thinks...*

'His lordship's paying.'

She thinks I've slept with him, that now he's paying me off. 'It will be a loan. Just as soon as I have employment and a wage, I'll repay him.'

Mrs Semple made a noise that might have been agreement, might have been disbelief. She was looking out of the window with a frown that wrinkled her brow.

'Mrs Semple, I am not his mistress. What you saw last night—'

'Was quite innocent on your side. Yes, I know.' The housekeeper turned and smiled.

'On both sides.'

'He's a man, and I doubt he's been an innocent for many years, Miss Ellery. No, don't bristle up, he's no predator on decent girls, he won't be after seducing you. Or worse. But, like I say, he's a man, you are a woman, and a pretty one under all that drab clothing and bandages. If he didn't take an interest I'd be worried about his health.'

A half delighted, half shocked snort of laughter escaped Tess. 'You know Lord Weybourn very well?'

'Since we were both six years old. My father was the Earl of Moreland's estate manager. Alex is a good man. Stubborn as his sire, though.' The frown was back.

'You worry about him, don't you? What has gone so wrong with his family?'

Mrs Semple's mouth twisted into a wry smile. 'That's his story to tell you. But I will tell you something. He is flagellating himself for leaving you somewhere that wasn't safe for you. You'll hurt his pride, if nothing else, if you make a fuss about paying him back for a few bits and pieces and a decent wardrobe of clothes.'

'He wasn't to know there would be any problem,' Tess protested. 'And he certainly wasn't to blame.'

'If he had taken you to the canal boat in time, then none of this would have happened, and I know you should have insisted and so on and so forth, but Alex Tempest has an over-developed sense of responsibility for all that care-nothing air he pretends to have. So are you going to make him miserable or are you going to swallow your pride and enjoy some decent clothes?'

'I'll swallow it,' Tess conceded. *I'm so far down that Primrose Path I may as well face the fact that I'm ruined and have a man buy me clothes. It was a pity I couldn't be ruined properly while I was at it though...* The thought caught her unawares and she scrabbled in her purse for a handkerchief to turn her gasp into a cough. 'But nice clothes aren't suitable for someone looking for a post as a governess.'

'We'll see. I suspect when Lord Weybourn puts his mind to it he'll be able to steer you in the direction of something rather more elevated than your convent might have done.' Mrs Semple's gaze rested on her speculatively. 'Hmm. Yes, I can see all sorts of possibilities.' The frown vanished to be replaced with a mischievous smile. 'Now let's get this kitten settled and make a list of what you need. And call me Hannah, please.'

Chapter Eight

'Where the blazes is my coffee?' Alex enquired of thin air. The dining room was bereft of footmen, his coffee jug had been empty for ten minutes, there was no sign of his toast and the fire needed making up. He should have known it was too good to last, the peace and quiet and order that had reigned for almost a week since the departure of Tess and the kitten.

He wasn't helpless and it wasn't above his dignity to grapple with the coal tongs, but even so… With a sigh he got up, mended the fire and then gave the bell pull a prolonged tug. Silence. The hall, when he looked out, was deserted, the front door still bolted.

It was not unheard of for housebreakers to raid London houses, tie up the staff and make off with the silver with the owners none the wiser for hours. Breakfast time was a strange time to attempt it, though. Feeling slightly melodramatic, Alex retrieved his cane from the hall stand and walked softly to the service door under the stairs.

He was halfway down, wincing as a tread creaked, when he heard a thump and a clatter and took the remaining stairs in three strides. In the kitchen, her back to him, was a strange woman in a green gown. He could see the large bow of the voluminous apron that was wrapped round her, her glossy dark hair was topped by a large white cap; she had a badly bent toasting fork in one hand and the remains of half a dozen slices of bread around her feet.

'You useless male *object*, you!' she announced in tones of loathing.

One glance around the kitchen was enough to show Alex that he was the only male in sight. 'Madam? If you care to tell me who you are I will endeavour to be of rather more utility.'

She whirled round, trampling the bread in the process. 'Oh, no,' Tess said flatly. 'You.'

'Me,' Alex agreed and propped the cane unobtrusively in a corner. So not burglars, but an invasion that was far less easy to deal with. He told himself that the feeling in his chest was the after-effects of stalking burglars. Or dread. 'What are you doing here—other than pulverising bread and breaking the kitchen equipment—and where is Mrs Semple?'

Tess moved into the light. *Oh, my God, her face.* The bruise was now multicoloured and she had the fading remains of a black eye. 'And you are supposed to be resting that ankle.' Alex trampled on the urge to scoop her up and make her lie down. She wouldn't thank him for mentioning the way she looked, and thinking about it would probably only make it hurt more. *And once I have my hands on her I may not be able to let go.*

'Hannah is very much under the weather and in bed with a headache, so I am attempting to make your breakfast. Everything was going well, wasn't it?' She tossed the toasting fork on to the table and frowned at him. 'The ham and eggs? The sausage? The hot rolls? They were all perfect, I thought. Only there is no more coffee and Noel knocked the bread off the table the moment I had sliced it and I bent the toasting fork when I made a dive for it.'

'Where are MacDonald and Phipps? Or Byfleet, come to that?' One end of the table was laid for four breakfasts with plates at various stages from egg smeared to laden but scarcely touched.

'MacDonald has run out for coffee and bread. I sent Phipps to the lodging house with some medicine that Hannah asked for. Byfleet has gone to Jermyn Street, I think. Buying shirts.' That was delivered in a rapid mutter from a crouched position on the floor where Tess was retrieving broken slices of bread.

'Dare I ask why he needs to buy shirts at this time in the morning?' The nape of her neck was exposed, soft and pale and vulnerable, begging for his lips. Alex took the toasting fork, braced the wrought iron handle against the tabletop and leaned on it. It was more or less straight when he squinted down the length. His brain was more or less in control of his animal instincts, too.

Tess stood up with her hands full of bread, flinched when she found herself facing the prongs and looked round for somewhere to deposit her load.

'On the fire,' Alex suggested.

'Throw food on the fire? I can't do that. Sister Peter says it goes straight to the devil if you do that.'

'And you believe her?'

'Of course not.' Tess found the slop bucket and tossed in the broken slices. 'But it's like not walking under ladders and tossing salt over your shoulder—one just gets into the habit.'

'And I suppose nuns get into more habits than anyone,' Alex observed, as he hitched one hip on to the table. He found a crust and buttered it lavishly. He should be both irritated and worried to find Tess back in the house; instead he felt oddly cheerful. Uncomfortably aroused, but happy.

Tess's harassed expression transformed into a grin. 'That is a terrible pun!' She picked up the toasting fork and studied it. 'My goodness, you are strong.'

'It is all the exercise I get tossing nuns about. Shirts?' Alex prompted, resisting the instinctive grin in return. It would be dangerous to let things get too cosy.

'All your clean ones were in the ironing basket in the scullery this morning, apparently. Then Noel found them.'

'Ah.'

'More *urgh*, actually, although Mr Byfleet expressed himself rather freely on the subject.' She eyed him warily. 'I can make you some tea and bring it up if you like.'

'No, I would not like. I will sit down here and wait to find out why my infallibly efficient housekeeper has run out of coffee, why when she has never, in all the years I've known her, succumbed to a headache, she has taken to her bed with one and why, when she has, she sent you to make my breakfast.'

'Hannah has been spending a lot of time with me, I'm afraid, buying clothes and settling me in. I expect she's been distracted and forgot to check the store cupboard. And she was very quiet yesterday evening. I thought she was simply deep in thought, but perhaps it was the headache.'

'Have you had your breakfast?' Alex found the honey and spread it on another crust.

'I had mine first.' Tess began to gather up the dirty crockery and took it through to the scullery. He noticed her limp had completely vanished. 'Hannah says a scullery maid will come in later.'

'So I believe. Tess, come back here and sit down.' He waited until she returned and sat, neat and composed in her new dress and clean white apron. She folded her hands in her lap and regarded him, head on one side, like an inquisitive bird or a child waiting for an eccentric adult to do something entertaining. Very meek, very attentive. Why did he have the suspicion that she was laughing at him? 'You shouldn't be here.' All he had to do was put his foot down; it should be a simple enough matter.

'I am a perfectly good plain cook.' Now she was managing to look wounded, blast her. 'You would never have known I was here if it wasn't for the problem with the coffee and the toast. Your staff are highly respectable.' Alex opened his mouth, but she sailed on. 'And who is to know?'

'I know.' *And I am finding it decidedly unsettling.* 'You are not a servant.'

'I am acting as your housekeeper. That is at least as respectable as being a governess in many households.'

'Not for an unmarried lady, it isn't.' Alex dusted crumbs off his fingers and stood up. 'I'll call a hackney to take you back to the lodging house.'

The door to the area opened and Phipps came in, gawped when he saw Alex and whipped off his hat. 'Good morning, my lord.'

'Good morning. And how is Mrs Semple's headache?'

'Not good, my lord. I didn't see her, only Mrs Green, the lodging house keeper. She says it's the influenza and two more of her lady lodgers have it.'

'I must go and nurse Hannah.' Tess was on her feet, pulling off cap and apron.

'No, miss. Mrs Green said that she and her girl will look after the ladies and that Mrs Semple said you weren't to go back and risk catching it. She's had your bags packed and I've brought them here with me.'

'Absolutely not. You cannot stay here,' Alex began as the door opened and a thin woman came in.

'Morning, all. I'll get the copper on the boil and— Oh!' She stopped dead at the sight of Alex and Tess. 'Where's Mrs Semple? I'm Nelly 'Odgkins, come to do the weekly wash.'

'She's sick,' Tess said before Alex could intervene. 'Can you carry on as usual, please, Mrs Hodgkins?'

'Right you are, mum.'

'Miss Ellery—'

'I've got the coffee and three loaves, Miss Ellery... My lord?' MacDonald grounded the shopping baskets and stared at Alex as a scrap of a girl slid into the room through the door behind him.

'Mornin', Mr MacDonald, Mr Phipps. Ooh...' She stopped and stared, wide-eyed.

'You must be Annie. Off you go to the scullery and start on the breakfast dishes,' Tess said firmly.

Alex strode round to shut the door in the hope of stemming the flood of incomers and, hopefully, the evil draught of cold December air.

His shove met with resistance against a brawny shoulder and a head covered with a battered low-crowned hat appeared round the door. 'Morning, all. I've got some fine mutton cuts here, Mrs Semple. Er?'

'Good morning.' Tess waved the butcher inside, then turned to Alex. 'You need a housekeeper, my lord,' she said, low voiced, then clapped her hands for attention. 'Annie, come out here for a moment, please. Mrs Semple is down with the influenza, I'm afraid, and I am Mi—*Mrs* Ellery, the housekeeper in her absence. Phipps, please get a kettle boiling for his lordship's coffee. MacDonald, pass me the loaf, then you can start making the toast. I'll be with you directly, Mr—?'

'Burford, mum. Don't you worry yourself, I'll be fine over here till you're all sorted.' He took himself over to a bench in the corner, grounded his basket with a grunt and sat down, hands on knees, with every appearance of settling down to watch a play, much to Alex's irritation.

'I'll see you in the study after breakfast, *Mrs* Ellery,' Alex said. Any trace of pleasure at being alone with Tess had vanished. Who, he thought bitterly, was going to appear next? The parish constable? He scooped up the kitten, who had bounced out in pursuit of the butcher's trailing bootlaces, and retreated upstairs with as much dignity as he could muster.

'Routed from my own kitchen, Noel. Now what am I going to do with her?'

Noel yowled and bit Alex's thumb.

A fresh pot of coffee, hot toast and the last pot of what Phipps assured her was Mrs Semple's best strawberry conserve would surely soothe a troubled male breast at breakfast time, Tess thought. Halfway up the back stairs she remembered her apron and went down again to take it off and straighten her cap, which showed a tendency to slide on her tightly coiled hair.

'You look the part, Miss…er…Mrs Ellery,' MacDonald said with an encouraging smile that only confirmed that what she *looked* was in need of encouragement.

At Alex's door she knocked. *I must stop calling him that, even in my head.*

'Come.' It was hardly welcoming. Perhaps the jam had been a mistake, too obvious a peace offering.

Tess walked in, wishing this was rather less like being summoned to Mother Superior's study and that she could manage a confident smile. But that still made her cheek ache. 'My lord.' She bobbed a curtsy, folded her hands and waited.

'For goodness' sake, Tess, sit down and stop play-acting.' He was using the point of a paperknife to flip over a pile of gilt-edged cards on his desk.

'I am not. I am endeavouring to behave like a proper housekeeper in front of your staff and any visitors.'

'You cannot be my housekeeper. You cannot stay here.' Alex jammed the paperknife into a jar of pens. 'You are most certainly not going to come into contact with any visitors.'

'I am perfectly competent and they taught us house-keeping and plain cookery at the convent. This is a small house. I can manage very well.'

'That is not what I mean.' His gaze, those hazel eyes shadowed, was on her mouth, his own lips were set in a hard line.

They had felt firm, yet soft on hers. Strong, yet questioning. They had asked questions she… Tess closed her eyes and Alex made a sound, a sudden sharp inhalation of breath. She blinked and he was still staring at her.

'It's about that kiss, isn't it? You think I was throwing myself at you.' The words were out before she could censor them. She had been so certain he knew it had been a mistake, so certain that he had disregarded it with an ease she could only dream of managing herself.

'No. Yes. Partly.' Alex had his elbows on the arms of his chair. Now he clasped his hands together as though in prayer and rested his mouth against his knuckles, apparently finding something interesting on the surface of the desk. When he dropped his hands and looked up she could see neither amusement nor desire in his expression. 'You should not be in a bachelor household, it is as simple as that. I am not in the habit of pouncing on my female staff and, although I can find explanations for what happened the other night, they are not excuses, not acceptable ones.'

He frowned. 'I can't imagine what Hannah was thinking of, sending you here. She was as set on moving you out as I was.'

'She is ill and perhaps she'd had long enough to think about it and know I was perfectly safe here.' Tess stopped herself pleating the fine wool of her skirt between her fingers. 'I think she was more worried about you than about me, at first.'

'About me?' That at least wiped the brooding expression off his face. Alex sat up and stared at her.

'I suspect she thought I was attempting to seduce and entrap you,' Tess said primly. It was ludicrous, of course.

Alex threw his head back and laughed, a crack of sheer amusement. 'You?'

'I know. Ridiculous, isn't it?' *Of course it is.* So why did his laughter twist inside her with a stab of what was perilously close to shame? She managed a little cackle of her own, just to show how funny it was.

'She was obviously sickening for the influenza even then,' Alex said, with a shake of his head for the preposterousness of it.

Yes, *preposterous* was the word. Teresa Ellery, as ignorant as Noel was about the big wide world, battered and bruised, dressed as a convent orphan, might arouse Lord Weybourn's chivalrous instincts, but not his amorous ones. That kiss, the one she'd built all those castles in the air about in her dreams and daydreams, was nothing more than the instinctive reaction of any man to a woman in his arms foolishly pressing her lips to his.

'Anyway, I cannot go back to the lodgings. As well as the risk of catching the influenza myself, the landlady is quite busy enough as it is with sick nursing,' Tess said. 'If I am not seen above stairs when you have visitors, who is to know?'

He scrubbed one hand across his face, an oddly clumsy gesture for such an elegant man. 'I suppose I can hardly send you off to an hotel. There's a bedchamber above mine you could use,' he said with evident reluctance. 'None of the male staff sleep on that floor and it has a door that locks. We must get a maid for you, one to sleep in the dressing room.' He reached out and pulled the bell, then fell silent until MacDonald came in. 'Take Mrs Ellery to our usual domestic agency and assist her in finding a suitable lady's maid.'

'A *lady's* maid?'

'You are a lady, aren't you?' One brow lifted.

'Well, yes.' *No, I'm not.* 'But a housemaid would do.'

'We have two housemaids. They come in three times a week to do the cleaning. We do not require any more.'

'Yes, my lord.' To wrangle in front of the staff was impossible. Tess stood up, dropped a neat curtsy and waited for the footman to open the door for her. 'We will go immediately, if you have finished your current tasks, MacDonald.'

* * *

'It's a very good agency,' MacDonald confided as they stood outside the door with its neat brass plate. 'His lordship gets all his staff here.'

Twinford and Musgrave Domestic Agency. Est. 1790. It certainly sounded established and efficient, Tess told herself. They would guide her, which was a good thing, because she had only the vaguest idea of the details of a lady's maid's duties.

MacDonald opened the door for her. 'Mrs Ellery from Lord Weybourn's establishment, requiring a lady's maid,' he informed the man at the desk, who rose after a rapid assessment of Tess's gown, pelisse and muff. She was grateful for Hannah's insistence on good-quality clothes or presumably she would have been directed to join the queue of applicants lined up on the far side of the hall herself.

'Certainly, madam. Would you care to step through to the office? My assistant will discuss your requirements and review the available—'

He was interrupted by a baby's wailing cry. The door opposite opened and a young woman backed out, clutching the child to her breast. 'But, Mr Twinford, I can turn my hand to anything. I'll wash, I can sew, scrub—'

She was of medium height, neatly and respectably dressed, although not warmly enough for the weather, Tess thought, casting an anxious look at the baby who was swathed in what seemed to be a cut-down pelisse.

'You've turned your *hand* to more than domestic duties, my girl.' The voice from the office sounded outraged. 'How can you have the gall to expect an agency with our reputation to recommend a fallen woman to a respectable household?'

'But, Mr Twinford, I never…' The woman was pale, thin and, to Tess's eyes, quite desperate.

'Out!' The door slammed in her face and she stumbled back.

'I do beg your pardon, Mrs Ellery. Shocking!' The clerk moved round the side of the desk. 'Now, look here, you—'

'Stop it. You are frightening the baby.' Tess stepped between them. 'What is your name?'

'Dorcas White, ma'am.' Her voice was quiet, genteel, exhausted. Close up, Tess could see how neatly her clothes had been mended, how carefully the baby's improvised coverings had been constructed.

'Are you a lady's maid, Dorcas?'

'I was, ma'am. Once.'

'Come with me.' She turned to the spluttering clerk, who was trying to get past her to take Dorcas's arm. 'Will you please stop pushing? We are leaving.' She guided the unresisting woman out to the street and into the waiting carriage. 'There, now at least we have some peace and we are out of the wind. You say you are a lady's maid and you are looking for a position?'

'I was, but I can't be one now, not with Daisy here. I'll do anything, work at anything, but I'll not give her up to the parish.'

'Certainly not.' All that was visible of the baby was a button nose and one waving fist. 'Where is her father?'

Dorcas went even whiter. 'He…he threw me out when I started to show.'

'What, you mean he was your employer?' A nod. 'Did he force you?' Another nod. 'And his wife said nothing?'

'He told her I'd… He said I had…'

She would get the full story later when the poor

woman was less distressed. 'Well, we won't worry about that now. I need a lady's maid. You can come and work for me. Or for Lord Weybourn, rather.'

'You are Lady Weybourn?' Dorcas was staring at her as though she could not believe what she was hearing.

'Me?' Tess steadied her voice. 'No, I am his new housekeeper, but it is an all-male household and I need a maid for appearances, you understand.' She looked at the thin, careworn face, the chapped hands gently cradling the baby, the look of desperate courage in the dark eyes. 'It would be more like a companion's post, really. Would you like the position?'

'Oh, yes, ma'am. Oh, yes, please.' And Dorcas burst into tears.

Chapter Nine

'Where is Miss…*Mrs* Ellery?' After the chaos of the morning, the previous day had passed uneventfully. Alex had dealt with his paperwork, visited some art dealers and then gone to his club, where he had dined and spent the evening catching up with acquaintances and what gossip there was in London in early December. A good day in the end, he concluded, one mercifully free from emotion and women.

He'd had some vague thought of calling on Mrs Hobhouse, a particularly friendly young widow. When he had last been in London she had sought him out, had been insistent that only Lord Weybourn with his legendary good taste could advise her on the paintings she should hang in her newly decorated bedchamber. It was so important to get the right *mood* in a *bedchamber*, wasn't it? It had impressed Alex that she could get quite so much sensual innuendo into one word.

At the time he had considered assisting her with viewing some likely works of art from a variety of locations, including her bed, and yet somehow, when it came to the point of setting out for Bruton Street, he found he'd lost interest.

This morning's breakfast had been excellent. Alex folded his newspaper and listened. Everything was suspiciously calm. It was surely too much to hope that Hannah had made a miraculous recovery and was back at her post.

'Mrs Ellery is in the kitchen, my lord.' Phipps balanced the silver salver with its load of letters and dipped it so Alex could see how much post there was. 'Shall I put your correspondence in the study, my lord? Mr Bland said to tell you that he has gone to the stationer's shop and will be back directly.'

'Very well.' Alex waved a vague hand in the direction of the door. His secretary could make a start on it when he got back; he wasn't ready to concentrate on business yet.

So Tess had spent the night upstairs in the bedchamber above his own, had she? Alex picked up the paper, stared at the Parliamentary report for a while. Hot air, the lot of it. The foreign news didn't make much more sense.

Spain, West Indies, the Hamburg mails… He hadn't heard so much as a footstep on the boards overhead, but then she'd doubtless been fast asleep when he'd arrived home and had risen at least an hour before he was awake. So far, so good. The heavens hadn't fallen and he had obviously been worrying about nothing.

Alex tossed down the *Times*. He was wool-gathering, which was what came of having his peace and quiet interrupted. What he needed to do was turn his mind to the possibilities for offloading a collection of rather garish French ormolu furniture that he was regretting buying. He made his way down the hall towards the study, then stopped dead when an alien noise, a wail, wavered through the quiet.

A baby was crying. Alex turned back towards the

front door. Surely no desperate mother had left her off-spring on his blameless front step? Well, to be honest it was hardly blameless, but he had made damn sure he left no by-blows in his wake.

The noise grew softer. He walked back. Louder—and it was coming from the basement. Then it ceased, leaving an almost visible question mark hanging in the silence.

When he eased open the kitchen door it was on to a domestic scene that would have gladdened the palette of some fashionable, if sentimental, genre painter. Tess was sitting at the table with a pile of account books in front of her. Byfleet was standing by the fireside, polishing Alex's newest pair of boots, while Annie sat at the far end of the table, peeling potatoes.

And in a rocking chair opposite Byfleet was a woman nursing a baby while Noel chased a ball of paper around her feet. The stranger was crooning a lullaby and Alex was instantly back to the nursery, his breath tight in his chest as though arms were holding him tightly.

A family. They look like a family sitting there. Alex let out his breath and all the heads turned in his direction except for the baby, who was latched firmly on to its mother's breast. The woman whipped her shawl around it and stared at him with such alarm on her face that he might as well have been brandishing a poker.

'My lord.' Tess sounded perfectly composed, which was more than he felt, damn it. 'Did you ring? I'm afraid we didn't hear.'

There was a pain in his chest from holding his breath and he rubbed at his breastbone. 'No. I did not ring. I crossed the hall and I heard a child crying.'

The stranger fumbled her bodice together, got to her feet and laid the baby on the chair. 'My lord.' She dropped a curtsy and he noticed how pin neat she was, how thin. 'I am very sorry you were disturbed, my lord. It won't happen again.' Her voice was soft and her eyes were terrified.

'Babies cry,' he said with a shrug. Admittedly, they weren't normally to be found doing so in the kitchen of a Mayfair bachelor household. Himself, he'd been brought up in a nursery so remote from the floors his parents occupied that a full military band could have played there without being heard and he'd had his earliest lessons in a schoolroom equally distant where no parent would have thought of dropping by. 'I was not disturbed, merely curious.'

'This is Dorcas White, my lord.' Tess moved over to stand beside the woman. Did she think she needed to protect her from him? 'She is my new lady's maid.'

'And the baby?'

'Is mine, my lord.' Dorcas looked ready to faint.

Alex looked down at her hands, clutched together in front of her. No ring. He met Tess's blue gaze and read a steely defiance in it that took him aback.

'The baby's name is Daisy, my lord.'

'Thank you, Mrs Ellery. I am aware that babies are people, too.' She coloured up. Annoyance, he supposed. That made two of them. 'So we have acquired another stray, have we? I suppose I must be thankful that the baby is already with us or I have no doubt I would be expected to house oxen and a donkey in my stables come Christmastide.'

Tess drew in a deep breath through her nose and narrowed her eyes at him. 'I suspect that verges on blasphemy, my lord. Dorcas is very well qualified as a lady's maid.'

'And comes with excellent references, no doubt?' It

came out sharply and Tess's chin jutted. So she didn't like his tone? There was still an ache in his chest that he didn't understand, memories of childhood he thought he had locked away in his head. His tight, small, bachelor household had become full of women, virtually a crèche. He was entitled to snap—he was amazed he wasn't shouting.

'Might we have a word, my lord?' Tess enquired with a sweet, false smile. 'Upstairs?'

He held the door for her and followed her stiff back along to the study. Tess did not wait for him to get behind the barrier of his desk and sit down before she attacked. 'No, Dorcas White does not have references. A man who forces himself on a servant and then tells his wife that *the slut* flaunted herself at him when he'd had a few drinks, that she'd been *asking for it*, is not someone who writes a reference for his victim.'

'Are you certain?' Even as he said it he felt ashamed of himself. Those thin, desperate hands, those wounded eyes, the way she had held her child... No, that was not some little hussy who had taken advantage of Tess's good nature. 'Yes, of course you are, and I can see you are right,' he said before the angry rebuttal was out of her mouth. 'What does she need for the child? Buy it for her, whatever it is.'

If he had been looking for a reward, which he hadn't, he told himself, he would have got it in the smile that transformed Tess's face.

'Who is the father?' He suppressed his own answering smile. This was not a laughing matter.

'I have no idea. I didn't ask her. Why?'

'Because he needs dealing with,' Alex said, startling himself. What was he, some knight errant, dispensing justice for wronged damsels? 'Still, I suppose you'll never get the name out of her and I don't want her worried that the swine will find out where she is.'

'Oh, thank you,' Tess said and clutched his hand. 'Thank you for understanding. I knew you were Sir Lancelot really, however much you grumbled about Noel and things.'

Her hand was small and warm and strong in his and he closed his fingers around it, even as he said, in tones of loathing, '*Sir Lancelot?* Do I look like some confounded idiot clanking around in armour? And besides, he was a decidedly dubious type—making love to his king's wife like that.'

'I thought when you hit that sailor that you were a storybook knight and then you were grumpy with me so I changed my mind. But it is all a front, the grumpiness, isn't it?' Her eyes were dancing; it seemed she was as amused by her nonsense as he was.

His meek little nun was teasing him, he realised, and this time could not suppress the answering smile. Alarm bells were ringing even as he lifted her hand and pressed the back of it against his cheek, her pulse rioting under his fingers. *Charm and sweetness. You cannot let yourself enjoy them, not for your sake and definitely not for hers.*

'Yes,' Alex agreed. 'It is all a front, but behind it is not your *preux chevalier*, there's a real, live, flawed man with many masks and many, many faults.' He moved her hand so he could nip lightly at her fingertips in warning and felt, more than heard, her shuddering indrawn breath. 'A man who is hypocrite enough to despise the father of the child down there and yet who cannot forget the feel of your mouth under his, your body in his arms.'

Tess became still, her eyes wide and questioning. *She's an innocent*, he told himself. *Even if she can deal with illegitimate children and speak frankly about what has happened to Dorcas. She needs warning, scaring a little, even.*

He loosened his grip on her fingers and her hand slid up to cup his cheek. She was not wary, not at all alarmed by him. The touch was not sexual, not even sensual. It was intended, he realised with something like shock, to comfort. When was the last time anyone had touched him like that?

'You are very hard on yourself, aren't you, Alex?' Tess murmured. 'You aren't a saint, you certainly aren't a monk, so why do you expect it of yourself?'

'I am a gentleman,' he said, his voice harsher than he'd intended. 'The least I can do is try to behave like one around decent women.'

'You are trying. Very hard, I think.' She cocked her head to one side with that questioning look he was learning to beware of. 'I may be a virgin, and that may have been my first kiss, but I am quite capable of recognising sensual attraction when I experience it. There is something between us, isn't there?'

Alex found himself incapable of answering her as she wrestled so honestly with things no young lady was supposed to think about, let alone articulate.

'I am quite capable of saying *no*, at least, I am when I haven't been hit on the head and frightened half out of my wits,' Tess said decisively. She lowered her hand and stepped away. 'We got carried away, we both did. But the onus should not be all on you to be prudent.'

'*Prudent?*' Alex found he had to move away from her. If it was a retreat, he didn't care, and the big desk was a reassuringly solid barrier. 'Naturally it is down to me to behave properly.'

'If I was the sort of young woman who has a hope of

marrying, then of course it is,' she agreed. Tess perched on the arm of a chair and he wondered if, for all her calmness, her legs were a bit shaky. 'But I'm not, am I? So I need to make decisions based on different criteria, such as, do I want to be your mistress? What would make us happiest, while it lasted?'

'Tess, stop this! You cannot discuss being my mistress, and happiness is the last thing we should be considering.'

'Is it?' She frowned at him, her brow wrinkled. 'But what is the point of a...liaison if it doesn't make people happy? What is the point of life, come to that?'

'Frankly? I do not know about the meaning of life. I just get on with living it as best I can. But a liaison? It is about sex on one side and financial gain on the other,' Alex snapped. He drove his fingers through his hair and tried to get his feet back on solid ground. This was like finding oneself knee-deep in fast-flowing water when one thought all one was doing was having a stroll beside a stream. 'It is commerce. It is not something you should even think about.'

Her expression seemed to indicate that she was thinking about it, very carefully, very seriously.

Alex fought the urge to run his finger around a neckcloth that seemed far too tight. He coped with sophisticated ladies, wanton widows, expensive high-fliers, all without turning a hair. Why the devil was he finding it hard to deal with one outspoken innocent? 'Look, Tess, men and women find themselves physically attracted all the time. We have to deal with it like everyone else does. You just pretend it isn't happening.'

She nodded. 'I can see that is usually best. But this isn't making you happy, is it?'

'It is making me damnably confused, if you must

know.' Did she think he expected sexual favours as a payment for giving her shelter? Did she think that in return for shelter she had a duty to make him *happy*, whatever she meant by that? She certainly wasn't casting out lures or flirting, although he doubted she knew how. 'But that is beside the point. You are a lovely young woman, Tess. I would have to be a plank of wood not to be attracted to you.'

That made her smile, at least. 'Thank you. It wasn't that I had decided we should have an *affaire*, you understand. But I don't want you feeling guilty all the time if things happen. I expect I will learn not to notice when we touch by accident, or when I meet your eyes and I seem to read things in them.'

She could read him like a book, he was sure, even if she didn't understand some of the long words. 'It will do me no harm to feel guilty occasionally.' Alex made his tone lighter. 'We'll not speak of this again.' *Who do I think I am deceiving?* 'Now, about Dorcas—make certain she understand she's safe here. I'm not going to throw her out if the baby cries. I won't have her hiding it away for fear of that. A baby should be with its mother.'

'Yes, of course. Thank you, I will reassure her.' Tess stood up. 'Thank you for letting me stay. I know it is disrupting things, even if we leave aside…you know. But I work hard and I'll earn my keep, I promise.'

'You don't have to work at all.' Alex put as much bored languor into his tone as he could. 'You could stay in your room with Dorcas to chaperon you until Hannah is well again or we find you a post. As you are well aware, if I'd delivered you where you asked, on time, none of this would have occurred.'

'I have my pride, too, you know.' Tess bobbed her infuriatingly proper curtsy and went out as though they had discussed nothing more momentous than a minor staffing problem.

Alex sat down took a deep breath and pulled his pile of correspondence towards him. Tess had been brought up to tackle issues head-on and without hypocrisy, it seemed. But hypocrisy was one of society's main safeguards, and without it she was vulnerable. So was he. The widow who wanted to buy pictures was looking increasingly tempting. It was too long since he had been with a woman; that was all it was, this need to hold Tess, to take the pins from her hair, the clothes from her body, to lie down with her and…

She had shocked Alex, Tess realised. Seeing the baby had upset him for some reason, and it wasn't the fact that little Daisy's crying had annoyed him. He was angry with Dorcas's employer, which was understandable, for any decent person would have been, but there was something else, something deeper in his reaction.

And that moment when she had taken his hand had been…startling. She'd had no intention of flirting and she had no idea how to. She certainly hadn't thought of trying to provoke him into kissing her again, but the energy that had flowed between their joined fingers still sparkled along her veins. It had seemed to her important to try to understand where they stood, to tell him how she felt. But that had been a mistake. He had not wanted that kind of honesty from her. And she couldn't simply take his protection, his money, and do nothing in return. She expected to work for her living, and she owed it to Hannah to keep her from worrying about the household while she was ill.

When Tess got to her feet and went into the kitchen it

was empty except for Dorcas, who was hemming handkerchiefs with the baby fast asleep in a makeshift crib by her side. She looked up. 'Is he…is his lordship very angry?'

'Not at all, just startled. He says we are to buy whatever Daisy needs and you are not to be afraid that he will be annoyed if he hears her crying.' Tess sat down on the other side of the fireplace. 'Lord Weybourn is simply not used to having women about the house, that is all.'

Chapter Ten

'Are you sure you wouldn't rather come back to Half Moon Street? I could make up the room across the passage from mine, and now I have Dorcas with me we can nurse you easily.'

'That is thoughtful of you, Tess.' Hannah Semple groped for a handkerchief as she began to cough. 'Oh, drat and blast this! We sound like a colony of seals I once saw on the coast.' From the room opposite came the echo of the same sound. 'But I'm better here in my own home with my things around me. And no one is very sick now, just laid low with this wretched chesty cough, so Mrs Green and her girls are managing to look after us easily enough.'

She curled her fingers around the cup of tea that Tess handed to her and sipped, her nose glowing pinkly though the steam. 'Besides anything else, I'd drive Lord Weybourn mad with the coughing.'

'He doesn't seem to be disturbed by the baby.' Tess poured herself a cup and settled back in the fireside chair. 'And she cries a lot, bless her.'

'I find it hard to imagine, Alex taking in a baby.'

'You thought he would send her away? He wasn't

pleased, not at first, but that just was the surprise, I think.'

'Oh, I don't mean he would send them off into the night. But I'd have expected him to find her lodgings or something, not have them live in.' Hannah sneezed, then sat regarding Tess over the top of the handkerchief. 'You've turned his house upside down with your strays by the sound of it. I'm amazed he hasn't reacted more strongly.' She sat up against the pillows. 'Has he had any visitors?'

'No, he goes out a lot and there have been endless invitations, but there've been no callers. I don't think he's issuing invitations with me there.'

'Perhaps that's why he's being so tolerant. After all, kittens and babies underfoot wouldn't do much for his carefully maintained image.'

'What image?'

'Elegant, imperturbable, languid and cultivated. A fastidious pink of the *ton* on the surface. He's a serious sportsman on the quiet, but unless you saw him after a hard round at Gentleman Jackson's you'd be forgiven for not noticing.'

Tess laughed. 'That's just a mask. Underneath he's funny and very kind. And the sparring explains the muscles.'

'Hmm. You've noticed them, have you?' Hannah gave her an old-fashioned look. 'He's thought about nothing but himself for ten years.' Despite the thickness of her voice she sounded remarkably tart.

'But he *is* kind.'

'I didn't say he wasn't. He's charming, he treats people well—and he organises his life so no one gets behind the mask or disturbs his well-ordered life.'

Tess kicked off her shoes and curled up in the chair.

Outside the rain was threatening to turn into sleet and the wind howled in the chimney, making the flames dance and reminding them that December had most definitely arrived. Inside all was snug and comfortable, she had thought. Now Hannah was making her uneasy.

'His mistresses must,' she suggested with the sensation of jabbing her tongue against a sore tooth. 'Get close, I mean.'

'I very much doubt it. They can get inside those well-cut clothes, they can rumple his sheets—but lay bare the man underneath? No.'

'But...' *But I get to the real man sometimes. I can touch more than his skin.* She almost said it, then realised how pathetic it would sound. *I'm different. He lets me in. He trusts me. And Hannah, who has known Alex for most of their lives, will smile and be kind about my illusions. She might even think I'm developing a* tendre *for him. How humiliating.*

'Why does he need a mask?' she said instead. 'What is he hiding?'

Hannah laughed and set off a coughing fit. She waved Tess back to her chair when she reached for the water glass. 'I'm all right. He isn't hiding, he is creating. He has remade himself from scratch these past ten years.'

'Ten? But he's twenty-seven now. What happened when he was seventeen?'

'He left home.' Hannah frowned at a harmless print hanging over the fireplace. 'For good, I mean. He'd been at university for one term. He came home for...he came home for a visit, and when he returned to Oxford he never went back to Tempeston again.'

'But seventeen is very young.' What had she been like at seventeen? Full of questions and uncertainties, her body no longer that of a girl, her emotions torn between a yearning to be back in the safety of childhood and an uneasy impatience to discover the world. What must it be like for a boy, out by himself in that big, dangerous world?

'Yes, it is young,' Hannah agreed. 'But he had friends and anger and intelligence to keep him going.'

Anger. 'What happened? What drove him away?'

Hannah shook her head. 'As I said, it is not my story to tell. If Alex ever does tell you about that Christmas, then you will know you really have got under the mask, under his skin. If he trusts you with that, then he has entrusted you with his soul and everything fragile within that tough carapace he has built around himself.'

They sat in silence. Hannah seemingly worn out after her outburst, Tess unable to find words. So it had been Christmas. Was that why he was so cynical about the festival? Eventually she said, 'But don't his parents want to be reconciled with him?'

'Have you ever wounded someone badly?'

Tess shook her head. 'I don't think so. I hope not.'

'If you had, then perhaps you would understand. If you injure a person close to you so cruelly that your own conscience is riven, then sometimes you become angry with them for making you feel so guilty. His father did something inexcusable, something that resulted in a death, something that slashed Alex to the heart. Lord Moreland is a man who never found himself at fault, who has never been known to own a wrong or to apologise. I expect nothing has changed.' She shrugged, a complicated heaving of blankets and shawls. 'Therefore, if he is not at fault, then Alex must be. If he had hurt Alex, then Alex must have been to blame. Do you understand?'

'I think so. How dreadful.' The words were inadequate, but she could find no others. Tess reached out a hand to the fire for some warmth. 'Could Alex not make the first move to reconcile?'

'You know those horse-drawn tramways? There are iron or wooden rails and the horse can draw a heavy load quite easily along them?' Hannah did not wait for an answer. 'To move from that exact track would need huge effort and would most certainly overturn the cart, injure the horse, possibly kill the driver. Should the driver try to leave the tracks, drive a new path, risk that injury, just on the off chance it might work?'

The silence stretched on. Tess looked up and found Hannah's eyes were closed, her breathing slow and deep. She had fallen asleep, worn out, perhaps by emotion.

Tess uncurled herself and put on her shoes, found her things and tiptoed out.

'I don't think Mrs Semple is well enough to come back to work, not this side of Christmas. I know it is almost three weeks away, but there is all the preparation to be thought of.' Tess folded back the notebook she was using to keep lists of things to be done. Now a fresh page was headed *Christmas??* and she had caught Alex just before William Bland, his secretary, arrived. She was determined to pin him down for some answers.

'I thought she was not seriously ill.' He stopped mending the end of his pen with a pocket knife and looked up. 'I must send the doctor round again.'

'She *is* getting better, but the infection seems to have settled on the lungs of all of the sufferers and they are worn out with coughing. She needs a holiday somewhere she can be looked after. What would she usually do at Christmas?'

'Go back to her husband's family in Kent. It's a big family and she's very fond of them.' Alex squinted at the pen nib, then stuck it in the standish. 'I could send her down early, in the coach with rugs and hot bricks and one of the men to escort her.'

'That sounds like a good idea. Shall I arrange it?'

'No. I'll go and talk to her, if that dragon of a landlady will let me, a dangerous man, into her female fortress. Anything else in that very efficient little notebook?'

'I need to know exactly what happens here at Christmas. What the arrangements for the rest of the staff are, whether you'll be entertaining, whether you'll be out much. I need to plan for meals, shop for provisions,' she added when he looked at her blankly. 'Phipps and Mac-Donald tell me they don't have family in the south and then there's the coachman and your grooms.'

'What happens is that I don't expect to see them from the morning of the twenty-fourth until the evening of the twenty-sixth. They fill the coal scuttles and leave the place tidy and I eat out at my clubs. I can cope with making my own bed once a year,' he added, presumably in response to her opening and closing her mouth like a landed carp. 'I told you—I spend Christmas by my own fireside with a pile of books and a bottle or so of good brandy. All of my friends of a sociable disposition will be out of town.'

'Then, you do not mind what happens below stairs so long as it does not disturb you?'

'Or burn the house down or bring in the parish constable. Exactly.'

'Right.' Tess closed her notebook with a snap. This house was going to have a proper Christmas regardless of what his lordship expected. 'And above stairs you just want appropriate preparation made?'

'Certainly. You can manage that?'

'Oh, yes, especially if you are out most of the time.'

'That would be helpful, would it?' Alex asked absently. He was already running one finger down a column of figures. 'I'll be at the club a lot of the time.' He flipped open his desk diary and made a note as there was a knock at the door. 'Come in!'

'My lord?' Mr Bland looked in, his arms full of papers. 'I have the auction catalogues from Christie's you wanted, but I can come back when it is convenient.'

'No, we've finished, haven't we, Mrs Ellery?'

'Indeed we have, my lord.'

When she went down the indoor staff were all below stairs. 'MacDonald? Please ask the stable staff to join us. All of them. Annie! Leave the scullery cleaning a moment and come in here.'

They crowded into the kitchen, Annie still clutching her scrubbing brush, Byfleet the flatirons he'd been about to set on the grate. The grooms brought the rich, warm smell of horses to mingle with the aroma of baking bread as they stood awkwardly by the back door.

How long had she been here? Tess wondered as she surveyed their faces. Scarcely a week? It was hardly much more since she had staggered in, battered and exhausted, and yet this was beginning to feel like home, and she was gaining a confidence she never expected to find. In the new year, when Hannah was well again, she could set out on her quest for employment feeling so much better equipped.

The staff were waiting patiently. Tess jerked her thoughts away from the prospect of employment agencies and smiled. 'I have been discussing Christmas with his lordship. Mrs Semple is much better, you'll be glad to hear, but she'll be going off to her in-laws in Kent very soon to recover. Now, how many of you will be spending Christmas at home with your families?'

Annie held up her hand, realised it was holding a dripping brush and gulped. 'Me. I'll be at me lodgings, I s'pose, Mrs Ellery, ma'am.'

'No one else?' Heads shook. 'And who's at the lodgings, Annie?'

She shrugged. 'The other lodgers, ma'am.'

Tess had a fairly good idea what home must be like for Annie. 'Do you think you would like to join us for Christmas, Annie?' The girl's jaw dropped, then she nodded energetically. 'You can have one of the upstairs rooms for a few nights. What do the rest of you usually do?'

'Make do,' Byfleet volunteered. 'We're all men, so we get in some food from the cook shops, his lordship lets us have extra money and plenty of beer and a bottle or so from the wine cellar. We smoke, play cards, yarn a bit.'

'We'll be a mixed party this year,' Tess said briskly. 'I can cook a proper Christmas dinner if I have some help.' *I hope.* She glanced at the row of cookery books on the mantelshelf. 'Then we can go to church afterwards, for midnight service. Christmas morning we'll exchange presents and enjoy ourselves for the rest of the day.' She looked around the room. 'What do you say?'

'I say *yes*,' MacDonald said with a broad grin. 'I'll get out my fiddle and Will there has got his flute. And with the youngsters we'll have a proper Christmas.' He started counting heads. 'There's the three from the stables, me and Phipps, Mr Byfleet, Dorcas and little Daisy, Annie and you, ma'am.' He grinned. 'That's ten, a snug little party, Mrs Ellery.'

'It is indeed,' Tess said. *And if I can work a miracle there will be eleven of us. So far, so good. We have a party. Now we need presents.*

Alex tossed the sale catalogue aside. Nothing in it got his acquisitive juices flowing. He felt bored, he realised incredulously. No, not *bored* exactly. Stale? Tired of London, tired of routine. Unsettled. It was ridiculous. He was normally so involved with his work and with his social round that Christmas was a welcome opportunity to sit back and relax. He regarded his drawing room with disfavour. It was too damn tasteful, too blasted orderly.

It was Tess who was responsible for this mood, he suspected. She was turning the place upside down. Hannah had been efficient, but mostly invisible. She left him to himself except for the occasional evening when she would shed her housekeeper's cap and come and curl up in a chair in the drawing room and gossip over a glass of wine. She was an old friend, she had a busy life of her own beyond his front door and she left him alone to live his life as it suited him.

But Tess was there, in the house, day and night. And she expected things of him beyond the regular payment of housekeeping money and a list of meal times when he wanted to be fed at home. She expected him to *react*, to involve himself with the concerns of the other staff. And she was up to something with this Christmas obsession of hers. And that was leaving aside the nagging awareness of her physically, the effort it took not to think of the slim figure, the soft mouth, those wise, young, blue eyes.

There was a tap on the door, the modest yet definite

knock he was learning to associate with his temporary housekeeper.

'Come in.' Yes, it was his little nun with her confounded notebook. He got up from the sofa where he'd been sprawled and waved her to the chair opposite.

Not such a little nun now, he thought as she settled her well-cut skirts into order. With good food and a warm house she had lost that pinched, cold look. Taking command suited her, put a sparkle in those blue eyes and a determined tilt to that pointed chin. And the food had done more than keep her warm, it had given her curves that were most definitely not nun-like.

My staff, my responsibility, he reminded himself, sat down and dumped the Christie's catalogue firmly onto his lap.

'Are you all right, my lord? I thought you winced just now.'

'Alex, for goodness' sake.' He smiled to counteract the snap. 'And it was just a touch of…er…rheumatism.'

'Rheumatism?'

He shrugged and the catalogues slid helpfully, painfully, into his throbbing groin. 'What can I do for you, Tess?'

'Christmas presents,' she said. She flipped open her notebook, produced a pencil and stared at him as though expecting dictation.

'Whose Christmas presents?'

'For the staff. The men, of course, Dorcas and little Daisy. And Annie. I think Annie should stay for a few nights, I don't like to think of her having to go back to that lonely lodging house.'

'Who the blazes is Annie? The scullery maid? No,

don't answer that. Do what you want about staff meals, but why presents? I give them all money on St Stephen's Day.'

'Of course you do and I am sure it is very generous. But Christmas presents are special, don't you think? Personal.'

Alex considered a range of things he could say and decided it was probably safer not to utter any of them, not when faced with a woman armed with a notebook. 'I'll give you some money and you can buy them.'

'I think the staff would really appreciate it if you chose them yourself.' He could feel himself glowering and could only admire her courage as she continued to smile. 'It is more in the Christmas spirit, don't you think?'

'Tess, you know perfectly well what I think about Christmas spirit. Codswallop. Humbug. Ridiculous sentimentality.' Anyone else would have backed down in the face of that tone and his glare. All the men he knew certainly would have done. They obviously raised them with backbones of steel in convents.

'But I know you value your staff,' she said in a voice of sweet reason. 'We could go out this afternoon unless you are very busy.' By not so much as a flicker did her eyes move towards the pile of discarded journals, abandoned catalogues, crumpled newspapers and the other evidence of a lazy morning. 'It isn't raining. And I have a list.'

'I'll wager you have.' Alex got to his feet. 'I surrender. Wrap up warmly, I'll get the carriage sent around.'

Half an hour later when he met her in the hall she was wearing a smart mantle that matched a deep-blue bonnet and she had decent gloves on. *How pretty she is with the bruise gone and that bonnet framing her face.* 'Where is Dorcas?' he snapped.

'Daisy was fretful and Dorcas has a lot of work on her hands hemming petticoats for me and it would only distract Annie from her work if she has to watch the baby, as well. We don't really need Dorcas, do we?'

The innocent question, the questioning tilt of her head to one side, got to him every time. He just wanted to kiss her silly. *Which is not going to happen.* 'Not if you feel comfortable alone in a closed carriage with me.' Alex kept his voice neutral, but she still turned a delicate shade of pink.

'Of course I do. We discussed…that. I thought we had forgotten about it.'

Forgotten that kiss? Forgotten that you admitted that the attraction wasn't just one-sided? When you become prettier and happier with every day that passes? When hell freezes over. Alex wasn't going to lie to her. 'I think we are doing a very good job of pretending it doesn't exist,' he said drily. 'Best put that veil down in case anyone sees you. Now, where to?'

'A music publishers first, there's one in Albemarle Street. I want music for MacDonald and Phipps—good tunes, ballads, dances. MacDonald can play the violin and read music and Phipps plays the flute, but only by ear, so MacDonald's going to teach him to read music. They've only got one or two pieces now.'

Alex helped her out of the carriage and into the shop, his ears ringing, while Tess talked. He had learned more about his footmen in ten minutes than he'd known in five years, he realised as he stood back to let her go through the door into the shop in front of him.

Chapter Eleven

'That was easy,' Tess said fifteen minutes later as she gave a satisfied pat to the brown paper parcel on the carriage seat. 'Now then, tobacco jars for Perring and Hodge. John Coachman says he'll not be responsible for his actions if he has to deal with two grooms squabbling over which tobacco is whose much longer. And he takes snuff, so a new box for him, don't you think?'

Alex directed John to Robert Lewis's tobacconist shop in St James's Street and sat back to digest the discovery that he was actually enjoying himself. Part of it, of course, was Tess's company. Her enjoyment of the shops, her enthusiasm and cheerful goodwill was infectious, and he found he had no objection at all to the image he saw reflected in shop windows of the two of them arm in arm. But strangely, it was more than that.

'Do you know, I find this oddly satisfying, like working out the attribution of a painting,' he confessed as they emerged later from Gray's the jewellers with a coral-and-silver teething ring for little Daisy. 'Are we done now?'

'Not yet.' Tess looked back over her shoulder as she got into the carriage.

Alex closed the door behind him and then stayed on his feet to shift parcels on the seat. 'More?'

'Well, yes. There's—' Tess began as the carriage started off, then stopped with a lurch.

Alex twisted round, caught his balance and lost it again as the vehicle jerked forward, accompanied by a vigorous exchange of curses from on top of the box. He just missed the seat; Tess grabbed for him and he hit the floor with her on top, one sharp elbow planted firmly in his midriff. *'Ough.'*

'Alex? Oh, I am so sorry, I've hurt you.' She was sprawled down the length of him, the two of them wedged on the floor. He looked up, through eyes watering from the impact, into her face, so close. The tip of her nose was pink from the chill, her lips were parted, her eyes were wide with concern. *Adorable. She's adorable.* And outrageously arousing with every inch of her pressed to him.

'Winded...' he managed. 'That's all.' He closed his eyes the better to enjoy the sensation of her curves, the erotic, impossibly innocent, scent of plain soap and a dab of lavender water.

'Alex! Alex, can you hear me?' She squirmed, trying to get to her feet without, he supposed, trampling all over him. 'Have you hit your head?'

Alex groaned, opened his eyes and found himself still nose to nose with Tess. *This is more than any man can be expected to withstand,* he told himself, gritting his teeth.

With a dolphin-like heave she got herself up at the expense of no more than an inch or two of skin scraped from his shin bones. 'I am so sorry I squashed you, Alex. Just lie still. I'll pull the cord and tell John Coachman to drive direct to your doctor.'

'No need.' He found his voice from somewhere and

sat up before Tess observed the interesting effect her squirming had produced on his body. 'I'm fine. Just...' *Hanging on to my self-control by my fingernails.* Alex put both hands on the squabs and pushed himself up and onto the seat next to her. 'Winded, as I said. What were we talking about?' *Something, please God, dull and non-inflammatory.*

'A donkey!' For a moment he thought she meant him, which was nothing but the truth, given that he was an experienced man about town reduced to a quivering mass of sexual frustration by a chit from a nunnery.

'Oh, isn't it sweet?' Tess pointed out of the window to a costermonger's barrow pulled by an improbably fluffy little donkey.

'Yes,' Alex agreed cautiously. It was not the word he would have used. 'But we do not need a donkey.' The way she collected things he could expect to come home to find an ass and an ox in the stables, just for Christmas. He wouldn't put it past her to go to Pidcock's Menagerie and borrow a camel for atmosphere.

Tess smiled at him, apparently able to read his mind. 'Of course not.'

Alex was seized with a contrary urge to buy her one, just to see that smile again. He repressed the whim. 'Now where?'

'A toyshop. I want a doll for Daisy.'

The shop, whose owner had obviously stocked up well for the approaching season, was a treasure trove. Alex restrained himself from buying a full set of lead soldiers just to arrange on the study mantelshelf. The display of dolls was astounding, and he blinked at the array of miniature femininity. Tess was studying the far corner where the plainest examples were arrayed.

Alex made for the most magnificent, complete with real hair and elegant clothing. 'There's no need to stint, I don't expect Dorcas can afford to give the child many toys.'

'She's too young for one, really, but I think it is nice if she grows up with a doll who will become an old favourite. But a baby needs a simple, soft doll, like those.' Tess lifted down a medium-size rag doll, then turned back to the counter past a row of wooden dolls, their hair and features painted on. She stopped and touched one, just with the tip of her finger, and something in her smile sent a cold shiver down Alex's spine.

'What's wrong, Tess?'

'Nothing. Only memories.' Her hand hesitated for a moment over the brightly coloured skirt, then she gave herself a little shake and took the rag doll across to the counter. 'I had a doll like that once.' Tess was looking at the wooden dolls again. 'Mama gave it to me for Christmas when I was six.'

'What happened to it?'

'The nuns took it when I went to the convent.'

'But you were, what, twelve by then?'

'Thirteen, and far too old to play with dolls, of course. I didn't play with her, though, I talked to her. She was my friend,' Tess said simply.

When they were outside on the pavement she blinked as if she had been miles away. Or years, perhaps, Alex thought. 'Did you not have friends?'

'Not really.' Her expression went blank. 'We moved an awful lot. And not when we were travelling, of course. I was perfectly happy,' she said hastily when he opened his mouth. 'I had Mama and Papa. But you know what it is like when you are a child, you need an ear to whisper your secrets into, someone to tell your troubles to. Some children have imaginary friends, Patty was my confidant, that is all.'

Yes, I know. Peter was all of that to me, but he was real. Friend, confidant, someone to tell my troubles and my secrets to. Only he hadn't been able to tell me his biggest secret and because of that, he's been cold in the ground these ten years.

'Where do you want to go next?' Alex asked and fished out his clean handkerchief for Tess.

She blew her nose briskly, stuffed the linen square into her reticule and said, 'A bookshop. Dorcas enjoys novels.'

Alex left Tess browsing amidst the stacked tables in Hatchard's in Piccadilly. 'Will you be all right here for half an hour? I've just remembered something I need to do.'

By the time he came back she had accumulated a pile of six books, two new notebooks and some sheets of wrapping paper with gold stars stamped on it. 'The notebooks and two of the books are for me,' she explained as he carried them to the counter for her. 'You must take those out of my wages.'

'Don't be foolish.' Alex looked at the spines. 'Cookery books and notebooks are essential housekeeping equipment.' He waved aside the assistant waiting to carry the parcel out to the carriage. 'Now we are going to Bond Street and Madame Francine's.'

'Madame—a modiste?' Tess stopped dead on the pavement. 'I am not going to help you choose garments for your light of love, my lord!'

'Foolish,' he repeated, marching her firmly towards the carriage. 'Garments for you. Hannah gave me a list, said that she had not finished outfitting you.'

'She had. I have everything I need.' She was beholden to him enough.

'What do you know about it, little nun?' He waved a folded sheet of paper under her nose.

'But—'

'But nothing. Here we are.' He helped her down, swept her into the shop, deposited her firmly in a chair and proceeded to charm the pantalettes off Madame Francine, as Tess said bitterly to Dorcas later.

She was taken off to a fitting room, measured, clucked over and finally allowed back to where Alex was waiting, perfectly at his ease on a spindly gilt chair, his nose in a copy of *La Belle Assemblée*.

'All will be ordered as you desire, my lord.' Madame Francine glanced at the list. 'We have taken foot tracings so the shoes will be delivered at the same time.'

Tess knew better than to make a scene in the shop, but she began to protest as soon as they reached the carriage. 'Alex—my lord—I cannot have you buying me more clothes. It is not at all proper, beside any consideration of the cost.'

'Do I appear to be poverty stricken? Unable to afford a modest wardrobe for a lady housekeeper?'

'No, but that is not the point.'

'Those old crows sent you out into the world dressed like a skivvy. Do you expect me to leave you like that?'

'You outfitted me as you would have a footman with his livery. That is understandable. And what you gave me was quite sufficient.'

'*Sufficient* is a mean, tight, word. You are a pretty

young woman, Tess, not a footman. It gives me pleasure to see you dressed nicely. You bring colour to the house.'

She felt the blush burn upwards and with it the anger. 'Pretty. I see. You expect me to show my gratitude, I suppose? Madame Francine knows you very well, doesn't she? I suppose that is where you take all your mistresses.' As soon as she said it she knew she had misjudged him.

'Yes, I have taken mistresses there before. You think that is how I regard you? You think that of me?' Alex's face was an expressionless mask.

'No. No, I do not. I am sorry, I reacted without thinking. I hate the idea of some sort of financial transaction, but... You want me. I may be inexperienced, but when we fell on the floor of the carriage...' Her vocabulary failed her.

'You noticed I was aroused?'

It was possible that a thunderbolt might strike, or the carriage horses bolt or the king pass by in procession. No miracle occurred to save her. Tess jerked up her chin and made herself look Alex in the eye. 'Yes.' *Yes, I did notice that hard ridge of flesh pressed into my stomach. Yes, I do know what it means and, no, I was not shocked. I was excited. Shamefully, achingly, excited.*

'You may also have noticed that I did nothing about it.' Now his voice was as colourless as his expression. 'I would have to be...a completely different kind of man not to be aroused by you. I can ignore this, just as any gentleman can. We are not all the victims of our animal natures like Dorcas's previous employer.'

'I know.' She kept her chin up, even though she wanted to bury her face in the carriage rug. 'It is on my mind because...' *Because I wish you were not such a gentle-*

man. Impossible to say it. Tess closed her eyes and swallowed. 'I wonder why you are not married.'

'I do not intend to marry,' Alex said, as calmly as if he was stating that he had no intention of visiting Germany.

That snapped her eyes open. 'You don't intend to marry? But that's ridiculous!'

'So is being quizzed on the subject by a convent-reared gentlewoman in my own carriage.' There was a definite edge to his voice now and colour up over his cheekbones. If he resembled any of the mythical creatures of Sister Moira's fairy tales, it was no longer a benevolent one. 'Why is it ridiculous that I do not intend to marry? Are you of the opinion that everyone should?'

'Of course not. In my case, for example, it should be obvious that I will not wed.' One dark brow lifted, but she pressed on. 'I am a penniless nobody with a living to earn. You are an aristocrat, heir to a title. Surely marriage is expected of you?'

'Exactly. I do not choose to do the expected.' There was an unfamiliar, bitter twist to his mouth now.

'Then, it is simply a self-indulgent whim?'

Alex turned those slanting hazel eyes on her. 'Throwing brickbats now I have made you uncomfortable, Tess? It is not a whim, it is a deliberate act by someone who is otherwise powerless to avenge a crime.'

His father. Hannah said someone died that Christmas ten years ago. 'You are depriving your father of the hope of the succession, aren't you? But you have a brother.'

His lips curved into a smile that sent cold chills down her spine. 'Indeed I have. Let us just say that if I were a stockbreeder I could not hope for a more willing stallion nor fear having one who has proved so unproductive so far. According to gossip Matthew has spent his wild oats over three counties without so much as one bastard to his name.'

'I do not think I like you very much in this mood, Alex Tempest.' Tess dragged the carriage rug close around her legs.

'Nor do I,' he said, the dangerous smile vanishing. 'I do not think I have ever come across a lady who is prepared to speak as frankly as you, Tess.'

'Perhaps I just see the future more clearly. I will not marry and I am unlikely ever to find myself in a situation where I can discuss such subjects so openly with a man. I will be gone soon after all. Hannah will return after Christmas and I will have to take myself off to the employment agencies.

'Are you not cutting off your nose to spite your face? After all, you are not a virgin, are you, my lord?' There was a woman in the carriage who looked like her, sounded like her. The Tess Ellery who was listening to what this other Tess was saying, who seemed to be able to see her through Alex's eyes, shrivelled inwardly with shock.

A sudden, surprised gasp of laughter escaped him. 'No.'

'I thought not, not after the mention of mistresses. Nor a monk, either, I imagine?'

'No, not a monk, either.'

'So you are not proposing a life of sacrificial celibacy. You will punish your father and wallow in sin at the same time.'

'Wallow in sin? Tess, what *have* you been reading?'

'No doubt I am very naive, but I do not think you are happy.'

'And marriage would make me happy? I very much doubt it. I haven't the models for doing it right, besides anything else. If I've inherited anything from my father, it is probably an ability to make an appalling husband and father. Don't look at me with those great innocent eyes, full of righteous indignation, Tess.' He studied her face for a moment, then smiled, a smile free from the bitterness and mockery. 'Are you by any chance attempting to seduce me into happiness by using sweet reason?'

She thought about it for a moment. 'Yes, I believe I am.'

'I have to tell you it is not very erotic.'

'It is not intended to be erotic!' *Infuriating man, to be able to make me blush even more deeply than I already am.* 'I am not talking about *that* kind of seduction.'

'Your arguments have their merits, but for other men, I think. And I have to tell you that successful seduction requires passion and recklessness and surprise.' His lips were twitching now. It was not laughter directed at her, she guessed. Hoped.

'I would need to catch you unawares?' Tess suggested. There was a flicker of something inside her, a warm, fidgety glow. 'Be more passionate with my arguments?'

'Indeed you would. And I am not easily caught with my guard down.'

Tess pondered on seduction over the next week in the intervals between ordering supplies, puzzling over whether one goose, one turkey and a ham would be enough for the Christmas meals and negotiating the use of the boiler in between wash days in order to dangle the cannonballs of plum pudding in the cavernous pot.

Alex had been amusing himself by teasing her and, perhaps, flirting a little, she guessed, although she had no experience of such a thing. According to the nuns seduction applied to sin, to devils luring souls into doing wicked things. In Minerva Press novels seduction was all to do with love and lust. Between the pages wicked women dressed in trailing silks lured the hero into their toils and then…the chamber door closed with a resounding thud, even in the most daring tale. Tess very much doubted she'd know a toil if she fell over it; she possessed no trailing silks and Alex would probably laugh himself sick at the sight of her slinking about in her very sensible flannel wrapper.

I am thinking about seducing him into bed, not into happiness, she thought. But that *would* be sin, not because she truly believed that making love was wrong, but because his conscience would hurt him if he took her virginity.

But if he was convinced it would do no harm… It was a delicious daydream, one that brought back the heat and the tingling feelings and the ache to be held, very close, very tight.

How would one go about seducing Alex Tempest? It was safe enough to weave fantasies, surely? Laughter seemed to lower his guard. Laughter and being close enough to touch might work. Catching the man at home and alone, though, that would the first step, and Alex was very, very good at being elusive.

'What I want for Christmas is an earl,' she informed Noel, who was in her room helping her to wrap Christmas presents by tangling the ribbons and hiding in boxes. 'Just the once. I know I'd have to give him back. I only want to borrow him. I suppose I would be quite hopeless at making love, but all the gossip says that men enjoy being with virgins. Which seems strange. But then men are strange, I'm beginning to find.

'I suppose I shouldn't be telling you this. You are much too young for such wicked conversation.' Tess scooped up the kitten, who was trying to eat silver paper, and tickled him until he was a limp, purring handful of fur. 'But I wish I could make Alex happy. He isn't, you know, not deep down. He's angry and hurting. I wish I could give him his family for Christmas, then he might settle down and find a wife and have children of his own.'

Noel made an ambiguous noise somewhere between a mew and a yowl. Tess lifted him up so his pink nose was inches from hers and his eyes crossed as he looked at her. 'You think we need a fairy godmother? They are in short supply in London, I fear.'

'What is in short supply?' Alex's voice said from behind her.

Chapter Twelve

Tess spun round on her knees and ended up on her bottom in a tangle of ribbons. 'You made me jump.' How long had Alex been standing there, one shoulder against the door frame of her room, listening to her? 'If you have been eavesdropping, then you'll know.'

'I have just arrived, was about to knock and the door swung open onto you complaining about shortages. What do you need?'

Unless he was an actor good enough for Covent Garden Theatre then he had only heard those few words. Tess offered up several prayers of thanks, one in Latin. 'Fairy godmothers. They are scarce, you must agree.'

'Why do you need one of those?' Alex pushed the door right open with his foot, but stayed where he was, pleasingly framed in the space. 'Just ask and I'll sort out your Christmas wishes.'

He was flirting, she was almost certain. There was certainly a wicked gleam in his eyes.

Tess got to her feet with as much grace as was possible, given that she had a kitten clinging to her skirts, and assumed her best housekeeper's expression. 'You wanted me?' she enquired.

Alex's gaze seemed somehow heavier, warmer as his eyes rested on her. It must be the different angle she was seeing him from now she was on her feet.

It was a moment before he replied. 'Only to tell you that I am dining at Brooks's tonight and I will be out to dinner at Lord Hawthorne's tomorrow night.' He flashed her his rapid, wicked smile. 'My last fling of dissipation and sociability before Christmas descends like a pall on London.'

'It is still only the thirteenth.' *What is he going to say when he sees what I have planned for Christmas?*

'I know, but everyone will start leaving for the country by the fifteenth, if they have not already gone.' He turned to leave, then glanced back over his shoulder. 'I've got a carpenter to make a proper cradle for Daisy. He'll deliver it tomorrow.'

'Oh, thank you.' Tess started forward, to touch his hand, kiss his cheek, then stopped as the realisation of what she was doing hit her. *No, it isn't fair, don't make it harder for him to behave like a gentleman.* She turned the movement into a clap of her hands. 'That's wonderful—an old drawer isn't really deep enough to keep out the draughts.'

He smiled and turned to leave. 'Thank you,' Tess whispered again as the sound of his footsteps across the hall faded away. It had taken thoughtfulness to notice the makeshift crib and to do something about it. It had involved him making an effort, *personal* effort, when he could have easily ignored a servant's child as something that was not his concern. 'There's hope for you yet, Lord Weybourn.'

The sound of the key in the latch froze Tess on top of the ladder. Around her in the hall both footmen and Dorcas stopped dead, their arms full of evergreens.

'Oh, my God, it's only seven o'clock, he's not due back for hours.' Phipps clutched the foot of the ladder, making it sway and Tess yelp and clutch the hanging lantern with both hands. The bunch of mistletoe she had been attempting to fix fell on to MacDonald's head, Phipps burst into laughter and Dorcas gave a small shriek.

The front door swung open slowly to reveal Lord Weybourn standing on his own front step, fog swirling around him as he held his latch key in one hand and a large wreath tied with scarlet ribbons in the other. 'This just fell off,' he said. 'I caught it. It appears to consist entirely of holly. Exceedingly prickly holly.'

'I knew I should have used wire, not string, to hold it to the knocker. Sorry, my lord.' MacDonald tossed the mistletoe to Phipps and strode forward to take the wreath. 'Ow. Oh, bug—I mean, ouch.'

'Oh, bug—ouch, indeed.' Alex came in and closed the door behind him. 'Phipps, do you intend to kiss me under that mistletoe or to take my hat and coat?'

'Take your hat, my lord.' Phipps threw the mistletoe to Dorcas and reached for Alex's cane. From her perch Tess could see the tops of Phipps's ears were bright red.

'And what, exactly, is this?' Alex enquired as he shrugged out of his caped greatcoat.

'Christmas evergreens. It is the twentieth after all.' Tess looked down into Alex's upturned face and tried to read his mood. Obviously arms full of prickly holly and his hallway in chaos was not how he expected to be welcomed home, but was he annoyed beyond that? 'We were not expecting you to return yet.'

'That much is obvious. Why are you up a stepladder, Mrs Ellery, when there are two able-bodied males here and three more in the stables?'

Because Phipps is scared of heights and MacDonald is clumsy was the truth, but she couldn't betray the footmen. 'A woman's artistic touch?' she ventured.

'I see.' Alex retrieved the now somewhat battered bunch of mistletoe from Dorcas and held it up to her, took a firm hold on the ladder, waited until she had tied the angular fronds in place and then said, 'Now come down, please.'

'Yes, my lord.' Tess attempted her best meek and obedient voice.

'Did I order Christmas evergreens?' he enquired when she was standing in front of him.

'You didn't forbid them, my lord.'

'A major oversight. I did not forbid massed carol singers, handbell ringers and a full-size yule log in the front room either. Are those to be expected?'

'No, my lord. At least, there will be carols downstairs. But no handbells, I promise, and the fireplaces are too small for yule logs.'

'And are any other rooms infested with fir cones?' Were his lips twitching? Just a little, perhaps.

'No, my lord. Just the hallway and below stairs.'

'I think I could tolerate a sprig or two of holly in the study. And fix that wreath back on the front door, MacDonald. We don't want the neighbours to think we are lacking in Christmas spirit, now do we?' *Yes, there is a definite twitch. Almost a smile.* 'You, Mrs Ellery, are a very bad influence on my household.' His gaze flickered up to the mistletoe immediately over her head. 'And on me,' he added softly.

Tess took three very deliberate steps backwards. 'Shall I have tea brought up, my lord?'

'Tea? No, brandy to the study, MacDonald. Is my post there?'

'Yes, my lord.' The footman doubled away; Alex vanished into the study.

Tess looked round at her remaining helpers. 'We are almost done, I think. Phipps, just let me have that remaining holly, the pieces with lots of berries, and I'll arrange it in a vase for the study. Dorcas, if you could tidy up and, Phipps, you remove the stepladder—' From the study there was the clatter of something metallic falling, then rolling. Then silence. 'What was that?'

'Sounded like the silver salver, Mrs Ellery.' Phipps hesitated, his arms full of stepladder. 'Should I go and see?'

'No, it is all right, carry on tidying up, I'll go.'

One of the few advantages of the Christmas season was a definite reduction in the amount of correspondence, Alex mused as he hitched one hip on to the corner of the desk and spun the salver round to pick up the bundle of post that had arrived since Bland had left after lunch.

He began to shuffle though the pile. Invitation, bill, bill, circular, tickets from the Opera House, letter from Rivers, a journal… And a letter on thick cream paper with a heavy seal. He turned it in his hands, saw the impression in the blue wax, a jagged line of lightning against a stylised cloud. *Tempest.*

For a moment he was tempted to toss it onto the fire unopened. Alex looked down at it in his hand. His shaking hand. *Coward.* With an effort of will he stilled the tremor then broke the seal.

Weybourn. Alexander. I do not know whether this will find you in London or what to do if it does not. Or what will befall us if you will not come.

It was his mother's handwriting. He hadn't seen it since he was seventeen. Alex stood up and the salver went spinning off the desk, hit the polished boards, spun and fell with a clatter.

Your father is very ill. He will not admit how ill, or how weak he is. Dr Simmington tells me he will not recover, that it is only a matter of time.

The elegant handwriting faltered and became less controlled.

Matthew is not capable or able to take control of everything that must be done here. Alexander, I need you to come home. Your family needs you to come home. Your father will never admit he cannot cope, that he needs you. But despite everything, despite what your father did and said and what you vowed, I beg you, if you have any affection left for your poor afflicted mother, return to Tempeston.

Lavinia Tempest.

The letter slipped from his fingers, drifted down to the carpet like a great falling leaf. *Return to Tempeston. Come home.* He closed his eyes.

'My lord? Alex?' A whisper of movement, a scent of lavender water, a touch on his arm.

Alex opened his eyes. Tess stood before him, the letter in one hand, the other resting on his forearm. Her face, puzzled and anxious, was turned up to his. 'What is wrong?'

'My father. Read the letter if you want.' He didn't seem able to move away, to think. *Your family needs you.*

'Oh, Alex.' There was a rustle of paper and then Tess's arms were around him, her hand pulling his head down to her shoulder, her breath warm against his neck. 'I am so sorry. What terrible news.'

She held him as though he needed comfort, as though he had broken down. What was wrong with her? Didn't she realise he didn't care? He hadn't seen them for ten years.

Tess was murmuring nonsense in his ear, rocking slightly back and forth as she held him. Alex found his arms would move, that he could hold her, too, soft and warm and fragrant. Feminine and sweet and, under it all, a backbone of steel. 'I do not need comforting,' he said. But he let his cheek rest on the soft mass of her hair while he got his balance back.

Tess leaned back against his arms and looked up at him. 'Of course you do, you stubborn man. You love them and they hurt you and now they need you and it hurts all over again.'

'Tess.' There were no words and no coherent thoughts either, just wanting. Alex bent his head and kissed her and the world righted on its axis. She opened to him with the generous innocence that was Tess, untutored, a little clumsy as their noses bumped. He remembered the taste of her, slightly tart under the sweetness, like new cherries.

Her hands cupped his head, her fingertips stroked his nape and her curves nestled against him as though a tailor had cut her to fit him. Only him. She gave a little gasp as he touched her tongue with his own, then bravely stroked back, gave a little wriggle and pressed closer.

He was going to have to stop. Through the incoherence that were his thoughts that imperative took shape, became urgent. *Stop, stop now. This is Tess.* And that, he realised, was why he did not want this to end.

When he lifted his head she blinked up at him, deliciously tousled and pink.

'Tess, we must—'

'Plan, I know.' She released his head, stepped back out of his arms. For a moment he was shocked by how easily she could set aside what had just happened and then realised this was the only way she could cope with it: pretend it hadn't happened, at least for a while.

'I'll ring for tea. There is a great deal to be done if you are to leave early tomorrow.' She went to the bell and pulled the cord, then sat down on the far side of the desk and regarded him with, he thought, some anxiety.

At least he could put a decent distance between them. Alex sat down in his desk chair. 'Your mother is going to need help,' she went on. 'An invalid in the house makes extra work for the male staff, I imagine, so our two footmen will be useful. Do your sisters live at home?'

'Laura's married and lives in Edinburgh. Maria is not at all practical. At least, she never used to be. She is… was, sensitive.'

'You'll need John Coachman and the grooms.' She was thinking aloud, frowning as she reviewed the staff.

'I take them all away and leave you alone?'

'There's Dorcas to keep me company. And Annie. The poor child is living in some lodging house. I cannot abandon her at Christmas after I promised she could come here. Three of us will be quite safe together for a few days.'

He'd have to go, he knew that. He couldn't ignore his own mother in the face of a plea like that. 'Come with me.'

'Come… You think your mother will need help sick nursing? Dorcas and I could assist with that, I suppose. But your mother isn't going to want to have strangers descend on her.'

'Tempeston is a big country seat, and it has the room to absorb an entire house party and all the additional servants. It can certainly cope with this household.'

She bit her lip and he wondered whether she was nervous about the thought of the big house, or of being with him. Then she took a deep breath and smiled. 'If you think I can help, then of course I will come, and Annie and Dorcas, too. We'll all come. It's the least we can do.'

Brave Tess. 'At least we have not got far to go, only into Hertfordshire, and the weather is fine.'

'Hertfordshire?'

'Yes, the Hertfordshire-Buckinghamshire border.'

She went very still, then gave herself a shake. 'Tempeston is so close? That *is* good news, we will be able to do the journey in the day.' There was a tap on the door and MacDonald came in before he could query why the mention of Hertfordshire seemed to take her aback.

'Tea, please. And some of the cake, thank you.' Tess waited until the door closed behind the footman. 'We will have to think about how to explain me.'

'And a baby. That might well need some explanation, also.' Alex found the everyday lunacy that was now his household was helping him get a grip. He realised with a jolt that he intended to go…*home.* He had jested about the family vault to Hannah; now there seemed to be a very real possibility that he would be expected to lay his father to rest in it in the near future.

'We could try a version of the truth,' he said, forcing himself to think of strategy and practicalities and not of the morass of emotions and anger and misunderstandings. 'I escorted you to England from Ghent for you to stay with an elderly lady as her companion. The elderly lady has died, you are stuck in London with no friends or relations and only Mrs White, your companion. I put you up, all very shocking, but what is one to do right before Christmas? Dorcas is the widow of a man who died very shortly after Daisy was conceived, which is why she is out of mourning now. You'll have to work out the details between you. If anyone asks me about you I can look convincingly blank—after all, I'm only acting as a courier.'

'That is brilliant, Alex.' Tess poured tea and passed him a cup. Her blushes had subsided, but her smile when she looked at him was still shy. He tried not to look at her mouth, pink and slightly swollen from his kisses. 'You will organise the carriages? There are rather a lot of us, and the luggage and the Christmas presents and the food.'

'Food?'

'We can't leave a goose, a turkey and a ham to rot, let alone all the puddings and the cakes. It will be less of a burden on your mother's cook if we take it.'

'Then, that's both of my carriages and the wagon for the heavy luggage.' Alex put down his cup, demolished a jam tartlet in one mouthful and stood up. Tess and her entourage were like an anchor, tethering him to safety. There were practical things to do, things involving a baby and a fat goose, things to keep his feet rooted in reality and the nightmares at bay. 'Tess?'

'Mmm?' She looked up, blushed and dropped her gaze to her notebook, already open on her lap.

'Thank you. Thank you for the comfort and the practicality. Thank you for that kiss.'

Alex locked away the thought of how much more he wanted than her lips as he pushed open the kitchen door. 'We are going to Tempeston tomorrow, all of us,' he announced. 'We're taking our perishable food, the Christmas presents, everything. Mrs Ellery will be down in a moment to give you instructions.' He looked round at their expressions, confused, excited and, in Annie's case, awestruck. 'And when we leave this house you will kindly remember that I never had a housekeeper named Ellery and if I did, she has nothing to do with Miss Teresa Ellery. Is that clear?'

There was a moment while they all stared at him, taking in the enormity of what he was asking, then Dorcas said, 'Annie, you run home and pack your bags then be back here, sharpish. I'll pack for Mrs…*Miss* Ellery, then I'll come down to help out here.'

Alex did not stop to give any orders. They were competent and Tess would take control. He went out to alert the grooms, then, as they hurried to check over harnesses and dust off the wagon they usually used for transporting the bigger pieces of statuary and furniture he dealt in, found himself alone in the stall with Trojan, his hunter.

The big chestnut, apparently delighted with the company, rested his shoulder against Alex's and leaned his weight on him. 'Daft fool.' Alex rubbed him under the chin in the sweet spot that always reduced the animal to jelly and put up with having his palm dribbled into. It was peaceful here, smelt of warm horse and straw and saddle soap. Horses were an indulgence that still gave him a lot of pleasure. His father, having decided that his willowy elder son would never make a horseman, had lavished the best mounts on Alex's brother, Matthew.

Strange that he had never felt jealous of his brother. His father's opinion that Alex was a disappointment had hurt, but then, he had never known anything else. As a child he was the undersize one, the dreamer, the reader. He'd retreated back into his own head, his own company when punished or lectured, which must, he could see now, have made him even more infuriating to his noisy, energetic, utterly nonintellectual father.

His mother had worried and fussed—which had only made his father more dissatisfied and irritable. But the man hadn't been a monster; he'd obviously wanted to be proud of his sons and yet he hadn't been able to cope with one of them not fitting his mental image of the perfect heir. Were all parents like that, wanting perfection, expecting too much? Would he be like that in his turn if he was ever rash enough to contemplate a family? It was one of the unpleasant night thoughts that weighed against marriage.

Now his parents needed him; even Matthew needed him, although he was unlikely to admit it. Alex suspected he was going to be a bit of a shock to all of them. 'That's an interesting thought,' he observed to Trojan, who merely snorted. 'The power balance has shifted. What do I want now? An apology, but not for me. To be loved? Ridiculous. To be approved of? Now, there's the rub. There's some part of me that's still seventeen and wants approval, that hasn't learned that the only approval worth having comes from people whose opinion you value.'

And that was quite enough introspection for one evening. He slipped Trojan a carrot and shut the stable door.

He had his mother to worry about—she'd sounded at her wits' end—and Tess. Tess, who, for reasons he failed to understand, trusted him. Desire was one thing; he understood that. But what possessed the foolish chit to trust him? It was that quality of innocence about her, he suspected. She had decided that he was redeemable from his cynicism and his self-centred lifestyle. Seduce him into *happiness* of all the wild ideas. It was going to take more than a few wreaths of evergreens and a wassail bowl to do that.

Chapter Thirteen

'Tired?' Tess stifled her own yawn and smiled at Dorcas, who perched, heavy-eyed, on the seat beside her. Opposite them Annie was already asleep again, one hand on little Daisy lying securely swaddled on the carriage's plush upholstery.

'Retiring at two and up at six is not my favourite choice of bedtime, Miss Ellery.'

'Not following on from the evening we had, that is certain.' Tess held on tight to the strap as the carriage rounded the corner on to the Edgware Road and headed north.

'It feels like a dream, packing everything and everybody up and leaving in such a procession.' Dorcas stroked the upholstery with the reverence she would accord fine silk as she peered out of the window into the gradually lightening morning gloom. 'And his lordship looking so dashing.'

Now Dorcas had drawn her attention to their outrider Tess allowed herself to stare. It was the first time she had seen Alex on horseback, and she was not at all certain she was glad she had seen him now. He was magnificent, so at home on the big chestnut that it would only add to her store of delicious, and thoroughly uncomfortable, images to be taken out for daydreaming and then severely closed away again. Ever since that kiss yesterday it had been even more difficult to close the mental door on those fantasies.

'I wonder why he chooses to ride. It is such a damp, chill day and I doubt it is going to get much more pleasant.' How easy was riding? It had never occurred to her before, but Alex was controlling the big animal with no apparent effort at all. *Those muscles again, that deceptive strength.*

'Perhaps he does not want to be sitting with us because of the baby,' Dorcas said, jerking Tess back from her reverie.

'He could always tell Annie to take her to the other carriage if she became fractious,' she pointed out.

'I am sure he would not do that. He is such a gentleman and patient with her.'

Impossible man. He is nice to babies and kind to kittens, he looks wonderful on a horse. And he kisses like every sort of temptation I could imagine and more.

'Do you think they'll believe it, about me being a widow? Daisy's so very young.' Dorcas nibbled a fingernail as she looked at her daughter, fast asleep and blowing bubbles.

'Of course they will. We worked it out that you'll just be out of mourning. But you do need a wedding ring.' Tess pulled the chain that hung around her neck out from her bodice and unfastened it. 'Here, borrow this, it was my mother's.'

'But I can't take something so precious.' Dorcas put out her hand and then snatched it back.

'Try it on.' It was loose on the thin finger, but the knuckle was enough to hold it securely. 'She would have been glad of you wearing it if it helped someone, and that is what we are doing, isn't it?' *After all, it has never been a real wedding ring.* 'We are preserving my reputation and at the same time helping Lord Weybourn.' That was what the thin gold band had represented, the appearance of respectability. The lie.

They reached the market town of Watford in the early afternoon and pressed on into rolling hills clad with the golden brown of beech trees that held their dead leaves into springtime. Finally, as the light hung at the edge of dusk, they halted outside an inn on a small village green.

Tess watched Alex dismount, hand his reins to one of the grooms and then go inside, followed by Byfleet carrying a portmanteau.

'Strange,' Tess mused, but Dorcas was feeding Daisy, and Annie tidying up all the paraphernalia from changing the baby, and both seemed to welcome the stop.

When the two men emerged again Alex was transformed. Gone was the rider in the low-crowned hat, the many-caped overcoat, the breeches and the long boots. In his place was a London swell, as exotic in the little village as a peacock in a barnyard.

Alex climbed into the carriage while Tess managed to close her mouth and stop goggling like a yokel.

'Ladies.' He settled onto the seat next to Annie, chucked Daisy under her fat chins with one exquisitely gloved forefinger and crossed his legs. Cream pantaloons. Skin-tight pantaloons. Tess shifted her gaze to the Hessian boots with silver tassels, then up to a waistcoat of cream moiré silk embroidered with lavender flowers. His coat was dark blue and his intricate, pale lavender neckcloth was secured by an amethyst stickpin. There was a gold seal ring on his left little finger, a quizzing glass hung around his neck and the subtle smell of his cologne filled the carriage.

He has shaved again, Tess realised, feeling travel-soiled and unkempt in contrast. 'Lord Weybourn. Did you have an enjoyable ride?'

'I did, thank you. Are you ladies comfortable?' Annie giggled and he lifted his quizzing glass, reducing her to blushing confusion. 'Miss Annie, chief nursemaid.'

No one would guess he was within miles of a reunion he was dreading and a meeting with a dying father, Tess thought. Although his manner was…strange. Almost artificial. The young ladies at the convent had once been allowed to attend the theatre to see an improving play. Tess, who had tagged on to the party, found her way backstage and watched from a corner, fascinated, as the actors transformed themselves from ordinary people into creatures of fiction.

And that was what Alex was doing, transforming himself. He was becoming more mannered; his accent carried a subtle affectation. He wore his beautiful clothes like a mask, she realised. Or armour.

She knew before he spoke when they were nearing their destination. Alex sat up straighter against the squabs and his eyes followed the line of the high wall to their left. The carriage turned between a pair of lodge cottages and began to follow a winding road through parkland. Tess watched Alex, saw the mildly bored expression on his face and saw, too, the way his hand tightened on the strap, the white knuckles.

'Have we arrived?' It was an inane question, but she could stand the silence no longer.

'Yes. Welcome to Tempeston.' Alex was looking

through the misted glass with an intensity that was a kind of hunger.

She glanced at the other two women, engrossed with the baby. 'You love it.' It was not a question.

'The river and the streams are my blood, the soil is my flesh, the stones of the house are my bones as they have been for generations of Tempests.' He stopped. 'And you have just caught me out in ludicrous sentimentality expressed in the most purple of prose. Forget it.'

Tess bit her lip to keep herself silent and leaned forward to rub her cuff across the window. Before her was the sprawling bulk of a house that formed a rough arc around a paved forecourt. The central block was lit, but the flanking wings were two dark arms waiting to close on them. She shivered as their carriage pulled up at the foot of the double flight of steps.

'Yes, it takes me like that,' Alex said, then smiled at Annie, who was visibly overawed. 'Nothing to worry about, it is only a house.'

The stones are my bones... And what waits inside? His soul? Tess tied her bonnet ribbons and collected up her reticule. 'Come along, Annie, make sure Miss Daisy is well wrapped up and stay close behind Mrs White all the time.'

'Yes, Mrs…Miss Ellery.'

The baby, mercifully, seemed settled and not inclined to grizzle. Tess imagined Alex's reception if he arrived with not only a strange young woman but an entourage that included a wailing babe in arms.

Light spilled down the steps as the double doors opened and two footmen ran down and opened the carriage door. Alex stepped out. 'Lord Weybourn and party. My mother is expecting us.' The second carriage drew up. 'My people.' Alex waved one hand in the general direction. 'A wagon is also following. See to it that everything is unloaded.'

'My... Yes, my lord. At once.'

One footman stood by to hand down the other occupants of the coach; the other doubled away and up the steps. By the time Tess reached the top, her hand on Alex's arm, a butler and two other footmen had appeared. The butler, she noted, had his expression perfectly under control; the two footmen were having trouble keeping the avid interest off their faces.

'My lord, it is a pleasure to see you at Tempeston once more.' The butler bowed.

'Garnett, good to see you. Mrs Garnett well?' Alex might have been away for a month, not ten years.

'Very well, my lord, thank you for asking. James, his lordship's coat. William, the ladies. John, see to his lordship's people.' Daisy woke up and produced a loud gurgle. 'I see we must have the nursery readied. I will—'

'*Weybourn.* Alexander, you came.' A tall woman, slender and grey haired, came down the stairs, her hands outstretched. 'My dear boy, I knew you would not fail me.'

Alex stepped forward and caught her as she almost stumbled on the bottom step. 'Mother, take care.' He steadied her, then withdrew his hand. 'Fortunately I was in the country.'

It seemed to Tess that Lady Moreland made a conscious effort to control all emotion. She was more than slender, she was thin—her wrists seemed too fragile to support the weight of the rings that sparkled on both hands. The older woman looked past her son. 'We have guests, how delightful.' Tess could only admire the implacable mask of courtesy that enabled her to sound genuinely welcoming in the face of unexpected strangers at such a time. 'Alexander, you did not tell me you were—'

'Escorting Miss Ellery. Yes, indeed. I assured her that she could rely on your hospitality. This is Miss Ellery and her companion, Mrs White. I brought them from Ghent on behalf of a mutual friend. Unfortunately the arrangements in London fell through.'

If anyone was going to lie to Alex's mother it was going to be her, not him. Tess stepped forward, hand outstretched. *She thought I was his wife, or at the very least, his betrothed. That mask slipped a little just then.* 'I do beg your forgiveness for my intrusion at a difficult time, Lady Moreland, but I found myself quite abandoned in a strange city with no hope of resolving my problems until the New Year. I hope I may be of assistance to you, and my companion, Mrs White, also. I am experienced in sickroom nursing.'

Good breeding was obviously enough to prevent Lady Moreland demanding why Tess found herself in such a predicament. 'Not at all,' she murmured, darting a glance at Alex. 'I thought for a moment that you were... Oh, and a baby, too?' There was the briefest betraying flicker of pain and hope in the fine hazel eyes. *Alex's eyes.*

'Mrs White's child, ma'am.' The hope died, leaving only the pain. 'I trust she will not disturb anyone. We have her nursemaid with us.'

'I have ordered the nursery to be put in order and the fires lit, my lady,' Garnett murmured. 'Young woman, if you follow John he will show you the way. His lordship's rooms are readied as you ordered, my lady. I thought the Chinese Bedchamber and the adjoining Rose Chamber for the ladies?'

'Excellent. If you and Mrs...er...White would like to

go with Garnett, Miss Ellery? Alexander, I must speak with you in my boudoir.' She turned back up the stairs with a distracted smile in Tess's direction.

Alex turned to Tess, a perfectly pleasant, perfectly judged expression on his face. 'Do ask Garnett for whatever you require, Miss Ellery. I will see you both before dinner.'

'Thank you, Lord Weybourn.' Tess dropped the ghost of a curtsy and turned to the butler rather than watch Alex's erect back as he climbed the stairs behind his mother. *He's a grown man, he can cope.* But at what cost?

'Alexander.' His mother sank down on a chaise and pressed a scrap of lace and lawn to her lips. 'I hardly dared hope you would come.' She looked as though only the boning of her stays and sheer willpower were keeping her upright. 'I missed you so much, my son. Your letters have been a godsend, but I so longed to write back.'

His mother was fifty years old, he knew that, but looking at her now he could believe she was ten, twenty, years older. Her hair was almost entirely grey, she looked fragile to the point of breaking and the skin around her eyes was papery with a strain that was caused by something deeper and longer-lived than her husband's recent illness. He had missed her with a deep ache he had learned to ignore as best he could, as he would an amputated limb. The realisation that she had been hurting, too, was a stab to his conscience.

He had written to her once a month, knowing his father would have forbidden her to correspond with him and that he could expect no answer to his letters. It was desperation that had made her disobey now.

'You look tired, Mother.'

'I look old, you mean.' Her chin came up. 'And you look well. More than well. How you have grown, matured. Who is that young woman? I thought, no, I hoped, you were going to introduce her as your wife or your betrothed.'

'Really? After what my father says about me?' She winced and he bit his lip. She was not the one who deserved to be punished.

'Your father can be a great fool,' his mother said. It was the first time he had ever heard her utter a word of criticism of her husband.

'And a stubborn one. But, no, Miss Ellery is just what I told you, a young lady adrift in London because the arrangements made for her reception went awry.' He shrugged. 'At any other time of the year I could have found half a dozen ladies of my acquaintance to look after her, but you know what London is like before Christmas. And I could hardly deposit her in a hotel. And before you ask, no, the baby is not hers and most certainly not mine. The child is Daisy White. Now tell me what is wrong with my father.'

His mother sagged a little, then straightened her spine. 'The doctors say your father has a disease of the blood, one they cannot cure. He is deteriorating steadily.'

'Has he asked for me?' He kept the hope out of his voice, ashamed of the weakness.

'No.' She did not seem to realise that she was shredding the fragile Honiton lace of her handkerchief.

'And Matthew?' His brother, the perfect Tempest. Big, strong, physical. A hard rider, a hard drinker, a hard gambler, a hearty philistine. A man's man and always the apple of their father's eye.

'Matthew drinks, gambles, whores,' his mother said,

her lips stiff with distaste for the words. 'He was never an intellectual.' Her raised brow dared Alex to comment. 'Now it is obvious that he incapable of taking up the work of the earldom. The agents do their best, but your father was always a man who kept his hand and his eyes on every aspect of all the estates, the business interests, the finances. He thought that Matthew took after him.'

'And that—as he did not believe I would marry, let alone father an heir, then—Matthew, or his son, would one day inherit it all. When did he realise?'

'That Matthew was incapable of managing a great inheritance? Not until he became so ill and even now he will not admit he needs help.'

'Of course not. That would mean calling me back.' Alex settled back in the chair, took a deep breath, found some sort of control of his voice. 'And possibly apologising. I imagine he is a very angry man.'

'You must be angry yourself.' His mother met his eyes. 'You must be angry with me.'

'You were in an impossible position.' He had known that right from the beginning. His mother was of a generation that would support their husbands whatever kind of tyrant they were. It was simply how she had been raised. 'Do you believe I am what he says I am?' *Lord, the last thing to discuss with one's mother.*

'That you are…not interested in women? Of course not. I have eyes in my head, I knew you went sneaking out of the house at night down to see Mary at the White Swan.' For the first time something like a smile twitched at her thin lips. 'I imagine I could tell you the date you lost your virginity. And while your letters to me contain nothing that might shock a maiden aunt, I do have my old friends in London. I hear the gossip.'

Alex had thought himself beyond blushing like a youth, but it seemed he was wrong. 'Does he know you sent for me?'

His mother got to her feet, as elegant and feminine as he always remembered her. 'I told him I would, but he did not believe me. I have never disobeyed him before, you see.'

I never knew she had the courage. That I did not remember. 'When will you tell him I am here?' He got to his feet, went to take her arm.

The door banged open with no warning knock. 'Hell's teeth and damnation.' The man on the threshold stared at Alex and then laughed. 'It really is you, my popinjay big brother, all grown up. Come to see if the old man's dead yet?'

'No. And do not swear in our mother's presence. Do you not knock on her boudoir door, or are you perhaps no longer a gentleman?' Alex found himself toe to toe with Matthew without realising he had moved. 'I will see you at dinner, Mama. You come with me.' He took his brother's arm, twisted it and had him out of the door before he could get his balance. He closed it behind them and pushed Matthew down the corridor out of earshot before he let him wrench free.

'Get your hands off me.'

Alex held both of his up, palm out. 'I imagine my appearance is a shock to you. Mother asked me to come.'

'The hell she did! And Garnett says you've got women with you and a baby.'

'There are two *ladies*. Gentlewomen, and you'll do well to remember that,' Alex said, keeping his voice soft, his hands by his sides. 'The baby belongs to Mrs White, the widow who is the companion to Miss Ellery. They find themselves unfortunately stranded in London. Mother has kindly offered them hospitality for the Christmas season.'

'We'll see what Father has to say about this.' Matthew turned on his heel and strode off towards the East Wing.

'You do that, brother mine,' Alex murmured as a door slammed violently in the distance. 'I just hope your reflexes are good enough to duck whatever he hurls at your head.'

Chapter Fourteen

'I am petrified,' Dorcas whispered. 'I've never been anywhere this elegant. I've never been anywhere except as a servant,' she added with a tremble in her voice.

'You told me your father was a doctor, Dorcas. You speak nicely, your manners are correct, your gown is perfectly acceptable. Besides, I don't think companions are expected to do more than sit in the background under these circumstances.'

'Good,' Dorcas muttered, her eyes on the back of the liveried footman sent to collect them for dinner. 'I'm glad we have an escort, this place is huge.'

The footman stopped, opened a pair of double doors. 'The Green Salon, ma'am.'

Tess took in a breath down to her toes. *I can do this.*

'Ah, good evening, ladies.' Lady Moreland held out one hand, gloved to the elbow in lavender kid. 'Do come and meet my younger son. Matthew, Miss Ellery, Mrs White.'

'Mr Tempest.' Tess inclined her head to the man who stood on the other side of the fireplace. She could see the resemblance to Alex, although he was shorter and stockier, but he had none of Alex's elegance or air of sophistication. He looked, she thought, sulky.

'I will leave Matthew to keep you company for a few moments while I make sure my husband has all he requires. I know you will excuse him eating in his chamber.' Lady Moreland shared a brittle smile between them and left the room.

'Miss Ellery. Absolutely charmed to meet you.' Matthew Tempest's gaze flickered over her figure, lingered on the bare skin exposed by the neckline of her simple evening gown. Tess felt her own smile congeal. She was not used to wearing anything so revealing and she was certainly not used to being ogled. Occasionally she caught a gleam of masculine awareness in Alex's eyes when they rested on her—more than occasionally, if she were to be honest—but not this blatant assessment. 'A bore for you to be landed with my brother's company,' he added.

'You think so, Mr Tempest? Lord Weybourn has been all that is kind.'

'He is hardly a ladies' man.' Mr Tempest appeared to find that an inordinately amusing remark.

'He is, however, a gentleman,' Tess said as sweetly as gritted teeth would allow.

The laugh this time was a trifle forced. Not such a fool, Matthew Tempest, that he could not recognise an insult when it was offered. 'No doubt you feel very *safe* with him.'

Tess stared at him, then noticed the knowing smirk. He didn't mean… He couldn't. Yes, he did. She resisted the urge to box his ears and lowered her lashes coyly instead. 'As safe as a lady wishes to feel with a handsome gentleman.'

His jaw dropped and she strolled away to where Dorcas had perched on one end of a sofa. 'That poisonous little toad,' Tess whispered as she sat down beside her. 'He is jealous of his brother.'

'Oh, hush, Miss Ellery, he is coming over.'

Matthew Tempest had, it seemed, recovered his temper, or at least his composure. *Or else he thinks we are whispering about him and wants to find out what we are saying*, Tess thought as he strolled over to their sofa.

'May I fetch you ladies a glass of Madeira? Or sherry, perhaps? Ratafia?'

'Nothing, thank you,' Tess said as the door opened and Alex came in.

'Miss Ellery, Mrs White, forgive my tardiness. Matthew, now I see you in good light, how you have changed.'

'Hardly surprising, given that I was fifteen when you walked out on the family.' Neither brother made any move towards shaking hands, let alone embracing, Tess noticed. 'I had expected quite the court card, if not a fop.' There was reluctant admiration in Matthew's expression, Tess realised. Or perhaps envy. 'Tell me, who is your tailor? Weston?'

'Of course.' Alex's smile became more natural, as though to take the edge off the words. His clothing was so plain as to be almost austere. He wore black and white, his shirtfront with barely a ruffle, his only ornament the gold of his watch chain, the dull gleam of the intaglio seal ring and the glow of the amethyst in his neckcloth. 'Do you get up to town much?'

'No.' Matthew's voice was sulky. 'I'm kept tied to this place, at Father's beck and call.'

'He is sick after all. I have no doubt you're a help to him.'

'Ha! He's got perfectly good stewards and agents, but nothing will satisfy him but that he has to have a finger in every pie, read every report, send me out to check on this and that, and then what I tell him is always wrong, or too short in some tiresome detail or I've missed the point. Again.'

Tess felt a twinge of reluctant sympathy for the young man. His father must be seething with impatience at his own limitations and nothing Matthew did was going to be good enough. 'What would you prefer to be doing, Mr Tempest?' she asked him.

He shrugged, then seemed to realise he was speaking to a guest and a lady and took the sullen look off his face. 'Breed hunters. Hunt.'

'Be a country squire, in effect,' Alex said.

'Nothing wrong with that. I'm the younger son after all.' The aggression was back in his voice and Tess cast around for a neutral topic of conversation.

'I am so looking forward to seeing something of the English countryside. I have lived in Ghent for years.' From the hallway came the sound of raised voices and she broke off as the door opened.

Lady Moreland came in, still speaking over her shoulder as she did so. 'John, James, do be careful. Moreland, I do think—'

'I am going to eat dinner at my own board and see what this nonsense about that popinjay Alexander coming back is about.' The earl entered, batting irritably at the two footmen who were attempting to steady him on either side. 'Get off, damn it, I'm not in my coffin yet.' He stopped dead and stared. 'My God, he really is here. I thought Matthew must have been drinking. *Alexander?*'

'Father.' Two syllables. Two perfectly civil drops of ice.

Tess, her gaze flickering between the men, wondered if Alex was as shocked as his father. He had made a barely discernible movement when the earl came in. Now he was stock-still.

It must be like staring into a looking glass, one that aged the viewer on one hand and stripped years away on the other. They were obviously father and son. Everything proclaimed it—their height, their bone structure with those high cheekbones and thin nose. Alex had his eyes from his mother, but that was all. Lord Moreland had once had the physique to match his son; now the broad shoulders seemed bony and, despite the careful tailoring, his evening clothes looked loose, as though he had lost a lot of weight recently. His hair was still thick, but faded into grey now, and the heavy eyebrows were almost white. How old was he? Fifty-five, sixty? He should be in his prime, and he certainly resented its loss as much as he suffered from his symptoms.

'What in the blazes are you doing here, Weybourn?' Lord Moreland wrenched his arm from the grip of the supporting footman, took two steps and sank down on to the nearest chair.

'I have come to celebrate Christmas in the bosom of my family.' A nerve jumped in the angle of Alex's jaw, but his tone was bland. 'And, naturally, to enquire after your health.'

'Measure me for my coffin, more like. How did you hear I've had my notice to quit?'

'A well-wisher wrote to me that you were unwell.'

The silence seemed to shimmer, or perhaps she was feeling faint with tension. Tess caught the involuntary movement of her hand towards Alex and willed herself to stillness.

'And you brought guests with you.' Hooded eyes turned in her direction.

Tess made herself step forward. Her curtsy, by some miracle, did not waver, nor her knees fail her. 'My lord. I am most grateful for your hospitality to myself and my companion Mrs White at a most awkward time for us.'

'Miss Ellery, Father. Miss Ellery, the Earl of Moreland.'

'You'll forgive me if I do not rise.' The dark eyes assessed her gown, her lack of ornament, her ringless hands, then lifted to her face. 'Ellery? One of the Buckinghamshire Ellerys, I presume, by the look of you.'

Now she really might faint. Tess clenched her hands until the nails bit into her palms and the sting steadied her. 'I am not acquainted with the family you speak of, Lord Moreland.' And they were most certainly not acquainted with her; they had made quite sure of that.

'Very wise,' the man in front of her said. 'A top-lofty crew.'

'They do have a duke in their ranks, which probably accounts for it, Papa.' A pale version of Lady Moreland wandered into the room and blinked short-sightedly at its occupants. 'They are most dreadfully proud. Is that really Alexander?'

'Of course it is Alexander,' the earl snapped. 'Why don't you wear your spectacles, you foolish chit?'

'I've misplaced them.' The young woman drifted closer and squinted. 'Alexander, you've changed. How lovely to see you.'

'I should hope I have changed after ten years. And so have you, Maria.' Alex stooped and kissed her on the cheek. 'You were eight when I left. When do you have your come-out?'

'Oh, this Season, I expect.' She smiled and Tess was suddenly aware that for all her vagueness and pallor the girl had intelligence and more than a share of Alex's charm.

'Unless I cock up my toes, which is more than likely, the way you crows all fuss and flap around me.' The earl appeared to take a perverse pleasure in the prospect of ruining his daughter's debut with a year of mourning.

Alex, ignoring the interjection, turned to Tess. 'Miss Ellery, may I introduce my sister, Lady Maria?'

'How do you do?' Close up the hazel eyes focused and the air of vagueness disappeared. What had Alex said? That his sister was sensitive. Tess had taken that as meaning foolish or hysterical, but she rather suspected he had meant she was attuned to other people. 'Mama told me what a fix you are in, Miss Ellery. Such a pity. Never mind, you'll be comfortable here. Shall we sit down?' She went over to the sofa and held out her hand to Dorcas, who shot to her feet and took it as though it was red hot.

Tess joined them, ready to deflect attention before Dorcas melted with nerves. Behind her she heard the earl growl some comment to Alex, but she was too grateful to be able to sit down to listen to his words.

'Sit down, Weybourn.'

Alex took the chair opposite his father and made a business of crossing his legs, smoothing a wrinkle from his thin silk evening breeches, tugging a cuff. It gave him something to do with his hands and, after all, one could not hit one's own father, not when the old devil was ill.

'Why have you come back? To apologise?'

'Certainly I owe my mother and sister an apology for my absence,' Alex conceded. 'I am not aware of any other apology owing. From me, that is.'

He had remembered his father's eyes as brown. Now they seemed black against his pale skin. 'You expect *me* to apologise?'

'It is normal, when a gentleman wrongs another.' Alex kept his tone mild and found to his surprise that it was easy. He was confronting the bogeyman of his memories and his nightmares and here was a sick, frustrated, angry man, old before his time. Someone to be pitied, if he could find it in himself. If he wanted to find the capacity to pity. There was Peter to remember and avenge. Peter, who was ten years in the cold ground thanks to the man in front of him.

'But this is not something to discuss now.' Alex glanced around him, saw his mother's eyes on him, felt the weight of Tess's anxiety behind him. She was upset and by more than tension over this scene or their deception. He tried to recall when he had first noticed it, then set the puzzle aside. He could not focus on it, not now, with his father's sardonic gaze on his face and the hostility coming off Matthew in palpable waves.

'Certainly not in front of the ladies,' his father agreed with a bitter twist of his lips that negated the reasonable tone and words. 'In my study at ten tomorrow.'

'Naturally. The usual place and time.' That was always the summons at dinner time whenever one of his sons had done something wrong, and that was usually Alex, not Matthew. Ten the next day, a time carefully chosen to ensure a night of anxiety and a lack of appetite at breakfast.

'Dinner is served, my lady.'

Alex rose and offered his hand to his father to help him stand. The big hand with its rider's callouses still hard on the palm hesitated, then closed around his and gripped, shifting over the evidence of Alex's own hard riding, the strength that endless practice with the foils gave, the healed scars on the knuckles.

The older man allowed him to get him upright, then he shook off Alex's grip. 'Take your mother in.'

'Of course, sir. Mama?' Alex gave her his arm and saw his father turn to Tess, hesitating behind.

'Miss Ellery.'

She came forward and rested her fingertips on his forearm. Had she ever sat down to a formal dinner before, even a small family affair? He doubted it. But her chin was up and she seemed confident enough. The woman who could stand up to loutish sailors and fight off randy attackers could cope. *Not my little nun anymore*, he thought with a twist of something remarkably like regret.

With four ladies and three men the table was, of necessity, unbalanced. Alex took the seat on his mother's right and smiled encouragement at Dorcas, pale but determined, opposite him. Tess, diagonally across on his father's right, was looking composed and appeared to be discussing Brussels lace, of all things, with Matthew, but the table was too large to hear clearly. She was on her own.

What was it his father had asked her? Whether she was one of the Buckinghamshire Ellerys, that was it; that was what had discomposed her so. *Strange*.

The meal seemed endless, with the quality of a dream.

It was as though ten years had passed in ten hours with the wave of some malevolent sorcerer's wand. The table was the same, the china service the familiar one, the decoration and pictures in the dining room unchanged and yet everyone in the room had aged and altered.

And then Tess turned her head, looked directly at him and smiled. If she had reached out and touched his hand, he could not have felt the gesture more directly. *This is the right thing*, the smile told him. *Take courage, you can do this.*

Somehow they all got through the meal, maintained a light, empty social chatter through every course. When his mother rose to lead the ladies out Matthew went to take his father's arm and supported him from the room. Alex did not make the mistake of offering his own assistance.

He went to present himself in the drawing room, but found only Maria. 'Miss Ellery and her companion have gone to bed and Mama is with Papa.'

'Not very entertaining for you.'

'I am used to it,' Maria said with a shrug and her faint smile. 'Matthew will be off to some local alehouse or another, I have no doubt, so at least we may be comfortable and I am all agog to hear about your life in London.'

It was almost eleven before Maria yawned her way off to bed, to dream, she assured him, of mantua makers, Almack's and strolling in Hyde Park with her brother, to the envy of every other young lady.

Alex found the decanters, poured himself a brandy and made his way to the library. It still had the old familiar look of neglect, despite having been polished and dusted. Alex trailed a finger along the edge of a shelf and it came away clean. No doubt his mother and sister had their own books in their boudoirs and bedchambers, not in this bastion of male importance with its leather bindings and gold tooling, massive furniture and imposing lecterns and atlas stands.

Did his father or Matthew ever set foot in here? When he had lived at Tempeston the library had been one of his refuges, a treasure trove of stories and facts, imagination and mind-stretching realities. No time for those now.

He found the massive volume bound in red leather and lifted it down, flipping through the pages. Eden, Eldridge…Ellery. James Augustus Finmore Ellery, third Marquess of Sethcombe, married…had issue… Four sons, five daughters. One son and two daughters died in infancy, the other three sons married with families of their own. Two of the surviving daughters also married. No familiar names amongst that host of hopeful youngsters. His finger reached the bottom of the list.

Jane Teresa Ellery, born 1775, died, unmarried, 1809.

1809. Died unmarried. This was Tess's mother, surely. He stood there, his fingernail scoring a line under the name. Why did that matter so much, to him? To Tess, obviously, the stigma of illegitimacy must be why she was so resigned to a life in service. But for him? He could pity her, admire her stoical determination to overcome her heredity and make a living for herself, but it was more than that—he felt winded as though he had received a blow in the diaphragm.

When the reason hit him it rocked him back on his

heels. The heir of the Tempests did not marry anyone but a pure-bred aristocratic heiress. But *marriage*? Where had that come from? Surely he had not been thinking of Tess in those terms? The door handle rattled. Someone was coming.

Chapter Fifteen

The room was deserted, but there was a branch of candles on the table next to a untidy pile of journals that seemed out of place in the rigidly ordered space. Tess lifted them and flicked through. *Notes and Queries*, *The Gentleman's Magazine*, *Proceedings of the Royal Society*. She straightened them into a neater pile and set it next to the thick red book they had been balanced on, the *Peerage*.

'Drat the man. Where is he?' It seemed as she stood there that she had been mistaken and the silent room was not empty after all. Tess told herself firmly that there was nothing to be alarmed about. This was not a Gothic novel, there were no ghosts and her nerves were merely a trifle overset. She had disturbed a servant setting things to rights, or perhaps the earl employed a librarian or—'Alex!'

'I'm sorry, did I alarm you?' He rose to his feet and emerged from what must be an alcove behind a massive atlas stand, an open book in one hand. He seemed pale in the candlelight.

'Oh. Oh, Alex.' Tess was not conscious of moving, let

alone running, but somehow she was in his arms, her own tight around him. And she was crying, with no idea why.

'Hey, what's this? Tess?' His fingers were under her chin, tipping her head back. She managed a comprehensive, unladylike sniff and blinked the tears away. 'Who has upset you?'

'No one. Everything. I'm so sorry, I should never have come here with you. Your mother doesn't need us— Dorcas and me, that is. Your father is… I had some stupid idea that you only had to walk in and he'd forget whatever had made him reject you and he would welcome you with open arms. But he is hard and angry and bitter.' She stared fixedly at the amethyst in the folds of his neckcloth. 'You were quite right. I am sentimental and foolish. There isn't some Christmas magic that will make this all right. It is hard enough for you without having me and all your staff here.'

'Tess.' Alex pulled her in closer, apparently careless of the effect of her wet cheeks on his crisp linen. 'If it wasn't for you this would be a hundred times more difficult. I want to rant and hector and lay down conditions. My instinct is to give my father an ultimatum, to force him to surrender all the business of the earldom into my hands, to pay him back by making him weak and dependent on me and to kick Matthew out on half his allowance and see how he fends for himself. Then I look at you and tell myself not to do anything that would make you think less of me.'

There was a weight on top of her head, and she guessed he had rested his cheek there. What was it that his father had done? Whatever it was it must have been dire indeed to generate this much resentment and confusion.

'You are a very civilising influence on me, Miss Ellery,' Alex murmured. Warmth stirred her hair as his breathing steadied.

'The earl hasn't shown you the door,' Tess ventured, wondering why his father might do such a thing. Alex seemed quite content to stand there all night holding her. It was lovely, but not…*easy.*

'He knows he needs me. He is going to pretend he doesn't know my mother went against his prohibitions to write to me because if she had waited much longer he would have had to do it himself and this saved his pride. My father might be stubborn, belligerent and bigoted, but he is not a fool and he is devoted to the earldom. He will do his duty by it and he is not going to cut off his nose to spite his face.'

'It will make a great deal of work for you.' It would turn his world upside down, the world that Hannah said he had created for himself from nothing. 'You are going to do it, aren't you? You'll stay.'

'I don't see what else I can do. This is my duty. Not to him, but to the estate, and to my mother, of course. I will certainly not be able to concentrate on anything else. I'll have to stop my own business, stop travelling, stop dealing.'

'But you love it,' Tess protested, pulling back against his arms to look at him.

'I've had ten years of freedom.' Alex shrugged. 'Now it is time to bend my neck to the yoke.' He made a disgusted sound. 'Listen to me, full of self-pity for having to do my duty, for having to accept privilege and make some return for it. My family needs me, my inheritance needs me, our tenants and dependents need me. I can do some good for my mother and sister and for Matthew, if he'll let me. And heaven knows, there should be satisfaction in mastering something I should have been learning from my majority.'

'You are a good man, Alexander Tempest.' Tess lifted her hand to his cheek so she could turn his head and look into his eyes. 'A very good man.'

For a moment, as he met her gaze, she thought he was going to swear at her, throw her hand aside. When he spoke his voice was low and angry and fierce. 'No, I am not a good man. If I was, then I'd forgive him and I'd do this willingly. But I cannot forgive, I cannot forget and I want to make the old devil beg me to do both. Does that make me any better than he is? I doubt it.'

It cost her an effort of will to keep still, keep her tongue silent with the questions clamouring for an answer. 'I let myself dream about a life on my own terms,' he added. All the old cynicism was back in his voice, his expression. Once she had believed he genuinely did not care. Now… 'It was only an illusion, of course. This place, this title, was always waiting for me.'

'It is not all bad.' She made herself put into words the truths that had been haunting her. 'You will marry now, have a family.'

The shadowed face became even starker. He turned abruptly, went to the table, picked up the *Peerage* and slammed it back into a gap on the shelves, one hand lingering on the spine as though to trap it there. 'Go to bed, Tess,' Alex said without looking round.

'I wish I could help.'

'You cannot help, little nun.' His back was still a blank barrier. All she had to read was his voice, and that had lost all its flexibility, all its music.

She ignored the words, answered only the pain under them, went to him, pressed herself against that long, strong spine and held on to the broad shoulders, her cheek against his shoulder blade. She could hear his sharply in-drawn breath, the hammer of his heartbeat.

'I am not a nun.'

'I wish you were.'

'Why? Why on earth should you want that?' She stayed wrapped around him as though touching would make him easier to understand.

'Because then you would be out of reach, forbidden, protected by your vows. I want you too much, Tess. I want you in my bed, I want you naked under me, to be inside you, possessing you. Is that clear enough?

'Yes.' *Oh, yes.*

'Then, run. Cling to Dorcas, stay at my mother's side, make Maria your inseparable companion, because I am just about at the end of my tether, Tess, and I want you to be safe.'

I love you. Her lips formed the words, silently. Why had she not admitted it to herself before? It wasn't simple desire, or even liking that she felt for him, it was love. Should she say it? No. *Alex is not for me and never could be, not forever. But for one night, two or three, while he needs me...*

It went against everything she had been taught about morals and virtue. But where was the morality in deny-ing Alex comfort? Where was the virtue in denying her own feelings for him? Tess lifted her hands from his still body and stepped back, away. 'I would never run from you, Alex. I would never feel I had to. But I will go now.'

In the luxury of the Chinese Bedchamber, with its painted scenes of exotic gardens and groups of fig-ures, Tess surrendered to the ministrations of the highly trained lady's maid that the countess had allocated to them. She wondered how Dorcas had coped with being waited on for the first time in her life. Well enough, she supposed, for when she eased open the door and looked into the Rose Chamber Dorcas was fast asleep in a nest of pink satin bedcoverings.

After she had washed and undressed, the maid helped her into her nightgown and robe and then proceeded to let down her hair and brush it. 'One hundred times, Miss Ellery?'

'Yes, thank you.' It would give her time to gather her courage. There were bottles of scented waters on the dressing table and she sniffed each in turn and wondered whether to dab something more exotic than her usual lavender water behind her ears. No, it was the unsophisticated Tess whom Alex seemed to want, not some elegant lady. It was going to be nerve-racking enough without pretending to be anything but what she was.

The first thing was to find Alex's bedchamber, otherwise she would be wandering about blind and, knowing her luck, would probably end up in the earl's room. 'This is such a large house,' she remarked. 'I have never been in one so extensive. I suppose all the family rooms are clustered in the middle for convenience and the guest rooms out in these wings.'

'Oh, no, miss, they are all spread out. Lord Moreland has his suite in the West Wing, her ladyship and Lady Maria are in the central block and Mr Matthew prefers the tower rooms. Lord Weybourn has the suite with the park view, just at the other end of this wing.'

Hardly a close and loving family, Tess mused as she made conversation about the lovely views from all aspects. But it was wonderfully convenient for her. She had been quailing at the thought of tiptoeing through the silent corridors, no doubt patrolled by attentive servants, but now she knew exactly where she was going.

The maid tucked her up in bed, moved the Argand reading lamp to the most convenient side and tried Tess's patience to screaming point by enquiring if Miss Ellery required some hot milk? Or some biscuits? More blankets, perhaps?

Alone at last Tess lay still, listening to the clock ticking. Finally it struck the half hour. Past midnight. Surely everyone would be in bed by now? Alex always sent Byfleet off once he had changed for dinner, apparently preferring the solitude to having someone help him out of his evening clothes, so there was not even that to worry about.

When she opened the door all was quiet, the corridor dimly lit by a shielded lamp on a table. Tess walked rapidly, her bare feet silent on the polished boards. She found the door, eased it open and tiptoed into a dressing room. It was unoccupied and she stood listening, inhaling the faint aroma of Alex's cologne. When she plucked up the courage to try the door the bedchamber was deserted, also. She crossed to the far side and found a sitting room, equally empty.

Where was Alex? Surely not still in the library? The room was lit by three Argand lamps, the fire was banked up behind a guard and decanters were ranged on a dresser, so he was obviously expected to be sleeping there. Tess unfastened her robe and folded it on to a chair, climbed into the bed and sat there, prey to nerves. Should she take of her nightgown, as well? That seemed very bold, but then, being here in the first place was so shocking that nudity could hardly make things worse.

Besides, it was hardly a very seductive garment—always assuming Alex would need seducing. Tess wriggled out of it and got back under the covers. She had never slept naked before.

The clock struck one. It felt very…gauche, sitting there bolt upright, the sheets clutched under her chin. Tess lay down. She could try to relax, just close her eyes. He wouldn't be much longer, surely?

She woke to the sound of someone moving around the room. Glass clinked against glass, someone sighed, as though weary, there were two thuds that she recognised as shoes being tossed aside. *Alex.*

Tess eased herself up against the pillows and found he was standing with his back to her. He took off his coat, dropped it on a chair and began to untie his neckcloth one-handed while the other held a glass with a finger of dark liquid in it. He set down the glass, took off his waistcoat and then started to unfasten his evening breeches.

I should say something. But her mouth was too dry. The breeches dropped to the floor and, thank heavens for maidenly nerves, the hem of his shirt dropped, too. Even so, even covered to mid-thigh, the sight of a pair of strong, muscled, hairy male legs was shocking. *Exciting… I cannot sit here spying on him.* Tess cleared her throat.

Alex spun round. 'What in Hades are you doing here?'

He sounded both angry and confused, but there had been one moment, one blink of an eye, when his face had lit up with welcome, with pleasure. It gave her the courage she needed to speak. 'I wanted to be with you. I need to be with you, Alex.'

Now she could not read his face at all. Alex grabbed a robe from the end of the bed and dragged it on, yanked the sash tight. 'If anyone discovers you are here, even if I come no closer than this, then you are ruined, Tess.'

'Ruined for what, exactly? I am not some young miss about to embark on her Season, someone whose virtue and purity is as important as her bloodlines and her dowry. I am destined to earn my living, not to wed. Will knowing what it means to lie with a man make me any less able as a companion, any less competent as a teacher?'

'No.' Alex picked up his glass again, stared at it, then slammed it down.

'I will not go from your bed to some den of vice to take part in wild orgies,' she said. 'I am not going to sell my body as a result. I know you desire me. I did not need you to tell me that in the library this evening. I desire you, too, and you know that, also.'

'What if I get you with child?'

'Then, you will provide for us, I imagine.' She felt calmer as his vehemence grew. 'I would never make any further claim on you and you are not betrothed, or even courting another woman, are you?'

'Tess, desire is not enough reason to risk your reputation.' Alex stood at the end of the bed, his hand on the post supporting the canopy. She knew him too well now to believe he was furious with her for being there, or that he wanted her to leave. But he was angry with himself for wanting her to stay, for wanting her at all: that she could believe.

'No, it is not,' she agreed, her fingers cramping on the edge of the sheet. 'But the need for comfort is, the need to be with someone. Curiosity is, too. I am never going to marry, Alex. I am never going to find another man I trust as I trust you, one that I could risk an affair with. I would wish for memories to warm my future dreams and I think you would welcome some warmth now.'

He was so still that time might have stopped if it were not for the tick of the clock, the crackle of the fire, the beat of her heart echoing the pulse she could see in his throat.

'No,' Alex said.

She had one card left in her hand, and she had no idea whether it was an ace or worthless. It cost enough to hazard, so perhaps it had some value. Tess released the sheet, threw back the covers, slid from the bed and stood naked before a man for the first time in her life. She closed her eyes.

'Tess.'

Was that good or bad? She was no beauty, she knew that. She was skinny and her breasts were small and she knew men liked breasts. But her hair was down and perhaps that covered some of the sharp angles.

'Tess.' Right in front of her. She could smell him now, smell his warm skin, his familiar citrus cologne, the plain soap from the bath he must have taken before dinner. 'Look at me.'

She opened her eyes, knowing she must be one whole blush, not having any idea what to do with her hands. Alex was so close she could see his irises were dilated, so close she could hear his breathing, see his slightly parted lips.

'I told you to run.' His hands were on the knot of his sash.

'I did. I ran here. I am a grown woman, Alex. I know what I want, what I need. Must I plead with you?'

'No. Never that.' He untied the knot at his waist, shrugged off the robe, pulled the shirt over his head and stood in front of her as naked as she was. Behind him the glow of the fire cast a nimbus of gold around his body. From in front the steady light from the little lamp threw sculpted muscles, long bones, taut tendons into sharp relief.

He was beautiful. Her exploring, fascinated gaze moved lower, stopped. This, then, was what an aroused man looked like. The fashion for tight evening breeches was revealing enough to demonstrate to even the most ignorant young woman that there was a difference between the man who had been at dinner that evening and the same man now. *Magnificent.* She managed not to say it aloud. There were other words—*alarming, impossible*—she did not say those, either.

'Do I frighten you, Tess?' His voice was husky with repressed emotion.

'No. Another man would, I think. Never you. Tell me you want this, too, that you are not doing this because I asked you.'

He laughed, a gasp of pure amusement. 'Tess, I can't feign this.' His gesture was graphic enough not to need words. 'Are you sure?'

'Nothing, except the most dire need, would have me standing in front of a man without a stitch of clothing on,' she assured him. *It is going to be all right. He wants me, I want him, we can be together, like this, for these few days.*

'You are smiling.' So was he. 'Come to bed, Tess, before you get cold.'

Chapter Sixteen

Such a prosaic thing, to scramble into bed, to feel the mattress dip under Alex's heavier body, to see his big, capable hands pull up the covers.

'I was quite nervous,' she confided. 'I still am. I have no idea what I am supposed to do.' If she wasn't careful she'd be chattering with nerves and that was the last thing he wanted, she imagined. Bad enough a gauche innocent; a wittering female would be even worse.

'Then, spare a thought for the virgin male.' He slid farther down the bed and pulled her with him to snuggle against his side. The slide of warm skin against skin was delicious. She itched to explore with her hands, but did not want to be clumsy.

'You know the theory, or at least, you think you do,' Alex said, his tone reminiscent. That was good, nothing was going to happen quite yet, not until she had her breath back. 'But the fellows who impart these facts are probably boasting. You hope they are. And you're the man, even if you are only fifteen and you haven't grown into your feet yet and your body and its reactions are certainly not under your control. So you think you ought to know what you are doing, you are sure you have it all straight…and then you encounter the female body.'

The hand that was curved around her ribs began to stroke, the fingers caressing slowly down the side of her breast. Alex continued speaking as though unaware of what his hand was doing. Tess kept very quiet and still in case he noticed and stopped.

'So soft, so responsive and so…complicated. There are curves, you know that, you have ogled them secretly for long enough. But then you discover the weight of a breast in your palm.'

He shifted, moved his arm and her small breast was lying cupped in his hand. 'It is heavier than you imagine it will be and so unexpectedly erotic it takes your breath away. Then you discover this.' His thumb moved, fretted back and forth across her nipple.

Tess gasped as the sensation arrowed down into her belly and her flesh became hard under the pad of his thumb.

'You see?' Alex shifted again so that he was half over her, his weight on one elbow. 'Not only does it feel good, not only are you rewarded by that little miracle of a re-action, but you discover you have given her pleasure, too. So you try the other breast, only this time you find yourself doing this.' He bent and took her other nipple be-tween his lips, his tongue rubbing against her tight flesh while his fingers continued to tease the other nub. 'And you discover for the first time how good a woman tastes and you wonder if she tastes the same all over. You for-got to kiss her at first because you were so nervous and so clumsy in your eagerness.'

He moved until his mouth was a fraction from hers. 'So you taste her mouth.'

Tess arched against him as their lips met. He squashed her breasts into his chest, squeezed the nipple he was still fondling tight between his fingers, which should have hurt, but strangely only made the deep ache inside better, and worse. His tongue was talking now, showing her how he would go about exploring her taste, sweeping over hers, teasing the inside of her cheeks, withdrawing to stroke along her lips. He nibbled at them until she began to shift under him, restless, aching, and he lifted his head.

'You discover that her mouth tastes different from her skin. Delicious, uniquely her, but different. So you want to taste more and you go adventuring.' He slid down, pausing to lick across her breasts in great, wet, sweeping strokes of his tongue that made her want to giggle and moan all at once. Then down to her belly. His tongue traced her hip bones, her bony hip bones, she thought in despair. It tickled impertinently into her navel, which did make her giggle.

Alex shrugged off the bedcovers, which had tented over his head, and looked up, his face alive with the old familiar smile that she had despaired of seeing again. 'And this is different again. But now you are getting impatient because you haven't learned that restraint increases pleasure and you are still terrified that you are going to get this all wrong, so you start to shift, thinking about what has to go where and worrying that you aren't the right size, or shape or...'

'Or?' She could still speak. Just. Something was happening to her body and whatever it was, she seemed to have no control over it at all.

'Or...you don't know, just that you are scared to death and in heaven, too. So she, this beautiful, generous, wise, woman gives you a nudge in the right direction. Put your hand on my head and push.'

'Push?' His head? Confused, she did as he asked.

Alex slid down another foot or so, pressed her thighs apart and kissed her.

Tess opened her mouth to scream, but all that emerged was a long, groaning purr of pure, wicked pleasure. His tongue foraged into the secret folds, his teeth nibbled, his lips sucked and kissed and... *'Ooh!'*

Tess came to herself to find Alex lying on her, his weight on his elbows, his legs between her spread thighs. He lodged perfectly in the cradle her body made. 'That was...'

'Good, isn't it?' He grinned, obviously pleased for both of them.

'I had no idea. I thought you just...' She blushed. 'Um, put it...'

'We can do that next.' He shifted his hips and something pressed against her. Alex frowned when she wriggled, eager. 'It might not be so good, not the first time, I understand.'

'Have you never made love to a virgin before?' The pressure was more of an intrusion now, but this was Alex, she told herself, he would be as careful as he could be.

'No, so this is a first time for both of us. I think...' He nudged forward a little. 'Yes, quick might be good.'

'Ow!' They both went still. Tess considered how she felt. 'Go on.'

So he did. Things went from tight and sore to tight and wonderful to a glorious confusion of sensation and movement. 'Oh, Alex! *Yes.*'

She felt him go tense, then pull away and then groan as he held her and she slipped into a haze of pleasure.

* * *

'Tess, sweetheart.' A whisper in her ear, a hand gliding over her hip, then settling between her thighs.

'Hmm.' She wriggled against Alex's fingers. 'Again?'

'No, wicked one. Time for you to go back to your own bed.'

She sat up and found the beside lamp still burning and illuminating the very gratifying sight of one large naked man stretched out on the bed beside her. Alex even managed to look elegant with morning stubble and not a stitch of clothing. *My lover. My love.*

He got up and bent to retrieve her nightgown, affording a magnificent view of taut buttocks and trim waist. 'What?' he enquired as he turned.

'I was ogling you.' Tess put on the nightgown. 'You are a very pleasing shape.'

To her delight colour slashed across his cheekbones as he reached for his robe, then made a business of finding hers. 'No slippers?'

'No, I was tiptoeing. Look at all those muscles.' She reached for his arm and curled her fingers around his biceps as far as they would go. 'I think I was seduced by your shoulders from that first evening.'

'I was trying very hard to think of you as a nun,' he confessed as he removed her hand from his arm and pulled her to her feet. 'It was overly exciting to discover that nuns do not wear corsets.'

'I do now.' Tess tied the sash of her robe.

'That can have its moments, too. Now hush.'

He delivered her back to her door. As she closed it she heard a muffled sound as though a hand had been laid against the panels, then the soft pad of his footsteps.

'I love you,' she whispered. 'Sleep well, Alex.'

* * *

Alex strolled along the corridor to the study, consciously slowing his pace to distance himself from the anxious scurry of the nervous youth he had been the last time he'd been ordered here.

He had given up on sleep at the first faint sound of servants moving discreetly around the house. Before he had taken her back to her room he had dozed with Tess in his arms, too shaken by the experience to lose himself in unconsciousness. Besides, it was a new pleasure to lie like this with a lover and to watch over her, observe the flicker of her eyes beneath those fragile lids as she dreamed, the soft, parted lips, the way her hair lay like silk on his shoulder.

She had been right; this had made them both happy. Now he had to make certain nothing went wrong for her. He was most certainly not going to allow her to go off to some employment agency in the new year and tie herself to some form of genteel drudgery. Somehow he had to persuade her to accept his support without her firing up and declaring it was payment for coming to his bed.

Now, despite the lack of sleep, he felt alert and much calmer than he had last evening. More accepting of a fate he could not, in all honour, avoid, he supposed, although a desire to forgive still eluded him.

The clock struck ten. He knocked and entered. 'Good morning, Father.' He would not give way to the urge to say *my lord*. The man was his parent.

'Sit down.' His father sat behind the great mahogany desk that still looked vast, even from an adult's viewpoint. 'Let us not beat about the bush. Your mother would have me understand that you are not the effeminate pervert I accused you of being.'

'Well, that is certainly to the point.' Alex settled himself in the chair opposite. 'Let me be equally clear. I have never been attracted to my own sex. I have never been with a member of my own sex. However, I do have—and had—friends who have that sexual inclination and I will not stay in this house to hear them insulted in the terms you have just used.'

His father's pale face flushed an unhealthy red. 'It is a hanging offence.'

'Indeed it is. And let us be clear about something else, as well. You accused Peter Agnew, my best friend, of being my lover.'

'He was older than you, he had a reputation—'

'He was my friend. Never my lover.' Alex fought to keep rational, not to shout and rant, throw all the anger that had seethed inside over the blind prejudice that had led his father to leap to conclusions. 'We had grown up together and he was like an older brother to me. He knew very well that I was attracted to women, and only women. God, I must have bored him to tears, pouring out all my youthful infatuations with this girl and that, confiding all the things that worried me before the first time.

'He would have no more tried to seduce me than any man of honour would attempt to seduce the daughter of a friend. In my ignorance, I had no idea how he felt about me until I read the letter he sent me before he blew out his brains. And he did that because you'd broadcast his name around the neighbourhood. Would you have had the restraint and the decency to suppress everything you felt for someone because it was for their own good? Would I? That keeps me awake at night sometimes, wondering. I have no idea if I can ever forgive you for it.' Somehow he had said it without losing his temper, without raising his voice.

He had never spoken of it except to his four friends at university. He had fled back to Oxford, angry, guilty, racked with shame and grief. They'd listened, Cris and Grant and Gabriel. Cris had simply flung his arms around him in a bear hug and then Gabe handed him a large brandy and Grant had said, 'Whatever you want to do, we're with you.' He knew then he could stand on his own two feet and that they would always have his back, just as he would have theirs.

His father was still glowering. Strangely it made it easier to stay calm. 'I really do not understand why you feel I had to fit into the mould of hunting, drinking, wenching masculinity you favour in order to be an adequate heir to the earldom. I was bookish, interested in art. That was, apparently, enough to label me less than manly.' Alex shrugged. 'If you had taken the trouble, you might have discovered that I am an excellent fencer, a more than adequate rider and that I actually perform quite well in the boxing ring. I just tend to do it all rather quietly and while dressed with elegance.'

His father glowered at him. 'You had no idea about young Agnew? Damn it, rumours were flying about his behaviour at Cambridge. I assumed…'

Alex stared back at the red face opposite him. If his father was going to bluster and rant, refuse to accept he had been wrong, then he was going to walk out of this house and never come back.

'I was wrong.' Gradually the hectic colour in his father's face subsided.

Alex let out the breath he had been unaware of holding, unclenched his hands from the arms of the chair.

You stubborn, thickheaded old devil. Why not just ask *me?* Alex got up, poured a glass of brandy and set it by his hand. 'You look as though you could do with that.'

'What are your debts?' the earl snapped.

'Debts? None at all. I am a rich man, Father. I don't need your money. I most certainly do not need this aggravation.'

'So doing your duty is an aggravation, is it?'

'Certainly. I doubt I'll have any time for my own business or for travelling, not if I'm to do this properly.'

'You'll need a wife. Time you were setting up your nursery.' He narrowed his eyes in calculation. 'Not that young woman you've brought with you. Pleasant chit, unspoiled, I like that. But no family from what I could extract from her.'

'No.' No family that would acknowledge her, that was certain. The heir to an earldom did not marry an unknown miss straight from a convent. He certainly did not marry the illegitimate offspring of the daughter of a near neighbour. It had not struck him that he might want to marry Tess until he had seen the evidence of her parentage in black and white in the *Peerage.* Foolish that, to be so attracted to a woman, to feel so protective of her, so aroused by her and not realise that he was developing feelings that went far deeper than affection. Foolish and damnably painful.

It was tempting to announce that he would never marry and to stick the knife in that way, but that, too, was foolish. He had to wed; he knew that now. All he had to do was accept it.

'I'll squire Maria around for her Season. That will expose me to all the eligibles.' It would make him feel like a buyer at a cattle market. How the devil did you come to *know* a woman that way? He knew Tess right through to her heart, and after last night he thought he probably knew her soul deep, as well.

He couldn't just abandon her, not after she had given him everything, and all because she saw him as another stray to care for, like Dorcas and Annie or that damned kitten. Somehow he had to get her to accept an allowance.

'What's making you look so sour?' The earl tossed back a mouthful of brandy.

My guilty conscience. And this damn pain round my heart. 'The thought of Almack's.' Alex looked at his father and dug deep into his reserves of patience and diplomacy. He was far from forgiving, an infinity from accepting, but he had to make this work for the sake of his mother and sister, for the earldom. 'Tell me what needs doing and we'll work this out.' *Somehow.*

Tess made her way to the drawing room, feeling absurdly conspicuous. No one had observed her whispered consultation with MacDonald, Dorcas and Byfleet, but she was sure Lady Moreland would thoroughly disapprove. What she would think about how her son had spent the previous night, Tess shuddered to think. The shudder turned into a *frisson* of remembered delight at the thought of Alex's hands on her body, just as she turned a corner and walked straight into him.

'*Alex.*'

He pulled her close and bent his head. 'I need you.'

'Alex, we can't—not here.' *Yes, please, right here. Kiss me...* 'But we must talk, urgently.'

'What is wrong?' He opened the nearest door and bundled her into what proved to be a small, cold sitting room. 'We shouldn't be disturbed here, it was never used except in the summer.' He sat down on a settee and pulled her on to his lap. 'Snuggle up, you'll get cold. Now tell me what is wrong. Is it about last night? I can't regret it, although I know I should. Are you sorry this morning, Tess?'

'No, certainly not. It was very...'

'Nice? Adequate? Alarming?'

'Stop fishing for compliments.' She curled into his embrace and butted him gently under the chin. 'It was surprising and wonderful and I feel very *womanly* this morning.'

'Hmm.' He nuzzled against her neck. 'I think you feel very womanly, too. So what is concerning you?'

'Christmas and our—your—staff. We had promised them a whole day to themselves—now what do we do? The staff here seem to expect to have to spend the entire day looking after the household.'

'I suppose they do.' She could hear the frown in Alex's voice. 'I never thought about it as a child, or a thoroughly selfish youth. Christmases just happened and they were crowded, noisy and involved a lot of people who spent most of the time arguing and eating and drinking too much. Are you sure you want to bother with this?'

She sat up straight and frowned at him. 'I thought you'd accepted that we were going to celebrate Christmas. You bought presents, you let us decorate the house...'

'That was back in London. You could have your Christmas downstairs, do what you like. If we start something here, goodness knows where it will end—the entire family glowering at each other around the dinner table while the carol singers serenade us, I expect.'

'It might help bring everyone together,' she ventured.

'I don't want bringing together.' There was silence. 'I suppose you are going to be disappointed.'

'Yes.' She was not letting him wriggle out of this.

'Very well. I'll talk to Mama. In fact, we'll both talk to her. I'll explain that you were organising it for me because Hannah was sick.'

He did not seem to be in any hurry to move. 'Alex?'

'Wriggle like that again.' His huff of laughter tickled her ear, his good humour apparently resorted. 'Come on, then, let's find Mama.'

Lady Moreland was in her sitting room with her household accounts spread out before her. 'Alexander, can you explain why we appear to be consuming three times more wax candles than this time last year?'

'No idea, I'm afraid. Mama, I brought my household staff with me as you know. I had promised them the whole of Christmas Day off for their own celebrations, now I find myself in a difficulty because we are here.'

'The entire day? You are very generous, Alexander.'

'I normally just have a cold meal that day. Miss Ellery and Mrs White profess themselves willing to make do, as well.'

'We wondered,' Tess ventured, 'if perhaps a hot luncheon would be sufficient for above stairs, with a cold buffet laid out for the evening. All of the downstairs staff could then celebrate together.'

'We could forgo dressing for dinner, just this once, Mama,' Alex said. 'An afternoon and evening doesn't seem too extravagant, once a year.'

'Unless that would be too disruptive for Lord Moreland?' Tess said, suddenly wondering how that sickly and irritable despot would take to the idea.

'If Alexander can persuade his father, then I have no

objection. To tell you the truth, a quiet Christmas would be a blessing just now.'

'Forgive me, Lady Moreland. I do not wish to presume, but would it be helpful if I speak to the staff about it—provided we have his lordship's consent? I would wish to be of assistance.'

The countess looked at Tess, a small, considering smile on her lips. Tess shifted under the gaze. Was *no longer a virgin* emblazoned on her forehead? Or perhaps she was allowing her feelings for Alex to show. But his mother was definitely smiling. 'Thank you, my dear. I think that would be very...appropriate. Alexander, tell your father I am in favour of this scheme.'

Tess glanced at Alex, relieved, but surprised, and found that he was looking at his mother with a quizzical expression as though he, too, was taken aback by those smiles and her agreement. She shrugged inwardly. Provided no one found out that she was sharing Alex's bed and no one discovered who she was, then there was nothing to worry about.

Chapter Seventeen

'We will go and find Garnett and take his advice on how to proceed with our party.' Alex steered Tess in the direction of the main hall.

'Your mother… I expected her to be reluctant,' Tess confessed. 'And yet she seemed quite approving of it.'

'I suspect the approval is for you rather than the scheme,' Alex said.

She wished they were in private so she could rub away the lines from between his brows. It took her a moment to realise just what he was frowning about. 'For me? She thinks you and I… But surely she knows I am a nobody?'

'Does she? Besides, you are not a nobody, you are very much yourself.'

How could he pretend to make light of it? 'I mean, does she realise that I am quite ineligible?'

'Probably not,' Alex conceded.

So there goes that foolish little daydream, the one where your King Cophetua falls for you, the beggar maid, marries you and defies all convention. Of course Alex has more sense than that. 'Then, you had better tell her before she comes to any embarrassing conclusions,' Tess said, more snappishly than she intended. It wasn't Alex's fault that he was heir to an earldom and she was the illegitimate child of a scandalous liaison. *Not that he knows that*, she mused as they came out into the hallway. *He knows I am ineligible enough, even if he believes I am legitimate. No money, no connections...*

'Alex! What in blazes do you think you are doing?' Matthew thudded down the staircase, his boot heels like thunder on the old polished oak.

'Organising Christmas dinner, since you ask,' Alex drawled, coming to a halt under a trophy arrangement of swords and rapiers that fanned out across the entire wall.

'To hell with Christmas dinner. What do you mean by thinking you can exile me to the other end of the county, give away property—'

'You will kindly mind your language in front of Miss Ellery. I have neither the power nor the inclination to exile you anywhere and I certainly do not have the ability to give away any of the lands, although why you are objecting since they would end up in your hands, I have no idea. I merely suggested to Father that as you wanted to set up your own estate, he give you one of the unentailed properties to the west.'

'To get me out of the way? And the old fool thinks that because you boast about your swordplay and your riding that you're a fit heir all of a sudden?' Matthew was pacing up and down, hands clenched, shoulders hunched, for all the world like an angry bull, Tess thought.

'Excuse me. This is obviously a family matter.' She stepped back into the passageway, then stopped behind the shelter of a screen. She did not want to eavesdrop, but nor did she like the edge of violence in Matthew's ranting.

'I *am* the heir. It is not a matter of choice.' Alex was

hanging on to his patience somehow. 'I suggested he double your allowance, set you up with a good property in recompense for the fact you've been landed with all the work up to now. If you hate the idea, then stay here.'

'And watch you mincing around?'

'I do not mince.' It sounded to Tess as though Alex's patience was stretched to breaking point. Why his brother seemed to be constantly jibing about his masculinity baffled her.

'Of course, I was forgetting you were a great swordsman. So show me.'

There was the sound of metal scraping against metal, then Alex said sharply, 'Take care, Matthew, there are no buttons on those foils.'

'All the better to prick you with, brother dear.'

Tess looked round the screen in time to see Mathew, foil in right hand, throw a second at Alex. He caught it by the hilt and pointed it at the floor. 'Don't be a fool.'

'What, scared of a little sport?' Matthew was in a fighting stance, feet spread, left arm out behind, the unblunted foil pointing directly at Alex's heart.

'Not at all, but do tell me, are you attempting to alter the succession?' Alex enquired and lifted his own weapon, adopting the same position. Tess could not see his face, but his posture seemed dangerously relaxed. She recalled how he had looked just before he'd hit the sailor on the ship and felt reassured.

'Alter the succession? No, you're welcome to it, but I would be interested to see whether you bleed water or red blood.'

'At this time in the morning, coffee.' Alex moved suddenly, a flickering lunge with the blade, and Matthew jumped back. Tess winced at the clash of metal and the two stopped talking and began to fight, it seemed to her, in deadly earnest.

Matthew was more aggressive, stockier and heavier and, to her ignorant eye, far more serious. Alex moved less, but with more grace, and he used his foil with an economy and accuracy that seemed to expend far less effort.

His brother was panting now, with sweat on his brow. Alex, as the fight brought him circling round to face her, looked cool. Matthew lunged straight for Alex's ribs. Tess clapped her hand over her mouth to stop the scream as Alex stood stock still, let the blade come, then sidestepped at the last moment. His left hand came down to fasten on Matthew's wrist and with a twist the foil went clattering against the wall.

In the ringing silence Tess braced herself for Matthew to lash out at his brother, but he straightened, his wrist still in Alex's grasp. 'Where did you learn to fight like that?'

'Germany. Where did you?'

'Father. We've been wrong about you, haven't we?' Matthew seemed half sullen, half embarrassed.

'Because I can use the foils?' Alex grinned. 'You should get around more, little brother. The man who taught me swordplay fought, shall we say, for the opposition. So does the man who gave me that in Gentleman Jackson's boxing ring.' He touched a finger to the thin scar on his cheekbone. 'But yes, you were wrong about me. I hate to break it to you, but an interest in the arts and a disinclination to slaughter everything with fur, feathers or fins is not a reliable indicator of very much, I'm afraid.'

Tess wondered what on earth they were talking about. But whatever it was, it had changed Matthew's attitude. 'You've boxed with Jackson? *The* Jackson?'

'There is only one.' Alex stretched up to hook the foils back in their place on the wall. 'Come on, let's go and have a look at the maps, discuss which of those two manors you want and I'll show you a really tricksy cross-buttock throw the Gentleman taught me.'

He had certainly forgotten she was there if he was discussing buttocks.

Alex waited until Matthew closed the library door behind him and was looking at him before he knocked him on to his backside with a sharp right to the jaw.

'What the hell was that for?' Matthew stared up at him, rubbed his jaw, but seemed disinclined to get up and return the punch.

'Swearing in front of Miss Ellery, fooling about with unguarded foils and generally being an ass.'

'Fair enough.' His brother grinned, then winced. 'At least, for the first two, guilty as charged. But what am I supposed to think when Father loses his temper, throws accusations at you and you walk out and are never seen again?'

'Let me think.' Alex leaned back against the edge of the long table. 'That he'd severely wounded my feelings? That his temper tantrum ended up with a young man blowing his brains out? That your seventeen-year-old brother didn't take kindly to having his manhood called into question? And I could have been easily seen if you'd bothered to look. There was no secret about where I was, and I've never been out of contact with our mother.

'You could have come and visited me in London any time you chose, when I was in the country. Or did you think the house would be full of macaronis and fops and we'd drag you off to some molly house and make you wear *macquillage*?'

'Er, yes, more or less.' Matthew got to his feet and showed admirable common sense, in Alex's opinion, by putting the width of the table between them. 'At least, thought it might be damned embarrassing.'

'Have you ever been to London?' Matthew shook his head. 'Long past time you did, then. Come and stay for the Season and I promise I'll protect your virtue.'

'Don't need it protecting.' Matthew hunched a shoulder, then burst out, 'I wanted to go, but the old devil wouldn't let me. Says there's nothing there for real men, no decent sport, just a lot of fancy balls and boring crushes.'

'Our father has an eye to his pocketbook. You'd enjoy London. I'll put you up for a couple of my clubs, introduce you around, get you some decent boots—'

'Hoby?' Matthew looked as though someone was waving gold coins in front of his nose.

'Hoby,' Alex agreed. 'Gentleman Jackson's, Purdey's or Manton's, some of the less stuffy places of entertainment. Just don't get into the claws of some Captain Sharp in gambling dens, because I'm not covering your vowels if you do.'

There was dead silence. Matthew opened and closed his mouth, then managed, 'I've been a bloody fool.'

Alex shrugged. 'So have I, I suspect. But I had a good time while I was at it and I don't think you have.' Matthew was growing up, wanting to achieve something of his own and emerge from under the shadow of his parent.

'Father approves of your sporting prowess, he thinks you are a real man in his image, but I'll wager he makes you feel you're second best because you aren't the heir.' His brother's face darkened. 'It's true, isn't it? He's obsessed with having an heir who is just like him. I'm not a sporting Nonpareil and you can never feel for the earldom as I do. Both of us miss being what he wants.'

Matthew stared at him, growing comprehension on his face. 'You're right. Damn it, I never could work out why nothing ever seemed to be quite good enough. And I'm bored here. I want something that's my own. And when he said you suggested just that, I suppose…'

'You were angry because I'd suggested it and it wasn't his idea? I think we had both better stop hoping that one day our father is going to declare himself proud of the pair of us. I suggest we just get on with our lives the way we think we ought to live them.'

He had surprised himself by how calm he felt when the realisation came into his head, and it seemed he had surprised Matthew, too. 'What has come over you? You have to be angry about the way you've been treated in the past and you've had a damn unfriendly welcome home from Father and me. Why are you being so forgiving?'

'I'm not, not about Peter. But…I don't know.' He shrugged. 'Christmas spirit, I suppose.' *Tess's influence is more likely.*

'The love of a good woman?' Matthew said with a grin. 'Miss Ellery's a very pretty girl, you lucky devil.'

She's more than that. The odd pain under his breastbone was aching again, as though something was tight and fearful inside him. 'You know perfectly well I'm expected to make a good match.'

Matthew's grin became wicked. 'Who said anything about—?'

His brother flinched when he saw Alex's expression. 'Do not say it. Do not think it. Miss Ellery is a guest under our roof.' Perhaps the pain was simply his conscience.

'Yes, of course. Sorry. Shall we have a look at the estate plans? If I can really choose one of the unentailed manors, I've got some ideas.' Matthew began to unroll the maps from the end of the table and weight the corners with books. 'I'd appreciate your advice.'

Alex found, suddenly, that it was difficult to speak. His brother wanted his advice, wanted what he had been able to give him, wanted to work with him. He had thought he had all the friendship and companionship he would ever want or need but this, he discovered, was different. This was family.

'Sorry, frog in my throat. Yes, of course, although you know far more than I do, I've no doubt. Is this the one you favour?'

'There you are. I've been looking everywhere.' Tess kept her voice cheerful as she bustled into the library. Alex's silhouette against the darkening grey sky beyond the wide windows looked bleak and brooding, and she made herself straighten her suddenly sagging shoulders as the flame of the candle she carried dipped.

She had been worrying about Alex and what was happening between him and his brother all afternoon, braced for the sounds of a fight or even, in her more anxious moments, a gunshot.

But as she touched the flame to the wicks of the unlit candelabras that stood around the room he turned and smiled at her, and the relief was enough to make her sit down with a thump on the nearest chair.

'I'm sorry, I have been neglecting you.'

'Not at all, only I have so much to report about my discussion with Garnett, Mrs Garnett and Cook that I wanted to tell you as soon as possible. I have a list, but essentially they think it an excellent idea and the staff are very enthusiastic. I spoke to your mother again and promised I would help organise the buffet upstairs in the evening, but we will have plenty of time to spend with our people. I mean your people.' *Lord, what a slip to make!* 'Handing out presents and so forth.'

She produced a notebook and Alex came over and sat next to her. 'Ah, the infallible notes.' Tess passed it over and watched him covertly while he read. He looked different, she realised. Younger almost, as though years had been lifted away.

'Is everything all right?'

'With this? Yes, excellent as far as I can tell—you know I have no recent experience of Christmas festivities. I have no doubt everyone will have a splendid time. You are a born organiser, Tess.'

'I meant with your brother. I was rather worried. He seemed so angry.'

Alex gave a snort of laughter. 'A masterpiece of understatement given that he made a spirited attempt to spit me on a blade. Yes, everything is all right with Matthew. I've found my way back to my little brother, Tess, and he needed me.'

'I am so glad. Oh, Alex, that is such good news.'

'It is all because of you, little nun.' His smile was decidedly lopsided now, as though he was attempting to cover deep emotion with a joke. 'You've infected me with your Christmas spirit. I am probably doomed. It will be handbell ringing and carol singing next and then I will be beyond help.'

'You are such a good man.' Tess leaned over to emphasise the warmth of her praise with a kiss on Alex's cheek just as he turned his head towards her. She found herself on his knee, twined in his arms, his mouth on hers, not returning the warm affection she had intended, but with the hard demand of a lover.

It seemed a very long time since he had taken her back to her bedchamber in the pre-dawn gloom. It seemed an endless evening stretched before they could be alone together again.

'I'll come to your room tonight, if you still want me to.' Alex traced the line of her eyebrows. 'Don't frown at me, little nun. If you don't want me I will stay away. My heart will break—'

'I am not a nun and your heart will do no such thing,' Tess snapped. She got up and paced down the library. 'Don't give me all that flummery. There is a mutual attraction, that is all it is. I am not one of your society flirts who needs seduction wrapped up in sparkly ribbons.' *Of course I want you, you darling man. Are you blind? And I want your heart, not your teasing. And if I got it I would have to give it back*, she thought drearily.

Safely on the other side of the table she took a deep breath and found a smile. 'Now, we haven't talked about all the details for the Christmas arrangements. We require a cartload of evergreens and then I'll need to know when you'll be coming downstairs to give your staff their presents. Do you think your family would enjoy it if they came upstairs at some point and sang carols? They've been practising.'

'If you need evergreens, ask Matthew.' Alex was on his feet, his face stony. 'I don't imagine for a moment that the staff want me down there, they'll have much more fun if left to their own devices, and if you organise carol singers then don't expect me to stay and listen to the caterwauling.'

'Then, that will be your loss. I will go and speak to Mr Tempest.' *Pull yourself together, Tess*, she scolded as she picked up her candle and left, managing not to sniff until she was outside the door. *You knew he only tolerated your interference to be kind.* Lady Moreland had been enthusiastic about the idea of evergreens and this was her house. She set out to look for Matthew.

Chapter Eighteen

Alex arrived five minutes late at the dinner table in a mood that more than matched his father's.

'You are late,' the earl snapped.

Alex inclined his head to his father and smiled at his mother. 'My apologies, Mama, ladies.' He took his seat and slapped his best amiable mask over an inner scowl. An afternoon of mingled sexual frustration, irritation, awareness that he had blundered with Tess and the necessity to write a ream of instructions to his secretary was enough to both kill his appetite and leave him longing for the brandy bottle.

Tess spared him a glance and a smile, then turned back to Matthew, with whom she was apparently deep in discussion about holly.

'I gather we're to have a traditional Christmas.' His father regarded Tess from under lowered brows and, as she answered, Alex braced himself to come to her rescue.

'Only if it will not disturb you, Lord Moreland.'

'Not at all, my dear.'

My dear? What had come over the old curmudgeon? It appeared he approved of Tess.

'The best berry-bearing holly are those trees along the

west boundary of Tom's Covert,' his father said to Matthew. 'You should find something for a yule log in that area— three oaks went down in the big storm last year.' He stared down the table at Alex. 'What are you snorting about?'

'Was I? I am sorry. But yule logs, Father?'

'If Miss Ellery wants a proper traditional country Christmas, then we need a yule log. I gather she's not seen one in all that time she's been in Ghent. Don't do these things properly over there. Foreigners.'

'Their traditions are simply different, Father.'

'I suppose it is too much to expect you to be getting your expensive boots dirty.' Alex resisted the temptation to produce an artistic shudder. 'You can go and tell the vicar he's welcome to bring the carol singers round on Christmas Eve, that'll liven the place up.'

'And the handbell ringers, too, I suppose? Father, you should be resting, not having half the village in to create a racket.'

'We haven't had a proper traditional Christmas since you left. I think I'd like one this year.'

As if they were days of joy and harmony before! Alex took in the set of his father's mouth and realised this was more than the desire to give orders. *Hell, he thinks it will be his last one.* 'Of course, sir, if it would please you.' He was rewarded by a speaking look from his mother and warm smiles from Maria and Tess. He still thought it sentimental nonsense, but if it gave his family pleasure he would smile and pretend. Which might put Tess back in charity with him, too.

Alex scratched on Tess's bedchamber door as the clock struck one, slipped inside and braced himself for a thrown slipper.

'Alex?' She had blown out all the candles and the room was lit only by the glow from the banked fire. It turned the white bedcovers patchily to rose and gold and threw her shadow flickering across the bed hangings.

'No, the headless ghost of the first earl. Who do you think?' He turned the key in the door and padded over to the bed.

Tess gave a little snort of amusement and sat up. 'I thought you wouldn't come after we quarrelled.'

'Was that what it was? A quarrel? I thought I was being chastised for insensitivity and a lack of Christmas spirit.'

'And I was being snappish. You were kind to your father at dinner tonight.'

'He may not see another New Year. I'm still angry with him, but barring the door to carol singers isn't going to bring Peter back.'

'Peter?'

Hell and damnation, she doesn't know why I left home. She doesn't know about Peter. 'He was a friend of mine and he had a secret, rather a dangerous one. When I left home my father said things about him that led him to commit suicide.'

'*No.* How dreadful.' Tess reached out and caught his hand, tugged him towards the bed. 'But what on earth could the earl have said for him to do that? Had he committed some crime?'

'No, but he had wanted to. Tess, I can't explain.' He looked down on her bent head as she studied their joined hands and felt her concern and kindness like a caress.

'Was he in love with you?' she asked.

'What?' Alex realised he had almost shouted it and dropped his voice to a whisper. 'What did you say?' He tried to tug his hand away, but Tess held tight.

'There was a scandal last year, the brother of one of the boarders. He wrote a very indiscreet letter to his sister and told her what had happened. He ran away to Italy with his friend.'

'I had no idea sheltered young ladies knew about such things.'

'Some of us do, and we aren't idiots, Alex. It makes sense of the way Matthew was goading you. But they were wrong, weren't they? I mean, you and I…'

'Yes, they were wrong. My father's an intolerant old bully and I was too artistic, too neat and precise for his liking. Then when he realised what Peter felt—which was more than I did in my innocence—he put two and two together and made fifty. I stormed out full of thoroughly embarrassed righteous indignation, stopped on the way to rant at Peter about the stupidity of my father, then left for Oxford without any idea of the bombshell that I'd dropped at his feet.'

'If that hadn't happened, then both you and your father would have calmed down, reconciled,' Tess said.

The sadness in her voice was like a jab in the solar plexus. What had she to be sad about? Was he just another of her lame dogs to be taken in and cared for? It was *his* grief, *his* anger, and he hadn't asked her to care, certainly hadn't asked a sheltered young woman to understand variations of sexual preference that should have sent her into strong hysterics. Alex found he was becoming weary of maintaining an unruffled front, of not revealing his feelings, of appearing tolerant and self-assured and all the things that right at that moment he most certainly did not feel.

'Are we going to bed or am I going to stand here all night discussing my family?'

Tess blinked at him, obviously startled by the harsh edge to his voice. Well, damn it, it was about time she realised that he wasn't a nice man hiding bounteous goodwill to all God's creatures behind a cynical exterior. Nor was he some hapless victim of cruel fate. Just at that moment he was a man who wanted a woman and who was on the edge of losing his temper for reasons he was not at all sure he understood.

'Yes, of course.' Tess flipped back the covers and moved across. She was wearing a nightgown tonight, he saw. A prim and proper flannel abomination, tight to the throat and the cuffs without a single frill or ornament to its cream plainness. 'I hoped you would come,' she added as he tossed his robe aside.

Her eyes widened. Had she seen him erect last night? Surely she had. Was she frightened? Then Tess ran the tip of her tongue over her lips and a surge of primitive power jolted through him. When he joined her on the bed she reached for the hem of her nightgown and pulled it over her head without hesitation, turned into his arms and lifted her face for his kiss. No, not frightened.

He took the lips that were offered to him, caressed the quivering, urgent body, found, without conscious intent, that he was already over her, nudging against the wet heat that was so ready for him. There was a rushing in his ears, a thunder of blood mingling with their panting breaths. Her mouth was open to him, sweet and fierce, her body closed around him, urgent, yielding, demanding. He surged in her, riding the pleasure like a wild horse, focused only on the turmoil of their two bodies, heard her cry and, somehow, found the focus to pull from her body before he crashed into his own shattering climax.

* * *

Pleasure, exhaustion, sticky heat, softness, the beat of a heart under his. Alex lay still, let his lax body come to itself while he gathered his wits, rubbed his cheek against the soft one next to it.

Gradually the human part of his brain gained some ascendancy over the triumphant, sated, animal part. He was sprawled with all his weight on the slender figure beneath him.

Tess. God, what have I done. He rolled off with a contraction of muscles that almost sent him off the far side of the bed. *She was as near as, damn it, a virgin, and I used her like a courtesan.*

'Alex?' Tess blinked her eyes open onto a chilly world where the lovely, big, muscled body that had been squashing her so deliciously was gone. Alex's lovemaking had been a revelation. The excitement, the urgency, the sheer vibrant sexuality of it, had shaken her in a different way to his tenderness and care the night before. That lovemaking could be so varied had never occurred to her. What would it be like tomorrow?

He was staring at her across the width of the bed. 'Tess, I am sorry. I hurt you.'

'No, not at all.' Why wouldn't her come to her, hold her?

'I was a brute. An animal.'

'Alex, don't—'

'I won't, don't be afraid that after that I would touch you. No, don't try to tell me it is all right, you are too forgiving, Tess.'

I will come over there and show you the opposite of forgiveness if you won't let me get a word in, Alex Tem-

pest! She opened her mouth to override him, shout him into being forgiven for whatever male sin he thought he had committed, if that was what it took to wipe that look from his eyes.

'I meant to say this after Christmas, but it is best now. Tess, I can't have you going back, dragging round agencies, finding yourself a position as some sort of drudge to a cantankerous old lady or a house full of screaming brats.'

'But—'

'I will find you a house somewhere, a pleasant market town, perhaps. Somewhere you and Dorcas can settle down respectably. I'll give you an allowance. You won't have to see me again. My man of business will handle it all discreetly.'

You won't have to see me again. At first her brain could not make sense of what he was saying, then it was as though her body realised at some deeper level. She began to shiver. 'You are paying me off? A house and an allowance is very generous in exchange for two nights in my bed, especially considering my complete lack of skill or experience. My goodness, what might I ask for if I acquire some more tricks?'

'Tess, it is not like that.' Alex swung off the bed and stood up, over six feet of naked, angry male. 'You didn't expect me to marry you. We talked about that. And don't flinch. Do you think I am going to hit you next?'

'I am not flinching. I am recoiling from a man I thought I knew and now find I do not. How dare you treat me like a whore! How dare you offer me money!' She scrambled from the bed in an ungainly lurch, picked up his robe and threw it at him. 'How dare you suggest that I am angling for a marriage so far above my station!'

Alex caught the bundle of red silk one-handed. *'Tess.'*

'Miss Ellery to you, my lord.' The shivering had stopped, replaced by a strong desire to be sick. 'Now get out of my bedchamber.'

At least he had the sensitivity to go without saying another word. It was difficult to move after the door closed behind him. After a while she became conscious that she was cold, so she moved round to the side of the bed nearest the fire and stood there, watching the dull glow of the coals. Then it occurred to her that she would like to wash, so she did, all over, in the water that had cooled almost to the temperature of the room.

There were marks on her body, red pressure marks where Alex's weight had lain on her, a roughness on her shoulder that his evening beard must have left. Yesterday the slight soreness and stiffness that lovemaking had created had been exciting, welcome. Now she moved gingerly as though she were ill, trying not to send those aftershocks of pleasure through her belly, through her limbs.

When she was sure she had scrubbed the scent of his body from hers she turned to the bed, pulled on her nightgown, flapped the sheets, found several brown-gold hairs that she threw on the fire. Then she climbed back into bed on the far side from the one they had made love on and curled into a tight ball while she waited for sleep.

'Miss Ellery, are we overworking you?' Lady Moreland put down the teapot and looked at Tess in a way that made it quite clear that her mirror had not lied. She *did* have dark circles under her eyes and she was pale and, try as she might, her cheerful expression looked as though she had cut it out of a print and pasted it on.

'No, not at all. I simply had one of those inexplicable sleepless nights. You know, I am sure, the kind where you toss and turn and can't drop off.'

'Oh, dear, that is so annoying when it happens. I wouldn't mention your looks if any of the men were down to breakfast of course, but Alexander and Matthew have gone out with the workers from the Home Farm to cut evergreens and my husband is staying in his room.'

'Alex—Lord Weybourn has gone out to cut evergreens?'

'Yes, and I hope some fresh air and exercise will put him in a better mood,' Maria said as she heaped eggs on her plate. 'He looked positively grim this morning. I thought he and Matthew had been arguing again, but they seem perfectly in charity with each other.'

'I think perhaps he is a little low because of having to give up his art business,' Tess suggested. 'It must be making a great deal of correspondence.' She wanted to throw the entire contents of an art gallery, preferably one full of marble busts, at his head, but it would be unfair on the rest of his family if she let her misery show. They had to live with Alex and she did not want their reconciliation spoilt by a sordid squabble.

'That will be it,' Lady Moreland agreed as she passed a cup of tea to Tess. 'It must be very difficult, and I never expected him to make as much of an effort to be civil to his father.' Tess's expression must have betrayed something of her feelings for she added, 'I do not scruple to mention the estrangement in front of you, Miss Ellery. I can tell you will be most discreet.'

Tess mumbled something that she hoped conveyed discretion, sympathy and a total disinclination to hear more. Lady Moreland steered the conversation on to London fashions and plans for Maria's wardrobe for the Season and Tess was left to make interested noises and look out of the window onto the carriage sweep at the front of the house for the return of the brothers.

When they did come back it was on a wave of cold air and a bustle of servants all loaded with branches to heap in the entrance hall. Matthew was in high spirits and Alex's unsmiling face was a healthy pink from the chill. He glanced at Tess and then looked back again, a long stare while, she supposed, he took in just how dreadful she looked. She nodded politely, then joined Maria and Matthew in a discussion of what needed to go where. Alex stalked off.

'Don't know what the matter is with Alex,' Matthew commented as soon as the sound of boot heels on stone had died away. 'Like a bear with a sore head.'

Maria offered Tess's suggestion about the heavy workload with the art business and Tess was able to retreat into a corner with a pile of holly, stout scissors and wire to fashion some wreaths. She wanted to think calmly about Alex, but she was so tired that the same hurtful, jangling thoughts just kept circling and knotting in her head until all she was conscious of was pain and a deep sense of loss. *Which is irrational*, she told herself. *He was never yours. You know there never was any hope of that.*

At luncheon she managed to sit between Maria and Dorcas and listened to Maria's anxieties about Almack's, her hopes that she would make friends easily and her despair of ever winning her dancing master's approval. On the far side of the table Alex endured his father's trenchant views of the government's foreign policy and then politely demolished them.

Tess, conscious that the four women at the table were all holding their breath, expected that outright opposition would send the earl into an apoplexy, but he grunted, 'You don't toad-eat, I'll say that for you, Weybourn. You're a damn fool Whig, of course, but at least you can construct an argument.'

Alex took the backhanded compliment with a wry smile and began to discuss felling some of the Home Wood. Across the table Lady Moreland exchanged a knowing look with her daughter.

Last night had apparently made no impact on Alex's thought processes or his intellectual alertness. He obviously had slept perfectly soundly, Tess thought resentfully. A touch on her arm drew her attention to the fact that Matthew was speaking to her. 'Shall we put up the mistletoe after luncheon, Miss Ellery?'

'Why, yes. That would be fun.' She managed a bright smile and was rewarded by a cold look from Alex. *If he thinks I'm going to flirt with his brother under the mistletoe, then more fool he*, she thought. Although it might be soothing to her bruised heart if Matthew wanted to flirt with her.

Chapter Nineteen

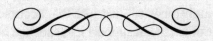

Alex told himself he was far too busy to waste time strewing greenery about the place, releasing spiders and earwigs and making every corner prickly with pine needles and holly.

If Tess wanted to giggle under the mistletoe with Matthew, then she was welcome to him. His brother was unlikely to offer her assistance that she could then wilfully misunderstand and throw back in his face, leaving him feeling like some kind of unsavoury rakehell preying on innocent young women and then buying them off.

Righteous indignation could only get him so far. Alex stopped halfway along the Upper Gallery and slammed his fist down on to a fragile side table, sending a vase rocking wildly. 'Hell and damnation!'

Tess had been an innocent young woman and, in virtually every way, she still was. Thanks to her gossipy schoolgirl friends she might have knowledge of some things that society thought were kept from unmarried ladies, but her understanding of the big, dangerous wide world was virtually nonexistent. He had surrendered to temptation and had taken her virginity, and now he had made that world far more perilous for her.

He steadied the vase, ran his thumbs over the fragile white purity of the Wedgwood medallions that decorated it. Tess had rocked his life, unsettled his certainties. She had taught him a tolerance and forgiveness that made this painful reconciliation with his family negotiable. She had burrowed into his affections and curled up there, trusting and straightforward, just like that accursed kitten.

His offer of financial support had shocked her in a way that his uncontrolled lovemaking had not, he realised as he paced down the Gallery. She had told him the truth when she came to his bed. She had wanted, and asked for, the right simply to be with him for a short while, to share whatever it was between them.

The portrait he was staring at came into focus. Lucinda, wife of the second earl. Beautiful, the daughter of a duke, well dowered and, by all accounts, a profligate little madam who had brought her besotted husband to the brink of financial ruin. He walked on a few paces to Wilhelmina, the first countess. Impeccable breeding, the face of a horse and the temper of a cornered cobra, so legend said.

For all their blue blood, what had those two carefully selected brides done for the Tempests, other than bring unhappiness? 'Damn it,' Alex said in the face of Wilhelmina's haughty disapproval. 'I'll marry the girl, bring in some affection and honesty and caring, and society can damn well think what it likes.' She might not think much of him any longer, but with good fortune he would give her children to love and, God willing, she'd stop him being such a disastrous parent as his own father had proved.

The prospect should have filled him with satisfaction, not a faint feeling of queasy foreboding. Nerves. He turned on his heel and strode towards the double doors. A man proposing marriage had a right to feel a degree of anxiety. He would sweep her off, down to the stables, take her up in front of him and ride off to the old castle, propose there. Tess would like that, enjoy the romance of it.

He diverted to his room, shrugged into his greatcoat and took his hat and a heavy cloak for Tess.

'My lord?' Byfleet hurried out of the dressing room. 'I'm sorry, I did not hear you ring.' He stopped at Alex's gesture of dismissal. 'Are you quite well, my lord? Only you seem a trifle pale.'

'Need some fresh air.' Was he coming down with something? Alex caught a glimpse of himself in the mirror, dark under the eyes, white around the mouth. He hadn't looked as bad as this, or felt as bad, before his one and only duel, an affair involving an Italian contessa, a dubious Old Master drawing and a jealous husband.

Then his life had been at stake, reason enough to feel a cold lump in the pit of his stomach and an encroaching sensation of dread. Now there was no excuse. All he had to do was make his peace with an intelligent, sweet and forgiving young lady who would be swept off her feet with joy at the thought of finding herself a future countess.

Tess was in the dining room, filling vases with holly and trails of ivy. No servants, he was pleased to see and, thankfully, no sign of Matthew, either.

She dropped the ball of twine from which she was cutting lengths when he marched up to her and stopped in a swirl of coat-skirts and cloak. 'My lord.'

No one who did not know her as well as he did now could have told that she was unhappy. Her self-control was as impeccable as ever, and it gave him no pleasure to see the tension in the way she held herself, the slight droop of her mouth. 'Tess, come riding with me.'

'I cannot ride.'

'I'll take you up in front of me. Tess, I am sorry, I should not have offered you what I did. I should have offered you marriage.' So much for a romantic interlude on horseback, a gallant knight making a powerful declaration to his lady in the castle ruins.

Her eyes were huge and dark and deep. A man could drown in those eyes. She was amazed that he had offered marriage; she was in shock. At any moment a smile would dawn and she would be in his arms.

'No,' Tess said. *'No.'* She backed away from him, her hands clenched tight by her sides. 'You must not. No.'

Alex made no move to stop her when she ran from the room. From him. So that was that. He had disgusted her with his violent rutting and insulted her with his crass offer and she had punished him in a far more effective way than she could ever have dreamed, leaving him unable to do the honourable thing.

I can't. I mustn't. Tess ran blindly away from temptation, ran as though all the devils in hell followed after her whispering inducements and false promises. She pushed open panelled double doors and found herself in a long gallery. It was mercifully empty, so she sat in one of the window seats and uncurled her cramped fingers. There was blood in her right palm where the nails had bitten in. She had wanted to say *yes* so much. Had wanted to reach for him, be held close, kiss that tight unhappiness from his face. She wanted to have her Alex back, her knight in slightly tarnished armour, her cynic with a soft heart, her lover with magic at his fingertips.

'No,' she told herself again. 'You will not take advantage of his honour.' She was being watched. The uneasy feeling stole over her as she sat there and she sat upright, got her face under control. How shameful to be found huddled miserably in a corner by the servants, or worse, her hosts.

When she looked around her the long chamber seemed empty, peopled only by the ranks of portraits with their guarded, careful expressions. It was foolish to imagine they were all staring with disapproval at her.

Chin up, back straight, Tess walked over to confront one particularly haughty dame. 'Wilhelmina, Countess Moreland', the gilded label on the frame read. 'Daughter of Hugo de Vane, Third Marquess Peterborough'. Wilhelmina stared down at Tess as though she was a junior housemaid who had upended a chamber pot on the best Wilton carpet.

Her bloodlines would be traceable back to some uncouth and sweaty Norman baron who had come over at the Conqueror's heels, Tess had no doubt. The countess would have been the culmination of centuries of dynastic breeding, careful alliances, political manoeuvring. There could have been no blots on her escutcheon or the earl would not have wed her. *She* was not illegitimate, let alone the product of a scandalous union.

Tess wondered rather drearily if she was ever going to find a place where she actually fitted, belonged. Everyone else knew their place, it seemed. She only wished Alex would let her find hers and stop filling her full of hopeless dreams.

She pulled a face at Wilhelmina. It was juvenile, but it relieved her even more childish desire to fling herself down and have a tantrum about the sheer unfairness of life. She had experienced what she had wished for—to lie in the arms of the man she loved and to share physical passion with him. Now she had to live with the consequences.

'What I need,' she informed Wilhelmina, 'is a baby to cuddle and a kitten to play with. I will wager you never said that in your life. And I know where I can find both of those things.'

Baby Daisy was in the nursery with Dorcas and Annie. She had just been fed and changed and was at her adorable best, all gummy smiles and tiny waving fists. Ten minutes of cuddles and cooing restored Tess's spirits enough to pay some attention to her companions. Dorcas looked plumper, healthier, happier than Tess had ever seen her and little Annie was acquiring quite alarming confidence with her new role of nursery maid.

Tess cradled Daisy and watched the other two women together. Annie had the rudiments of reading and writing, but Dorcas was encouraging her to read the newspaper and to keep basic nursery accounts. What was going to happen to them when the new year came? It would be a criminal waste for Annie to go back to her role as Alex's scullery maid and Dorcas, with no references and the baby depending on her, could never hope for respectable employment.

'Dorcas, may I tell Lady Moreland about your circumstances? I hope she may give you both a reference, and I will ask Lord Weybourn if you may both stay at the Half Moon Street house until you find employment.'

They both shot her startled glances. 'But, Miss Ellery,

won't you be staying here? So can't we stay, too?' Annie said and was promptly nudged in the ribs by Dorcas. 'What?' she demanded inelegantly. 'Miss Ellery and his lordship are all April and May, anyone can see there's a wedding coming.'

'I cannot marry Lord Weybourn.' Annie opened her mouth so Tess snapped, 'Because I am not eligible. I am illegitimate.'

'But you love him,' Annie protested. Little Daisy began to grizzle and she scooped her out of Tess's arms. 'And he loves you.'

'He doesn't and my feelings have got nothing to do with it,' Tess stood up, the good effects of cuddling Daisy vanishing. All she could think of now was the children she could never have with Alex. 'Lord Weybourn has his duty and he is perfectly well aware of it.' He would be, and be relieved, once he had got over his momentary fit of gallantry. And as for the suggestion that he loved her, why, that was simply Annie's romantic nonsense.

'I am going down to the kitchens and then to find Noel. I will see you at dinner, Dorcas.' She was running away, she knew that.

The kitchens were all a bustle with preparations for the Christmas Eve dinner, but Cook assured her that the sweetmeats she had made as gifts for the family were safe and sound in the coolest larder. One skill that Tess possessed to the satisfaction of the nuns was making the traditional candies that they sold in the town. She had created strong peppermint drops for Lord Moreland and Matthew and delicate rose pastilles for Lady Moreland and Maria, and Cook had found some pretty paper boxes for her to pack them in.

That just left Noel to find. He was drawn to the stables, but Tess worried that the bigger, fiercer stable cats would hurt him and fetched him back whenever he strayed.

She left by the kitchen door into the service yard, dodged the laundry maids lugging wet washing into the drying rooms, waved to the woodsmen delivering a load of logs and went through the archway into the stable yard. There was no sign of the kitten but she could hear Alex's voice coming from the tack room and went close to the door to listen. She should go before he saw her, but she needed to find out how he was after that last, fraught declaration.

'I think we'd do better running them unicorn.' When she peeped though the gap between open door and hinge she saw Alex was sitting on a saddle horse, his back to her as he spoke to one of the Tempeston grooms.

'Showy, my lord, I'll give you that, especially with the three greys. But Mr Matthew's been having a devil of a time with them and unicorn is a tricky configuration.'

'But it will remove the gelding who's proving most troublesome. The remaining three work well together.'

Obviously he wasn't nursing a broken heart, or even wounded pride, if he could chat so casually about carriage horses.

Tess began to back away, then her heel caught an upturned bucket and it tipped over with a clang on the flagstones.

The groom leaned sideways and saw her. 'There's Miss Ellery, me lord.'

Alex swung one long leg over the saddle horse and turned to face her. 'So I can see. I wondered what had happened to you, Miss Ellery. You had seemed a little discomposed earlier.'

'Oh, I have been busy, my lord.' Tess smiled politely. 'A little art appreciation, a visit to the nursery and the kitchens, then I thought I must see where Noel had got to.'

'I saw him in the hayloft a while ago,' Alex said. His voice was calm, his eyes were stormy.

Tempest eyes, Tess thought. 'I was concerned, but I see I was mistaken to be so. Life goes on, does it not, whatever emotional distractions confuse us.'

'You can call what there is between us an emotional distraction, Tess?'

She threw up a warning hand to remind him the groom was somewhere close.

Alex turned and called, 'Hodgkin, see if you can find Miss Ellery's ginger kitten, will you?' The sound of booted feet faded away. 'You have it all worked out now, do you, Tess? I cannot say I have.'

'You are suffering from a fit of quixotic gallantry. I am utterly unsuitable for you, you know that. It is not just that I am an orphan with no connections, no dowry and no qualifications whatsoever for a place in society.' She braced herself. Time to tell him, time to see the shock and distaste on his face. Time to watch the man she loved disentangle himself from this coil with cool finality. 'I am—'

'Illegitimate, I know.' Alex looked impatient, as though that bombshell was merely a minor irritation, a firecracker going off.

'But my mother—'

Again he cut in before she could finish. '"Jane Teresa Ellery, born 1775, died, unmarried, 1809." Yes? That is what the *Peerage* says and she was your mother, I assume? The date and her middle name seem too coincidental.'

Silence. 'Am I allowed to finish a sentence now?'

'Of course.'

'There is no *of course* about it. You do not listen to me. You have not right from the beginning. If you had, I would never have missed that boat, none of this would have happened. Now you will not allow me to finish a simple explanation when you must see how difficult it is for me.'

'I'm sorry.' Alex moved away abruptly, as though to leave, then swung back. 'I am unused to difficult discussions with women. With a lady,' he corrected himself. 'But James Ellery, third Marquess of Sethcombe, is your grandfather, is he not?'

'Yes. Is he still alive? My grandmother? I never met them, you see, or my aunts or uncles.' And that sounded pathetic, as though she was pining for a family to love, whining that she wanted their love, admission to their charmed circle of belonging. *Pathetic and true. Yearning for the moon.*

'Your grandfather is alive and, from what I gather, in his usual state of unarmed combat with my father over fishing rights on the river between the two estates, over fences, straying cattle, poaching tenants. My father said he inherited Sethcombe as a neighbour along with the title—like a bad debt or a mad relative in the attic. The old man was a cantankerous so-and-so even then. He must be a considerable age now if your mother was his youngest child. Your grandmother, I'm afraid, died some years ago.'

Tess blinked away the tears. She would never know whether her grandmother had cast her own daughter out and never forgiven her the horrible scandal or whether, like Alex's mother, she had secretly tried to keep in touch, to send her loving thoughts. 'It is a malign coincidence that your family's lands march with the Ellerys', is it not?' She kept her voice hard.

'Not really.' Alex shrugged. 'The aristocratic families are so entwined that it would be surprising if we did not adjoin some relative or another of yours.'

'For my grandfather to be the enemy of your father, that has a certain…inevitability about it.'

'Only if you are writing some damn stage melodrama,' Alex snapped. 'The gods and Fates are not hovering about trying to make life as difficult as possible for us with some pre-ordained doom. If you want to insist on making a production out of this, then let us assume we are supposed to bring about a reconciliation.'

'*Making a production out of this?* What is *this*? The unfortunate fact that I have lost my virginity to you and now you have an attack of conscience about it?' Loving someone did not stop them being hurtful, it seemed. *I love you*. She wanted to scream it at him, throw it in his face, watch him deal with that along with all the complications of male honour, family honour, love affairs real and imaginary, sexual scandal.

'Miss Ellery, I've found your kitten.' The groom came into the tack room, Noel clinging like a furry ginger burr to his shoulder, and stopped dead. 'I'm sorry, my lord. I'm interrupting?'

'Not at all,' Tess said. 'Please could you take Noel to the kitchen for me?'

Alex slammed the door behind the man and shot the bolt. 'You are illegitimate, that is unfortunate, but if your mother's family will recognise you, even as a distant relative, things will not be so bad,' he said. 'Who was your father?'

'George Fenton, the younger son of Lord Melford.'

'Why the blazes didn't they get married then? I don't know Melford. I think they're a Cumberland family, aren't they? Perfectly good match for the youngest daughter of a marquess.'

'My father was married.' There, she had said it.

Alex frowned. 'Married? Then, you aren't illegitimate. Tess—'

Her turn to interrupt now. 'Married to someone else. And then he married Mama. It was bigamous. They were criminals.'

Chapter Twenty

'Bigamous? But I heard nothing of that.' Alex stared at her as though she had announced she was the love child of the Prince Regent.

'I think the Ellerys managed to hush it up,' Tess said. 'Mama didn't know, you see, that Papa's first wife was ill, with a disease of the mind. Apparently she became ill quite gradually and Papa tried to find medical help for her, but in the end she was completely deranged. He had her looked after in a quiet country house of his. It must have been awful for him. There was nothing he could do for her except give her good care. That's where all the money must have gone, I think. Then he met Mama and they fell in love.

'She thought he was a widower and couldn't understand why her father forbade Papa to even speak to her. If he had only explained it would have been a heartbreak for her, but at least she would have understood before it was too late. I suppose in those days daughters were supposed simply to obey and not ask questions.

'They loved each other. I do not know when Mama found out that his wife was still alive, but she must have forgiven him and they never told me, only that Papa had been married before and had loved his first wife, but he'd felt blessed to have found a new love with Mama. I think it must have been true. He was such a kind man he must have loved her until she changed into someone he no longer knew.

'I had seen their wedding lines, but I had no idea they were invalid until Mother Superior told me when I was sent to the convent.' *Bastard, child of sin, daughter of depraved criminals. Unworthy.* The words still rang in her ears. *Only through hard work, humble acceptance of who and what you are, can you aspire to move in respectable company. You have no rights to the place where your parents were born, you have no place either amongst decent, God-fearing humbler folk...*

Tess took a steadying breath. 'I thought my name was Fenton until then, but of course, as the marriage was illegal then I am a bastard and must use my mother's surname. So you see I am utterly impossible as a wife for you, or for any respectable man.'

She thought she could read Alex's face now, but all she could discern was furious thought. Perhaps he was trying to work out a way to remove her from the house before his mother discovered just what she was harbouring.

'Why didn't you tell me before?'

'Before you slept with me? Before you brought me into your family home?'

'Before I fe— What's the date?'

'The *date*? Why, the twenty-third, of course.' Perhaps she had tripped and banged her head and not realised. Or perhaps the shock had turned Alex's brain.

'No damned time,' he muttered. He looked at her, his expression unreadable, then he took her by the shoulders, pulled her towards him and kissed her with a hard, possessive urgency.

That was goodbye, Tess thought as he released her as abruptly as he had taken her.

'I knew Christmas was a bad idea,' he said, turned on his heel, shot back the bolt and was out of the door and across the yard before she could speak.

Christmas Eve had been a strange day, Tess decided as she waited in the drawing room for the family to assemble for dinner. The earl had kept to his bedchamber, resting, because he was determined to go to midnight service. Lady Moreland and Maria had been out visiting friends and neighbours with gifts, calling on tenants. The servants had been busy with preparations and Alex and Matthew simply did not appear.

Annie reported that they had ridden off early together. 'I heard Mr Matthew say, "I don't blame you for running out on all the fuss,"' she confided. 'And his lordship said, "I need to think and I'm damned if I can do it in the house, so come and act like a brother for once and keep me company." And Mr Matthew said a bad word and laughed and off they went.'

The earl, Maria and Lady Moreland came in as she was puzzling, yet again, about Alex. Was he simply finding excuses to avoid her? Tess stopped fiddling with her fan as she and Dorcas stood and curtsied, and then forced herself to make conversation while Dorcas retired to her usual corner.

'Where are those boys?' Lady Moreland said after half an hour of everyone avoiding staring at the door.

'My apologies, Mama.' Alex strode in, elegant in immaculate evening dress, Matthew, less polished but still correctly attired, at his heels. Both faces had high colour from having been rapidly warmed after long exposure to cold. 'We have only just got back.'

'From where?' Lady Moreland demanded. 'I shudder to think what state the goose will be in. Cook will probably hand in her notice this very night.'

'I wanted to look at the estate, Mama. It has been a long time.' He looked at his father and then at Tess. 'I found it put things in perspective. I apologise for leaving our guests, but I see the house is most festively garlanded, so I assume you must have found occupation, Miss Ellery.'

'I…I am sorry, Lord Weybourn, I did not quite catch what you said.' *Not with you smiling at me like that.* The curve of his mouth was tender; the look in his eyes was regretful… *Stop it. It means nothing. He is simply apologetic for leaving me all day without a word. That look is not...*

He had been out all day thinking, looking at the estate with his brother. He had been reminding himself who he was, what was owed to his name. She could not deceive herself by choosing to see only that smile. Because she was fraught and nervous and aching for him, she saw in his expression what she longed to see. And that was impossible. Must be impossible.

Alex took her into dinner and Tess got through the meal somehow. It was true what the nuns had drilled into the girls: good manners and polite observances would carry you through the most difficult social situations. They would even cover up heartbreak.

Alex sent her no more of those achingly tender smiles. He, too, kept to polite conversation, teased his sister gently, drew out Matthew on the subject of horse breeding and endured his father's observations on the state of the nation.

Finally Lady Moreland rose. 'Gentlemen, if you are willing to forgo your port, shall we all retire to the drawing room for an exchange of gifts?'

She received no protests. Even Alex went meekly, Tess noted with relief—and promptly walked straight into Matthew's arms. 'Mr Tempest!'

'Miss Ellery, behold, the mistletoe.'

She glanced up. 'That is not where I told the footman to put it.'

'Indeed not, but it is where I moved it to.' He bent his head, his intent obvious, and then Tess found herself whirled round into Alex's embrace.

'Poacher,' Matthew protested. 'I would call you out for that, brother, if I were not so dazzled by Mrs White's new Christmas finery.' He caught Dorcas's hand and, despite her squawk of alarm, pressed a bold kiss on her lips.

'No,' Tess whispered, caught in the circle of Alex's arms. 'It is not…kind.' He was strong and hard and so wickedly tempting. Just one kiss, a kiss his family would think of as innocent Christmas fun. One last kiss to break her heart.

'On St Stephen's Day, if you want to leave me, Tess, I will let you go. I will send you back to London, somehow find you respectable employment. But you gave yourself to me for Christmas and until then, you are mine.' His whisper was urgent, fierce against her lips. And he kissed her, a kiss as light as a breeze, a mere brush of his mouth, an exchange of breath that left her trembling and close to tears. Then he released her and kissed Dorcas, a wicked smacker that made her laugh and blush before he passed on to kiss his mother and sister on the cheek.

St Stephen's Day, the twenty-sixth of December. She had not agreed to any length of time to stay. But she had gone to his bed, given herself to him, agreed to come with him to his family for Christmas, so perhaps he was within his rights to make demands. Although to what end, she had no idea. Surely he would not want to make love to her now, not when he knew she was the skeleton in the neighbours' closet, not when he had settled in his own mind where his duty lay.

And she had not helped the family much, not as she had intended. The earl was not bedridden, Lady Moreland seemed to need no assistance and Alex and his father were on speaking terms, of sorts, without any intervention from her.

'Are you unwell, Miss Ellery?'

The earl's abrupt question made her start guiltily. *If he only knew who he is harbouring under his roof.* 'Not at all, Lord Moreland. I was deep in thought, that was all. This is all very different from what I am used to.'

'A nunnery, eh? Not much mulled wine there, I'll be bound.'

'No, my lord.' The footman opened the door on to a blaze of candlelight and a table laden with parcels and packages. The servants had been hard at work while the family ate. 'Oh, this looks so festive!'

Alex found he was smiling. Not at the decorations or the presents, but at Tess's obvious delight. She looked like a child for a moment, hands clasped to her heart with delight—and then she was a woman again, the woman he desired, the innocent whose life he had almost ruined. Might still, if he was not very careful, very lucky.

There had to be some way through this. He found he

was looking at the portrait of his grandmother above the fireplace. Another dynastic alliance, another proper match for the Earl of Moreland. He had been infected by Tess's ridiculous fantasy world of Christmas love and magic into thinking that, somehow, there was a happy ending to this. But if there was, he had to find it. He had fallen in love with a daughter of scandal, a woman disowned by her family who could bring nothing to the earldom.

Then his brain caught hold of his thoughts. *In love. So that is what it is, this pain in my chest, this ludicrous optimism and plunging despair. Not just liking, not simply lust. I love her.*

No one appeared to notice him standing like a stunned ox in the middle of the room. Alex shut his mouth with a snap and looked about him. His mother was ordering everyone to their places, grouped around his father like a conversation-piece portrait of a happy family. Maria had thought to send for little Daisy, so there was even the obligatory charming baby, he thought with a flash of his old cynicism. Even the dratted kitten had managed to find its way upstairs and was stalking a trailing ribbon on Maria's gown.

Matthew had apparently been chosen as the distributor of gifts. Alex squeezed into a place on the sofa between his sister and Tess and was rewarded by a sharp elbow in the ribs.

'You are squashing us,' Tess whispered. 'It is not kind.'

'To squash you or to sit with you?' he murmured back. Against his side she was warm and soft and smelled deliciously of rosewater and Tess. 'Trust me, Tess.' *To do what?* the cynical voice in his head jibed. *Ensure her ruin? Make her unhappy?*

'To do what?' Her voice cracked as she echoed his thoughts and he saw her hands clench together. 'To set me up as your mistress? To keep my secrets?' She had as much faith in him as he did in himself. Or perhaps she was just more realistic.

'I have no wish to make you my mistress,' he said, soft voiced in her ear. The soft curls tickled his nose; the scent of her was almost intolerably seductive. *I can't give you up.*

'Then, why keep me here—?' Tess broke off as his mother clapped her hands and ordered Matthew to begin.

Tess seemed flustered to be presented with a Kashmir shawl from his mother and a fan from Marie. Her own sweetmeats were received with expressions of delight, Daisy's doll was instantly seized and sucked and Dorcas expressed delight with her parcel of novels. The floor was soon strewn with sheets of torn paper and tangled ribbons and Noel was in kitten heaven, chasing imaginary mice through the crackling heap.

When was Matthew going to get to his own gift to Tess? She had retreated as far into the corner of the sofa as possible, the tension crackling off her until he felt as though a thunderstorm was about to break. *She'll hate it*, he thought with a fresh plunge into pessimism. *She'll think I am laughing at her.*

'For Miss Ellery!' Matthew produced a rectangular package with a flourish and peered at the label. 'With Christmas wishes from Alex.'

'Thank you.' Tess's smile was warm as she took the package, but she was biting her lip when Matthew turned away.

'Open it,' Alex urged as she sat there making no effort to untie the knots.

It was almost the last parcel. She seemed to realise that all eyes were on her and scrabbled at the wrappings with uncharacteristic clumsiness. The lid came off the box and she pushed back the tissue paper and lifted out the contents.

'A doll? Alexander, you've addressed a present for the baby to Miss Ellery,' his mother said with a laugh.

'No,' Tess said before he could speak. 'No, he hasn't.' Her hands were shaking as she held the stiff wooden figure with its froth of blue skirts and painted black hair. 'It has sentimental meaning for me...something I told Lord Weybourn about. A memory from my childhood. Thank you.' She turned to him and he saw her eyes were brimming with tears.

'Tess,' he said softly, taking the doll from her and making a production out of settling it back in its box to give her a moment to recover. 'I never meant to make you cry.'

'It was a lovely thought.' Her hand on his was steady now, but he could feel the pulse hammering as he closed his fingers around her wrist. 'And I know you do not mean to make me cry.'

It was not the doll that she referred to, he knew, as she set the box firmly on her knee and looked back at Matthew and the others with a determined smile. He had made her cry, even if she would not allow him to see it, even if she acquitted him of deliberate cruelty, or careless disregard of her feelings.

'One last package, and it is for Alex,' Matthew announced, handing over a small carved box.

Alex took it, puzzled. There was no wrapping, no label, just old dark oak rubbed smooth more by handling than from any refined finishing. He opened it and stared. 'This is the Moreland signet ring, the seal.'

When he looked up his father was watching him, his left hand spread out, the fingers twisted and cramped and unadorned. 'I cannot wear that ring any longer. I would rather give it to you now than have you take it from my dead hand. If you will stay, take on the business of the estate, then you will need it, Alexander.'

He found he could not speak. Beside him Tess made a little choking sound, perilously like a sob. Alex tugged his own signet off, moved it to his right hand, then slid the ancient ring onto his finger. It fitted easily. Looking down, he saw his grandfather's hand, his father's, and he found he could speak. 'Thank you, Father. Of course I will stay.'

For a moment he thought his mother would weep and, to his horror, his father, also. Then the door swung open, there was a scrabbling of claws on the polished wood, Noel shot up his leg and onto his shoulder and James the footman skidded to a halt on the rug in front of him, both hands clinging to a leash with a panting hound puppy on the end of it. 'Sorry, me lord, only I couldn't stop her.'

The pup rolled over onto her back, waving huge paws and ungainly legs in the air. She grinned upside down at him, all teeth, tongue and slobber, wriggling with excitement, a ludicrous pink satin bow tied to her collar.

'What the blazes is this?'

'Your Christmas present from me,' Tess said faintly. He realised she was suppressing laughter, probably hysterical. 'Her name's Ophelia.'

Chapter Twenty-One

'*O*phelia?' Alex leaned down and scratched the fat pink stomach and the puppy writhed ecstatically. 'What sort of name is that for a hound? If it is a hound,' he added dubiously.

'I think there is some hound in there,' Tess said. 'She's *mostly* hound. Perhaps the rest is mastiff. Look at the size of her feet.'

'I am looking.' And looking at the sullen gleam of the intaglio bloodstone in the ring on his hand. If he had been drinking hard all day he could not feel more dislocated from reality. He dragged himself back to the present, to one mongrel hound puppy busily licking his shoes. 'The thing is going to be as big as a horse.'

'Don't call her a thing.' Tess was still laughing, he could hear it in her voice. But she was wary, too. 'The poor creature has had a hard life and deserves a proper name. She was found in a sack in the cattle pond. She would have drowned if one of the grooms hadn't gone in and rescued her. That is why we called her Ophelia.' She shot him a sideways glance. 'All small boys should have a puppy. I thought a grown man might like one, too.'

He had never had a dog as a child. His father kept pedigree fox hounds, Matthew had been given a lurcher to go rabbiting with, but Alex had not expected to be allowed a dog, had not asked. He had never thought he wanted one. Ophelia rolled over and began to chew his shoe.

'Stop that.' He clicked his fingers at her and she sat up, tongue lolling out comically as she put her head on one side. 'I don't suppose you are house trained, are you?'

'Er, no,' Tess said. 'In fact I think it would be a good idea if James took her out for a walk now.'

'Thank you, Miss Ellery, for my present.'

The hound puppy gave his hand one last slobbery lick, then towed the footman out as his family got up, began to move about the room looking at each other's gifts, talking. Beside him Tess sat, cornered by his body, the doll in its box on her knee.

'I should have given you gloves or a reticule,' he said, twisting the unfamiliar ring on his finger. A week ago, if someone had told him he would be wearing it, that his father *wanted* him to wear it, he would have thought them insane, or that he was drunk.

'I should have given you a book or hemmed some handkerchiefs.' Her fingers stroked the doll's skirts and he imagined their caress on his skin like a remembered breeze.

You gave me something you knew was missing from my childhood, because you understand me. And you have given me something far more precious—your trust and your innocence. I only hope I can make this right for you, Tess. For us. Why couldn't he talk to her? Why were the words so hard to find, so difficult to say, even in his head? *I love you. I want to marry you. Can I make you happy?*

No one was attending to them. 'Tess, I wish you would let me do the right thing.'

She turned, her body shifting against his, firing all the memories of her naked in his arms, the passion and the trust. Where had the trust gone? 'And I wish you would let me do the same,' she murmured. 'I do not want to marry you, Alex.'

'Why not?'

'Why not? To even ask that shows a great deal of self-confidence, my lord, if you cannot think of any reason that would outweigh your attractions as a husband. What can we put in the scale? On one side a title, wealth, a charming manner, kindness and, undoubted skills in the bedchamber. On the other the fact that I would bring a scandal into your family, that I can bring nothing else. You have only just begun to reconcile with them, Alex. Why would you throw that that away simply to do the *right thing*?'

'If it were not for your birth, would you marry me?' he demanded, cursing himself for beginning this whispered argument in a room full of people.

'If wishes were horses, beggars would ride. A cliché, but a true one,' Tess retorted. 'I am no one, Alex. I have no family, no roots, nothing. I will not be your mistress and I cannot be your wife.' She pressed a sharp, well-placed elbow in his ribs and wriggled out of her corner and onto her feet. 'I am going to my room.' As Alex stood she added, 'And that was not an invitation.'

No, he could not make love to her again, not without fearing that he was putting unfair pressure on her, attempting to seduce her into doing what she did not think was right. Nor could he use words of love to her, not when he had no plan yet to counter the arguments she set out against a marriage. Tess, he was coming to realise, had as strong a sense of honour as he did.

It was all her fault for going to his bed. She was quite clear about that. There was no possible excuse. She had known that what she was doing broke every rule of good, modest behaviour and now she was reaping the reward.

Tess propped the doll up on her dresser and returned the beady-eyed stare. 'I have no one to blame but myself. Mama had no idea she was doing anything worse than eloping with the man she loved. I knew perfectly well what I was doing.' And, like the dreamer that she was, she hadn't thought beyond that moment in Alex's arms. She hadn't realised she was in love with him and that being with him would make that love real and painful. And impossible.

'I suppose I ought to call you Patricia, not Patty. Patty was a child's doll. You are a foolish grown woman's, confessional.' So sweet of Alex to remember her words in the toyshop, so like him to buy her a doll to replace the one taken from her. He pretended he was a cynic, that he didn't believe in Christmas and gifts and traditions, but he did yearn after the magic, deep under that glossy shell of uncaring sophistication.

He would make a wonderful father to those children she could never have. She imagined them growing up, the children of scandal, the rejected relatives of the neighbouring great house. If Alex had not been so careful then she might be carrying his child now. Tess folded her hands over her stomach, over her empty womb, as hollow as her heart.

'I have lost nothing,' she told herself, willing the tremor out of her voice. 'I could never have Alex, never be anything else but his mistress.' Imagine the anguish of seeing him court and wed another woman. She knew Alex—he wouldn't keep a mistress then; his marriage vows would be sacred. Nor could she be with a married man. *I have lost nothing, just a few weeks with him, perhaps. You see, it is not so bad, I am not even weeping.*

She lay down on the bed and closed her dry eyes. It would be prudent to rest for an hour before they left for the church and the midnight service. No one must guess how she felt, least of all Alex.

She must have drifted off to sleep because Dorcas's discreet tap on the door woke her with a start.

'The carriages will be at the door in thirty minutes, but Lady Moreland says to come down as soon as possible. Will that gown be warm enough, Miss Ellery? Or shall I find your flannel petticoat?'

'Goodness, no.' Tess went into the dressing room and splashed cold water on her face. She would never undress for Alex again, but she was not going to appear anywhere near him in such a garment as a flannel petticoat. Which was totally illogical and, she supposed, he would say it was feminine nonsense if he knew of it. She could imagine the mischievous expression on his face as he teased her.

'I must have the muff and the heavy cloak with the hood.' Both were garments that Hannah had bought for her with Alex's money. Should she try to pay him back? Or return them, perhaps? But she would never find respectable employment without respectable clothes on her back. He wouldn't laugh about that, he would say it was foolish pride, and perhaps it was.

It was difficult at first to keep the smile on her face when she went downstairs to join the family in the hall, but the view from the door when Garnett flung it open took her breath away.

It had begun to snow and there, in a semicircle at the foot of the steps, was a group of carol singers. They launched into 'Adeste Fidelis' as the light spilled out down the whitened steps and illuminated their faces and beside her a fine tenor voice picked up the verse.

"'Adeste fideles, læti triumphantes. Venite, venite in Bethlehem. Natum videte, regem angelorum. Venite adoremus...'"

It was Alex. Beyond him Lady Moreland added her contralto and Maria joined her. Tess began to sing, translating in her head. "'Come all ye faithful, joyful and triumphant...'"

Soon they were all singing, footmen and butler as well, and even a deep bass rumble from Alex's father. There was silence when the last notes died away, then the singers began another carol, one that Tess, raised on the convent's hymns, did not know: 'Christians Awake!'

The rest of the staff had come out, too, and gathered round behind the villagers. Everyone sang and she stood and watched Alex, saw him smile at his mother, heard his voice, clear on the cold air, and knew she would remember this for the rest of her life.

One more carol and the staff were passing round glasses of punch, the farm wagon came round to carry the singers back to the village and the family coaches pulled up.

'You are a dreadful fraud,' Tess said to Alex as he helped her into the first carriage. 'The things you said about carol singers!'

She expected him to joke, to pick up her rallying tone, but his face was serious as he settled her in the seat and stepped down. 'I had forgotten the simple beauty of it,' he said. Then he did smile. 'Mama, mind that slippery patch.' He helped his mother to her place, then Maria and his father. Matthew climbed in, assisting Dorcas, and Alex shut the door.

'Is Alex—Lord Weybourn—not coming?' Tess felt something like panic, which was foolish.

'He has gone up on the box. Said something about clearing his head,' Lord Moreland said with a grunt.

At least mine is clear enough, Tess thought. *No room for daydreams now. Two days to get through, then I can ask Alex to send me back to London. I can go to Hannah's lodging house. I have enough money to support myself for a few weeks. Perhaps Hannah will give me a reference.*

The church was ancient and simple, its interior glowing with candlelight and made festive with evergreen swags along the pews. Up in the gallery the band was readying their instruments; there was a scraping from the fiddles, the deep boom of the serpent, the quick tootle of a flute.

Tess followed the family to the great box pew at the front of the nave and settled into a corner created by the pew butting up against a medieval tomb, an ornate box with the full-size effigies of a knight in armour and his lady lying on the top.

'That's Hugo de Tempest,' Maria whispered.

Tess was grateful for the embroidered cushion on the hard oak bench seat and the carpet on the stone floor. The hassocks were embroidered, too, and she knelt on hers and did her best to calm her thoughts and turn them in an appropriate direction. Then she sat and fixed her gaze on the haughty profile of the recumbent Hugo and tried not to think about his descendant sitting four feet away from her.

Alex sat, knelt, stood and sang with his mind fixed on one thing, one person. As the congregation settled down for the sermon he shifted slightly on the pew so he could see Tess's profile.

She was no longer his little nun. She was groomed and well dressed and had found the confidence to fit in with his family. And she was beautiful, he realised, watching the still, calm profile set against the frigid stone carving of the tomb. He had fallen in love with a woman without once thinking about beauty, and yet he had always expected it of any of the women he had kept over the years.

He was dazzled by her body, there was no denying it, but it was Tess he had fallen in love with, not her face. His family liked her already, he had seen how competent, how caring she was with the staff in his own house. She would be a perfect countess—if only he could persuade her that she would be accepted. Damn the Ellerys. Why they had to build Sethcombe Hall next door and not in furthest Northumberland…

Alex was not certain afterwards when the idea had come to him. Possibly at some time between the end of the sermon and the blessing, certainly before he had shepherded his small flock down the aisle and abandoned his mother to Matthew's support while he took his father's arm.

'Stop fussing, Alexander.'

'As you say, sir. But I'd be grateful if you would be

careful of your health. I have no wish to be using this signet except at your direction for many a long day.'

'Ha! Humbug.' But he smiled.

His mother hustled the earl off to his bed the moment
they reached the house, Maria on their heels. Matthew
had vanished. In front of him Tess was climbing the stairs
slowly, back straight, cloak trailing behind her.

He followed her up quietly and caught her in the corridor. 'Tess.'

'Please, don't.' She did not turn. Her hood had fallen
back and he looked at the nape of her neck. It was pale, vulnerable, soft. He knew how her skin felt under his lips, he
knew how she smelled, just there, he knew the taste of her.
Not to touch her now, not to pull her back into his arms so
he could kiss that perfect place…that took an act of will.

'Tess, do you hate me?'

'Hate?' She turned abruptly, so close he could have
pulled her against his body if he had not linked his hands
hard behind his back. 'No, never. How could I? I—' She
broke off as his heart gave one hard thump.

What had Tess been about to say? *I love you?*

'I wish I had never come here,' she said fiercely. 'I
wish you had not skidded on those cobbles, that I had
not fallen, that I had not overslept. I wish I was cold and
lonely in that London convent because I knew my place
there, I knew who I was and what I was. You made me
dream impossible dreams.'

Alex dragged his hands apart, reached for her. 'Tess.
Darling Tess.' She dreamed, he made her dream. Despite
everything, despite her unhappiness, he wanted to cheer.

She stepped back. 'But I cannot blame you. It is all
my own fault. Mother Superior in Ghent explained very
clearly that I am not only a bastard, but the child of a

criminal liaison. I am old enough to understand that and to accept it, you would have thought.'

'Is there a convent on the coast of Greenland, do you think?' Alex enquired. He could feel the anger boiling up, only just in his control. 'Or on the slopes of some volcano somewhere? I would like to see her transferred there, I think. You are the child of parents who broke the law and you are an innocent in all of this.'

'None of this is fair,' Tess said. 'But it is the reality. I will not be your mistress. I could not bear it. And I cannot be your wife, however often you gallantly offer to ruin your name and alienate your family for a woman who will never be accepted in society, simply because your honour demands it.'

'My heart demands it.' He could not believe he was saying it. Tess would laugh at him, just as she had when he had joined in the carol singing. He had worn the mask of cynicism for so long that surely no one would be able to see behind it now.

'Oh, Alex.' She reached up and caressed his cheek and he closed his eyes against the pain of it. 'You were right. I was a silly romantic and now I have infected you with my sentimentality and you will be hurt, too. I am so sorry.'

Her fingers left his face, but he kept his eyes closed, standing in darkness as her footsteps faded away. The clock struck one. It was Christmas morning already.

Chapter Twenty-Two

His father did not appear at breakfast, which was hardly surprising. Everyone except his brother and sister and Dorcas had taken it in their room, it seemed. Alex made himself eat his way through bacon, eggs and toast, all of which tasted like straw. He finished a second cup of coffee before he asked Garnett if he knew the earl's plans for the morning.

'I believe his lordship intends to spend some time in the study, my lord.' The butler gestured to a footman to replenish Alex's cup. 'Her ladyship expressed her concern that he should rest, but he remarked in my hearing that he intended to deal with some social correspondence and would not overexert himself.'

'Inform me when his lordship comes down, please, Garnett.'

The butler effaced himself and Alex reached for some more toast he did not want.

'Are you going to marry Miss Ellery?' Maria's question sent the strawberry preserve dish crashing from his fingers into the butter.

There was a flurry of attentive footmen. Alex waved

them away. 'Thank you, you may leave.' When they were alone he rescued the spoon and dumped jam on the toast. 'Why should you expect me to do that?'

Matthew snorted. 'Because the pair of you look like agitated turtle doves, billing and cooing one moment and flapping about in a taking the next.'

Alex made himself bite off a mouthful of toast, chew and swallow. 'I do not bill, nor coo, nor, for that matter, flap.'

'But you love her,' Maria persisted.

'What do you know about love, Mar?' Matthew enquired.

'I have eyes in my head and I know more about it than you do with your raking about, I'll be bound. And don't call me *Mar*.'

'Stop squabbling, children. You make me feel old.' Alex found he was incapable of denying that he loved Tess. Even a prevarication refused to pass his lips.

'You are getting old,' Maria countered. 'And it is certainly time you married. Mama likes her.'

'I am not yet thirty and it is not that simple.' Alex pushed back his chair and retreated to the library. It *was* a retreat, a full-scale, cowardly rout, he admitted it, but he dare not risk meeting Tess before he had this settled.

He pulled the *Peerage* from the shelf again and sat studying it. There were no answers there; he had to rely on his own wits.

The clock was striking eleven before Garnett came into the room. 'His lordship has just entered the study, my lord.'

'Thank you.' This was it, then. Alex remembered the duel again and decided that had, in retrospect, been considerably less nerve-racking than this.

The study door was closed, as always. A cliff face of polished oak, armoured with brass knobs, massive hinges. The great gate to the ogre's fortress when he was a child and had stood here stiffening his nerve after the summons to yet another lecture on how inadequate, useless, unmanly and generally unsatisfactory he was as a Tempest.

Alex flung it open without knocking, then closed it behind him with a satisfying thud.

'What in Hades?' His father flung down his pen. 'Damn it, Weybourn, I've made a blot! What's wrong with knocking, might I ask?' He narrowed his eyes. 'Something's wrong.'

'You owe me a life, Father.' Alex made himself sit down in the great chair opposite the desk instead of leaning over and thumping his fist on the leather surface. He crossed his legs, smoothed a wrinkle out of his breeches. 'We have skirted around this, but it is time to confront it. A young man died because of you. My friend. There is a debt to be paid and you are about to pay it.'

He had prepared himself for a temper tantrum of monumental proportions. Instead, his father picked up the pen from the blotter and stuck it into the inkwell. 'That young woman, I suppose. Tell me. Tell me what you want.'

Alex resisted the urge to pinch himself. Apparently the reasonable tone was not an illusion and his father was actually prepared to listen. But this would be a negotiation and he would need all his skill. He took a long breath in through his nose, settled back in the chair and told his father what he knew about Tess and what he wanted the earl to do.

There was one explosion, a bellow of, 'You want me to do *what*?', a great deal of muttering and banging about, and then his father said, 'Order the carriage and ring the 'bell for my valet. And tell your mother we will not be home for luncheon.'

The earl hauled himself to his feet with a grimace that Alex saw as he turned from the bell rope. Before he could think he found himself at his father's side, his hand under the older man's elbow. He had come to the house never thinking to touch his father again, certain that he hated him. Now he realised he was anxious, fearful for his father's health. *I care about him*, he thought, confused by the rush of emotion.

'Perhaps this is not the way to go about it. I will go by myself. You should rest, sir.' His mother would never forgive him if he dragged his father out on a wintery journey and his precarious health suffered further as a result. 'You could write a letter, perhaps.'

'I'll rest in my tomb,' the earl snapped, even as he leaned his weight on Alex's arm. 'And I'll see this matter sorted out before I do.'

Luncheon was served at one o'clock as usual. And as usual all the ladies were present. Matthew also appeared, explaining that if this was going to be the only hot meal of the day he would forgo his usual pie and tankard of ale down at the Moreland Arms.

Tess assumed Lord Moreland and Alex would take luncheon also, for the same reason, but there was no sign of them. Her hostess did not comment and finally she could bear it no longer. 'I hope Lord Moreland was not too tired by the late night.'

'No, not at all. He and Alexander have gone out, apparently.' Lady Moreland sent Tess a disconcertingly straight look. 'Did Alexander not tell you where he was going?'

'I have not seen him since last night, after the service. And he said nothing then of going out this morning.' For a moment she thought that Alex must have gone back to London, then she realised that his mother knew where he was, but, for some reason, was being mysterious about it.

'Did he not?' Lady Moreland. 'No, I suppose he would not. He always was a secretive young man.'

'I would have said self-contained rather than secretive,' Tess said, more forcefully than she had intended. Lady Moreland's eyebrows rose slightly. 'But of course I have only known him as an adult.'

To judge by her faint smile Alex's mother was more amused than irritated by Tess's defence of her son.

Matthew removed his attention from a pile of lamb cutlets and potatoes. 'I saw them drive off in the coach. Father was looking dashed serious.'

'I hope Lord Weybourn returns before dinner time. His staff are expecting him to look in on their festivities below stairs.' Tess chased a slice of carrot around her plate and wondered where her appetite had gone. *Where Alex has gone, is more to the point. He is up to something.*

She missed him, even though it was only hours since she had seen him. That was irrational because, if he was not there, then he was not breaking her heart with gallant attempts to offer her marriage or thoroughly ungallant offers of quite another kind.

The meal dragged to a close without any sign of the returning carriage. Lady Moreland rang for Garnett and dismissed the services of the staff once luncheon had been cleared and the cold collation set out for supper.

'Maria, you and I must go and write letters. We have received so many with good wishes for the season I declare I am quite behind with my correspondence. Miss Ellery, I hope you and Mrs White will make free of the music room if you would like to play the pianoforte. Or there is a large selection of journals in the Blue Drawing Room. I gather you will be visiting the staff below stairs later?'

'Yes, ma'am. Thank you, we will be well entertained, I am sure.'

Dorcas went upstairs to play with Daisy, releasing Annie to join the other staff, and Tess curled up in the window seat overlooking the drive and waited.

My heart demands it, he said last night. What did that mean? If he loved her, then he would have said so, surely? *Please do not love me*, she pleaded, leaning close to the window so that her breath fogged the cold glass and she had to rub at it with her hand in case it obscured the first glimpse of the returning carriage. It would be unbearable to leave him if he loved her, but she must. If he had been the younger son and willing to live out of society, a country squire as Matthew aspired to be, then perhaps it would be possible.

But Alexander Tempest, Viscount Weybourn, was not an obscure country squire and never would be.

'Miss Ellery.'

Tess woke with a start to find Dorcas leaning over her. She had fallen asleep on the window seat, her forehead against the cold glass, which was probably why she had a headache. That and the dreams. Alex naked in her arms, Alex in ermine-trimmed robes and an earl's coronet being dragged into the House of Lords while all the peers turned their back on her. Mother Superior explaining patiently, while Noel and Ophelia chased each other around her desk, why Tess must be thankful for even a menial position in a respectable household.

'I have been having such muddling dreams. What time is it?'

'Past three.' Dorcas jiggled Daisy in her arms and the baby chuckled up at her. 'I can hear fiddle music from below stairs.'

'He isn't back yet, is he?' Of course not, she would know if Alex was in the house.

'No.' Dorcas did not have to ask who *he* was, it seemed. Was she so very transparent? Tess could only hope Lady Moreland could not discern that Tess was head over heels in love with her eldest son.

The party downstairs was in full flow when she and Dorcas went down the back stairs, carrying the baskets of presents. As they entered the kitchen the Moreland staff fell silent at the sight of guests in their domain.

'A Merry Christmas, everyone. Please excuse the intrusion, but Mrs White and I have gifts for Lord Weybourn's staff.'

'Of course, Miss Ellery.' Garnett, almost unrecognisable out of livery and with a smile on his face, ushered them through to a second room. 'They said that they were expecting his lordship, so we have made the servants' hall available to them until after he has been down.'

'His lordship appears to have been detained.' Tess put a slight question into the statement, but the butler was too skilled to be taken in by a fishing expedition.

'So it would appear, Miss Ellery. One trusts he will not be much longer as the light is fading fast.'

Tess was greeted with beaming smiles and a chorus of Christmas greetings. MacDonald played a flourish on his fiddle, then put it down. They all gazed at her expectantly.

'I'm afraid Lord Weybourn had to go out today, unexpectedly.' *Unexpected for me, at least.* 'I know you will all be wanting to join the other staff here for your Christmas celebrations together, but I thought I ought to bring your gifts down in case his lordship is further delayed.' She put her two baskets on the table and Dorcas added another beside them. 'We'll leave you to your festivities, and a very happy Christmas to you all.'

'Won't you stay Mrs…Miss Ellery?' Annie said. 'Hand the presents out, seeing as his lordship can't?'

'But they are from him and it isn't my place—'

'Reckon it is, Miss Ellery,' MacDonald said. 'You're the lady of the house in London after all.'

'But I was only acting as housekeeper while Mrs Semple was unwell…' she began. How could they imagine for a moment that she thought of herself as anything else? Dreams, yes, but no one could be blamed for their dreams.

'That's not what I mean, ma'am.' MacDonald pulled out a chair while she gaped at him. 'Here, Miss Ellery, why don't you sit by the fire?'

'I… Thank you, MacDonald.' To even protest at his words would draw attention to them. 'Lord Weybourn chose all the gifts,' she added as she lifted the first from the basket.

'All by himself, Miss Ellery?' someone called.

'*Mostly* by himself.' She found she could join in the laughter and, gradually, as the presents were handed out and greeted with exclamations of surprise and pleasure, she relaxed. But there was a sadness in it, too. These were her people in so many ways, and she was going to miss them, miss their warmth and kindness, their loyalty and humour.

Annie looked as though she had grown two inches, she was so much the confident nursery maid, and the other staff seemed more knitted together, almost a family.

I helped with that, Tess thought and swallowed a tear as MacDonald began humming an air from the new sheet music and Phipps picked up the tune on his flute.

'Miss Ellery.' What had come first—the prickle of awareness at the nape of her neck or the sound of Alex's voice?

'Lord Weybourn.' She was on her feet, turning, finding a smile that was merely polite and not a betrayal of what was in her heart. 'I hope you do not mind, but we did not know when you would return.'

Alex looked…strange. Then she realised he was radiating tension, although there was a smile on his lips for his cheerful staff. 'I apologise, everyone. I should have been here to wish you the very best for the season, but I had an unavoidable visit to make.'

He wanted to leave, she could tell, although she doubted anyone else did as they clustered around, thanking him for their gifts, pressing him to take a slice of plum pudding, a sugared almond. Annie wanted to tell him about Ophelia, Noel emerged from the safety of his basket to wind himself around his boots and all the time he smiled and laughed and teased while his long body seemed rigid with the desire to be gone.

Tess began to watch the clock. Five minutes, ten. Finally, after quarter of an hour Alex said, 'Miss Ellery, I am sorry to drag you away from this delightful party, but I am afraid you are needed upstairs.'

'Of course. Thank you, everyone, the pudding was delicious. Have a wonderful evening.' She smiled and laughed at their rejoinders and rescued Noel from under Alex's boots. She promised to take Ophelia for a walk the next day and followed Alex out, through a maze of corridors and up the back stairs to the hall.

'Thank you for distributing the gifts.' He sounded stilted, probably with annoyance.

'I am sorry if I presumed, but—'

'Presumed? Don't be so foolish, Tess.' It was definitely a snap and not in the slightest bit reassuring.

'Where are we going?' she asked after a moment. Apparently he had not marched her upstairs to reprove her for usurping his place with the staff in that little ceremony, but now they were in the draughty hall Alex seemed frozen in place.

'We have guests I would like you to meet.' He took her arm and made for the front salon. The grip was verging on the uncomfortable; his face was set. Tess almost tripped over her feet keeping up with him. At the door Alex stopped abruptly, looked down at her, then stooped and kissed her hard and fast. 'Forgive me, Tess.'

He opened the door and swept her in while she was still gasping and flustered from the kiss.

The occupants of the room were grouped around the hearth. Lady Moreland sat on one sofa flanked by an elderly man and a middle-aged one. Two ladies sat on the opposite sofa with a young lady of about Tess's age between them. Lord Moreland stood in the centre, his back to the fire. He looked as though he had been interrupted in mid-speech. The others all turned at the sound of the door closing and the two other men rose to their feet.

No one smiled, although their eyes seemed fixed on her.

Then Lady Moreland held out her hand. 'Miss Ellery, do come in.'

Alex's hand released its grip and moved to cup her elbow, guiding her across the deep pile of the carpet towards the fireplace. It felt like walking through sand in a dream. Perhaps this was a dream.

Then the nearest woman moved abruptly. Tess looked directly at her and the floor seemed to shift beneath her feet. 'Mama!'

Chapter Twenty-Three

'I do not faint.' Tess heard her own voice, weak but indignant, and managed to open her eyes.

'You had a shock, my dear, that is all.' Lady Moreland's face, thin, concerned, swam into focus above her.

'I need to sit up.'

'Is that wise?' Another female voice, unfamiliar.

'Yes. I want Alex... I mean, where is Lord Weybourn?'

'I am here, Tess.' His mother moved aside and Alex appeared in her place. 'Let me put a cushion behind you.'

She managed to sit up, her gaze fixed on his face. 'I thought I saw... I am seeing things. Ghosts.'

'No, not a ghost. You saw your aunt's eldest daughter. I think your cousin, Lady Wilmslow, must be about the age your mother was when she died. Apparently there is a strong resemblance.'

Oh. So I am not going mad, I am not seeing things. Oh, Mama, I wish it had been you. Then the implication of Alex's words penetrated her spinning thoughts. 'My aunt? My cousin? *Here?*'

'To meet you, yes.' Alex straightened up and stepped back.

There was a moment of hesitation, then the three ladies came forward, the youngest dropping to her knees beside Tess. 'I am your second cousin Charlotte. I am so pleased to meet you! I've been wanting to know all about my scandalous Cousin Jane and no one would tell me anything.' She sat back on her heels, blonde ringlets bouncing, and beamed at Tess. 'We're muddling you— are we a great surprise?'

'A…shock,' Tess confessed. She swung her feet down from the sofa and sat up. The room shifted queasily.

One of the older women came and perched by her feet, the other—the one who looked like Mama—stood with her hand on Charlotte's shoulder. 'My dear Teresa. Did Lord Weybourn not warn you?'

Tess shook her head, looked round for Alex. He was standing with his father, both of them withdrawn from the group around Tess. He was watching her intently. 'I do not know what to say. My aunt told me that the family wanted nothing to do with either of us.'

There was an uneasy silence. The three women all looked at the elderly man who was still on his feet. He stared at Tess from under beetling grey brows. Lord Moreland cleared his throat and the stranger shot him a fierce glare. 'Don't you presume to prompt me, Moreland. I'll make up my own mind. She looks like a lady, I'll say that, not a chit born in sin and raised by a Papist.'

Tess's confusion cleared, leaving her oddly calm and very, very angry. With everyone. She got to her feet, ignoring agitated sounds from her female cousins. 'Are you my grandfather, sir?'

'I am Sethcombe. This is your younger uncle, Lord Withrend.'

Tess straightened her back, lifted her chin and took a deep breath. *I will not break down. I will not scream at him.* 'My mother intended to make a legal marriage. If she was not in full possession of the facts, then you, my lord, must take responsibility for not advising her of them. As for my aunt, she was a good woman who followed her conscience and was true to her faith. I was raised as a gentlewoman and that is all I lay claim to. I most certainly have no wish to lay claim to a relationship with you, my lord.' She turned and dropped a slight curtsy to Lady Moreland. 'I apologise, my lady, for any embarrassment I may have caused. I had no idea who your neighbours were until after I entered this house.

'I will retire to my room now and I would be most grateful if you would allow me a carriage to take me to the nearest stagecoach halt in the morning.'

'Tess!' Alex strode across the room to stand between her and the door as she turned amidst an echoing silence. 'You cannot do that. Your family has come to meet you, to make their peace.'

'I see no sign of it. My cousins are most kind, for which I thank them. But my grandfather considers me a child of sin by one daughter, raised by another whom he cast out for following a faith of which he obviously disapproves deeply.' Her voice wavered and she brought it back under control with an effort that hurt her throat. 'My presence in this house must only be a strain on relations between neighbours. An embarrassment.' She side-stepped and reached the door before he spoke.

'You are not an embarrassment to me and you ever could be. I wish you to be my wife, Tess.'

She closed her fingers around the door handle, the moulded metal cutting into her palm.

'I thought you might care for me a little, Tess.'

How that must hurt his pride, to make a declaration in front of his parents, in front of their neighbours. 'I do care for you, Lord Weybourn.' She said it steadily and without turning. 'I care too much to stay and bring scandal on your family. You have only just found them again. I would not have you lose them.'

Somehow she made it to her chamber and rang the bell. Dorcas arrived five minutes later, pink cheeked and cheerful.

'I am sorry to disturb you, Dorcas, but I am leaving in the morning. Please could you ask one of the footmen to bring my portmanteaux down so I can pack?'

'But don't you want me to come with you, Miss Ellery?'

'I can't afford to pay you, Dorcas. I am very sorry. I will write a note for Lady Moreland and I am sure she will do her best to find you a respectable place where you may keep Daisy with you.'

'We'll come, too,' Dorcas said stubbornly.

'I have no money—only enough to afford some cheap lodgings until I can find a position. It wouldn't be fair to Daisy.'

'You can't go off to London by yourself. Look what happened before. We'll come with you—we can go to the lodgings you had with Mrs Semple—and we will find something we can do.'

'Dorcas—'

'I won't leave you.' Dorcas sat down on the end of the bed. 'You saved us. I'll get the bags.'

Oh, bless her. She was too grateful for the support to argue anymore. 'Knock when you come back. I am locking the door.' Not that there seemed to be any need. Alex was hardly rushing after her. He had probably realised all too clearly what a mistake he had made in bringing her grand—in bringing Lord Sethcombe and his family here.

She began to move about the room, opening drawers, piling her few possessions on the bed. She hesitated over the gifts from the Tempest family, then put them in the pile to pack. It would be ungracious to discard them.

Patricia sat stiffly on the bedside cupboard, blue skirts smooth, painted eyes beady. 'Oh, Alex. Of all the things to give me. I will talk to her, try to pretend I am back in an innocent childhood—and all the time I'll see you, look into your eyes, want to run my fingers through your hair.' She trailed her hand over the shiny painted scalp. 'I'll want to hear your voice and there will only be silence.'

'Tess!' There was a sharp knock on the door panels. 'Dorcas is standing here with your luggage. What the devil do you think you are doing?'

She found herself at the door, her hands pressed against the panels, as close to him as she would ever be again. 'I am leaving, as I said I would. Alex, how could you do that? How could you cause such embarrassment for your parents? You told me your father and Lord Sethcombe were not on good terms, and this can only make it far worse.'

'I thought it best to surprise you so you could not refuse to see them.' He sounded tense, but patient. 'He is an old man, Tess, and we are asking him to admit he blundered badly with two of his daughters and let blind prejudice estrange him from his granddaughter.'

'I am not asking him anything.'

'You will not forgive him, then? Not even for—'

Silence. 'For what?' Tess prompted. But it seemed Alex had gone. *For what—or for whom?*

* * *

It was the longest Christmas evening that Alex could remember. The Sethcombe ladies, distressed at losing Tess almost as soon as they had found her, were driven home by Lord Withrend. Lord Sethcombe stayed, apparently a fixture in the best chair in the study, drinking brandy with Lord Moreland, the two men exchanging occasional observations on matters that had no bearing on the problem whatsoever, so far as Alex could tell from his silent vigil by the window, hoping against hope that Tess would relent and come down.

At seven Annie presented herself, bobbed a curtsy that was one inch from insolent and announced that where Miss Ellery, Mrs White and Daisy went, she went and she hoped his lordship would take that as her notice because she didn't care whether he gave her a reference or not, she wasn't staying, not no how. At which point she burst into tears and fled the room.

'Excellent staff management, Weybourn,' his father observed.

'Annie's loyal,' Alex snapped. 'I'll not fault anyone for that.'

'That matters to you, does it not, Weybourn?' Lord Sethcombe said.

'Yes.' He shut his lips tight on the observation that if the older man had been loyal to his daughters this would not have happened.

'Do you love my granddaughter?'

'Of course I love your granddaughter!' Alex slammed the brandy glass down on the table beside him, sending liquid splashing across the polished surface. 'Do you think I'd have dragged my ailing father out on a bitter winter's day to try to make peace with you if I didn't?

Tess made me see the importance of family, the importance of forgiveness, but she didn't teach me well enough to forgive you for this, I fear.'

'You've a temper on you, Weybourn.' Sethcombe observed. 'Didn't expect that. They told me you were a languid, elegant, care-for-nothing fellow. You gave me a shock, I'll not deny it. I'm not an easy man to shift in my opinions.'

Lord Moreland snorted. 'You may say that again, Sethcombe.'

The marquess glowered at him. 'Your son wants to marry my granddaughter. I've no objection to that—'

'With respect, sir, you have nothing to say in the matter. Miss Ellery is of age. As you don't recognise her your approval is irrelevant,' Alex said, hanging on to the tail of his temper.

'But you want me to acknowledge her. Will that be enough to see her received?'

'It will go a long way. The problem may lie in getting Tess to acknowledge *you*.'

The glare swung round in an attempt to wither him. Alex glared back. *Tess. I'm going the wrong way about this, locking horns with this old devil. I love you. I think you love me. Can I convince you that is all that matters?*

He got to his feet and both older men jumped as though they had been off in a world of their own. They probably had, he realised. Thinking about old battles, old hurts. To hell with the past; he'd been entangled in it for too long. He had a future to build with Tess if he could only make her believe in it.

She had locked her door and he was not going to stand out there begging to come in. Nor would he act the lord and master by fetching a key and letting himself in. Tess's life had been short on romance. Well, he might not be able to do it in armour, but, by God, he was going to try something romantic for once.

Outside the moonlight was bright on the frosted grass, the shadows darkly dramatic where the topiary yews marched along the edge of the wide lawns. The trellis-work along the south front was bare, but the stems of the ornamental vines were thick and strong and he found no more difficulty climbing them than he had as a boy escaping from his tutor.

There was light in Tess's window, but when Alex reached it the room was empty. 'Tess!' He knocked on the panes, aware, suddenly, of the slippery soles of his evening shoes on the icy stems, the cold cramping his fingers. She was gone. 'You fool, you waited too long.' He let his head fall forward and banged it against the glass. *Idiot. She's run, gone off across the fields in this deadly weather.*

The despair was as bitter as the wind. Could he find her again? Dorcas and Annie would be with her, and little Daisy. They'd be careful for the baby, that was his only comfort. *Search parties—and the staff full of punch and mince pies. How long?* He slammed his fist against the window one last time and shifted to start the climb down.

His head was just below the level of the sill when the window swung open. 'Alex! What are you doing? Come in, for goodness' sake, or you'll fall.' Tess was leaning out, hands outstretched.

His hands opened with the instinctive urge to seize hold of her—safe and warm and *there*.

'*Alex!*'

Their fingers met, gripped, then he let go with his right hand and climbed up to face her. 'You are falling out of that gown, Miss Ellery.'

'Infuriating man.' Both tears and laughter trembled in her voice. 'You would be falling out if you were female and were leaning out of a window in an evening gown with an idiotic viscount dangling from your hands over rock-hard paving.'

'I thought you had run away.' He gripped the window frame and hauled himself through, then almost fell out again as Tess threw herself into his arms.

'I'm sorry.' Her face was buried in his neckcloth and the warmth of her body seeped into his cold skin like a caress. Alex held tight and prayed. 'You brought Grandfather here and it cannot have been easy and Lord Moreland went, too, even though he is so ill. And I'd wanted you to make up with your family, forgive your father—and I can't even forgive my own grandfather.'

'He's a curmudgeonly devil, but he's coming round. He knows he is in the wrong and he wants you to forgive him, but he's an old man and a proud one. I think you may have to meet him halfway, Tess.' He laid his numbed cheek against her hair and breathed in the scent of Tess, of woman. *My woman.*

'I had just gone out of the door on my way downstairs to see if he was still there when I heard the knock on my window,' she mumbled into his shirtfront as she began to burrow her nose between the buttons. 'Brrr, your chest is cold. What on earth were you doing?'

'I thought it might be romantic,' Alex said, attempting to resist the urge to pick her up bodily, toss her on to the bed and demonstrate that not all parts of his anatomy were frozen.

'To almost kill yourself?' Tess leaned back in his arms and glared at him. 'Of all the—'

He kissed her. Her mouth was hot and opened on a gasp of surprise, then she was kissing him back, stroking her tongue over his, sighing as she pressed close into his arms. She was here, she was his and he was home.

Alex broke the kiss when her knees were threatening to give way. Tess sagged into his arms and rubbed her cheek against his chest, the friction of the waistcoat edge a welcome irritation reminding her that this was real and not a dream.

'I know you wanted a knight in armour, a Sir Galahad, and all you had was a prosaic soul trying to do this by logic and negotiation. You needed sweeping off your feet.' His breath was warm in her hair as he nuzzled into it, pulling her close.

'I don't want a knight. I want my viscount—just as long as marrying me does not ruin you.'

'Truly, Tess?' Alex stepped back, let her go, his gaze fixed on her face. 'I love you. I want to marry you, raise children with you. It might still be difficult—I can't pretend it won't, even with our families' support. I won't be ruined, far from it, but there will be talk, and you might not be received at court.'

'I don't care. I only want you, only need you.' Once she had dreamed of seeing the Prince Regent. Once she had dreamed of a gallant knight. Now she had a family and a man she loved to build their own with.

'You showed me the way home,' Alex said. 'You gave me my father back.' A faint rumour of sound drifted in through the window with the cold breeze. The staff were singing carols. 'You gave me Christmas back.'

Tess held out her hand, tugged him towards the door. 'Let's go and tell them. How soon can we get married?'

'A month.'

'That long? Alex, I want to be yours the moment you can get a special licence.'

'And I want the biggest possible wedding.' He stopped at the head of the stairs and caught her in his arms, his smile a caress that made her dizzy with desire for him. 'A society wedding, an announcement that I love you, that our families love you and we are proud of you. I want you to have the pleasure of buying a trousseau and I want the pleasure of buying you jewels.'

'There's still my grandfather.'

'Just kiss his cheek, let him forgive himself.' Alex took her hand and led her downstairs, into the small dining room where Maria was filling a plate for Tess's grandfather and the rest of the family were carrying on what sounded like a desperately polite conversation.

'Teresa.' Her grandfather stood up. 'I cannot undo the past.'

'I know.' She found it easy to release her grip on Alex's hand, to go around the table and to stand on tiptoe to kiss the old man's cheek. 'But we can start afresh, can't we? I love Alex. We are going to be married. I want you to know your great-grandchildren.'

The cheek her lips were pressed to was wet and his voice was gruff as he said, 'I wish your grandmother was alive today.'

'So do I.' Tess put up one hand and wiped the tears off his cheeks. 'Alex will fetch me some supper and we'll talk about her.'

Maria was in tears, Lady Moreland fluttered a lace handkerchief, Matthew was slapping Alex on the back and Lord Moreland, seated at the head of the table, struck his knife against his wine glass.

'A toast to the future Lady Weybourn, my new daughter.'

Epilogue

'**Y**our attention, please!' Alex stood in the door of the servants' hall, Tess by his side. Faces turned; the laughter and chatter died away. 'I have the honour to introduce you to my betrothed. You all know her and many of you made her feel safe and welcome in a strange city. You will all understand why I cannot live without her—'

Whatever else he intended to say was lost in the hubbub. Dorcas, predictably, was in tears. Annie, her newfound dignity forgotten, was dancing up and down, the Half Moon Street staff were clapping, Garnett, his face split by a huge grin, was leading his people in a rousing chorus of cheers.

The noise showed no sign of abating. Alex eased back through the door, taking Tess with him. 'Father's told Garnett to open the champagne. Goodness knows if anyone is going to be sober by tomorrow.'

They reached the ground-floor landing of the backstairs, but Alex kept climbing. 'Where are we going?'

'To bed.' He stopped at the next turn. 'Unless you wish me to retire to my own bedchamber until the wedding night?'

'Alex, you are scandalous.' And a terrible temptation.

'I am in love.' He shrugged, the movement of those strong muscles sending a delicious *frisson* through her. 'There's nothing to be done about it but make love to me, or banish me.' In the dim light he looked almost convincingly downcast. 'Besides, I wanted to unwrap my Christmas present.'

'Which Christmas present? Oh!'

He swept her up, shouldered open the door and strode down the passageway to her room. 'The one in my arms. The one the Fates sent me.' He set her on the bed and went back to lock the door.

'You have already unwrapped it.' Tess sat up, the better to look at him as he crossed the room shedding clothing as he did so. Coat, exquisite waistcoat, neckcloth landed where he threw them. He dragged his shirt over his head, wreaking havoc with his hair, and kicked off his shoes.

'What are you laughing at?' Alex demanded, his hands on the fastening of his evening breeches.

'You. The elegant, exquisite Lord Weybourn, careless of his beautiful waistcoat, his perfect hair.'

He smiled. 'If you only want me because of my tailoring, I am afraid you are going to be disappointed.'

'I cannot tell you how deliciously exciting it is to see that perfection in disorder because of me.' She watched him, blatantly admiring as he pulled off trousers and stockings in a few urgent movements.

'You, Miss Ellery, are developing into a hussy. What would Mother Superior say?'

'She would faint away, I hope. Alex, I do love your shoulders.'

'Only my shoulders?' He knelt on the bed behind her and began to work on the tiny fastenings of her gown.

'That was the first thing I found attractive about you, even when you were being infuriating and not letting me get a word in edgeways and making me miss my boat.' She reached back and caressed as much of them as she could.

'Not my fine profile?' Alex was working on her corset strings now, his breath hot on her nape.

'I wanted to box your ears. Besides, at least two of your friends have more exquisite profiles than you do. I thought that *you* looked like a particularly wicked, rather dangerous, mythological creature.'

'A what?' In a flurry of skirts she was on her back, clad only in chemise and stockings.

'Mythological.' He was rolling her stockings down, pausing to lick and nibble at the most sensitive skin, the location of which he seemed to know by instinct.

'I am most definitely not mythological.' A nip. 'I do not have the hindquarters of a goat.' A nibble. 'Nor do I have horns.' A long, wet, wicked swipe of his tongue up the length of her bare right leg from ankle to mid-thigh. 'I am, however, having the most pagan ideas about what to do with you now you are unwrapped.'

He slid up her body and propped himself on his elbows to look down into her face. 'But first I just want to make love to you like this, so I can look at your face, drown in your eyes, kiss those lips.'

Without conscious thought she had parted her legs to cradle him where he fitted, where he belonged, against the core of her, his long, hard body pressed to her softness, his heart beating against hers.

'Yes, Alex.' Tess arched against him and he entered

her in one long thrust, then stopped, his forehead resting against hers.

'I'm home,' he murmured, his breath warm on her lips.

'So am I. At last. With you.' She kissed him, pulled down his head and clung to his lips as he moved within her, with her, pulling her into the whirlpool, the whirlwind. The storm crashed around them, tossed her into wave after wave of sensation and then drew her up into one perfect moment. *'Alex.'*

A minute, an hour, a year later she opened her eyes and found him watching her with his soul in his eyes. Her vision blurred. 'Welcome home, my love.'

He smiled and laid his head on her breast, and Tess felt his lips move against her skin. 'That is wherever you are, my love. Always.'

* * * * *

HIS CHRISTMAS COUNTESS

LOUISE ALLEN

Chapter One

December 24, 1819—the Scottish Borders

Becoming pregnant had been so easy, so catastrophically simple. An unaccustomed glass of champagne, a little unfamiliar flattery, a night made for romance, a careless, innocent tumble from virtue to ruin.

Somehow that ease increased the shock of discovering just how hard giving birth to the baby was. *It is because I'm alone, I'm cold, I'm frightened,* Kate told herself. *In a moment, when these pains stop, I will feel stronger, I'll get up and light the fire. If I can get there, if there is any dry kindling, if I can strike a spark.*

'Stop it.' She spoke aloud, her voice echoing in the chill space of the half-ruined bothy. 'I *will* do it because I have to, because I must, for the baby.' It was her fault her child would be born in a tumbledown cottage on a winter's day, her miscalculation in leaving it so late to run away, her lack of attention that had allowed the pickpocket to slip her purse from her reticule in the inn yard, leaving her penniless. She should have gone to the workhouse rather than think she could walk on, hoping for some miracle and safe shelter at the end of the rough, muddy road.

Her mind seemed to have turned to mush these past few days. Only one message had been clear: *get away before Henry can take my baby from me.* And she would do anything, anything at all, for this child, to keep him or her safe from her brother's clutches. Now was the time to move, while there was still some light left in the lowering sky. She tried to stand up from the heap of musty straw, but found she could not. 'Pull yourself together, Catherine Harding. Women give birth every day and in far worse conditions than this.' Beyond caring that she was reduced to a lumbering, clumsy creature, she managed to get on to her hands and knees and began to crawl towards the hearth and the broken remains of the fire grate.

The weakness caught her before she could move more than a few feet. It must be because she had eaten so little in the past day and night. Shaking, she dug her fingers into the dirt floor and hung on. She would gather a little strength in a moment, then she could crawl nearer to the cold hearth. Surely giving birth could not take much longer? Learning some basic facts of life would be far more useful to young women than the art of watercolours and playing the harp. Learning the wiles of hardened rakes and the consequences of a moonlit dalliance would be even more valuable. Most of all, learning that one could not trust anyone, not even your closest kin, was a lesson Kate had learned too late.

If the mother she could not remember had survived Henry's birth… *No.* She caught herself up before the wishful thinking could weaken her, before the haunting fear of what her own fate might be overwhelmed her. She was still in the middle of the floor. How much time had passed since she had thought to light the fire? Hours? Only minutes, from the unchanging light. Kate inched closer to the hearth.

Something struck a stone outside, then the sound of footsteps muffled by the wet turf, the snort of a horse and a man's voice.

'This will have to do. You're lame, I'm lost, it is going to snow and this is the first roof I've seen for the past ten miles.' English, educated. Not an old man, not a youth. *Hide*.

She backed towards the heap of straw, animal instinct urging her to ungainly speed. A plank table had collapsed, two legs eaten through by rats or damp, and she burrowed behind it, her breath sobbing out of her lungs. Kate stuffed her clenched fist into her mouth and bit down.

'At least water's the one thing we're not short of.' Grant Rivers dug a broken-handled bucket from the rubbish heap outside the tumbledown cottage and scooped it into the small burn that rushed and chattered at the side of the track. His new horse, bought in Edinburgh, twitched an ear, apparently unused to forming part of a one-sided conversation.

Grant carried the bucket inside the part of the building that had once been a byre. The place was technically a but and ben, he supposed, one half for the beasts, one half for the family, the steaming animals helping them keep warm through the long Border winters. There was enough of the heather thatch to provide some shelter for the horse and the dwelling section had only a few holes in the roof, although the window and door had long gone. At least the solid wall turned its back on the prevailing wind. He could keep warm, rest up. He was enough of a doctor to know he should not ignore the headache and the occasional dizziness, the legacy of that near-fatal accident a week ago.

He lifted off the saddle, took off the bridle, used the reins as a tether and tipped the bag of oats from his saddle-bag on to a dry patch of ground. 'Don't eat it all at once,' he advised the chestnut gelding. 'It's all you are getting until we reach civilisation and I've half a mind to steal it to make myself porridge.'

There was sufficient light to see by to clean out the big hooves and find the angular stone that had wedged itself into the off-hind. It looked sore. He gave an apologetic rub to the soft muzzle that nudged at him. His fault for pressing on so hard even though he suspected he would be too late for his grandfather. At least he had been able to send a letter saying the things in his heart to the man who had brought him up, letting the old man know that only dire necessity kept him from his side at the end.

He must also get back to Abbeywell for Charlie's sake. It was the last place he wanted to be, but the boy needed his father. And Grant needed his son, for that matter. Christmas was always going to be grim this year with his grandfather's health failing, but he had not expected it to be this bad—him bedridden in Edinburgh with his head cracked open and Charlie left with his dying great-grandfather. Grant had planned to leave the city on the seventeenth, but that was the day a labourer, careless with a scaffolding plank in the New Town, had almost killed him. As soon as he had regained consciousness and realised he was incapable of walking across the room, let alone travelling, Grant had written the letter. The reply had arrived from the steward two days ago. His grandfather was not expected to last the night.

Grant had hoped to be with his son for Christmas Day. Now he might make it by that evening if the gelding was sound and the weather held. 'We'll rest up, let the bruising ease, stay the night if I can get a fire going.' Talking to a horse might be a sign of concussion, but at least it made something to listen to beyond the wind whistling up this treeless Borders valley. Unless the direction of that wind changed, the makeshift stable was fairly sheltered and the horse was used to Scottish weather.

And for him the familiar cold of a Northumberland winter was no different from this. There was enough rubbish lying about the place to burn. He'd make a fire, pass the night with the food in his saddlebags and allow himself a dram from his brandy flask, or the illicit whisky James Whittaker had handed him as they'd parted yesterday in Edinburgh's New Town.

Something in the air... Grant straightened, arms full of dry scraps of wood, nostrils flaring to catch that faint rumour of scent. Blood? Blood and fear. He knew the smell of both from those weeks in the summer of '15. The killing days when he and his friends had volunteered to join the fight to see Napoleon finally defeated. The memory of them had saved his neck in more than a few dark alleyways before now.

A low moan made the horse shift uneasily. The wind or an animal? No, there had been something human in that faint wisp of sound. He did not believe in ghosts and that left someone hurt or in distress. Or a trap. The cottage would make a handy refuge for footpads. 'Eat your oats,' he said as he eased the knife from his left boot and tossed the armful of wood away.

He moved fast as the wood clattered into the far corner, then eased around the splintered jamb of the inner door to scan the single living room. It was shadowed and empty—a glance showed a broken chair, a scattered pile of mouldy straw, an overturned table, cobwebs and shadows. There was that soft, desperate sound again and the scent of fear was stronger here. Caution discarded, he took three strides across the earth floor and pulled away the table, the only hiding place.

It did not take several years of medical training to tell him that he was looking at a woman in labour and a desperate one at that. Of all the medical emergencies he might have confronted, this was the one from his nightmares. Literally. Her gaze flickered from his face to the knife in his hand as she scrabbled back into the straw.

'Go away.' Her voice was thready, defiant, and there was blood around her mouth and on the back of the hand resting protectively on the mound of her belly. She had bitten her fist in an attempt to muffle her cries. His stomach lurched at the sight. 'One step more and I'll—'

'Deposit a baby on my boots?' He slid the knife back into its sheath, made himself smile and saw her relax infinitesimally at his light tone. When he tossed his low-crowned hat on to the chair, exposing the rakish bandage across his forehead, she tensed again.

'Don't be ridiculous.' Her voice was English, educated, out of place in this hovel. She closed her eyes for a moment and when she opened them again the effort to stay focused and alert was palpable. 'This baby is *never* coming out.'

'First one?' Grant knelt beside her. 'I'm a doctor, it is going to be all right, trust me.' *There's two lies to begin with—how many more will I need? I'm not qualified, I've never delivered a baby and I have no idea whether* anything *is going to be all right.* He had, however, delivered any number of foals. Between theoretical knowledge, practical experience of female anatomy and years of managing a breeding stables, he would be better than nothing. But this child had better hurry up and get born, because he was trapped here until it was.

He was big, he was male, he seemed to fill the space and the bandage made him look like a brigand, despite the well-made clothes. But his quiet confidence and deep, calm voice seeped through Kate's cramped body like a dose of laudanum. *A doctor.* The answer to her incoherent prayers. There were miracles after all.

'Yes, this is my first child.' *And my last. No amount of pleasure is worth this.*

'Then let's get this place warm.' He shrugged out of his greatcoat and laid it over her. It smelt of horse, leather and man, all strangely soothing. 'We'll make you more comfortable when the fire's lit.'

'Dr…?'

'Grantham Rivers, at your service. Call me Grant.' He poked at the grate, went into the stable and came back with wood. His voice was pleasant, his expression, what she could see of it, unruffled, but she could sense he was not happy about this situation. For all the easy movement, the calm voice, he was on edge.

'Grantham?' Incredible the effect of a little warmth and a lot of reassurance, even if she was all too aware that her rescuer wished he was somewhere else entirely.

'I was conceived there, apparently, in the course of a passionate wedding night at the Bull Inn.' He was striking a flint on a steel cupped in his palm and surrounded by some sort of tinder. It flared up and he eased it into the wood, nursing the flame with steady, competent hands. 'It could have been worse. It might have been Biggleswade.'

She had never imagined laughing again, ever, at anything. Her snort of amusement turned into a moan as the contraction hit her.

'Breathe,' he said, still tending the fire. 'Breathe and relax.'

'Relax? Are you mad?' Kate lay back, panting. Breathing was hard enough.

'No, just male and therefore designed to be unsatisfactory at times like this.' His mouth curved into a smile that she could have sworn was bitter, but it had gone too fast to be certain. 'What is your name?'

Caution resurfaced. She was at his mercy now. If he were not the good man he appeared to be, then there was nothing she could do about it. Her instincts, sharpened by the desperate need to protect her baby, told her to gamble and trust him. But with her life, not with her secrets. Should she lie about her name? But that would serve no purpose. 'Catherine Harding. Miss,' she added as an afterthought. Might as well be clear about that. 'My friends call me Kate.'

Dr Rivers began to break the legs off the table and heap the pieces by the fire. Either it was very rotten or he was very strong. She studied the broad shoulders flexing as he worked and decided it was the latter.

'Where's the baby's father?' He did not seem too shocked by her situation, but doctors must be used to maintaining a neutral front, whatever their patients' embarrassing predicaments.

'Dead.' That *was* a lie and it came without the need for thought. Then, hard on the heels of the single word, the wariness resurfaced. This man seemed kind and promised to help her, but he could still betray her if he knew who she was. And, almost certainly, if he knew what she had been part of. He was a gentleman from his voice, his clothes, his manner. And gentlemen not only helped ladies in distress—or she hoped they did—but they also stuck together, protected each other against criminal conspiracies.

'I'm sorry about that.' Grant Rivers laid the tabletop on the earth floor, heaping up the drier straw on it. He was asking her something. She jerked her mind back to dealing with the present. 'Have you any linen with you? Shifts, petticoats?'

'In my portmanteau. There isn't much.' It had been all she could carry.

He dug into it, efficiently sorting through. A nightgown went on one side, then he began to spread linen over the straw, rolling her two gowns into a pillow.

'Dr—'

'Grant.'

'You are very efficient.' A contraction passed, easier than before. He was making her relax, just as he had said.

'I had a short spell in the army. Even with a batman, one learns to shift for oneself. Now, then.' He eyed her and she felt herself tense again. 'Let's get you into something more comfortable and on to this luxurious bed.' It was getting darker and she could not read his expression. 'Kate, I'm sorry I'm a man, I'm sorry I'm a complete stranger, but we have got to get you into a nightgown and I have got to examine you.' He was brisk, verging on the impatient. 'You're a patient and just now you can't afford to be shy or modest.'

Think of the baby, she told herself. *Think of Grant Rivers as a guardian angel. A Christmas angel, sexless, dispassionate. I have no choice but to trust him.* 'Very well.'

He undressed her like a man who knew his way around

the fastenings of women's clothing. *Not sexless, then.* She was out of her stained, crumpled gown and underclothing before she had time to be embarrassed. He'd placed the nightgown so it had caught a little warmth from the fire and soon she was into that and on to the bed, sighing with relief at the simple comfort of it, before she had the chance to realise her nightgown was up around her waist.

'There, we just place this so.' Grant swung the greatcoat over her. 'Now a light, something hot to drink. Lie back, concentrate on getting warm.'

Kate watched from between slitted eyes as he built up the fire, brought in a bucket of water and set it by the hearth. He lit a small lantern, then dipped water into a mug, adding something from a flask balanced on a brick by the flames, and washed his hands in the bucket. His actions were rapid, yet smooth. *Efficient* was probably the word. A man who wanted to get things done and who wouldn't waste time. A man who was forced to wait on this baby's schedule. Both his efficiency and, strangely, his impatience were reassuring. She was seeing the essence of this man.

'Where did the lantern come from?'

'I carry one in my saddlebags. I'll just find something else for water. We'll need a fair bit before we're done. Luckily the last occupants were fairly untidy and there's a promising rubbish heap outside.'

He ought to seem less than masculine, coping so handily with domestic tasks, but he merely appeared practical. Kate studied the broad shoulders and narrow hips, the easy movement, the tight buckskin breeches. She never expected to feel the slightest flutter of sensual need for a man again as long as she lived, but if she did, purely theoretically, of course, Grant Rivers was more than equipped to provoke it. He was definitely very— *'Ooh!'*

'Hang on, I'll be with you in a minute.' He came back in carrying an assortment of pots, water sloshing out on to the floor. He held out his hands to the fire. 'My fingers are cold again.'

What has that got to do with...? Kate sucked in an outraged breath as, lantern in hand, he knelt at her feet and dived under the greatcoat tented over her knees.

'It is remarkable how one can adapt to circumstances,' she managed after five somewhat stressful minutes. Incredibly she sounded quite rational and not, as she felt, mildly hysterical.

Grant emerged, tousled but composed, and sat back on his heels, shaking thick, dark brown hair back out of his eyes. He smiled, transforming a face she had thought pattern-book handsome into something approaching charming. 'Childbirth tends to result in some unavoidable intimacies,' he said. 'But everything seems to be proceeding as it should.' The smile vanished as he took a pocket watch from his waistcoat and studied it.

'How much longer?' She tried not to make it sound like a demand, but feared it had.

'Hours, I should think. First babies tend to be slow.' He was at the fire, washing his hands in yet another container of water, then pouring something from a flask into a battered kettle with no handle.

'Hours?'

'Drink this.' He offered the brew in a horn beaker, another of the seemingly inexhaustible contents of his saddlebags. 'I'll get some food in a minute. When did you last eat?'

That needed some thought. 'Yesterday. I had breakfast at an inn.'

Grant made no reply, but when he brought her bread
and cheese made into a rough sandwich, she noticed he
ate nothing. 'What are you going to eat? This is all the
food you have with you, isn't it?'

He shrugged and took a mouthful of the liquid in the
horn beaker. 'You need the energy. I can live on my fat.'

He rested his head against the rough stone wall behind
him and closed his eyes. *What fat?* With a less straightforward man she might have suspected he was fishing
for compliments, but it did not seem to be Grant Rivers's style.

What was he doing as a doctor? She puzzled over him,
beginning to slip into a doze now the food was warm in
her stomach. He was educated, he had been in the army.
There was no wedding ring on his finger—not that there
was anything to be deduced from that—and there was an
engraved signet on his left hand. His clothes were good.
And yet he was riding over the Marches without a servant and prepared for a night of rough living.

A piece of wood slipped into the fire with a crackle,
jerking her fully awake again. 'How did you hurt your
head?' Was he fleeing from something?

'A stupid accident in Edinburgh. I'd been staying with
a friend in the New Town and the place is covered in
building sites. Some fool of a labourer dropped a plank
on me. I was out cold for a couple of days and in no state
to move much after that, but there's nothing broken.'

He closed his eyes and she did the same. She let herself drift off, reassured. She was safe while he was there.

Chapter Two

The night passed with intervals of sleep interrupted by increasing waves of contractions. At some point Kate was conscious of simply abandoning herself to Grant Rivers, to the competent hands, the confident, reassuring voice, the strength of the man. There was no choice now, but her instincts told her this was a good man, and if she was mistaken, there was nothing she could do about it. As time passed, on leaden feet, her trust grew.

She held on to his fingers, squeezing until she felt his bones shift under her grip, but he never complained. He was going to deliver her baby, he was going to save her so she could hold her child in her arms. He was her miracle. She was tired beyond anything she had ever experienced, this was more difficult than she could have imagined and she seemed to have been in this place for years. But it would be all right. Grant Rivers would make it all right.

It was taking too long. Kate was exhausted, the light was dreadful and he had no instruments. He knew full well that if there were complications, he did not have the knowledge to deal with them.

As dawn light filtered through the cobwebbed windows, Grant took a gulp of the neat whisky, scrubbed his hands over his face and faced down the fear. She was *not* going to die, nor was the baby. This time, at this crisis, he could save both mother and child. There was no decision to be made about it, no choice. He had only to hold his nerve, use his brain, and he would cheat death. This time. He stretched, went out to check on the horse, then saw the tree growing at the back of the bothy and smiled.

'Talk to me, Kate. Where do you come from, why are you here, alone on Christmas morning?'

'Not alone.' She opened her eyes. 'You're here, too. Is it really Christmas?'

'Yes. The season's greetings to you.' He showed her the little bunch of berried holly he had plucked from the stunted tree and was rewarded with a smile. *Hell, but she looks dreadful.* Her face was white and lined with strain, her hair was lank and tangled, her eyes bloodshot. She was too thin and had been for some time, he suspected, but she was a fighter.

'How old are you?'

'Twenty-three.'

'Talk to me,' he repeated. 'Where are you from? I live just over the Border in Northumberland.'

'I'm from—' She grimaced and clutched at his bruised hand. 'Suffolk. My brother is a…a country squire. My mother died when he was born, my father was killed in a hunting accident a few years ago. He was a real countryman and didn't care for London. Henry's different, but he's not important or rich or well connected, although he wishes he was. He wanted me to marry well.'

A gentlewoman, then, as he had thought. 'You're of age.' Grant wiped her face with a damp cloth and gave her some more of the warm watered brandy to sip. It should be hot sweet tea, but this was all he had.

She was silent and he guessed she was deciding how much to tell him, how much she trusted him. 'He controls all my money until I marry with his blessing. I fell in love and I was reckless. Naive. I suppose I had a very quiet, sheltered country life until I met Jonathan.' She gave a twisted shrug. 'Jonathan's…dead. Henry said that until I had the baby I must stay at the lodge near Edinburgh that he inherited from an uncle, and then he would… He *said* he would find a good home. But I don't trust him. He'll leave my child at a workhouse or give her to some family who won't love her…' Her voice trailed away. 'I don't trust him.'

It wasn't the entire story. Kate, he was certain, was editing it as she went along. He couldn't blame her. This probably happened all the time, well-bred young women finding themselves in a difficult situation and the family stepping in to deal with the embarrassment, hoping they could find her an unsuspecting husband to take her off their hands later. It was a pity in this case, because Kate, with her fierce determination, would make a good mother, he was sure of that.

He settled back against the wall, her hand in his so he would know when another contraction came, even if he drifted off. He was tired enough to sleep without even the usual nightmares waking him, but Kate's fierce grip would rouse him. How much time was this going to add to his journey? Charlie knew he was coming and he was a sensible boy for his age, but he'd been through too much and he needed his father. *He needs a mother, too.*

There was nothing he could do to hasten things now. He shifted, trying to find a smooth place on the craggy wall, and prodded at the other weight on his conscience, the one he could do nothing about now. Grant had disappointed his grandfather. Not in himself, but in his reluctance to remarry. Over and over again as he grew frailer the old man had repeated his desire to see Grant married. *The boy's a fine lad,* he'd say. *But he needs brothers, he needs a mother... You need a wife.*

Time and time again Grant had repeated the same weary excuses. He needed more time, he had to find the right woman, to get it right this time. He just needed *time*. To do what? Somehow learn to read the character of the pretty young things paraded on the marriage mart? Discover insights he hadn't possessed before, so he didn't make another disastrous mistake? His own happiness didn't matter, not any more, but he couldn't risk Charlie. *I promise,* he had said the last time he parted from his grandfather. *I promise I will find someone.* And he had left for the Continent, yet again.

He neither needed nor wanted a wife, not for himself, but Abbeywell needed a chatelaine and Charlie needed a woman's care.

'What will you do when the baby is born?' he asked, focusing on the exhausted woman beside him.

'Do next? I don't know,' she said. 'I can't think beyond this. There is no one. But I'll manage…somehow.'

She's not a conventional beauty, but she's got courage, she's maternal. Time seemed to have collapsed, the past and the present ran together. Two women in childbed, one infant he could not help, one perhaps he would save. But even if he did, nothing would prevent this child being born illegitimate, with all the penalties that imposed.

The germ of an idea stirred. Kate needed shelter, security for her child. Would she make a good governess for Charlie? He pursued the idea around. Charlie had a tutor, he did not need someone with the ability or knowledge to teach him academic studies. But he did need the softer things. Grant remembered his own mother, who had died, along with his father, of a summer fever when he had not been much older than his own son was now. She had instilled ideas about kindliness and beauty, she had been there with a swift hug and a kiss when male discipline and bracing advice was just that bit too harsh.

A mother's touch, a mother's instinct. Kate was not a mother yet, but he sensed that nurturing disposition in her. Charlie didn't need a governess, he needed a mother. Logic said…*marry her.*

What was he thinking? *I'm too tired to think straight, my brain's still scrambled.*

In the stable the gelding snorted, gave a piercing whinny. Grant got to his feet, went to the outer door and peered through the faint mist the drizzle had left behind it. A couple of men, agricultural workers by the looks of them, were plodding along the track beside a donkey cart. He went back inside and Kate looked up at him. Her smile was faint, but it was there. *Brave girl. Are you wishing for the impossible? Because I think it is walking towards us now.*

'We're still in Scotland,' he said, realising that his mad idea was possible to achieve. *Am I insane? Or are those strangers out there, appearing right on the heels of that wild thought, some kind of sign?* 'There are two men, farmers, coming along the track.' *Witnesses.* 'Kate—marry me.'

'Marry you?'
It was hard to concentrate on anything except what was happening to her, anything beyond the life inside

that was struggling to be free. Kate dragged her mind back from its desperate focus on breathing, on the baby, on keeping them both alive. She remembered the mix of truth and lies she had told him and stared at Grant.

In the gloom of early-morning light he did not appear to have lost his mind, despite the blow to the head. He still looked as much like a respectable, handsome English gentleman as might be expected after a sleepless night in a hovel tending to a woman in childbed.

'I am not married, I am not promised to another. I can support a wife, I can support the baby. And if you marry me before the child is born, then it will be legitimate.' His voice was urgent, his expression in the morning light intent. He smiled, as though to reassure her, but the warmth did not reach his eyes.

'Legitimate.' *Legitimate.* Her child would have a name, a future, respectability. They would both be safe and Grant could protect her from the results of Henry's scheming. Probably. Kate rode out another contraction, tried to think beyond the moment, recall *why* she couldn't simply solve this problem by marrying a complete stranger. He could certainly hide her, even if unwittingly. She would have a new name, a new home, and that was all that mattered for the baby.

She was so very tired now, nothing else except her child seemed important. Grant was a doctor living in the wilds of Northumberland, hundreds of miles from London. That should be safe enough. But why would he? Why would he want her and her baby, another man's child? *Legitimate. We would be hidden.* The tempting words swirled through her tired brain, caution fighting desperation and instinct. 'But there's no time.'

'This is Scotland,' Grant said. 'All we have to do is to declare ourselves married before witnesses—and two are heading this way. Say *yes*, Kate, and I'll fetch them and it will be done.'

'Yes.' He was gone before she could call the words back. She heard his voice raised to hail someone. *Yes, I will do it. Another miracle to go with my good angel of a doctor. A Christmas miracle. He never need find out the truth, so it can't hurt him. What is the term? An accessory after the fact. But if he doesn't know...*

'Aye, we'll help you and gladly, at that. I'm Tam Johnson of the Red House up yonder and this is my eldest son, Willie.' The accent was broad Border Scots. 'You're lucky to catch us. We're only going this way to do a favour for a neighbour.'

There was the sound of shuffling feet outside and Grant ducked back in. 'May they come through now?' Kate nodded and he stood aside for two short, burly, black-haired men to enter.

They seemed to fill the space and brought with them the smell of wet sheep and heather and peat smoke. 'Good morning to you, mistress.' The elder stood there, stolid and placid. Perhaps he attended marriages in tumbledown cottages every day of the week. Beside him the younger one twisted his cap in his hands, less at ease than the man who was obviously his father.

'Good day,' she managed, beyond embarrassment or social awkwardness now.

Grant produced a notebook, presumably from his capacious saddlebags. She wondered vaguely if he had a packhorse out there. 'I assume we need a written record that you can sign?'

'Aye, that'll be best. You'll be English, then? All you both need to do is declare yourselves married. To each other, that is.' The older Mr Johnson gave a snort of amusement at his own wit.

'Right.' Grant crossed the small distance and knelt beside her, took her hand in his. 'I, Grantham Phillip Hale Rivers, declare before these witnesses that I take you, Catherine—'

'Jane Penelope Harding,' she whispered. He was only a doctor. They did not put announcements of their marriages in London newspapers.

'Catherine Jane Penelope Harding, as my wife.'

Another contraction was coming. She gritted her teeth and managed, 'Before these witnesses, I, Catherine Jane Penelope Harding, declare that I take you, Grantham Phillip…Hale Rivers, to be my husband.'

'We'll write the record outside, I think.'

She was vaguely conscious of Grant standing, moving the Johnsons out of the room, then her awareness shrank to the pain and the effort. Something was happening, something different…

Where was Grant? She listened and heard him, still in the stable.

'Thank you, gentlemen.' There was the chink of coins. 'I hope you'll drink to our health. You'll bring the donkey cart back down here after noon?'

'Aye, we will, no trouble at all.' That was the older man, Tam Johnson. 'You'll not find it far to Jedburgh now the rain's stopped. You'll be there by nightfall. Thank you kindly, sir, and blessings on your wife and bairn.'

'*Grant!*'

He ducked under the low lintel and back into the inner room. 'I'm here.'

'Something's happening.'

'I should hope so.' He took up the lamp. 'Let's see what this child of ours is doing.'

Grant made her feel secure, Kate thought hazily. Even in those last hectic minutes she had felt safe and when the first indignant wails rent the air he had known just what to do.

'Here she is,' he'd said, laying the squirming, slippery, red-faced baby on her stomach. 'The most beautiful little girl in the world at this minute and very cross with the pair of us by the sound of her.'

Time had passed, the world had gone by somewhere outside the bubble that contained her and the child in her arms. She was conscious of Grant moving purposefully about. At some point he took the baby and washed her and wrapped her up in one of his clean shirts, then washed Kate and helped her into a clean nightgown and wrapped them both up in his coat.

There was something hot to drink, porridge to eat. Perhaps the Johnsons had left food or had come back. She neither knew nor cared. When Grant had spoken to her, asked her if she could bear to travel, she had nodded. He had sounded urgent, so she made herself agree, told herself that he would take care of them and all she had to do was hold her baby safe at her breast.

It was bumpy at first, and her nose, about all that was exposed, was cold, but that was all right because Grant was there. Then they were in his arms again and there was noise and people talking, women's voices, warmth and a soft bed. They must have stopped at an inn to rest.

Kate looked up at him standing over her, looking dishevelled and very tired. And...*sad*? This was the man she had married. It seemed unreal. 'Thank you.'

'My pleasure.' He sounded almost convincing. 'What are we going to call her?'

'Anna, after my mother.' She'd decided that in the course of the bumpy journey. *Anna Rivers. And I am Mrs Rivers now. We are safe and all at the cost of a few lies.* Not little, not white, but she would be a good wife to him, be happy in her modest home. He would never know.

'Anna Rosalind, then, for my mother.' When she looked up, surprised by the possessive note in Grant's voice, he shrugged. 'She's an important small person, she needs at least two names. I've found you a nursemaid. She's used to newborns.' A cheerful freckled face appeared at his side. 'This is Jeannie Tranter and she's happy to adventure into England with us. It isn't far now, only across the border into Northumberland.'

'Oh, good.'

I wonder whereabouts in Northumberland Grant lives...but it doesn't matter, we're safe now, both of us, hundreds of miles away from Henry, hundreds of miles away from a vengeful earl and the law. We can go anywhere and no one will take her away from me because she belongs to Grant now. That was all that mattered. *We both belong to him.*

The thought drifted in and she frowned. Her baby had a father, but she had a husband. A man she did not know, a man who had total control over her life, her future.

Something touched her hair and she opened her eyes. Grant was still looking down at them. She remembered to smile at him, then turned her attention back to the baby.

* * *

'I'll take a bath, then I'll be in the parlour if you need me,' Grant said to Jeannie Tranter.

The girl nodded briskly, her attention on the woman and baby in the bed. 'Aye, sir, I'm sure we won't need to disturb you.'

And that's put me in my place as an unnecessary male. It had been the same the last time. *Don't think about the last time.* The bathwater in front of the fire was still hot, the pleasure of scrubbing away the grime of the past twenty-four hours or so blissful. He soaped his hair, ducked under and came up streaming, then found he had no inclination to get out. Baths were good places to think.

Grant had dozed a little, then woke without any sensible thinking done at all to find the water cool. He splashed out to dry off and find something from his depleted wardrobe to change into. A childbirth used up an inordinate amount of clean linen.

By the time he was in the private parlour pouring a glass of wine, his legs stretched out on the hearthrug, his brain had woken up. Just what had he done? A good deed? Perhaps, although tying a woman, a complete stranger, to him for life was a risky act of charity. Or was it an entirely selfish act, a gesture to his guilty conscience, as though he could somehow appease his grandfather's shade by doing what the old man had so wanted and thus fulfilling his promise? The uncomfortable notion intruded that he had found himself a wife and a stepmother for Charlie without any effort at courtship, without any agonising about choices.

The easy way out? Too late to worry about motives, I've done it now. And the child's a girl, so no need to worry about the inheritance, should it ever arise, God forbid. He'd married a plain woman of genteel birth with a social-climbing brother who was going to be very pleased indeed when he discovered who his new brother-in-law was. That could be a problem if he wasn't careful. Grant rolled the wine around his mouth as he thought it all through.

Pushing doubts aside, he had someone to look after the household, someone who appeared to be bright enough not to be a dead bore on the occasions when he was at home. And Kate had courage and determination, that was obvious enough. He had a wife and only time would tell if it had been a wise decision or a reckless gamble.

There were fifty miles to cover tomorrow, over moorland and open country. If the roads were good and the weather held, they'd do it in the day and he would be only one day later than he had hoped. The inn had a decent chaise for hire, the stables held some strong horses by the looks of them—and they'd be needed, because there wouldn't be a change to be had until they were over the border. The gelding was sound now, it had only been a bruised hoof.

The rhyme 'For Want of a Nail' ran through his head. In that old poem the loss of the nail meant the loss of the shoe, the loss of the horse and its rider and, eventually, the loss of the battle and a kingdom. Because of his own haste his horse had been lamed, he'd had to stop and he'd gained a wife and child. Grant got up and rang for his supper and another bottle. He was maundering, comparing a disaster to—what? What crazy optimism made him think this marriage between two desperate strangers could be anything *but* a disaster?

Chapter Three

'Mr Rivers is a very good rider, is he not, ma'am?'

'Hmm?' From her position lying full length Kate couldn't see more than the occasional treetop passing by. 'Is he?'

Jeannie, the nursemaid, stared at her. 'But surely you've seen him riding, ma'am?'

'Yes. Yes, of course. I don't know what is the matter with me.'

'Not to worry, Mrs Rivers. My nana, who taught me all about looking after mothers and babies, she always said that the mother's mind is off with the fairies for days after the birth.'

My mind is certainly somewhere and I wish it would come back, because I need to think. Anna was sleeping soundly in the nurse's arms and Jeannie seemed exceedingly competent. The chaise had an extension at the front so that when the wall section below the front window was removed it could be placed in front of the seat to make a bed where a passenger could stretch out almost full length. Kate had slept heavily and although she felt weak and shaky she was, surely, in a fit state to take responsibility for herself. She should be thinking about what she had done and what the consequences would be.

I have married the man, for goodness' sake! A complete stranger. What is his family going to say? Grant was persuasive enough, but surely he couldn't convince them that he was the legitimate father of this child by a mother they'd heard nothing about before?

'I want to sit up.' Lying like this made her feel feeble and dependent. Besides, she wanted to see what Mr Rivers—what her husband—looked like on a horse.

Jeannie handed her Anna and helped her sit up. That was better. Two days of being flat on her back like a stranded turtle probably accounted for her disorientation. Kate studied the view from the chaise window. It consisted of miles of sodden moorland, four horses with two postilions and one husband cantering alongside.

Jeannie was a good judge of horsemanship. Grant Rivers was relaxed in the saddle, displaying an impressive length of leg, a straight back and a steady gaze on the road ahead. His profile was austere and, she thought, very English. Brown hair was visible below his hat brim. What colour were his eyes? Surely she should have noticed them? Hazel, or perhaps green. For some reason she had a lingering memory of sadness. But then she'd hardly been in a fit state to notice anything. Or anyone.

But she had better start noticing now. This was her husband. Husbands were for life and she had begun this marriage with a few critical untruths. But they could do Grant no harm, she told herself as she lay down again and let Jeannie tuck her in. There was this one day to regain some strength and get some sleep, then there would be a family to face and Anna to look after in the midst of strangers. But by then she would have her story quite clear in her head and she would be safe in the rustic isolation of the far north of England.

They stopped at three inns—small, isolated, primitive. Jeannie helped her out to the privy, encouraged her to eat and drink, cradled the baby between feeds. Her new husband came to look at her, took her pulse, frowned. Looked at Anna, frowned. Swung back on to his horse, frowned as he urged the postilions to greater speed. What was so urgent? Anyone would think it was life and death.

'I think we must be here, ma'am.' The post-chaise rocked to a halt. Kate struggled up into a sitting position and looked around. Darkness had fallen, but the house was lit and lanterns hung by the front door. Away from the light, the building seemed to loom in the darkness. Surely this was bigger than the modest home a country gentleman-doctor might aspire to?

She looked for Grant, but he was already out of the saddle, the reins trailing on the ground as he strode up the front steps. The doors opened, more light flooded out, she heard the sound of voices. She dropped the window and heard him say, 'When?' sharply and another voice replied, 'In the morning, the day before yesterday.'

Grant came back down the steps. 'In you come.'

'Where are we?' But he was already lifting her out, carrying her in his arms across to the steps. 'Anna—'

'I have her, Mrs Rivers. I'm right behind you, ma'am.'

'This is Abbeywell Grange, your new home.'

There was a tall, lean man, all in black, who bowed as Grant swept her in through the front door. A butler, she supposed, fleetingly conscious of a well-lit hall, a scurry of footmen. The smell of burning applewood, a trace of dried rose petals, beeswax polish, leather. There were evergreen wreaths on the newel posts of the stairs, the glow of red berries in a jug. She remembered Grant's offering of the holly sprig and smiled. This was an old, loved home, its aura sending messages of reassurance. She wanted to relax and dared not.

'Welcome home, my lord. We are all very relieved to see you. The staff join me in expressing our deepest condolences.'

Condolences? On a marriage? Then the whole sentence hit her. 'My lord? Grant, he called you *my lord*. Who are you?'

But the butler was already striding ahead towards the end of the hall, Grant on his heels. 'Master Charles… Lord Brooke, I should say, will be happy to see you, my lord. It has been quite impossible to get him to go to bed.'

'Who is Lord Brooke?' she asked in a whisper as the butler opened the door into a drawing room. A fire crackled in the grate, an aged pointer dog rose creakily to its feet, tail waving, and, on the sofa, a small boy sat up, rubbing his eyes.

'Papa!'

'Charlie, why aren't you in bed? You're keeping Rambler up.' Grant snapped his fingers at the dog. It was obviously an old joke. The boy grinned, then his eyes widened as he saw what his father was carrying.

Grant settled Kate in a deep armchair by the hearthside and Jeannie, with Anna in her arms, effaced herself somewhere in the shadows.

'Charlie.' There was deep affection in Grant's voice as he crouched down and the boy hurled himself into his arms. So, this was why he had been so impatient to get back, this was what the discovery of a woman in labour had been keeping him from. *He has a son. He was married? A lord?* This was a disaster and she had no inkling how to deal with it.

'You got my letter explaining about the accident?' The boy nodded, pushed back Grant's hair and touched the bandage with tentative fingers. She saw his eyes were reddened and heavy. The child had been crying. 'It's all right now, but I'm sorry I wasn't here when you needed me. Then on my way from Edinburgh my horse picked up a stone and was lamed with a bruised hoof, so I lost a day and a night.'

'Great-Grandpapa died on Christmas Eve,' Charlie said. His lower lip trembled. 'And you didn't come and I thought perhaps you'd… Your head… That they'd been lying to me and you were going to…'

'I'm here.' Grant pulled the boy into a fierce hug, then stood him back so he could look him squarely in the face. 'I'm a bit battered and there were a couple of days when I was unconscious, which is why I couldn't travel, but we've hard heads, we Rivers men, haven't we?'

The lip stopped trembling. 'Like rocks,' the boy said stoutly. 'I'm glad you're home, though. It was a pretty rotten Christmas.' His gaze left his father's face, slid round to Kate. 'Papa?'

Grant got up from his knees, one hand on his son's shoulder, and turned towards her, but Kate had already started to rise. She walked forward and stopped beside Grant.

'My dear, allow me to introduce Charles Francis Ellmont Rivers, Lord Brooke. My son.'

Kate retrieved a smile from somewhere. 'I… Good evening, Charles. I am very pleased to meet you.'

He bowed, a very creditable effort for a lad of—what? Six? 'Madam.' He tugged at Grant's hand. 'Papa, you haven't said who this lady is, so I cannot greet her properly.'

'This is Catherine Rivers, my wife. Your stepmama.'

Kate felt the smile congeal on her lips. Of course, if Charles was Grant's son, then she was his…

'Stepmama?' The boy had turned pale. 'You didn't say that you were going to get married again, Papa.'

'No. I am allowed some secrets.' Grant apparently agreed with the Duke of Wellington's approach: never explain, never apologise. 'You have a new half-sister as well, Charlie.' He beckoned to Jeannie and she came forward and placed Anna in his arms. 'Come and meet her, she is just two days old.'

The boy peered at the little bundle. 'She's very small and her face is all screwed up and red.'

'So was yours when you were born, I expect,' Kate said with a glare for Grant over Charlie's head. 'Why didn't you tell me?' she mouthed. *The boy isn't a love child. He's the product of a first marriage. I married a widower. And a nobleman.* She wrestled with the implications of Charlie having a title. It meant Grant was an earl, at least. Which meant that Anna was Lady Anna, and she was—what?

Earls put marriage announcements in newspapers. Earls had wide social circles and sat in the House of Lords. In London.

'There never seemed to be a good time.' Grant gave a half shrug that suddenly made her furious. He should have warned her, explained. She would never have agreed to marry him.

'What is her name?' Charlie asked, oblivious to the byplay. Anna woke up and waved a fist at him and he took it, very carefully.

'Anna Rosalind.' One starfish hand had closed on Charlie's finger. His face was a mixture of panic and delight. 'Would you like to hold her?'

'Yes, please.'

Grant placed her in Charlie's arms.

'Very carefully,' Kate said, trying not to panic. 'Firm but gentle, and don't let her head flop. That's it—you are obviously a natural as a big brother.' She was rewarded by a huge grin. She could only admire Grant's tactics. The surprise of a new baby sister had apparently driven Charlie's doubts about a stepmama right out of his head.

'Grant,' she said, soft-voiced, urgent, as Jeannie helped the boy to sit securely on the sofa and held back the inquisitive hound. 'Who *are* you?'

'The fourth Earl of Allundale. As of two days ago.'

'I suppose that was something else that there was no time to mention?' Again that shrug, the taut line of his lips that warned her against discussing this now.

Her husband was an earl. But he was also a doctor, and heirs to earldoms did not become doctors, she knew that. It was a conundrum she was too weary to try to understand now. All she could grasp was that she had married far above her wildest expectations, into a role she had no idea how to fill, into a position that was dangerously exposed and public. Even in her home village the social pages in the newspapers were studied and gossiped about, the business of the aristocracy known about, from the gowns worn at drawing rooms to the latest scandals. How could the wife of an earl hide away? But Grant had no need to fear she would make a scene in front of his son: unless they were thrown out into the dark, she found she was beyond caring about anything but warmth, shelter and Anna's safety this night.

'You are worn out. Charlie, give your sister back to her nurse and off you go to bed. I'll come and see you are asleep later.' Grant reached for the bell pull and the butler appeared so rapidly that he must have been standing right outside the door. 'Grimswade, can you dispatch Master Charles to his tutor? And you will have prepared my wife's rooms by now, I've no doubt.'

Grimswade stood aside as Charlie made a very correct bow to Kate, then ducked through the open door. 'Certainly, my lord. His late lordship had some renovation work done. In anticipation,' he added.

Grant stilled with his hand on the bell pull. 'Not the old suite?' His voice was sharp.

'No, my lord, not the old suite. The one on the other side of your own chambers. The doors have been changed. One blocked up, another cut through. His late lordship anticipated that you would wish to retain your old rooms even after he had...gone.'

Kate wondered if she would have to stand there all night while they discussed the interior layout of the house. She didn't care where she slept as long as it had a bed, somewhere for Anna, and the roof was not actually leaking.

'Very well. Have you made arrangements for the child and her nurse?'

'Yes, my lord.' Without any change in voice or expression Grimswade managed to express mild affront at the suggestion that he was in any way unprepared. 'My lady, if you would care to follow me.'

That is me. I am—what? A countess?

'I'll carry you.' Grant was halfway across the room.

'Thank you, no. Do stay here.' Something, Kate was not sure what, revolted at the thought of being carried. Grant

Rivers's arms—her *husband's* arms—were temptingly strong, but she was tired of being helpless and he was altogether too inclined to take charge. She had to start thinking for herself again and being held so easily against that broad chest seemed to knock rational thought out of her brain.

In a daze she managed the stairs, the long corridor, then the shock of the sitting room, elegant and feminine, all for her.

'I will have a light supper served, my lady. The men are filling your bath in the bathing chamber next to the dressing room through there.' Grimswade gestured towards the double doors that opened on to a bedchamber, one larger than she had ever slept in. 'And this is Wilson, your maid.'

'Luxury,' Kate murmured to Jeannie as the butler bowed himself out and the maid, a thin, middle-aged woman, advanced purposefully across the room. 'Too much. This is not real.' Fortunately the sofa was directly behind her as she sank back on to it, her legs refusing to hold her up any longer.

'You're just worn out, ma'am—my lady—that's all.' Jeannie's soft brogue was comforting. With a sigh Kate allowed herself to be comforted. 'It will all come back to you.'

The next hour was a blur that slowly, slowly came back into focus. Firm hands undressing her, supportive arms to help her to the bathing room, the bliss of hot water and being completely clean. The same hands drying and dressing her as though she was as helpless as little Anna. A table with food, apparently appearing from thin air. The effort to eat.

And then, as she lay back on the piled pillows of a

soft bed, there was Anna in her arms, grizzling a little because she was hungry, and Kate found she was awake, feeling stronger and, for the first time in days, more like herself.

'We might be confused and out of place,' Kate said as she handed the baby back to Jeannie after the feed, 'but Anna seems perfectly content.'

'You've not stayed here before, then, my lady?'

'No. I'm a stranger to this house.' *And to my husband.* 'Where are you to sleep, Jeannie?'

'They've set up a bed for me in the dressing room, my lady, just for tonight. It's bigger than the whole of the upstairs of our cottage,' she confided with glee. 'And there's a proper cradle for Lady Anna.'

'Then you take yourself off and get some rest now. I expect she'll be waking you up again soon enough.'

The canopy over the bed was lined with pleated seagreen silk, the curtains around the bed and at the windows were a deeper shade, the walls, paler. The furniture was light and, to Kate's admittedly inexperienced eye, modern and fashionable. The paintings and the pieces of china arranged around the room seemed very new, too. Strange, in such an old house. The drawing room, the hallway and stairs had an antique air, of generations of careful choices of quality pieces and then attentive housekeeping to deepen the polished patina.

Kate threw back the covers and slid out of bed. Deeppile carpet underfoot, the colours fresh and springlike in the candlelight. Grant had reacted sharply when her chambers were mentioned. Interior decoration seemed a strange thing to be concerned about, given the circumstances— surely a new wife who was a stranger, another man's baby carrying his own name, a bereavement and a son to comfort must be enough to worry about. *Another puzzle.*

She moved on unsteady legs about the room, admiring it, absorbing the warmth and luxury as she had with the food earlier, feeling the weariness steal over her again. In a moment she would return to the big bed and be able to sleep. Tomorrow she would think. There was a murmur of voices, just audible. Idly curious, Kate followed the sound until she reached a jib door, papered and trimmed so it looked at first glance like part of the wall it was cut into.

The handle moved easily, soundlessly, under the pressure of her hand, and it swung inwards to show her a segment of another bedchamber. Masculine, deep-red hangings, old panelling polished to a glow, the glint of gilded picture frames. Grant's bedchamber. For the first time the words *husband* and *bed* came together in her mind and her breathing hitched.

On the table beside the door was a small pile of packages wrapped in silver paper. She glanced down and read the label on the top one. *Papa, all my love for Christmas. Charlie.* It was obviously his very best handwriting. Her vision blurred.

Grant's voice jerked her back. He must be speaking to his valet. She began to ease the door closed. 'Thank you for coming by. Tomorrow I'd be grateful if you'd take a look at my wife and the baby. They both seem well to my eye, especially given the circumstances—Kate must be very tired—but I won't be easy until a doctor has confirmed it.'

Another doctor? Kate left the door an inch ajar. There was a chuckle, amused, masculine, with an edge of teasing to it. 'It seems to me that you did very well, given that you've never been trained for a childbirth. Or were you, in the year you left Edinburgh?'

'I observed one. I had, thank Asclepius and any other gods that look after inept medical students, studied the relevant sections of the textbooks before I did so and some of it must have stuck. I'd just about reached the limits of my book learning, though, and after the last time—'

The other man made some comment, his voice low and reassuring, but Kate did not register the words. *Grant is not qualified? He is not a doctor.* The embossed metal of the door handle bit into her fingers. *He lied to me.* The irony of her indignation at the deception struck her, which did nothing for her temper.

'I thought perhaps so much experience with brood mares might have helped, but I can tell you, it didn't,' Grant confessed.

Brood mares. He thought he could deliver my baby as though she were a foal.

She heard Grant say goodnight to his visitor as she set foot in his bedchamber. He turned from closing the door and saw her. 'Kate, what's wrong? Can't you sleep?'

'You are not a doctor.' He came towards her and it took only two steps to be close enough to jab an accusing finger into his chest. 'You delivered my baby, you told me not to worry. You fraud!'

Chapter Four

Grant stepped back sharply, the concern wiped from his expression. 'I have two years of medical training, which is more than anyone else within reach had. There *was* no one else to deliver your baby.'

'You might have told me.' She sat down abruptly on the nearest chair. 'You thought you could treat me like a brood mare.'

'Ah, you heard that. Damn. Look, Kate, you were frightened, in pain, and you hadn't the first idea what to do. You needed to be calm, to conserve your strength. If I had told you I had never delivered a baby before, would that have helped you relax? Would that have helped you be calm?'

She glared at him, furious that he was being perfectly reasonable, when something inside her, the same something that had latched on to those words, *husband* and *bed*, wanted nothing more than to panic and make a fuss. And run away.

Grant stood there, patient—and yet impatient, just as he had been in the bothy. He was good at self-control, she realised. If he wasn't so distracted by grief for his grandfather and worry for his son, she would not be allowed a glimpse of that edginess. And he was right, perfectly right. He had some knowledge and that was better than none. He had kept her calm and safe. Alive. Anna was healthy. Kate swallowed. 'I am sorry. You are quite correct, of course. I am just...'

'Embarrassed, very tired and somewhat emotional.'

'Yes,' she agreed. *And confused. Damn him for being so logical and practical and right, when I just want to hit out at something. Someone.* 'You did not tell me you are an earl.' She had wanted to hide, go to ground. Now she was in the sort of marriage that appeared in society pages, was the stuff of gossip.

Grant ran his hand through his hair. He was tired, she realised. Very tired. How much sleep had he had since he had walked into that hovel and found her? Little, she supposed, and he was travelling with a recent head injury. 'I didn't think it relevant and you weren't in any fit state for conversation.' His mouth twisted. 'My grandfather was dying, or had just died. I was not there and I did not want to talk about it. Or think about it. All I wanted was to get back to Charlie.'

'Were you too late to see your grandfather because of me?'

Grant shook his head and sat down opposite her. It was more of a controlled collapse than anything, long legs sprawled out, his head tipped back, eyes closed. The bandage gave him a rakish air, the look of a pirate after a battle. 'No, I wouldn't have reached him in time, not after the accident in Edinburgh. But even so, there was no choice but to stay with you—he would have expected it himself.'

No, she supposed there hadn't been a decision to make. No one could walk away from someone in the situation she had been in. No decent person, at any rate. She had married a decent man. Her agitation calmed as she looked at him, studied his face properly for the first time. She was thinking only of herself and Anna, but she owed him a debt. The least she could do was to think about his needs. 'I'm sorry. Go to bed. You are worn out.'

Grant shook his head and opened his eyes. They were green, she realised with a jolt, seeing the man and not simply her rescuer. But a warm green verging on hazel, not the clear green of a gemstone under water... 'Soon. I need to look in on Charlie.'

She was not going to exhaust him more by complaining about the fact he had not told her he had been married, that he had a son as well as a title. That could keep until the morning. She was certainly not going to look for any more resemblances to Jonathan. 'I will go back to bed, then. Goodnight.'

There was silence until she was through the jib door. She wondered if he had fallen asleep after all. Then, 'Goodnight, Kate.' She closed the door softly behind her.

'Goodnight, Kate. Goodnight, *wife*,' Grant added in a whisper as the door closed. Perhaps he should have kissed her. Poor creature, she looked dreadful. Pale, with dark shadows under bloodshot eyes, her hair pulled back into a mousy tail, her face pinched with exhaustion and a confusion of embarrassment and uncertainty. He could only hope that when she was recovered and suitably dressed she would at least look like a lady, if not a countess.

He hauled himself to his feet and stripped off his clothes with a grimace of relief. He felt as if he'd spent the past year in them. Naked, he stood and washed rapidly, then rummaged in the clothes press and pulled out loose trousers, a shirt and a robe, dressing without conscious thought. Comfort, something he could catnap in if Charlie needed him to stay and chase away nightmares, these would do. His eye caught the glint of silver paper and he went to investigate. Christmas presents. He picked them up, torn between grief and pleasure.

When he slid quietly into Charlie's room the mounded covers on the bed heaved and a mop of dark blond hair emerged. 'Papa!'

'I had hoped you were asleep by now.' Grant sat on the edge of the bed and indulged himself with a hug that threatened to strangle him. 'Urgh! You're too strong for me.'

Charlie chuckled, a six-year-old's naughty laugh, and let go. He looked up at Grant from under his lashes. 'I'm glad you're home.'

'So am I. I'm sorry I was not here when Great-Grandpapa died.'

'Dr Meldreth took me in to see him. He was very sleepy and he told me that he was very old, so he was all worn out and he wanted to go and be with Great-Grandmama, so I mustn't be sad when he left. But I am.'

'I know, Charlie, so am I. And we will be for a while, then we'll remember all the good times we had, and all the things we used to talk about and do, and you won't feel so bad. What did you do on Christmas Day?'

'We went for a walk and to church, and then I opened my presents because Great-Grandpapa said I must do so.' He sniffed. 'He gave me his watch. I…I blubbed a bit, but it made me really proud, so I'm glad. And thank you very much for the model soldiers and the castle and the new boots. Then we had Christmas dinner and Mr

Gough showed me how to make a toast. So I toasted *absent friends*, for both you and Great-Grandpapa.'

'It sounds to me as if the household was in very good hands with you in charge, Charlie.' Grant managed to get his voice under control, somehow. 'I found my presents— shall I open them now?'

Grant went to retrieve the gifts and they opened them together. His grandfather had given him a miniature of his parents, newly painted, he realised, from the large individual portraits that hung in the Long Gallery. He read the note that accompanied it, blew his nose without any attempt to conceal his emotion and turned to Charlie's gift, which he had set aside.

'This is excellent!' It was a large, enthusiastic and almost recognisable portrait of Rambler, his old pointer dog, framed in a somewhat lopsided, and obviously home-made, frame. 'I will hang it in my study next to the desk. Thank you, Charlie. You go to sleep now. Do you want me to spend the night here?'

'I'm all right now you are home, Papa. And Mr Gough let me talk to him all I wanted. He thought it would be better after the funeral when we can say goodbye again.'

The tutor had proved as sensitive as he had hoped when he hired him. 'You know where I am if you want to come along in the night.' Grant tucked his son in, bent down and gave him a kiss that, for once, didn't have his son squirming away in embarrassment. He seemed to understand and to be taking it well, but he was so young. Grant felt a pang of anxiety through the haze of weariness that was closing in like fog. Perhaps he would sleep without nightmares if he was this tired.

'I didn't know you were going to get married again,

Papa.' The voice from under the blankets was already drowsy.

Neither did I. 'Go to sleep, Charlie. I'll explain in the morning.' *Somehow. And I hope to heaven that you take to your new mother and sister, and she takes to you, because if not I've created the most damnable mess.*

'She's being a little angel, my lady.' Jeannie tucked the sleeping baby back into the crib she had brought into the sitting room while Kate was feeding Anna. Fed, clean and cuddled, she truly was sleeping like a small, rather red-faced cherub.

Kate, fresh from Wilson's best, and exhausting, efforts to turn her into something approaching a respectable lady, retreated to the sanctuary of the sofa next to the crib. Wilson was handicapped by an absence of any gowns to dress her in, to say nothing of Kate's figure, which, it was obvious, was not going to spring back instantly into what had been before. A drab, ill-fitting gown that was seriously the worse for wear was not helped by a headful of fine mousy hair that was in dire need of the attentions of a hairdresser.

She looked a frump, and an unhealthy one at that, she knew. Her husband, once rested and with a view of her in a good light, was going to be bitterly rueing his impetuous, gallant gesture.

His knock came on the thought and Kate twitched at the shawl Wilson had found in an effort to drape her body as flatteringly as possible. A harassed glance at her reflection in the glass over the fireplace confirmed that the wrap's shades of green and brown did nothing to help her complexion.

'Good morning. May I come in? Did you sleep well?'

The dark smudges were stark under Grant's eyes and the strong-boned face seemed fined down to its essentials. The rakish bandage had gone, leaving the half-healed cut and angry bruising plain across his forehead.

'Good morning. Yes, of course.'

She was not going to huddle on the sofa, trying to hide. She might look a fright, but she had her pride. Kate swung her feet down to the floor, pushed her shoulders back, lifted her chin and curved the corners of her mouth up. That felt very strange, as though she had not smiled properly in months. Perhaps she had not, except at Anna.

'Dr Meldreth is here, Kate. I think it would be a good idea if he checked you and Anna over.'

'He studied with you in Edinburgh, I gather?' He nodded. 'But unlike you is actually qualified?' That was a sharp retort—she could have bitten her tongue. If it were not for Grant's time at the university, he would have been far less capable of helping her bring Anna safely into the world.

'Exceedingly well qualified,' Grant said before she had a chance to soften her words. He kept any annoyance out of his voice, but his expression hardened. He must think he had married a shrew. 'I'll show him in, shall I?'

He didn't wait for her nod, but ushered in a short, freckled, cheerful man about his age. 'My dear, Dr Meldreth. Meldreth—Lady Allundale. I'll leave you together and I'll be in my study when you've finished, Meldreth.'

Kate summoned her two female supporters and managed to produce a calm, friendly smile for the doctor. He examined Anna and then, swiftly and tactfully, Kate, maintaining a steady flow of conversation while he did so. *Excellent bedside manner,* Kate decided. She felt confident in having him as their doctor.

'You are both in excellent health and the little one is just as she should be,' he assured her when she rejoined him in the sitting room. 'But you need to rest, Lady Allundale. Rivers told me what a rough time you've had of it and I don't think you have been eating very well, have you? Not for quite a while.'

'Probably not, Doctor.'

He closed his bag and straightened his cuffs with a glance at Wilson and Jeannie. It seemed he wanted privacy. Kate nodded to the other women. 'Thank you, I will ring when I need you.' When they were alone she made herself look him in the eye. 'There was something you wished to say to me?'

'I will be frank. I am aware that your marriage only just preceded little Anna's birth. I am also aware that Grant will fudge the issue, making it seem that yours was a long-standing relationship and that the marriage took place some time ago, but was kept quiet. Probably his grandfather's ill health can be made to account for that.'

'I assume that, as a doctor, you will exercise professional discretion.'

'Certainly.' He did not appear surprised by the chill in her voice. 'I simply wished to make the point that—' He broke off and cursed softly under his breath. 'This is more difficult than I thought it would be. I wanted to assure you that I will give you all the support I can. I also wonder just how much of Grant's past history you are aware of.'

She could freeze him out, look down her nose and assume the air of a thoroughly affronted countess or she could take the hand of friendship he appeared to be offering her. She needed a friend.

'I know nothing. I was not even aware that he was the

heir to an earldom when I married him. Nor that he was a widower with a child.'

'He will tell you himself, I am sure. But he was close to the old earl—Grant's parents died when he was not much older than Charlie is now. His grandfather brought him up and did a good job of it, for all that he probably leaned too much on the side of tradition and duty. Grant married a suitable young lady, to please his grandfather and do what it seemed was his duty, and talked himself into believing that was how marriage should be.' He pushed his hand through his sandy hair. 'I am saying too much, but you have to know this—Madeleine was a disaster. Possibly the only thing that could have made the situation worse was the way she died.'

'What happened?' Somehow Kate made herself sit quietly attentive for the answer. She had thought she was coming to some safe, comfortable home. A doctor's household, decent and respectable. Modestly prosperous. Instead she found herself married to an earl, with his unburied predecessor somewhere in the house. Her husband had married tragically, she had a stepson—and a new baby. And she had the overwhelming feeling that she could not cope with any of this. But she had to. Grant had thrown her a lifeline and she had a duty to repay him by being a proper wife, a good stepmother to Charlie— and, somehow, a passable countess.

'There was a fire. Rivers was…injured, but he managed to get Charlie out. They couldn't save Madeleine.'

'When?'

'Four years ago. We do not think Charlie remembers any of it, thank God.'

'That is a blessing.' *Poor little boy.* 'Thank you.

Forewarned, at least I can try not to blunder into sensitive areas.'

'Some blundering might be a good thing, frankly.' Dr Meldreth stood up. 'Rivers took it too well, too stoically, for the child's sake. I am not sure he ever really put it behind him. And now he is bone-weary, he's exerted himself sooner than he should after a blow to the head and he's feeling as guilty as hell because he didn't get back in time to see his grandfather before he died.'

'I will try to make him rest and hope he feels able to talk to me.' Kate rose and held out her hand to the doctor. 'Thank you. It is good to know he has a friend close by.'

'I'll be back in a couple of days, unless you send for me earlier.' Meldreth shook hands briskly. 'I wasn't sure whether to mention anything, but Rivers said you've got courage, so…' He shrugged. 'I'll see myself down to the study. Good day, Lady Allundale.'

After that it was hard to sit with any composure. So, the situation was such that the good doctor would not have said anything unless he thought she had courage. That was hardly reassuring.

But perhaps it was time she started drawing on that courage, assuming she did actually possess any. If only she did not feel so ignorant. She had experienced the upbringing of any country gentlewoman, with the neighbouring wives doing their best to support a motherless girl. But, although her manners would not disgrace her, she had no experience of the kind of social life Grant would be used to. Now she was presumably expected to know how to greet a duke, curtsy to a queen, organise a reception and look after scores of tenants and staff.

Well, there was no time like the present to begin. Kate rang for Wilson. 'I do not know when the funeral will be, but I must have respectable mourning clothes.' If they were going to have to improvise and dye something with black ink, then the sooner they started, the better.

'It is tomorrow, my lady. His lordship said not to disturb you about it. There'll just be gentlemen there, no ladies, so you can stay in your rooms.'

Her little burst of energy deflected, Kate sat down again and gazed out at the grey skies, trying to make sense of the world she found herself in and her place in it, and failing miserably. Luncheon was brought up. Grimswade delivered a pile of novels, journals and newspapers. She fed Anna and cuddled her, dozed a little, tried to pay attention when Wilson suggested they make a list of all the essentials she needed to buy. Dinner arrived, a succession of perfect, luxurious little courses. Kate refused the red wine, but found she had the appetite to demolish virtually everything else that was put in front of her. The doctor had been correct. She had been neglecting herself out of worry.

Grimswade appeared as the footman was carrying out the dishes. 'Is there anything else you require, my lady?' Butlers, she knew, cultivated a bland serenity under all circumstances, but she thought he looked strained. The whole household seemed to be holding its breath.

Was there anything she could do? *Nothing,* Kate concluded as the door closed behind the butler. Just keep out of the way. Charlie was with his father and a stranger's clumsy sympathy would be no help to them. She should have asked Grimswade when the rest of the family would arrive. At least they could take some of the burden off Grant's shoulders. How lonely this felt, to be in the middle of so many people and yet completely cut off from their fears, their hopes.

She gave herself a brisk mental shake for the self-pity. She and her child were safe, protected and, at least for a few days, hidden. They had a future, even if it was shrouded in a fog of unknowns. Grant and Charlie were mourning the loss of someone dear to them and the best thing she could do was to intrude as little as possible. Grant had made it clear he did not want her involved or he would have confided in her, wouldn't he?

Chapter Five

She had slept well, Kate realised as she woke to the sound of curtain rings being pulled back. In the intervals when Jeannie had brought her Anna to feed she had listened for sounds from Grant's bedchamber, but none had reached her.

The light was different. She sat up and saw the heavy snow blanketing the formal gardens under a clear, pale grey sky. 'What a heavy fall there must have been in the night, Wilson. Is the house cut off?'

The maid turned and Kate saw her eyes were rimmed with red. She had been crying. *Of course, the funeral.* She felt helpless.

'Very heavy, but the turnpike road is open, my lady, and the men have cleared the path to the church.' Wilson brought a small tray with a cup of chocolate and set it on the bedside table, then went to make up the fire. 'I'll be back with your bathwater in half an hour, my lady.'

The luxury, the unobtrusive, smooth service, suddenly unnerved her. She was a countess now, yet she was the daughter of an obscure baronet, a girl who had never had a Season, who had been to London only three times in her life, who was the mother of a child conceived out of wedlock and the sister of a man who had embroiled her in unscrupulous criminality. *I can't do this...*

The door opened as she took an incautious gulp of hot chocolate and burned the inside of her mouth. 'Wilson?'

'It is us. Good morning.' The deep voice held grief and weariness under the conventional greeting. 'I came to tell you that we will be leaving for the church at ten o'clock. The procession will go past the window, if you wish to watch.' Grant stood just inside the room, one hand resting on Charlie's shoulder, the boy pulled close to his side. Charlie's eyes were red and he leaned in tight to his father, but his chin was set and his head high. Grant looked beyond exhausted, although he was clean-shaven, his dark clothes and black neckcloth immaculate.

'I am so very sorry.' The cup clattered in the saucer as Kate set it down and Grant winced. She threw back the covers, slid out of bed and then just stood there in her nightgown. What could she do, what right had she to think she could even find the comforting words? Her instinct was to put her arms around the pair of them, hug them tight, try to take some of the pain and the weariness from them, but she was a stranger. They would not want her.

'There will be local gentlemen in church, those who can make it through the snow. And the staff, tenants and so on. There will be a small group returning for luncheon, but the staff have that well in hand and you should not be disturbed.' He might as well be speaking to some stray guest who deserved consideration, but was, essentially, an interloper. 'There will be no relatives, no one to stay. We only have cousins in the West Country, too far to attend in this weather, and a great-aunt in London, who likewise could not travel.'

Kate sat down on the edge of the bed. 'I am so sorry,' she repeated. 'Is there anything I can do? Letters to write, perhaps? You will want to spend your time with Charlie.'

'Thank you. My grandfather's... *My* secretary, Andrew Bolton, will handle all the correspondence. There is nothing for you to do.' Grant looked down at the boy as they turned towards the door. 'Ready? We should go down to the hallway now.'

'I'm ready.' Charlie's straight back, the determined tilt of his head, were the image of his father's. He paused and looked back at Kate. 'Good morning, Stepmama.'

Kate watched the procession from her window. The black-draped coffin was carried on the shoulders of six sturdy men, cushions resting on it with decorations and orders glittering in the pale sunlight. Grant walked behind, his hand on Charlie's shoulder, the two of them rigidly composed and dignified. Behind paced a crocodile of gentlemen in mourning clothes followed by tenants in Sunday best and a contingent of the male staff.

She found a prayer book on a shelf in the sitting room and sat to read the burial service through quietly.

By the time luncheon had been cleared away Kate decided that she was going to have to do something. She had cracked the jib door into Grant's bedchamber open a fraction so that she would know if he had come up to rest, and by four o'clock he had not. She handed a fed, gurgling Anna to Jeannie, cast a despairing glance in the mirror at her appearance and set off downstairs.

'Have the guests left?' she asked the first footman she

encountered. He was wearing a black armband, she noticed with an inward wince for her own lack of mourning.

'Yes, my lady.'

'And where is my husband?'

'In his study, my lady.'

'Will you show me the way, please?'

He paused at the end of the hallway outside a dark oak door. 'Shall I knock, my lady?'

It looked very much closed. Forbiddingly so. 'No, I will. Thank you…'

'Giles, my lady.'

She tapped and entered without waiting for a response. The room was warm, the fire flickering in the grate, the curtains closed against the winter chill. There were two pools of light, one over a battered old leather armchair where Charlie slept, curled into a ball like a tired puppy, the other illuminating the papers spread on the desk.

It lit the hands of the man behind the desk, but left his face in shadow. 'Grant, will you not come to bed?' she asked, keeping her voice low.

There was a chuckle, a trifle rusty. 'My dear, that is a most direct suggestion.'

Kate felt her cheeks flame. 'I was not trying to flirt, my lord.' *I would not know how and certainly not with you.* 'Surely you need to rest, spend a few hours lying down. You must be exhausted.' She moved closer, narrowing her eyes against the light of the green-shaded reading lamp. The quill pen was lying on its side on top of the standish, the ink dry and matte on the nib. Grant had run out of energy, she realised, and was simply sitting there, too tired to move.

'Perhaps I am.' Grant sounded surprised, as though

he had not realised why his body had given up. He made no attempt to stand.

'Why did you marry me, if you will not allow me to help you?' Kate sat down opposite him, her eyes on the long-fingered, bruised hands lying lax on the litter of papers. They flexed, then were still. Beautiful hands, capable and clever. She had put those discoloured patches on the left one. She had a sudden vision of them on her skin, gently caressing. Not a doctor's hands any longer, but a lover's, a husband's. Could he see her blush? She hated the way she coloured up so easily, was always consumed with envy for those porcelain-fair damsels who could hide their emotions with ease.

'You felt sorry for me, I can see that. It was a very generous act of mercy, for me and my child,' she went on, thinking aloud when he did not answer. 'And, for some reason, your grandfather was anxious to see you married again and you would do anything to make him happy.' Still silence. Perhaps he had fallen asleep. 'But I cannot sit upstairs in my suite for the rest of my days.'

'Not for ever, no. But for now you are still a new mother. You also require rest. Is there anything you need?' he asked.

At least he was not sleeping where he sat. Kate did not wish to bother him with trivial matters, but he was talking to her, maybe she could distract him enough to consider sleep… 'I have no clothes.' His expressive fingers moved, curled across a virgin sheet of paper. 'Other than two gowns in a sad state and a few changes of linen,' she added repressively. 'I need mourning.'

'It can wait.' The words dropped like small stones into the silence, not expecting an answer.

At least he was not sleeping where he sat. If she could

rouse him enough, she might persuade him to get up and go to his bed. 'Not for much longer. I cannot appear like this, even if it is only in front of the servants.'

He focused on her problem with a visible effort. 'The turnpike is clear. Tomorrow, if the snow holds off, Wilson can go into Hexham and purchase enough to tide you over until you are strong enough for a trip into Newcastle.'

'Thank you.' Kate folded her own hands in her lap and settled back in the chair. If he thought he could send her back to her room with that, he was mistaken. The silence dragged on, filled with the child's breathing, the soft collapse of a log into ash, her own pulse.

'Are you going to sit there for the rest of the afternoon and evening?' Grant enquired evenly when another log fell into the heart of the fire.

'Yes, if you will not go and rest.' She kept her tone as reasonable as his. 'You will be no good to Charlie if you make yourself ill with exhaustion.'

'So wise a parent after so few days?' There was an edge there now.

'One needs no expertise, only to be a human being, to know that the boy will need your attention, your presence, while he grieves. You are in no fit state for anything now, after so many days without proper rest. And you cannot deal with your own grief by drugging yourself with tiredness.'

'How very astringent you are, my dear.' Grant moved suddenly, sat up in his chair and gathered together the papers in front of him. 'No soft feminine wiles to lure me upstairs, no soft words, only common-sense advice?'

'If you wanted the sort of wife who deals with a crisis by feminine fluttering, who feels it necessary to coax and wheedle, then you have married the wrong woman, my lord.' She kept her voice low, conscious of Charlie so close. But she could not rein in the anger entirely and she knew it showed. 'I do not know what your first wife was like, although I am sure she was raised to be a far more satisfactory countess than I will be, I am afraid. But I will try to enact little scenes of wifely devotion for you from time to time, as you obviously seem to expect them.' *His first wife was a disaster, Dr Meldreth said. I will be one, too, although a very different kind of disaster.*

'Demonstrations of wifely devotion would certainly be a novelty. However, if you can refrain from enacting scenes of any kind, I would be most grateful.' Grant pushed back his chair, went to lift Charlie in his arms and murmured, 'If I could trouble you for the door?'

I must make allowances for his exhaustion, for his bereavement, Kate told herself as she followed the tall figure through the hallway and up the stairs. Giles the footman was lurking in the shadows and she beckoned him over. 'His lordship is going to rest. Please let the rest of the household know that he is not to be disturbed until he rings. It may well be that this disrupts mealtimes, so please pass my apologies to Cook if that is the case. Perhaps she can be ready to provide something light but sustaining at short notice?'

The footman's gaze flickered to Grant's unresponsive back. Kate waited, eyebrows raised as though she found it hard to understand his hesitation. She had never had to deal with superior domestic staff of this calibre and she suspected he knew it. The way she looked wouldn't help. But, like it or not, it seemed she was mistress of this household now and she must exert some authority or she would never regain it.

'My lady.'

'Thank you, Giles.' She nodded as though never doubting his obedience for a moment and climbed the stairs. By the time she reached the landing Grant had turned off down a side passage. She followed him to the doorway of what must be the boy's bedchamber. A tall, fair-haired young man came out of an inner doorway and turned down the covers. Between them they got the child out of most of his clothes and into bed, exchanged a few words, and then Grant came out.

'That's his tutor, Gough. He'll sleep in the side chamber in case Charlie wakes.' Grant kept going into his own rooms. Without conscious thought Kate followed him. '*I* do not require tucking up in bed, Kate.'

'I do not know *what* you require, my lord.' She turned abruptly, in a way that should have sent her skirts whirling in a dramatic statement of just how strained her nerves felt. They flopped limply about her ankles, adding to her sense of drabness. 'Your son has both more sense and better manners, from what I can see.'

She reached the jib door to her room, pulled it open, and a hand caught the edge of it, pushed it back closed. Grant frowned down at her. 'What is wrong?'

'*Wrong?*' Would the man never give up and just lie down and sleep? Kate turned back, raised one hand and began to count off on her fingers. 'Let me see. You do not tell me you had just inherited an earldom. You do not tell me you are a widower with a son. You drive yourself to the brink of collapse trying to do everything yourself. I find myself mistress of a great house, but the servants do not appear to expect me to give them orders...' *I need to hide and I find myself a member of the aristocracy.*

'You have just given birth, you should be resting.' Grant pushed the hair out of his eyes with one hand, the other still splayed on the door. She rather suspected he was holding himself up.

'I am quite well and I have a personal maid and an excellent nursery maid. I do not expect to talk about all those things now, but I do expect my *husband* to go and rest so we can discuss them sensibly in the morning.'

'Very well.' He turned back through the door with all the focus of a man who was very, very drunk with lack of sleep. He walked to the bed. Kate followed him and watched as he sat down and just stared at his boots as though he was not certain what they were.

'Let me.' Without waiting she straddled his left leg with her back to him and drew off the boot. Then switched to the other leg. 'Now your coat.'

Grant's mouth twitched into the first sign she had seen of a smile for days. 'Undressing me, wife? I warn you, it is a waste of effort just now.'

Is he flirting again? Impossible. She caught a glimpse of herself in the mirror, a drab creature with a lumpy figure, a blotchy complexion and a frightful gown, next to Grant's elegant good looks. Mocking her was more likely. 'Stand up. I am not going to clamber about on the bed.'

He stood, meekly enough, while she reached up to push the coat from his shoulders. She was slightly above average height for a woman, but he was larger than she had realised, now she was standing so close. No wonder he had lifted her so easily. She found herself a little breathless. Fortunately the coat, like the boots, was comfortable country wear and did not require a shoehorn to lever off. The fine white linen of his shirt clung to his arms, defining the musculature. He had stripped off his coat in the bothy, she recalled vaguely. Doubtless the other things she had to focus on had stopped her noticing those muscles. Ridiculously she felt the heat of a rising blush. Kate unbuttoned his waistcoat, pushed that off, then reached for his neckcloth.

Grant's hand came up and covered her fingers as she struggled with the knot. She looked up and met his gaze, heavy-lidded, intent. 'You have very lovely blue eyes,' he murmured. 'Why haven't I noticed before?'

He was, it seemed, awake. Or part of him was, a sensual, masculine part she was not ready to consider, although something fundamentally feminine in her was certainly paying attention.

It is my imagination. He is beyond exhausted, too tired to be flirting. Certainly not flirting with me. Kate shot another glance at the mirror and resisted the urge to retort that at least there was something about her that he approved of.

'I was quite right about you.'

'What?' she demanded ungrammatically as she tugged the neckcloth off with rather more force than necessary, pulling the shirt button free. The neck gaped open, revealing a vee of skin, a curl of dark hair. It looked…silky.

'You have courage and determination.'

Kate began to fold up the length of muslin with concentration. 'I am trying to get you to rest. What about that requires courage?'

'You don't know me.' He sat down. 'I might have a vicious temper. I might hit out at a wife who provoked me.'

'I think I am a reasonable judge of character.' She had wound the neckcloth into a tight knot around her own hand. Patiently, so she did not have to look at him, Kate began to unravel it. This close she could smell his skin, the herbal, astringent soap he used, the tang of ink on his hands, the faint musk that she recognised as *male*. But Grant smelt different, smelt of himself.

She walked to the dresser and placed the neckcloth on the top, distancing herself from the sudden, insane urge to step in close, lay her head on his chest, wrap her arms around the lean, weary body. *Why?* To comfort him perhaps, or because she wanted comfort herself, or perhaps a mixture of the two.

When she turned back Grant was lying down on top of the covers, still in shirt and breeches. He was deep, deep asleep. She stood looking down at him for a moment, studied the fine-drawn face relaxed into a vulnerability that took years off his age. How old was he? Not thirty-two or -three, as she had thought. Twenty-eight, perhaps. His hair flopped across his forehead, just as Charlie's did, but she resisted the temptation to brush it back from the bruised skin. The long body did not stir when she laid a light blanket over him, nor when she drew the curtains closed slowly to muffle the rattle of the rings, nor when she made up the fire and drew the guard around it.

My husband is a disturbingly attractive man, she thought as she closed the jib door carefully behind her. Anna was crying in the dressing room, she could hear Jeannie soothing her.

'Mama will be back soon, little one. Yes, she will, now don't you fret.'

A husband, a stepson, a baby. Her family. She had a *family* when just days before all she had was a scheming brother who had always seen her as wilful and difficult and the babe inside her, loved already, but unknown.

Anna, Charlie, Grant. When her husband woke, refreshed, he would see her differently, realise he had a partner he could rely on. She owed him that, she owed Anna the opportunity to grow up happily here. The anxiety and the exhaustion had made her nervy, angry, but she must try to learn this new life, learn to fit in. As the pain of the funeral eased, she would be there for them all. Charlie would learn to like her, perhaps one day to love her. And somehow she would learn how to be a countess. She shivered. How could a countess stay out of the public eye?

When tomorrow comes, it will not seem so overwhelming, I'll think of something. 'Is that a hungry little girl I can hear? Mama's coming.'

Chapter Six

Hunger woke Grant. One minute he had been fathoms down, the next, awake, alert, conscious of an empty stomach and silence. Gradually the soft sounds of the household began to penetrate. The subdued crackle of the fire, someone trudging past in the snow, the distant sound of light, racing feet and the heavier tread of an adult in pursuit. Charlie exercising his long-suffering tutor, no doubt. Close at hand an infant began to cry, then stopped. *Anna. I have a daughter.* And a wife.

There was daylight between the gap in the curtains, falling in a bright snow-reflecting bar across the blanket someone had draped over his legs. Grant pushed the hair out of his eyes, winced and sat up, too relaxed to tug the bell pull and summon food and hot water.

Now, today, he must take up the reins of the earldom. That was perhaps the least of the duties looming before him. He had known for nearly twenty years, ever since his father died, that he would inherit. His grandfather had run a tight ship, but had taught Grant, shared decisions as he grew older, explained his thinking, given him increasing responsibilities. There were no mysteries to discover about the estates, the investments or the tenants and he had inherited an excellent bailiff and solicitor along with the title.

Charlie was going to be all right, given time and loving attention. Which left Kate. His new wife. What had he been thinking of, to marry her out of hand like that? She was certainly in deep trouble, all alone with a new baby and no means of support, but he could have found her a cottage somewhere on one of the estates, settled some money on her. Forgotten her.

His grandfather had been fretting himself into a state over Grant's first marriage. Blaming himself for ever introducing Grant to Madeleine Ellmont, worrying that Grant was lonely, that Charlie had no mother, that the future of the earldom relied on a healthy quiverful of children. So much so that Grant had come to hate the house that had always been his home. But he could have lied to him, made up a charming and eligible young woman whom he was about to propose to, settled the old man's worries that way.

What had prompted that impetuous proposal when he already knew his grandfather must be beyond caring about his marital state? Something about Kate had told him he could trust her, that she was somehow *right*. He had glimpsed it again yesterday when he had looked into her eyes and seen a spark there that had caught his breath for an instant.

A clock struck ten. Lord, he'd slept more than twelve hours. Grant leaned out of bed and yanked the bell pull. He had to somehow get everything right with Kate. She was unsettled to discover she was a countess with a stepson and that was understandable. He had an edgy feeling that he had disconcerted her when she was helping him to undress. He kept forgetting that while she might be a mother she seemed quite sheltered, not very experienced. What had he said? Nothing out of line, he hoped. For the first time he wondered about Anna's father and just what that love affair had been—a sudden moment of madness, a lengthy, illicit relationship, or…

'You rang, my lord?' said Giles the footman.

Grant frowned at him for a second. It took some getting used to, being *my lord* now. 'Hot water, coffee. Ask Cook to send up some bacon, sausage… Everything. She'll know.'

When the water came he washed and then shaved himself while Giles found him clean linen and laid out plain, dark clothes. That was something else to add to the list, a valet.

When he tapped on the jib door and went through into Kate's suite he found her in the sitting room, the baby in the crib by her side, her hands full of a tangle of fine wool. She was muttering what sounded like curses under her breath.

'Good morning. Cat's cradles?'

'Oh!' She dropped the wool and two needles fell out of it. 'Mrs Havers, the housekeeper, brought me this wool and the knitting needles. She thought I might like to make a cot blanket, which was very thoughtful of her. I didn't like to tell her I haven't tried to knit since I was six.' She grimaced at the tangle. 'And *tried* was the correct word, even then. Did you need me, my lord?'

'Grant, please. I came to see how you are and to thank you for persuading me into bed yesterday. I had gone beyond being entirely rational on the subject.' There was colour up over her cheeks and he remembered making some insinuating comment about luring him into bed. *Damn.*

'I hope you feel better this morning.' She bent her head over the knitting once more, catching up the dropped stitches. 'Charlie was up and about quite early, testing the bounds of his tutor's patience. He seems a pleasant young man, Mr Gough.'

'He's the younger brother of a friend from university. I thought he would be a good choice as a first tutor—he has plenty of energy and Charlie seems to have taken to him.'

Kate picked up the wool and began to wind it back into a ball, her gaze fixed on her hands. 'You slept well?'

'Yes, excellently. How is Anna this morning?'

Grant sat down and retrieved a knitting needle from the floor as Kate answered. He might as well order the teapot to be brought and some fancy biscuits—this seemed like a morning call, complete with stilted, meaningless polite chat, achieving nothing.

'Tomorrow, I intend going down to London. I must present myself at the House of Lords, the College of Heralds and at Court.' He was escaping.

'Oh.' She set down the wool and sat up in the chair as though bracing herself. 'I am sorry, I had not realised we would be leaving so soon. I am not certain I feel up to the journey yet.'

Surely that was not panic he saw in her eyes? He shook his head and realised Kate had taken that as a refusal to listen to her objection.

'But…if we must, may we stop in Newcastle on the way? Then I can buy a respectable gown or two to tide me over.' She looked around, determined, it seemed, to obey his wishes. 'Where have Jeannie and Wilson got to? I am sure we can be ready in time.'

'There is no need for you to disturb yourself. I had no intention of dragging you away. I will take Charlie and

Gough with me, I don't want to leave the boy without me yet. They can come back on the mail after a few weeks, once I am certain he is all right.' Kate closed her eyes for a moment and he felt a jab of conscience at not realising how exhausted she must be. 'When you feel up to it you will find Newcastle will serve for all your needs while you require only mourning clothes.'

'Very well. As you wish, my lord.' Kate picked up the wool and needles again with a polite smile that seemed to mask something deeper than relief. 'And you will send Charlie back, you say?'

'The moment I am certain he doesn't need me. In the longer term I will be too occupied with business to give him the company he needs and the house and servants will be unfamiliar to him. He will be better here, where he feels secure. I will send for him again after a month or two—travelling long distances will be no hardship for him, he'll find it an adventure—but I want him based here.'

'Of course. As you think best. I can see that London might not be a good place for a small boy in the longer term if you cannot be with him most of the time.'

Grant told himself he should be pleased to have such a conformable wife, such an untemperamental, obliging one. Perversely, he felt decidedly put out. Through yesterday's fog of tiredness he seemed to recall the sparkle that temper had put in Kate's eyes, the flush on her cheeks, the stimulus of a clash of wills. Women were moody after childbirth, he knew that. This placidity was obviously Kate's natural character.

'Grant?' She was biting her lip now. 'Grant, will you put a notice about the marriage in the newspapers? Only, I wish you would not. I feel so awkward about things...'

Newspaper announcements had been the last thing on his mind, but he could see she was embarrassed. 'No, I won't. An announcement of the birth, yes, but it will give no indication of the date of the marriage. "To the Countess of Allundale, a daughter." All right?' Kate nodded and he hesitated, concerned at how pale she had gone. Then she smiled and he told himself he was imagining things. 'If you'll excuse me, my dear, I have a great deal to do.' She would no doubt be delighted to see the back of him—and why should it be otherwise?

May 5, 1820

Home. Warmth on his back, clean air in his lungs, the sun bathing the green slopes of the Tyne Valley spread out before him. Grant stood in his stirrups to stretch, relishing the ache of well-exercised muscles. However ambiguous his feelings about Abbeywell, he had been happy here once and perhaps he could be again, if only he could blank out his memories and find some sort of peace with his new wife.

His staff had obviously thought he was out of his mind to decide to ride from London to Northumberland instead of taking a post-chaise, but he knew exactly what had motivated him. This had been a holiday from responsibility, from meetings and parties, from political negotiating and social duty. And a buffer between the realities and reason of London and the ghosts that haunted this place.

If he was honest, it had also been a way of delaying his return to his new wife and facing up to exactly what his impulse on that cold Christmas Day had led to.

'I like her,' Charlie had pronounced on being questioned when he came on a month's visit to the London house in March. But he was too overexcited from his adventurous trip on the mail coach with Mr Gough to focus on things back in Northumberland. He wanted to talk to his papa, to go with him to the menagerie, to see the soldiers and the Tower. And Astley's again, and…

'You get on together all right?' Grant had prompted.

'Of course. She doesn't fuss and she lets me play with Anna, who is nice, although she's not much fun yet. May we go to Tatt's? Papa, please?'

Doesn't fuss. Well, that would seem to accord with Kate's letters. One a week, each precisely three pages long in a small, neat hand. Each contained a scrupulous report on Charlie's health and scholastic progress, a paragraph about Anna—she can hold her head up, she can copy sounds, she can throw her little knitted bunny— and a few facts about the house and estate. *Millie in the kitchen has broken her ankle, the stable cat caught the biggest rat anyone had seen and brought it into the kitchen on Sunday morning and Cook dropped the roast, it has rained for a week solidly…*

They were always signed *Your obedient wife, Catherine Rivers*, each almost as formalised and lacking in emotion as Gough's reports on Charlie or his bailiff's lengthy letters about estate business. And never once did she ask to come to London or reproach him for leaving her alone.

He replied, of course, sending a package north weekly, with a long letter for Charlie, a note for Gough, answers to Wilkinson's estate queries. And there would always be a letter one page long for Kate, with the kind of gossip that Madeleine, his first wife, had expected. What the royal family were doing, what the latest society scandal was— omitting the crim. con. cases, naturally—the latest fads in hem lengths and bonnets as observed in Hyde Park. Signed *Your affct. husband, Grantham Rivers*.

The parkland rolled before him like a welcome carpet and the road forked, the right hand to the house, the left to the rise crowned with the mausoleum his great-grandfather had built in the 1750s. The chestnut gelding was trotting along the left-hand way before Grant was conscious of applying the reins. No rush, it was only just noon, no one was expecting him to arrive on any particular day.

The classical monument sat perfectly on its hillock, turning the view into a scene in an Arcadian painting. It was a Greek temple with its portico facing south, its basement full of the ancestors his great-grandfather had removed from the church vault, its inner walls made with niches for the future generations of Rivers. 'So we can admire the view,' the first earl had reportedly announced. 'I'm damned if I'm spending eternity in that damp vault with some dullard of a preacher sermonising on top of me.' The countess of the day had had mild hysterics at the sentiment and had been ignored and now she, too, shared the prospect.

Grant tied the gelding to a ring on the rear wall of the building and strolled round to the front. There were stone benches set under the portico and it would be good to rest there awhile and think about his grandfather.

The sound of laughter stopped him in mid-stride. He recognised Charlie's uninhibited shrieks, but there was a light, happy laugh he did not recognise at all. He walked on, his boots silent on the sheep-cropped turf, and stopped again at the corner.

A rug was spread out on the grassy flat area in front of the temple steps and a woman in a dark grey gown was sitting on it, her arms wrapped around her knees, her eyes shaded by a wide straw hat as she watched Charlie chasing a ball. An open parasol was lying by her side.

'Maman, look!' Charlie hurled the ball high, then flung himself full length to catch it.

The woman clapped, the enthusiasm of her applause tipping her hat back off her head to roll away down the slope. Long brown hair, the colour of milky coffee, glossy in the sunlight, tumbled free from the confining pins and she laughed. 'Catch my hat, Charlie!'

Maman? Grant started forward as Charlie caught the hat, turned and saw him. He rushed uphill shrieking, 'Papa! Papa! Look, Maman—Papa's home.'

The woman swung round on the rug as Charlie thudded into Grant, his hard little head butting into his stomach. He scooped him up, tucked him under his arm and strode down to her. She tilted her head back, sending the waves of hair slithering like unfolding silk and giving him an unimpeded view of an oval face, blue eyes, a decided chin and pink lips open in surprise.

'My…my lord, we did not expect to see you for another day at least.' Her face lost its colour, her relaxed body seemed to tighten in on itself.

Kate? Of course it is Kate, but... He did something about his own dropped jaw, gave himself a mental shake and managed to utter a coherent sentence. 'I made good time.' He set Charlie on his feet. 'Maman?'

'Stepmamas are in fairy stories and they are always wicked. So I asked Mr Gough for the words for *mama* in lots of languages and we looked them up and I chose *maman*. Maman likes it,' his son assured Grant earnestly. 'She said it was *elegant*.'

* * *

'Will you not sit down?' It was extraordinary how it was possible to sound quite calm outwardly when her insides were in a jumble of feelings, the overriding one of which was confusion. Kate gestured towards the open basket and managed what she hoped was a welcoming smile. 'Do have some luncheon. We have enough food to withstand a siege. Charlie, as always, assured Cook that we might be lost in the woods for days. We never are, but Cook does not like to take the risk.'

When in doubt when dealing with a man, feed the beast, her mother had always said with a chuckle. Kate kept her tone serious and was rewarded by the slight upward tilt of one corner of Grant's mouth. He had a sense of humour, then. It had not been possible to detect it in his dutiful letters, which had not been made any less dry by the fact they contained nothing but gossip. Presumably that was all wives were supposed to be interested in.

Wives, of course, were perfectly capable of reading the news-sheets and keeping informed that way, although that simple fact did not seem to occur to men. Her brother, Henry, had always been amazed when she revealed an opinion on anything from income tax to child labour and he firmly believed that thinking led to weakening of the feminine brain. Kate pushed away the resentment and watched her husband as he moved round to drop to the rug at her side and discovered Anna lying under the parasol, kicking her legs and chewing on a bone ring.

Grant reached over and tickled her and the resentment retreated some more. He was good with the children, she must remember that.

'She has grown and she looks to be thriving. As do you,' he added. 'I scarcely recognised you.'

From the way Grant shut his mouth with a snap he realised that was a less than tactful remark. Instead of saying so Kate wrestled her hair into a twist and jammed the hat back on top. 'Babies tend to grow in the natural course of things. But she is very well, as am I.' She sent him a considering, sideways glance, making sure he saw it. 'You look much better than I remembered.'

That very forward remark obviously caught him by surprise. Grant tossed his low-crowned hat aside and shifted round to look directly at her, eyes narrowing. 'Thank you. I think.'

She had known him to be a good-looking man when she married him, but not this attractive, with a London gloss on his hair and clothes, his face tanned from his long ride north. 'In December you looked haggard, bruised and exhausted. You were recovering from a blow to the head and you were grieving,' Kate said with a slight shrug. His eyes moved down to her breasts as she moved and she caught her breath at the answering flare of heat in her belly. The fact that she had a figure obviously interested him. No doubt it was the transformation of her bosom; men could be very predictable.

It was nearly five months since Anna's birth now. She had passed through exhaustion to a conviction that when she felt stronger she never wanted a man to touch her again. After all, her first, and only, experience had not been so pleasurable as to have her yearning for more.

And that comfortable state had lasted for three months until the moment when she had looked up from the dinner table to see Grant's portrait hanging on the opposite wall, just as it had since the day she arrived. It had been part of the decoration of the house, hardly regarded, but that evening she had felt a startling stab of attraction as she met the direct green gaze. The feeling had been so visceral, so unashamedly physical, that she'd choked on her fish terrine and Mr Gough had rushed round the table to offer her water.

Since the arrival of Grant's letter announcing his return she had been in an unseemly state of confusion, alarm and anticipation. This was her husband—and husbands expected their *rights*.

Chapter Seven

'After all, I was in the process of giving birth,' Kate continued calmly, hoping the frankness of her words accounted for the heat in her cheeks. The thought of Grant exercising his husbandly rights made her positively breathless. 'It is hardly surprising that we both now appear to be tolerably well looking in comparison. Of course, I could tell that you were a well-favoured man, even then, but it must be a relief for you to discover that I am not *quite* as bracket-faced as you feared.'

'It is difficult to know how to reply to that.' Grant was not used to being left at a loss for words, she could tell. Possibly he was slightly flattered, although he must be accustomed to being regarded as good-looking. Possibly also he was feeling a trifle awkward about letting her see what he had thought of her before.

'There is no need to say anything.' She was not a conventional beauty, she never had been, but she thought that these days she looked at least tolerable, and, if Grant now thought so, too, she was content with that.

'I have been away a long time, longer than I intended.' He had decided to get all the apologising over at once, it seemed. Kate wondered if the length of his absence had anything to do with his mental image of his new wife. Had he escaped to London and the arms of a beautiful mistress? As apologies went, it was not very effusive, more a statement of fact than of regret.

'We have managed very well and you were a most regular correspondent.' *Not that I understand you any better now than before you left. And you are a man, not a saint, so I must not feel jealous of a mistress—she is only to be expected. But if you take one up here, one that I know about, that will be a different matter.* The stab of jealousy was unexpected and she diverted it into a vicious cut at the pastry in front of her. 'Would you care for a slice of raised pie?' she enquired to cover the impulse to snap out a demand to know all about this theoretical other woman. 'It is chicken and ham.'

'Papa, are you home for long?' Charlie had been sitting almost on his father's feet, obviously on the point of bursting with the effort to Be Good and not interrupt the adults.

'For the summer. Ough!' Grant fell back on the rug under the impact of Charlie's flying leap and hug. 'You are too big for jumping on your poor father. Big enough to come out with me and start learning about the estate, I think, provided you keep up your lessons to Mr Gough's satisfaction. Now, sit quietly and eat your picnic while I talk to your stepmama.' Grant settled the boy between them and against her side Kate could feel her husband's encircling arm and the child's skinny little body quivering with happiness like an overexcited puppy.

The arm was warm and it was tempting to lean into it, to feel the muscled strength braced to support her.

Kate sat up straight and filled a plate for Grant from the picnic basket.

'Thank you. Have you heard from your brother yet?' he asked as he took the food from her.

'No. I have not written to him and I would, of course, have mentioned it in my letters if I had. I do not want him to know of this marriage. I do not want him to know where I am. To be perfectly frank, we were not close. We did not part on good terms and it would be awkward...' She'd scoured the newspapers daily, looking for the arrest or trial of Sir Henry Harding, baronet, for blackmail. But perhaps aristocrats had other ways of dealing with the potentially explosive matter of extortion. She shivered. But there had been no notice of Henry's death, either.

'Awkward to have him asking questions about our marriage?'

She nodded, grateful that he had jumped to the wrong conclusion. She did not want Henry to know about her marriage because, beside him embroiling her any deeper in his schemes, she had no idea how he would react. At best, he would attempt to borrow money from his new brother-in-law. At worst, he could cause the most dreadful scandal and she could not inflict that on Grant.

'I would be much happier if you did not make contact with him.' *And find out who Anna's father is and realise just how I came to lose my virginity to the man and became an accomplice in blackmail.* Grant was the kind of principled gentleman who would never allow such dishonesty to go unpunished, whatever the scandal. *Let sleeping dogs lie...*

Grant shrugged. 'We are going to have to deal with him sooner or later. In the meantime, are you opposed to entertaining a small house party? It had not occurred to me to propose it, but now I see you looking—'

'More the thing?' Kate suggested, swallowing the hurt. Had he really thought to shut her away up here, an unpaid housekeeper and guardian for his son, simply because he considered her plain and awkward? Now, it seemed, he did not fear she would embarrass him in front of his friends. The fact that she had welcomed the seclusion was neither here nor there.

'More rested,' Grant supplied smoothly. 'And from your letters it sounds as though you have the household well in hand.'

'Your staff are well chosen and well trained. Once they had accepted that I really was your wife, and not some stray you had picked up on the moors, they have proved most cooperative.' Not that she would have stood for any nonsense. She had been used to helping run a small household, so she knew the principles, and she was all too aware that if she did not secure the respect and loyalty of the staff of this much larger one right from the start, then she never would. It was another mark in Grant's favour, the loyalty and affection they showed for him.

'How small a house party?' she enquired, leaning away from him to give Anna a quick kiss and to hide the uncertainty that she could manage the sort of gathering an earl might hold. Provided it was here, on what had become her own turf, she was not too anxious.

'No more than three close friends of mine, potentially with partners. I've had enough formal socialising in London to last me several months. Charlie, do you remember Lord Weybourn?'

'Uncle Alex?'

'Yes. He was married in January. I thought to ask

him and his wife to stay. And, if they are still in the country, Lord Avenmore and Lord Edenbridge. They are old friends,' he added for Kate's benefit. 'The two bachelors might bring their unmarried sisters, perhaps, to balance out the men.'

'That sounds delightful.' Kate took a bread roll from the basket, then sat with it in her hands, wondering why she had picked it up. The longer Grant sat beside her, the more her appetite deserted her. It was nerves, that was all. She was happy that he was back, for Charlie's sake if nothing else—only, there was a hollow feeling of anticipation, as though the air had been sucked out of her lungs. This was her husband and he was going to expect to begin a normal married life, with all that entailed. Part of that hollowness was apprehension, but a good part was excitement and she had been making herself face that ever since the arrival of the letter announcing his return.

She put the bread roll back untasted, handed Charlie an apple turnover and smiled as he ran off, mouth full, to retrieve his ball. Beside her Grant was silent and she sought for small talk to fill the void. 'It has been…quiet. I am glad you are back. The children are very absorbing, of course.'

'But they are not adults. You have been lonely.' When she murmured agreement he asked, 'Have none of our neighbours called?'

'Dr Meldreth and his wife and the vicar and his sister, that is all. Please, do not make too much of it. I am in mourning, after all, and in the country people do observe that very rigorously. I see them in church on Sunday, naturally, and I usually dine with Mr Gough.'

'Now I am back I will visit all our neighbours, let the

ladies know we are not in strict mourning any longer. You should get any number of calls within days.'

Charlie's voice floated down from the portico of the mausoleum. '...and now Papa's back I will help him with the estate, just like he helped you, Great-Grandpapa. You'll be proud of me when I do that, I expect, Mama.'

'What the devil?' Grant swung round, sending the lemonade jug rocking. 'Who is he talking to? My grandfather, his mother? Is the child delusional?'

'Of course not.' Kate grabbed his arm as he began to get to his feet. Grant shot her a frowning look, but settled back down beside her when she did not relax her grip. 'He missed his great-grandfather, so we started coming down here so that he could talk to him. And then he realised that his mama was here, too. He understands that we do not know what happens after death and he doesn't think he is talking to ghosts or anything unhealthy like that. But it comforts him, helps him to sort out his feelings. Rather like writing a diary, I suppose.' Kate came up on her knees beside Grant, her hand on the unyielding arm braced to push him to his feet. 'Did I do wrong? He is not at all morbid about it and this is a lovely place. A peaceful place, where he can remember happy times.'

'He cannot remember his mother, he never really knew her, she died when he was only just two.' Grant stayed where he was, but the tension radiated off him. Had he loved his first wife so much that he could not bear any mention of her? But that was not what Dr Meldreth had implied. The staff in the house acted and spoke as though Charlie's mother was a grief that could not be spoken about, becoming thin-lipped and awkward if Kate made any reference to her. There were no portraits, not even in Charlie's room.

'He says he remembers her scent and the fact that she always wore blue, but that is all. I have no idea whether it is accurate, but it helps him to have that faint image. He is certain that she was beautiful.'

'She was.' Grant's voice softened. 'Blonde and blue-eyed, which is why she favoured blue in her dress. She always wore jasmine scent and on a warm evening it lingered in the air like the ghost of incense…' Kate closed her eyes at the hint of pain beneath the reminiscent tone. 'Charlie would do well to forget she ever existed,' he said and turned so his back was to the little temple.

'Grant!' Kate stared at him, then scooped up Anna as the baby began to cry, as unsettled by his abruptly harsh tone as she was.

'She was a disaster as a mother.'

And a disaster as a wife? 'He need not know that,' Kate said fiercely.

'Of course not, what do you take me for?'

'I do not know. I do not know *you*. But he needs the confidence of knowing he had a mother who loved him, even if she was not very good at it in your eyes. What does it matter if *you* do not like it, if it is best for Charlie?'

'Damn it, Kate. You presume to lecture me on my own child?'

'Yes, of course I do.' She glared back at him over the top of Anna's bonneted head, aware that she was bristling like a stable cat defending her kittens. Then she saw the darkness in Grant's eyes, the memory of goodness knew what past miseries. 'I am sorry, but I am his stepmother and you left him with me to look after. He is still only a little boy, not ready for harsh truths.' She rocked the baby, trying to soothe her. 'What did she do that was so unforgivable?'

Grant got to his feet in one fast movement, a controlled release of pent-up tension. 'I am sorry, but I have no intention of raking over old history. Madeleine is in the past and there is nothing you need to know.' He bent to pick up his hat. 'If you will excuse me, Kate, I will ride on to the house and take Charlie with me. I assume a footman is coming out in the gig to collect you and bring the basket back?'

'Yes, I expect him very soon.' Kate was glad of Anna grizzling in her arms, demanding her attention. She did not want to look into those shadowed eyes and see his anger with her, or his pain over his beautiful, lost wife.

He called to Charlie and the boy came running to be hoisted up into the saddle in front of his father. Grant gave him the reins. 'Wave goodbye to your stepmama.'

When the sound of hooves died away and Charlie's excited chatter faded amongst the trees, Kate fed and changed Anna, packed away the baby things in one basket and the remains of the picnic in the other and got to her feet, too restless to wait for the footman and the gig.

She had to think about Grant, but not about what would happen that night. If she began to imagine that, then she would be in more of a state of nerves than a virgin on her wedding night. The virgin might have a little theoretical knowledge, but Kate knew exactly what would happen and the thought of being in Grant's bed made her mind dizzy and her body ache.

She had lain with Jonathan just once and she had believed herself in love with him, a delusion she now knew was born out of ignorance, a desperation to get away from home and the lures of an accomplished rake. And the experience had been a sadly disappointing one, even though she had not truly understood what to expect. But she hardly knew Grant, the man, at all, he had never so much as kissed her hand and she was most certainly not tipsy with moonlight and champagne. And yet, just the thought of him made her breath come short and an ache, somewhere between fear and anticipation, form low down. Goodness knew how she had managed a rational conversation with him appearing like that.

Kate tucked Anna more snugly into her little blanket, settled her into the folds of her shawl to make a sling and began to walk back to the house. It would take almost half an hour with her arms full of her wriggling, chubby baby. Time enough to think about something other than how long Grant's legs had looked, stretched out on the rug, how the ends of his hair had turned golden brown in the sunlight.

Time, in fact, to consider that locked door on the other side of Grant's suite of rooms in the light of what he had said about Madeleine, the beautiful wife who had been such a bad mother and who had died in a fire.

She had realised almost from the beginning that the forbidden suite must have been her predecessor's rooms. She could understand that the chambers would hold difficult memories for Grant, but even so, it was surely long past the time when they should have been opened up, aired, redecorated and put to use. What would happen when Charlie was old enough to be curious about the locked door? It was unhealthy to make a mystery out of his mother like that, and if he ever discovered that was where she had died, he might well have nightmares about it.

None of the keys on her chatelaine fitted the lock and all the servants denied having the right one, either. Eventually Grimswade told her that neither his late lordship nor his young lordship had wanted the rooms opened. 'The earl holds the only key, my lady,' he told her, his gaze fixed at a point over her head.

Since then Kate had tried hard not to allow the locked room to become a Bluebeard's chamber in her imagination, applying rigorous common sense to keep her own nightmares at bay. She had found her way around the house without looking at the door if she could help it, she had asked no further questions of the staff, but it refused to be forgotten. There were times when she seriously considered picking the lock with a bent hairpin, or seeing if a slender paperknife would trip the catch, then told herself to not even think about something so unseemly.

Now she wondered just what Madeleine's crimes had been. *A disaster as a mother.* That, somehow, did not make sense. Surely she could not have beaten the child— neither Grant nor his grandfather would have allowed her unsupervised access if they feared violence. And being a distant and cold mother was nothing unusual amongst the nobility, Kate knew. Many a child was raised almost entirely by servants without anyone accusing the parents of being a disaster.

The only explanation Kate could think of was that she was a failure as a wife and therefore morally unfit to be a mother. Had she taken a lover—had Grant found them together in her bedchamber? It was an explanation, but it was difficult to imagine Grant being cuckolded. In fact, her mind refused to produce an image of a more attractive alternative who might have tempted his wife to stray.

'Which is very shallow of me,' she admitted to Anna. The baby stared back at her with wide green eyes. 'Grant is intelligent, good-looking, and he was the heir to an earldom when she married him. But good looks and position are not everything. If Madeleine had found her soulmate...'

Then she should have resisted temptation. Madeleine was married, she had made vows, she had a child. Which is easy enough for me to say. Despite being a well-brought-up, respectable young lady, I gave my virtue easily enough. Of course, having a scheming brother who put her in the way of a man who could be trusted to yield to temptation when it was offered and who could not afford a scandal had helped her along the path to ruination. Her becoming pregnant was, as far as Henry was concerned, the perfect gilding on his plan to blackmail her lover. *What if Jonathan came back now, walked around that bend in the path ahead?*

Kate watched the bend approach. No one appeared around it, of course, least of all the rakish Lord Baybrook. And if he did, he would not be coming with protestations of undying love, with explanations of how she had entirely misunderstood his flat refusal to marry her when Henry had confronted him two months later, after she had been forced to confess her predicament.

Not that she had seen him then, of course. Henry, as befitted the male head of the household, had taken himself off to London to, as he put it, *deal with the matter.* Only, he had not dealt with it, not brought her a husband back. At the time it had struck her as strange that her brother had not been more angry, but she had decided that perhaps he had been relieved that he had not found himself facing the viscount at dawn on Hampstead Heath. Then she had found the letter in Henry's desk, the coldly furious response to blackmail, the counter-threats. But Lord Baybrook had not called Henry's bluff. He would pay, she thought, reading the letter. Pay—and then she was certain that one day he would find some way to make Henry pay and Kate, too, the woman Jonathan thought had deliberately set out to ensnare him.

Anna gurgled and Kate stopped, her feet sinking into the soft mulch of the path. There was nothing to be gained by brooding on it, fretting over the long arm of a vengeful aristocrat or wincing in shame at her own part in her brother's schemes. Most certainly, she was in no position to judge Grant's first wife on moral grounds. Equally certainly, if she had the choice between Grant Rivers, Lord Allundale, and Jonathan Arnold, Lord Baybrook, she had no doubt which man she would choose now.

Chapter Eight

Grant sat up in the marble bath and considered the tricky, but eminently safe, subject of plumbing. His grandfather had installed baths with a cold-water supply and drains for the main bedchambers, but he had not risked the newfangled systems of boilers and piped hot water. Grant had agreed with him at the time, but lugging the cans of hot water upstairs and along endless corridors certainly made a great deal of work for the servants.

He lathered the long-handled brush and scrubbed his back while calculating the safe location for boilers and the length of pipework one would need. It was technical, complicated, and was entirely failing to stop him brooding on the subject of his wife. His second wife.

He had been deep in discussion with his secretary and the steward when he heard her voice in the hallway that afternoon. Six months ago Mr Rivers would have pushed aside the piles of paperwork and asked the men to wait while he went out to greet her. But the Earl of Allundale could not do anything as unfashionable and demonstrative as interrupting an important meeting in order to speak to his wife for no reason whatsoever. A few months in London society had reminded him force-fully of that.

Madeleine had always said he was far too casual, not sufficiently aware of his own consequence, or of hers. Now he was the earl he should behave like one, and, given the circumstances of their marriage, Kate was going to need all the consequence he could bring her, he was very conscious of that.

Now he put aside the brush and lay back to critically survey what he could see of his body as he stretched out under the water. Toes, kneecaps and a moderately hairy chest broke the surface. No stomach rising above the soap suds, thank goodness. The London Season was enough to put inches on anyone foolish enough to eat and drink all that was on offer during interminable dinner parties, suppers at balls, buffets at receptions. But with rigorous attendance at the boxing salons, sessions with the fencing master and long rides in the parks, at least the elegant new clothes he'd ordered when he'd first arrived still fitted him by the end.

Alex had laughed at him for having a fashionable crop, but he had hardly noticed the teasing—contemplating his old friend Alex Tempest married to the woman he had believed on first sight to be a nun was enough to distract any man.

Alex and Tess had seemed happy. Blissfully so and physically, too. Shockingly they hardly seemed able to keep their hands off each other—Lord and Lady Weybourn appeared to have no reservations about appearing unfashionably in love.

Grant reached out and pulled the plug out, then, when the bath emptied, he put it back and turned on the cold-water tap. He made himself lie still until it reached his shoulders. It had dawned on him when he reached London that he was a married man again. Which meant that he should be faithful to his wife. It was not something that had entered his head when he made that rash proposal, and sex had not been exactly at the forefront of his mind for at least a month before that, what with the anxiety about his grandfather and then so much travelling, culminating in his accident in Edinburgh.

Now he lay in the cold water and made himself calculate. This was May. It had been mid-November when he had ended that pleasant little dalliance with the Bulgarian attaché's wife in Vienna. Nearly six months. Despite the chill of the bath, blood was definitely heading downwards with the realisation of such prolonged celibacy. Damnation. He could hardly sling a towel round his hips and stride off to his wife's bedchamber to deal with the matter. That was not the way to approach one's first night in the marriage bed. And what were Kate's expectations of that marriage bed anyway?

Grant climbed from the bath and stood in front of the fire while he towelled himself dry. The logical way to discover her feelings and views on any subject was simply to ask her. On the other hand, he hardly knew the woman. Wife or not, he could not just sit down and have a frank and open discussion about sex. She would be shocked.

He had been away a devil of a long time and he had a guilty conscience about that, he realised as he towelled his back. He could expect to receive, at the very least, some wifely remonstrance on the subject before he was forgiven. Yet when they had met in front of the mausoleum Kate had simply not acknowledged that there had been anything wrong, so he could neither justify himself nor be forgiven. Maddening. The question was, did she realise how awkward that was and was she administering a particularly subtle punishment? Or did she care too little to be annoyed with him? Probably the latter.

The faint sound of splashing stopped him, the towel still stretched across his shoulder blades. Of course, when the suites had been changed around, the two new bathing rooms had been carved out of a small, little-used retiring room and the walls must be simply lath and plaster. He padded across and applied his ear to the panelling. Definite splashing and the sound of Kate's voice.

Grant stepped back with a grimace. The next thing, he would be peering through the keyhole at his own wife. The sounds were certainly exercising his imagination in a thoroughly arousing way, as though his body needed any more encouragement. He gave his back one sharp slap with the towel and went out to the dressing room, where Griffin, his smart new London valet, was laying out his smart new London clothes. If nothing else, his wife would not be confronted by the travel-worn, battered, weary, grief-stricken man she had married. He gave a grunt of satisfaction as he lowered his chin the half-inch to perfect the set of the waterfall knot in his neckcloth, nodded his thanks to Griffin and headed for the drawing room and the start of his new marriage.

Kate paused at the head of the stairs for one last calming breath, twitched her black silk skirts into order and descended the staircase in a manner befitting a countess. She had waited nearly four and a half months for this evening and the unexpected encounter with Grant that morning had done nothing to make this any easier. The exhausted, kind, patient stranger she had married was now an alert, attractive, impatient, secretive stranger.

Nothing had changed for him, it seemed, except for the fact that he'd had nearly four and a half months' worth of town bronze, the status of an earl and an endless amount of time to regret marrying her. She had her looks back, her confidence as the mistress of a large country house and an inconvenient attack of physical attraction for the aforesaid stranger.

I want a proper marriage, not simply make-believe for the rest of our lives. But what does he want? She smiled at Giles as the footman opened the door for her and then checked on the threshold as Grant turned from the contemplation of a landscape painting she had placed over the hearth, a replacement for one of the old earl's more bloodthirsty hunting scenes.

'A definite improvement.'

For a moment she thought he meant her appearance, then he gestured to the painting. *At least he is smiling.* 'I am glad you think so.' Kate went to her usual armchair by the fireplace. The distance across the room had never felt so long, nor her limbs so clumsy. Grant moved as though he would intercept her, touch her, but she sat down before he could reach her side. With a feeling of relief that she recognised as sheer nerves she picked up her embroidery frame from the basket beside the chair. She wanted this man, but she had no idea how to cope with him.

'Naturally, I would not remove any portraits, but I found that sitting here every evening under the glazed eyes of a slaughtered stag was somewhat dampening to the spirits,' she said as she found the needle, then dropped her thimble.

Grant stooped to retrieve it and handed it to her. He moved back, but remained opposite her, one elbow on the end of the mantelpiece. In any other man she would

have supposed the pose was intended to draw attention
to his clothes or his figure, and it certainly did that, but
Grant's attention seemed to be all on her.

'That is a charming gown. Have you been sending to
London for the latest fashions?'

She had been pleased with it, although a trifle nervous of the low neckline, which the dressmaker assured
her was high by London standards. 'No, merely for the
latest fashionable journals. I have discovered a most accomplished dressmaker in Newcastle and an excellent
fabrics warehouse.'

'In that case you might wish to accompany me into the
city next week and choose something for half mourning.
I imagine you are weary of unrelieved black and grey
and the six months isn't too far away. I hardly feel the
need to apply the strictest rules, do you?'

'We are mourning *your* grandfather, it is for you to
decide, but I must confess that some colour would be welcome.' It would be a delight, to be truthful, even if it was
only shades of lavender and lilac. She placed a careful
row of French knots. 'Were your friends very surprised
at the news of your marriage?'

Grant's eyebrows rose at the abrupt change of subject
and it seemed to Kate that in moving to take the chair
opposite her he was taking the time to compose his reply
with care. 'My three closest friends know something of
the truth.' He shrugged. 'I could hardly deceive them
that our relationship was of long-standing, they know my
movements too well. But I would trust them with my life
and you may rely on their absolute discretion. As far as
acquaintances in town are concerned, I confided in a few
incorrigible gossips that Grandfather had not approved
of the match, hence a secret Scottish wedding and no

announcement. They were titillated enough by the disapproval not to question the date and one or two were
obviously on the verge of remarking that it was convenient that his death precluded an uncomfortable confession to him following the birth of our child.'

'How…distasteful.'

'Society can be like that, I find. The prospect of gossip
and scandal sharpens even the most respectable tongue.'
He shrugged. 'But it plays into our hands. They'll spread
the tale and provided no one has the effrontery to demand
to know the date of the wedding it will soon become of
no matter, and even if some conclude that we anticipated
the wedding, no one will hold that against you. It will
soon be old history.'

'They won't hold it against me because too many of
them have done the same, no doubt.' His lips twitched at
the tartness of her tone. 'Did you tell people who I am?'
she asked, trying not to sound as worried as she was.
'And what is supposed to be the reason for your grandfather's disapproval?'

'I mentioned that you were from a respectable minor
gentry family in Suffolk.' She managed not to let out a
long sigh of relief. 'The fact that your father was merely
a country squire without connections or an established
place in society was sufficient explanation for Grandfather to oppose the match. The old man was a product
of his generation—nothing less than the daughter of an
earl, and one bringing a substantial dowry and influence
with her into the bargain, was good enough for the Earl
of Allundale.'

'I see.' Kate unpicked the knot she had just set, which
had become unaccountably tangled. *So presumably*

Madeleine had been Lady Madeleine, even though she was married to a mere Mr Rivers.

'That was his view,' Grant said. 'I do not share it. Having married a lady with just those qualifications as my first wife, I know all too well they are no guarantee of anything. However, it makes a perfectly plausible reason.'

'Of course,' she agreed. *And the old earl was quite correct—what do I bring to this marriage? We could have a good marriage, as long as I can keep my secrets, but if they become public knowledge, it will make a scandal that would rebound on Grant and on the children.* She was pleased at how composed she sounded.

'Kate, you must write to your brother soon,' Grant said.

'No. I will not write to him. I do not want him knowing anything of my marriage.'

'Kate, why ever not? I would have asked you for his direction and done so myself if I had realised you would neglect to do so. I need to talk to him about the settlements,' Grant said. 'And I assume he is holding money for you that will be released on your marriage. I seem to recall you saying something.'

Did I? How foolish. 'There is virtually nothing. I do not want to make a fuss about it. He has control until I marry with his approval, that is all.'

'You think he will object to me? He may not know me by reputation, but he is hardly likely to turn up his nose at an earl.'

'He would be delighted with an earl,' Kate said drily. 'But he will be unpleasant. If you must have the truth, Henry has an expensive wife and ambitions beyond his means. He is quite unscrupulous.' That was all true enough. 'If he discovers who I have married, he would ask to borrow money—which I doubt you would ever see again. To encourage him to sponge off you would not be right.'

That was harsh, but it was a mild version of the truth. Henry would hold the scandal of Anna's parentage over Grant, try to entangle him in that mire. He would get a surprise if he tried it, she thought grimly. Grant would probably throttle him. But then there was the blackmail. What if Grant thought he must inform the magistrate? He was an honest, straightforward man. There was no way he could ignore it, surely? Then he would be smeared by association, by his marriage.

'He is my brother-in-law. I would not like to be unreasonable. Do not sound so apologetic, my dear. Brothers-in-law are almost expected to hang on one's coat-tails.' The tolerant amusement in Grant's voice was no help. 'Besides, there is the matter of the settlements, which I really should discuss with him. You should have what is yours.'

'It is very little, a few hundreds.'

'Settle it on Anna if you do not want it. It is always a mistake to neglect financial matters, however minor.'

Kate wondered suddenly just how wealthy Grant was. There was no stinting about the household, the land was obviously in good heart. But that might simply be because he was expending all he had on keeping things just so. Now, on top of the risk of her dubious brother touching him for loans, which would never be repaid, she had saddled him with the expense of a wife and a child. She had removed his opportunity for a much more advantageous marriage and all she could offer were the skills of any competent mistress of a country house.

For how much longer could she put Grant off about

contacting Henry? Or could she add to her deceit, tell Grant that she had written to her brother, but that he had cut the connection?

But then Grant would still want to pursue her money 'for her and, she suspected, he would try to heal the breach. And behind those fears was the lurking terror that sooner or later he would ask her to accompany him to London, take her place beside him in society as his hostess. Inwardly she quailed. A country mouse contemplating life amidst the birds of prey of fashionable London could not have felt as inadequate. She could not even dance the waltz, Kate reflected with a descent into gloom. The faint smile felt as though it was pinned to her face. She would manage if she had to. Somehow. But if Lord Baybrook was there…

'Kate, is something wrong?' Grant had obviously noticed the artificiality of her expression.

'No, of course not.' She made the effort to smile with her eyes when all she felt was queasiness.

'There is no need to be anxious.' There was something warm in his expression, some meaning in his tone. Kate stared back, puzzled, as he added, 'About tonight, I mean.'

He is talking about bed, about making love. Does he mean not to be anxious because he will come to me… or that he will not? I hope he comes. There was no hiding the truth from herself that she was attracted to this man, this stranger-husband. She felt the blush rising up her face and with it the shame that Grant would see her eagerness, think her a wanton. Or perhaps he would welcome that, expect her to be very experienced and to possess sophisticated skills in bed.

It was difficult to understand this feeling. After all, her

skills were non-existent and she had no idea what would be involved in sophisticated lovemaking.

'I am not anxious about tonight,' she said, rather too loudly.

'Dinner is served, my lady.' Grimswade somehow managed to sound even more smoothly efficient and bland than normal. When had he appeared in the doorway behind her? Had he heard? She wondered if it was possible to pass out from sheer embarrassment. Henry always said that one should treat the servants as though they were furniture and would discuss anything and everything in front of them—from an embarrassing rash to his gaming losses.

'Thank you, Grimswade.' She found a smile for the butler as she began to rise to her feet, then almost jumped in surprise to find her husband by her side, his hand outstretched.

'My dear.'

My dear. A conventional phrase, that is all. He means nothing by it. She put her fingertips on his wrist and resisted the urge to curl them around the strong tendons, to feel the jut of his wristbone. When she had seen him this morning her eyes had been drawn to his bare, tanned hands, a sharp contrast with her smaller, paler hands beside his on the rug. What would those long fingers look like on her body? How would they feel? Now she told herself that she could detect nothing through the fine kid of her evening gloves, not his body heat, not the pulse of his blood.

'I do hope you like the new recipe for veal ragout Cook has been trying,' Kate remarked as they walked through to the dining room. 'It is an old family one I remembered.' Discussing the food was utterly banal. He would think her so dull. But it was safe.

Giles the footman stepped forward to pull out her chair at the foot of the table for her, but Grant was before him. He pushed it in carefully as she sat, then laid one hand on her shoulder in a fleeting caress before taking his own place at the head of the long board. 'I am certain that whatever you suggest will be delightful.' That warmth was back in his eyes and behind it a question that had not been there before. Or perhaps a doubt.

Conscious of the attendant footmen, of Grimswade bringing the decanter to fill Grant's wine glass, Kate closed her lips on the impulsive questions—*What do you want of me? What do you expect of me?*—and focused her attention on the dishes arrayed on the table. At least her husband would have no reason to complain of her supervision of the kitchen, whatever he felt about her presence in his bed.

Chapter Nine

Kate was nervous. That blush when he had mentioned *tonight* had not been the faint glow of anticipated pleasure, but the embarrassment or nerves that Grant might have expected from a virgin. But she was not untouched—the presence of little Anna was proof enough of that. So what was it? An aversion to him, or painful shyness? One would be easy enough to overcome, the other, less so.

'Have you been dining here in lonely state every night?' he asked, casting round for some innocuous topic to discuss in front of the servants. He could send them away, of course, but that might only aggravate whatever fears Kate was harbouring.

'Usually I invite Mr Gough to join me. I find he is an intelligent conversationalist. Once a week we have an early supper with Charlie in the small dining room with all the leaves taken out of the table. He enjoys the grown-up treat.'

Grant felt a jab of something unpleasantly like jealousy and instantly regretted it. His wife had been lonely, Gough was a gentleman, intelligent and doubtless pleasant company, and he, too, was probably lonely and welcomed the opportunity for conversation.

But something in his expression must have betrayed that instinctive, possessive reaction. Kate bit her lip and glanced uneasily at the footmen as though expecting a rebuke in front of them.

'An excellent idea,' Grant said with casual approval. 'My grandfather would dine with Gough when he did not have company visiting and often when he did. I am glad you had congenial adult companionship.'

'We had a lot to discuss about Charlie's lessons. Mr Gough follows your instructions carefully, of course, but there is so much day-to-day detail. I hope you do not feel I am encroaching?'

It was a question, not an apology, and Grant was careful to keep his own tone light. 'Certainly not. You are his stepmama, after all, as I am sure you would have reminded me if I had objected to your involvement.'

Kate flushed up at that, but her voice was confident as she raised it to give an order. 'Grimswade, that will be all. We will serve ourselves and ring when we require dessert.'

'My lady.' The butler gestured to the footmen and closed the door softly behind the last liveried back.

Kate put down her fork and fixed him with a direct gaze, compelling his attention. 'My lord, I think we should be frank. I have a great deal of experience of being a daughter and a sister and of the limits of my authority and freedom in those roles. Since I have been here at Abbeywell I have gained several months' worth of knowledge of how to run a large country house. But I have no experience of a husband, of the limits he will impose on my actions, of his expectations of me.'

Ah, so now the recriminations come. Grant chewed his mouthful of beef, swallowed and decided that dodging the issue would not help. 'In effect you feel I abandoned you.' He had done just that, but he was damned if he was going to justify himself. Which was a good thing, because he was not certain that he could. He had left Abbeywell because he knew, once he was not drugged with exhaustion and grief, that he could not bear to be there. Now he was going to have to make himself endure. He owed it to Charlie, to the estate and to his neglected wife.

Part of him had been running away from confronting what he had done by marrying a woman without the qualifications necessary for a countess. He was beginning to suspect he was wrong about that judgement, but confessing that he had believed it could only be deeply wounding to Kate.

'You had a great deal to do in London, many responsibilities in connection with the earldom. I am not reproaching you, my lord.' Her smile was sudden, vivid, and took him completely by surprise. 'I merely explain my own…limitations.'

'I wish you would use my given name.' Grant smiled back, charmed, and realised he had never seen that open, uncomplicated smile from Kate before. She smiled at the children, at the servants, but never at him.

But why would she? He had hardly seen her except as a desperate woman in the throes of labour, or an exhausted one in its aftermath. Even that morning her smile had been polite and dutiful. But this expression transformed her. Strangely it did not enhance her beauty, as a smile usually did for a woman. Instead it emphasised the slight irregularity of her face, it crinkled up her blue eyes and showed the little gap between very white, otherwise even, front teeth. And yet…*charmed* was the only word for his reaction. This was a real woman, not a pretty, regimented society doll. A real woman he knew not at all.

'I see no limitations, Kate. There is nothing we cannot deal with by a little discussion, an exchange of views, greater familiarity.' He chose the final word deliberately.

That produced a blush that he had no difficulty interpreting as anything but one of sensual awareness. Kate's lips were parted and she did not meet his gaze, but glanced up, above his head, blushed even more rosily and reached for her water glass.

Grant suppressed the instinctive movement to turn and look at the wall behind his chair. Of course, that was where his own portrait hung. So what was there about that to make her colour up? Unless she had spent every mealtime sitting just there, looking at his image and liking what she saw. He bit his lip to repress a grin that could only be unworthily smug. He was used to hearing himself described as a good-looking man, women seemed to like to flirt with him, but he felt no conceit about that. He looked like his grandfather at the same age, which was good fortune and no merit of his. He could feel some satisfaction at the appreciation shown by his lovers, however, because he was confident that was due to practice and an interest in his partner's pleasure as well as his own, rather than to heredity.

His first wife had been more prone to burst into tears or tantrums at the sight of him than to blush prettily. The marriage had been an arranged one and they had hardly known each other before it. Grant had come to the conclusion that Madeleine was simply averse to sex and hoped that he was not the cause, but that it was something inbuilt in her character. She had been stiff and unresponsive in bed from the first, informing him, when he had asked her what was the matter, that her mama had explained to her that she must endure her marital duty and that was what she was doing. Enduring. It was hard work being a sensitive and imaginative lover in the face of that. And then he had made the grave tactical error of getting her pregnant too soon...

Grant pushed away the memory and focused on the very different wife facing him down six foot of polished mahogany. It occurred to him that it would be a pleasant novelty to be wed to a woman who took an interest in the physical side of marriage. He allowed himself to smile and decided that Kate was decidedly flustered.

Slowly, slowly, don't startle her, you are almost a stranger in her eyes, he reminded himself. Just because she showed sensual awareness did not mean that she was not shy. He must court this woman even though she was already his countess. 'I hope you will always feel free to discuss any thoughts you have about Charlie. As for the household, it is yours to command, and if the allowances I give you for those expenses and your own expenditure are inadequate, I will certainly amend them.'

'Thank you.' Kate had recovered her composure, it seemed. She took a sip of wine. 'It would be helpful to know when we might have regular discussions about day-to-day issues.'

'Of course. Would around ten each morning suit you? I am usually back from my morning ride about then and the steward and estate manager come to see me after luncheon.' She nodded, apparently happy with the proposal. 'Of course, we will have much more time together to discuss more...intimate matters.'

The charming smile vanished, but the equally charming blush persisted. How far down did it go? Below the decorous dip of her black silk evening gown? Down far enough to tint those sweet curves with rose? Grant shifted in his chair, feeling again the lash of his own arousal. Slowly, slowly might be wise, but the seduction of his countess promised to be a leisurely pleasure.

Kate watched her husband's face and tried to read the thoughts behind that handsome, intelligent surface. She suspected that he was clever enough to hide whatever emotions he did not want her to read, although the warmth in his gaze and the faint curve of his lips when that gaze strayed downwards from her face were less revealing of deep thoughts than of basic masculine instincts, that was certain.

She wanted him, although now the man was before her in the flesh and not simply as a fantasy fuelled by a two-dimensional image, that wanting was tinged again with apprehension. Kate reached for the silver bell that stood before her place. 'Time for dessert, I think, my lord.'

One dark brow lifted.

'In front of the servants I should not be too familiar, Grant,' Kate said repressively and was rewarded by a fleeting, wicked smile that vanished into an expression of aristocratic calm when the footmen re-entered.

Somehow Kate's increasingly fevered imagination had carried her directly from the dining table to the bedchamber and it came as a shock to see Grimswade setting the decanters on the sideboard when the dessert dishes were cleared, just as he always did when Mr Gough dined with her.

'I will leave you to your port, my lord.' She rose and Grant stood, too. She caught his reflection in the glass of the watercolour that hung by the door as she left and saw he was still on his feet, watching her. The glimpse of dark, shadowed eyes made her shiver deliciously.

Now what? Mr Gough would linger only long enough to drink one glass, more out of custom than pleasure, she suspected. Then he would join her for an hour, bringing journals with items he thought might interest her, or some written exercise of Charlie's that he knew she would approve.

She had come to enjoy the harmless, companionable interludes that were such a pleasant novelty. Her brother had never scrupled to leave the ladies waiting for him if he had a male companion to talk to or when he found a female guest tiresome. Sometimes, he would not join his wife and sister at all, disappearing to a cockfight in the village or to join his cronies for a game of cards without as much as a by-your-leave.

Kate picked up her embroidery, regarded the unsteady line of French knots with dismay and began to unpick them.

'If you scowl at that unfortunate piece of work much longer, it will scorch,' a deep voice remarked from just behind her.

She jumped, drove the needle into the ball of her index finger and said a naughty word under her breath. She switched the glare to Grant, who moved, soft-footed, to stand in front of her.

'You have pricked yourself. My fault for startling you.' He hunkered down, the silk of his evening knee breeches straining tight over muscular thighs, and took the wounded hand in his. 'Let me kiss it better.'

'I— Oh!' He lifted her hand, pressed his lips to the tiny bead of blood and then sucked the whole top joint of her finger into his mouth. Kate stared down at the fashionably barbered dark head bent over her hand, the wide shoulders in their blue superfine, the elegance of the man performing a small, insignificant, utterly indecent act.

Because it was indecent, she had not the slightest doubt of it. His fingers clasped lightly around her wrist, the ends over her pulse as if to monitor the effect he was having on her. She was shackled by the encircling grip as securely as if by iron manacles, because she could no more have moved her hand away than flown.

The sensitive tip of her finger was encased in the wet heat of Grant's mouth. His tongue caressed the pad until the sting of the needle prick was lost in the soft touch. She could sense the sharp edge of his teeth, carefully kept from her flesh as gradually, so very gradually, he drew her finger into his mouth as far as the middle joint. The suction pulsed, moving it in and out, his tongue tip curled and the heat rose through her as she realised what this action mimicked.

She needed to move, to squirm in her chair and push him away, draw him closer. She needed—

Grant sat back and she jerked her hand back against her bodice, the damp finger leaving a mark on the silk for a moment. 'Has that taken the sting away?' His lids were half closed, his eyes dark, his parted lips a little moist.

As if he has been kissing me, she thought wildly. *This is what he will look like when he holds me in his arms, when his body comes down over mine, pressing it into the bed. His* naked *body over mine, hot and hard and aroused.*

Somehow she found the composure to murmur, 'Perfectly, thank you', as though he had merely dabbed at the little puncture with his handkerchief. 'So careless of me. I might have got blood on the linen.'

Grant's lids lifted, his lips closed as he smiled and he stood up, looming over her for a moment. Kate found her eye level was precisely right for her to see that whatever he said, however coolly he might smile at her and however steadily he got to his feet, he was aroused. Impressively, alarmingly, aroused. *Just like my fantasies.*

'I think I will retire now.' It was the instinct to escape, to be alone to come to terms with what his touch was doing to her, but as soon as the words were out of her mouth she saw that Grant had interpreted them as an invitation, a direct response to what had just happened. Kate folded her embroidery into a careful square, put it into the sewing box and made herself rise with leisurely grace. Anything but let Grant see how excited and panicked he made her. Why she must hide it, she was not sure, because instinct told her he would welcome her awareness. It was pride, perhaps, or apprehension of her own limited experience disappointing him. Or was it fear that her own confused and heated fantasies would prove false and she would feel as let-down and unsatisfied as she had with Jonathan?

'Goodnight, my... Goodnight, Grant.'

His crooked smile was teasing. 'Goodnight, Kate.'

He doesn't mean it as a farewell. He'll come to my room, she told herself as she climbed the stairs and hurried to the nursery for Anna's goodnight kiss and a quick word with Jeannie. Then to Charlie's room, her fingers crossed that he would be asleep and there would be no battle over lights out. But he hardly stirred as she brushed the hair back from his forehead, kissed the smooth skin and pulled his tumbled covers back over his sprawled body.

Wilson, her maid, was already in Kate's bedchamber, alerted by the downstairs staff. 'The new lawn nightgown—' Kate began, then saw that it was already laid out on the bed, its matching robe beside it. Of Kate's usual comfortable plain cotton nightgown there was no sign. 'You already have it,' she observed lamely.

'Yes, my lady. With his lordship being home, I assumed this would be the right one.' The woman said it without the slightest hint of embarrassment. Apparently she took it as a matter of course that her master would visit his wife's bedchamber and that her mistress would want to look her best.

And why shouldn't she? Kate told herself, attempting to look as nonchalant as the maid about the fact she was preparing to receive her husband. *She thinks we are an established married couple who have been separated for months, not two virtual strangers who have not even exchanged a kiss.*

She submitted to the bath and the hair brush, made a choice at random from the array of scent bottles presented to her, rejected the robe and climbed into bed, wishing she had not read so many Gothic tales where the heroine, a virgin sacrifice clad all in white, awaits the arrival of the mysterious dark man, who may be the villain, or, perhaps, the hero.

She tried to calm herself with thoughts of her youthful fantasies about marriage. It had been a sheltered life in the Essex countryside. Motherless, her behaviour had been subject to more scrutiny by her father and brother and the neighbouring matrons than it might otherwise have been. So flirtations were very mild, her social circle limited, her daydreams of a husband vague and romantic. No wonder she had fallen so hard for Jonathan.

Minutes passed. Kate reached for the novel she had been reading and tried to focus on it so that she would not look too eager, or too nervous, when Grant came in. She read the same page four times. The clock struck the half hour. He would have gone to look in on Charlie and perhaps also Anna. He would have bathed, or at least washed. Shaved, perhaps. He was, she suspected, a fastidious man. *Another half hour, he'll come within the next half hour,* she told herself and frowned at the small print that seemed to dance before her eyes.

She pushed one shoulder strap down, then pulled it back. *Ting,* went the clock on the mantelshelf. *Ting, ting...* Kate counted to eleven. Grant was not coming. She tossed aside the book and made herself go through all the perfectly acceptable reasons why he might not. Then she threw back the covers and slid out of bed.

No patience with slippers, no patience with a wrapper and certainly no patience with a husband who'd left her for months, then behaved in a manner enough to fluster a nun, let alone a wife, and who then left the aforesaid wife to a lonely bed and a very silly novel.

Kate opened the connecting door without bothering to knock. Grant was sitting up in bed, bare-chested, the evening beard still shadowing his chin and what appeared to be a most absorbing book in his hands.

He looked up as she stepped into the room, but he did not let go of the book.

'What are you reading?' Kate demanded.

'Constitutional procedure,' he said so calmly that she wished she was wearing slippers so she could throw one. How dared he be all relaxed when she was a positive tangle of emotions? 'I am attempting to get my head around some of the trickier aspects of the working of Parliament.'

He closed the volume. 'Why? Are you looking for something interesting to read?'

'No. I am attempting to get my head around the trickier aspects of marriage,' Kate retorted. 'I see I may have to consult an encyclopaedia.' The door, when she turned and stalked back into her bedchamber, slammed with the most satisfying bang.

It opened again before she reached the bed. 'Perhaps I might assist,' her husband offered.

Chapter Ten

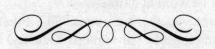

Kate kept walking on shaky legs, climbed into bed and only then turned. Grant was dressed, somewhat sketchily, in a heavy green silk robe, belted loosely at the waist over what appeared to be nothing but bare skin.

She took a strengthening breath down to her diaphragm. 'Assist? You, my lord, are the source of my confusion.'

'Because I did not come to your bed?' He moved to the foot of it, sat with his back against the post, legs stretched out parallel with hers, and studied her face.

Kate made herself lie still and not acknowledge the insidious pressure of his body. One long, bare, elegant foot pressed against her hip bone. She wanted to run a finger along the sharp cords of tendon, the curve of his instep. Instead she said, 'I told myself that Charlie might have had a nightmare, or that you were so tired after your journey that you had fallen asleep or that a crisis might have occurred on the estate. All those were perfectly reasonable excuses for flirting with a wife you had not seen for months and then failing to…to join her. But constitutional procedure? I am not a vain woman, but really, I had not placed myself below turgid reading matter of that sort.'

'I was employing it to take my mind off your presence in the next room. It was not very successful, and if I had been aware of that nightgown, it would have been even less so.' As Grant leaned back, the front of his robe gaped open to reveal the side of his muscular chest, dusted in dark hair.

'Why?' It seemed she was only capable of enough breath for one word at a time.

'I thought you were nervous. Shy. Flustered.' He shrugged and the robe gaped more. Kate held her breath. 'I did not want to pressure you.'

'Of course I was…*am* shy. I do not know you. We have never even kissed, let alone…that. How am I supposed to feel?'

'You are not a virgin,' Grant pointed out. He looked faintly wary, she was glad to see. *So he should be. He is lucky I am not throwing* The Caledonian Bandit *by Miss Smith at his head. It is all it is fit for.*

'Clearly not.' She had her breath back now the robe had ceased its descent. 'But I am not at all experienced. I…I became pregnant very quickly.' She tried to recall what she had told him about her lover. Lying was so alien and so difficult. 'And we could not meet often.'

'I'm not a virgin, either, of course. I don't expect you to hold that against me. But you are not at all experienced?' He seemed to be pleased by that. Men were strange creatures.

'Yes. I mean, no.' It had been lovely to be in Jonathan's arms, to be able to show her feelings for him, of course it had. While it lasted, before disillusion set in. But even at the height of her short-lived infatuation he had never made her feel so agitated, so confused as this did. And it had not been such a wonderful experience that she was desperate to repeat it, so why did she want Grant to shrug off that robe, come to bed and just— 'So, yes, I was apprehensive. I am still. But now I think it would be better to simply get it over with.'

'Get it over with,' Grant repeated, his voice flat. 'Your expectations do not appear to be very high.' His hands had gone to the ties of his robe. Now they stilled.

'I am sure you make love very nicely,' Kate said politely, wishing the soft feather mattress would simply swallow her up. Now she had insulted him. No man was going to take well the suggestion that his lovemaking was anything but magnificent. *Very nicely? Of all the things to say...*

'I have not had any complaints recently.' Grant straightened up from his relaxed slouch against the bedpost.

Recently? From his mistress, I suppose. Does that mean his late wife... Pride made her bite back the question. 'I just thought it would be better to—'

'Get it over with. Yes, I grasp the point that flirting and courting and giving you time to get accustomed to me may not be the best way to go about this and that you really wish it was all over.' He stood up and tugged the knot in the sash free. 'But you do wish me to come to your bed?'

'Yes. Of course. Lights?' It came out as a squeak. The branch of candles was still alight on her dressing table and the little oil lamp by the bed cast a warm, but revealing, glow over the snowy expanse of sheets.

'We have confided that neither of us is a virgin. I think we can cope with the shock of nudity.' Grant shrugged off the robe. He sounded less than happy.

Kate closed her eyes, then, when there was no sound of movement, opened them again. Grant was standing there, hands on lean hips, waiting, she supposed, for her to faint, scream or dive under the covers. She did none of those things, just stared at his admirably flat stomach, then, when she thought her breathing was under control, let her gaze slide lower.

He was not as aroused as he had been in the drawing room when he had been sucking her finger, but then he was probably finding her so infuriating that it was killing his desire. Kate realised suddenly that she did not want that. She wanted Grant to make love to her, here, now and with enthusiasm. His eyebrows lifted as she threw back the covers, reached for the hem of her nightgown and dragged it over her head in one ungainly movement.

When she made herself meet his gaze she found he had not moved, but the green eyes were dark beneath lowered lids and his mouth was curved into a crooked smile that held both approval and a promise.

'Right from when we first met, I knew you had courage,' Grant said as he closed the distance between them. He lay down beside her and, to her enormous relief, pulled the covers up over their bare bodies. She was very aware that the last time she had lain with a man she had not given birth to a child and that this man had once been married to a woman who, if Kate had discovered nothing else about her, had been a beauty.

The warmth of his body as he lay beside her was comforting, but her nerves were jangling and she just wished he would get on with it. 'Have you changed your mind?' she asked.

'No.' Grant turned so he was on his side facing her and moved closer, until the evidence of just how much he had *not* thought better of this was branding itself to her hip. 'I was giving you the opportunity to dive out of the other side of the bed if you had changed yours.'

Afterwards Kate had no idea whether it had been nerves, hysteria or simply her old sense of the ridiculous reasserting itself, but she found herself laughing. 'Like a scene in a French farce,' she managed between gasps of mirth. 'In and out of bedrooms, in and out of bed...'

'You have obviously been watching far more *risqué* farces than I have,' Grant said with a grin, and then, before she had stopped laughing, before the nerves could seize her again, he rolled her on to her back and kissed her.

Kate was open-mouthed on a gasp of laughter and Grant took advantage of her parted lips to take possession, his tongue sliding in to stroke hers, his lips warm and firm and demanding. For a first kiss it was anything but tentative, but nor was it impatiently demanding. *Here I am,* Grant seemed to be saying. *I want you, you want me. Shall we?*

Her body knew the answer, it seemed. Her arms curled around his neck, pulling him closer as her tongue stroked against his. *Yes.* He felt so different, so new. Taller and more muscular than Jonathan, his hands slower, yet more assured, his taste absolutely new and very arousing. Her hands slid over his shoulder and the right one encountered long, rough tracks of scar tissue. Grant shrugged away from her touch and she took the hint, curling her fingers around his neck instead. Then she forgot all about scars.

When Grant broke the kiss, gathering her in against his chest, she rubbed her cheek against the dusting of coarse hair, learning his scent. Citrus from the soap he had washed with, a faint hint of leather, a distant tang of brandy, a musk that was very male, very much him. The scent she remembered from that long desperate night when he had sat close beside her and she had clung to his hand, patterning it with bruises, spiced now with arousal.

'That tickles,' he said, his voice a rumble under her cheek. His hands were beginning to stray, down over her hips, up across her ribs, curving around her buttocks. Kate let her own fingers wander, exploring the flat stomach, dipping into his naval, which made him gasp with laughter, running up and down the thicker line of hair, not daring to follow it all the way.

Grant seemed content to let her roam, but his own hands became more purposeful, stroking up over the curve of her breasts, rubbing across her nipples just enough to make them peak and tingle, then down to brush the curls at the apex of her thighs.

Kate began to move, restless, and found her fingers were gripping Grant's hips. Jonathan had been faster, more urgent, rougher. Did Grant not want her with the same desire?

His lips closed over one aching nipple and she moaned, arching up against him. She felt his lips curve into a smile and then shivered with nerves as he shifted and pressed one hand gently between her thighs, opening her.

'Oh, yes,' he said, the words vibrating against the puckered skin of her nipple, and his teeth nipped gently as he slid one finger into her. Then his thumb found the place that Jonathan had rubbed against so impatiently. Only, Grant was gentle, teasing, and the raw, almost intolerable sensation became one of pulsing sweetness mixed with a desperation that had her squirming against his hand.

'Shh, slowly, slowly,' he murmured against her neck. But she did not want to be slow. She wanted him now, wanted the *more* that she could sense, just out of her reach. Her right hand moved from his hip, stroked down, touched the heated flesh and stroked again until he groaned aloud.

'If you do that—'

'Yes,' Kate urged. 'I want… I don't know. I need…'

Grant's weight was a fresh arousal as their bodies touched down their entire lengths, hot skin against hot skin. He shifted, lifted on his elbows and then, holding her gaze with his, sheathed himself within her.

'Ah…sweet Kate.' He closed his eyes, dropped his head so his forehead rested on hers and held still. She felt the tension vibrating through him as she grasped the broad shoulders, tilted her head so her lips found his. The urgent need to move became a longing for peace as she lay there, so close, so much at one with him. She let her body encompass his, ease around it, holding him within her.

When he began to move it was at first so slow, so gentle, that she hardly realised that her own body was rocking with his, yielding to the slow thrusts, the need building again as she released the hard flesh only to accept him back with a soft gasp of pleasure. The rhythm increased until she was clinging to him, gasping as they rode the gathering, building storm together.

Grant shifted, lifted her against him, and the pressure built until she was curled around him, her ankles locked at the small of his back, striving desperately to catch hold of whatever it was that was tormenting her so deliciously, promising something that was just out of reach. And suddenly she broke apart, heard herself cry out, felt Grant tense and arch over her, and then the world went black, save for the lights in the darkness behind her lids as she let go and flew.

What had just happened? Kate lay in the circle of Grant's arm, her cheek against his chest. His skin was damp, his heartbeat strong, rapid, but slowing as she sensed him drifting into sleep.

What had *happened*? she asked herself again, lying wide-eyed in the flickering candlelight. She hardly knew this man except as the Good Samaritan who had saved her that bleak Christmas. Saved her, saved her child, turned her life upside down. Yes, he was an attractive man, but a man with secrets, a man with barely hidden darkness in his soul.

She had married him, accepted the protection of his name, his status and his wealth. Accepted, too, that she had a duty as his wife to lie with him and perhaps, if she was fortunate, to bear a child of his. *And I had become excited by the thought of him,* she admitted to herself. *Aroused.* Which was good, because it would have been hard to accept lovemaking with a man for whom she could feel no attraction.

But this wonderful physical experience—where had that come from? She had known Jonathan a little, liked him, thought she loved him, considered him a handsome man and had been eager to go to his arms. Yet his passion had left her strangely untouched, unsatisfied, confused. *I talked myself into love with him, didn't I?* Kate told herself. But she did not love this man, either, so what was the difference? *Why did I not burn up in Jonathan's arms as I did with Grant?*

Because Grant is the better lover, of course. So it was all a matter of technique, of arousal, and in her imaginings when she met Jonathan she had told herself the romantic lies that it was all about love.

Kate turned away from the comfort of the warm, strong body beside her to lie on the edge of the bed on cold sheets. *I deserve the chill,* the nagging little voice of her conscience chided. *Wanton.* 'Jonathan,' she whispered. What a fool she had been, how eager to experience love, when really what she had been seeking was this, this physical delight. And as a result of her naivety and Henry's cynical scheming she had been ruined and was now hundreds of miles from home, living a lie.

That had been...incredible. Grant let himself drift in utterly relaxed drowsiness, his body boneless with sensual pleasure. He had never expected it, never thought that Kate would catch alight in his hands, that her body would answer his with that joyful, urgent sensuality.

She curled against him now, warm, soft. Kate, his wife, who did not react to his kisses and caresses as though forcing herself to yield to her duty, but as though she wanted to join him in creating magic. To find a compatible lover was not such a novelty, but to find that, quite by chance, he had married a woman who took and gave with such sweet, almost innocent, eroticism, that was a miracle.

Kate moved, turned away, and he woke fully to see she was lying, her back to him, on the edge of the bed. 'Oh, Jonathan...' He caught the faint whisper and even with that thread of sound, the unhappiness.

Something cold and heavy lodged in his stomach. Disappointment? Jealousy? So, Kate was still in love with Anna's father, still mourning him, which must explain her shyness and confusion earlier. Now she was feeling guilty for enjoying making love with her husband.

Because she had enjoyed it, that was not arrogance on his part—even the most accomplished courtesan could not have feigned that reaction. Grant reached out his hand to touch her shoulder, then drew it back before his fingers reached the curve of exposed skin. Reluctant to intrude, he turned on his side away from Kate's tense body and pulled the covers up over both of them. If he touched her now, she would think it was a demand for more sex. If he tried to console her, then she would know he had heard that whisper. He had no idea what to say to make things any better. At least now he understood her strange mood, the evidence of interest, of arousal, and yet the fear that forced her to ask for his presence in her bed had driven her to want to *get it over with*.

Grant got up, went to snuff the candles, doused the bedside lamp, pretended that he believed Kate was fast asleep as he fought down the dark mood that threatened to grip him. It was unreasonable, to feel…hurt. He was not in love with Kate and she had made no pretence of marrying him for anything other than the protection of his name for her child, so in no sense was he betrayed or deceived. She did not dislike him, he was certain, and she was certainly not repelled by him. It was simply that she had been in love with someone else, someone for ever out of her reach. And now she was making the best of the circumstances. In effect he had married a widow and done so before she'd had a proper chance to mourn.

But how to mend this marriage? He had the summer and the autumn, that was all. Then they must go to London, he would take his seat in the House of Lords and Kate must learn to be a peer's wife, a society hostess.

They could do it as virtual strangers—after all, many marriages functioned like that—but it was not how he wanted his marriage to be and it was not how he wanted the children to grow up, in a household with parents who were distant and cool with each other.

A hideous accident had taken Madeleine before Charlie's life could be blighted by his parents' unhappiness, but Grant was not prepared to risk it again. He could live without a wife's affection, certainly without her love, but somehow, for the sake of the children, he was going to have to make this work and make Kate happy, or, at the very least, content.

Chapter Eleven

When Grant opened his eyes on to the dawn light he found that, against all expectation, he had slept without his dreams being full of heat and flames and he had woken knowing how he was going to deal with his marriage. He would not let Kate guess he had heard her last night, he would not mention her lover, he would apologise for his long absence in London and then he would simply carry on as though everything was normal. He would make love to his wife, he would talk to his wife, he would ask his wife's opinions—and he would keep her so busy out of bed, so well satisfied in it, that she would not have the energy to mope over the man who had fathered Anna.

Beside him Kate stirred. He curled his arm around her and pulled her round to face him. She mumbled sleepily, eyes still closed, hair tousled, but she did not resist. Grant tightened his grip and bent to kiss her. 'Good morning, Lady Allundale.'

If she seems the slightest bit reluctant, then we'll have to talk... But Kate's lips opened under the pressure of his and her arms came up around his neck, her fingers sliding into the hair at his nape in a way that made him shiver with anticipation. It was a start. *Make love to her until she's dizzy,* he told himself, inhaling the scent of warm, sleepy woman. That would be no hardship.

Kate woke, stretched, blushed. She was alone in her bed, but Grant was still a powerful presence in the room. Her body ached pleasurably in the most intimate places, the musk of their lovemaking was heady in the air, the bedclothes were a tangle and, when she turned her head to look at the pillow where his head had rested, there was a single dark brown hair that curled around her finger when she touched it.

So, last night had not been a dream. They had made love twice and Grant had seemed to be very satisfied with the result. She most certainly was—physically satisfied, that was. Mentally she felt happy, guilty, confused and apprehensive. Happy, because to take that much pleasure in one's husband's arms must be a blessing—and the greatest good fortune. But she did not understand how it could be that she could do so. She did not love Grant and he did not love her. Would this last, or had it been a fluke? She wished she could talk to him about it, but how could she?

The conversation would be impossible. *I am overwhelmed by how good it is to make love with you. But why did I not feel like that with the man who took my virginity? Is it always going to be like that? Am I very ignorant and unskilled? Will you become tired of me soon? Am I disgracefully wanton?*

What if he agreed that, yes, she was lacking skill and sophistication, yes, the experience had been nothing out of the ordinary for him? 'I would sink with shame,' she murmured.

'My lady?' Wilson had entered from the dressing room with her usual quiet efficiency. The mistress of the house-hold might have had the most wonderful and confusing night of her life, but the routine continued as usual.

'Nothing.' Kate cast a despairing glance around the bedchamber as the curtains were drawn back and light flooded in, revealing the wrecked bed, the sash of Grant's robe, her own nightgown tossed to the floor. Wilson merely glided around, gathering things up. She folded the sash neatly and set it aside.

'Would you care for breakfast here in your room, my lady? Or will you be taking it in the breakfast parlour?' That was where Kate normally took it, along with Char-lie and his tutor.

'His lordship—'

'His lordship rode out about an hour ago, my lady. I understand from his man that it is his usual habit when in residence here.' There was not the faintest suggestion in her voice that his wife might be expected to know this. But of course, Grant had spoken of it last night and she had forgotten. For the past few months she had felt in control of herself, of this household. Now the arrival of one man meant, it seemed, that she could not even recall last night's conversation.

'I will take breakfast as usual in the parlour, after I have seen Lady Anna.' And Grant had suggested that they meet at ten to discuss practical matters. That had seemed an excellent idea at the time, now she could not imagine producing one coherent word when she had to face him again.

* * *

The harmless meeting still did not seem anything but an ordeal to be survived when she tapped on the study door on the stroke of ten.

'Come in!'

She pushed the door open and Grant came to his feet behind the big desk. 'My dear Kate, you have no need to knock.'

My dear Kate. 'Thank you.' She made herself meet Grant's eyes and smile. She at least felt rather more composed now she was dressed and had made a neat list of things to talk about. It was amazing how clothes made a barrier to hide behind. Last night she had been naked with this man, clawing at his muscled back, revelling in the hard thrust of his body.

Kate took a firm hold on her imagination and forced herself to be practical. This was broad daylight. She was the mistress of the house, coming to discuss harmless domestic matters. She should not feel awkward—after all, up until yesterday she had not needed to knock on any door in this house. Except for the one Grant kept locked. Bluebeard's chamber. Madeleine's rooms. She took the seat on the other side of the expanse of polished oak. 'I have several things I would like to discuss.'

'So do I. An early ride gives me the opportunity for some uninterrupted thinking, so I made some notes.' Grant picked up the sheet of paper from the blotter in front of him, frowned at it, then abruptly screwed it up and tossed it into the hearth. 'And I thought I had worked it all out, a plan for this marriage.'

'A plan? Why do we need a plan?'

'I did not think we did. I thought I would come back

here for the summer, join my wife and family, spend a pleasant few months getting to grips with the estate and then take us all back to London after Christmas when Parliament reconvenes. Then you could enjoy the Season.'

'And that is no longer your intention?' *Please, not London.*

'Certainly it is. And I thought that it would be easy enough to find a way to live together, to coexist and form a household, despite the way our marriage started.'

Her mouth felt dry. Kate willed herself to say calmly, 'So what has changed?' What had gone wrong that he had brooded about on his morning ride?

'Last night—' He broke off, looked out of the window and then back at her as though making the effort to meet her gaze. 'I was not going to say anything. I thought we could coexist, work together and simply put the past behind us. But in the light of day, I wonder if that is the best way forward for us.' He picked up a quill without looking at it and Kate watched as it bent in his grip. When it snapped Grant glanced down as though he was unaware he had been holding it.

'I see.' She could hear that her voice was colourless, but for the life of her she did not know how to inject any warmth into it. 'You must find me inexperienced, lacking in…sophistication.'

'In bed? Oh, hell.' Grant got to his feet, came round the desk and sat on the edge of it, close to her. 'No, that is *not* what I mean. Last night was very pleasurable for me, Kate. Very. But I heard what you whispered afterwards. You are still in love with him, aren't you? You are doing your duty as my wife, but you still love Anna's father.' He said *duty* as though it was a dirty word.

'I… No, I don't.' She realised how important it was

to make Grant understand that. He did not love her, he was not asking or expecting her to love *him*, but he must loathe the thought that he had taken to his bed a woman who was gritting her teeth and doing her duty—even if she discovered she enjoyed it.

If Jonathan had been a groom from the stables, a local farmer, a merchant from King's Lynn—any of those— she could tell the truth, admit he was alive and had re- fused to marry her. But how could she confess that her lover had been an aristocrat who was in all probability known to Grant? The awful thought struck her that they might be friends. What if Jonathan had confided in him? *I'm being blackmailed by some dirty little worm and his two-faced bitch of a sister.*

She had to keep lying even though she hated it. 'I had thought I must still love him, but I am not in love and perhaps I never was.' She stared up at Grant, trying to find the right words, create a safe fiction that would pro- tect her—and him—from the humiliation of the discov- ery that he had married not just another man's cast-off lover, that he had given his name, not to some fatherless baby, but a child with a parent who could very well sup- port it. A man who would probably want to see her and her brother tried for blackmail.

Kate tried to find a story that would satisfy him. 'Jonathan was going to America, and then he would send for me. But when no letter came, when I realised he must be dead, lost at sea, then I was frantic with worry. But not with grief. I was sad, but I wasn't devastated. And I would have been, wouldn't I, if I loved him?'

It was partly true. When Henry told her that Lord Baybrook had refused to marry her she had been fright- ened, but she had been more fearful that Henry would challenge him to a duel rather than shattered by his betrayal. If she had loved him, truly loved him, his refusal to protect her should have broken her heart. And when she had found out Henry's infamy, if she had loved Jonathan she would have gone to him, done everything in her power to put things right. As it was, to her shame, she had done nothing until she realised that Henry was a threat to her unborn child.

'I see.' Grant lifted a hand as though to touch her, then let it fall back to rest on his thigh. The broad hand gripped the buckskin-covered muscle and the movement sparked a dull gleam from the signet on his finger.

She could not raise her gaze from his hand. 'You are shocked.' Of course he was, what did she expect? 'It was scandalous enough that I slept with him, but if I did not even have the excuse of loving him... And now, to find such pleasure with a man I hardly know? You must think I am a wanton.'

'I think I am a lucky man.' Kate jerked up her head and saw Grant's smile—sudden, dazzling. Confusing. Then he bent down, pulled her into his arms and up to perch on the desk beside him. 'You are not wanton, Kate. You are sensual, passionate and desirable. I thought I was marrying a woman with courage and intelligence who would be a good stepmother to Charlie. I rather think I have been more fortunate than I deserve.'

'Desirable?' She was no traditional beauty, she knew that. And childbirth had made changes to her body, even though she had ridden and walked until her figure was trim again and her muscles taut.

'Desirable,' Grant confirmed and bent his head to snatch a kiss from her lips. 'Did you not notice how much pleasure you gave me last night?'

Kate felt ready to sink, but Grant was being frank with her, and very understanding, so she owed it to him to be equally frank. Besides, his arm around her waist, the pressure of his body against hers, gave her courage. 'I thought men didn't mind very much who they were with, once they were actually making love. That any woman would do.'

Beside her Grant made a sudden, suppressed sound. Laughter or outrage? 'Believe me, we mind.' It had been laughter. 'And, no, any woman will not do. Except for the sort of rutting beasts whom I hope you will never encounter.'

'You do not find being married to me as bad as you feared, then?' She let herself lean into him, reading his mood through the feel of the big body more easily than she could interpret his expression.

Grant stiffened, then she felt him relax. *He has decided to carry on being truthful.* 'I foresaw difficulties, and the bedchamber was one of them. I am much reassured.'

'And the others included the fact that you thought me plain, awkward and unfit to be an earl's wife?' Kate prodded.

'As you observed yesterday, neither of us was at their best last Christmas.'

'So you left me here rather than allow London society to see who you'd married.' As soon as she said it, she knew the fact that he had left her here had been a blow to her pride, even as she had been so relieved that he had done so. And it was very poor tactics to make him think she wanted to go there now.

Grant got to his feet and began to pace around the study. 'I could not... It was too soon after the birth for you to travel.' Perhaps he was not prepared for total honesty after all. At least, she pondered, he was careful not to hurt her feelings.

'You could have sent for me when Charlie went to London for the second time.'

'I told myself that Anna was too young, that she was better here in the country air.'

'You told yourself?'

Grant swung round and she saw his expression was rueful, not angry. 'You listen to what is behind the words, don't you? Yes, I *told myself* we were better apart. My reasons for marrying you were good, I knew that. But the risks, the drawbacks, seemed greater the longer I was away from you.'

And you did not come back, you left it months. Why? 'And now?' *This is the rest of our lives, the choice between happiness or, at best, a bitter toleration.*

'Now I wish I had come back sooner, begun to know my wife sooner. London and the Season may be a trifle… sticky, but we have months to build this marriage to be too strong for gossip to break it and for you to become a confident countess.'

It is to be happiness, then. She pushed away the thought of the Season, the threat implicit in those words. 'I have a list,' Kate said and smiled at her husband. For the first time since she had woken up to the enormity of what she had done, the word *husband* did not fill her with apprehension. And London was a long way away, time to worry about that later.

'And what is on this list? An increased dress allowance? I'm to make numerous morning calls with you?' He was teasing her, but his eyes held that familiar reserve. What did he think she would demand?

'I want you to show me the house and the estate

yourself. Tell me about it and what it means to you. Let me see it through your eyes.' That was what she had wanted, for all those months. She needed to understand Abbeywell and its importance to Grant and Charlie, then she would know how to live here, not as a visitor, but as part of it. There were changes she could see that needed making, projects that would improve the life of the tenants, the ease of using the house, the beauty of the estate, but she had no right to make them without consultation and some she would not even suggest if her idea for diverting the stream to make a water garden meant drowning Grant's favourite boyhood hideout or the suggestion for building a communal laundry for the village was simply too expensive. Opening the door to Madeleine's rooms was far down the list of what she could venture upon, even though it was becoming something dangerously like an obsession.

'You want me to show you around? But you have been here for months, running the household. Charlie must have dragged you all over the grounds, Mrs Havers will have covered the domestic side of things.'

'Yes, but it is your *home*, you grew up here. Now I am your wife I need to understand it as you do, if that is possible.' Grant still seemed surprised. 'It will help me understand you, too.'

'If that is what you would like, then of course.' He sounded merely polite, but Kate thought he was pleased. 'You realise that you will be undermining the main complaint of husbands everywhere—*my wife does not understand me*?'

'Is that what you men say to each other in your clubs to justify lurking there, drinking and gaming, or is it what you whisper in the ears of ladies who you hope will take pity on you and share their favours?'

Her relief at the change of mood between them had carried her into dangerous waters. Grant raised one dark brow and was suddenly no longer the amused, slightly flirtatious husband of a moment ago. 'Are you asking me if I am faithful to you?'

Kate slid from her perch on the desk. It was no longer the time and place to sit swinging her feet, behaving like a milkmaid with her swain. She must remember that she was a countess. 'No, I am not asking you that question and I do not think I ever would. But if you are asking if I wonder about other women, then, yes, of course I do. I know that men are not designed to be celibate, even the best of husbands.'

'I keep forgetting that you do not know me,' Grant said and she saw from the set of his mouth that she had managed to insult him again. 'I take marriage seriously. I may not have made vows to you in church, but I will act as though I have. I will be faithful to you and I have been since we wed, if you are wondering about a mistress in London, or even less reputable arrangements.'

'Thank you...' Kate managed. Her sister-in-law, Jane, had confided that no man could be trusted to be faithful, that it was in their very nature to seek out new excitements, new women. She had shrugged in the face of Kate's shocked disbelief and incoherent protests about honour and love matches. Men, Jane maintained, were all tomcats by nature and male honour did not preclude infidelity. Either her sister-in-law was wrong, or Grant was telling her what she wanted to hear. She trusted his honour, she realised. Grant would keep his vows.

'And I am sure I do not need to say that I do not

subscribe to any fashionable tolerance in regards to my wife.' He waved a dismissive hand when she opened her mouth to protest. 'I am sure you will be as faithful as a wife can be, Kate. I am just saying, for the record, that I will call out any man who lays a finger on you—and do my damnedest to kill him. And if your Jonathan had abandoned you and not drowned, then I would go after him and kill him, too.'

They stared at each other for a long moment, then Kate said, slowly, 'You may trust me with your honour and mine and I trust you in the same way.' She would never betray him with another man—but the pit was gaping at her feet. She had lied to him, she continued to lie to him, and if he realised that her lover was alive and was being blackmailed by her brother, she did not know what he would do.

'Enough of this serious stuff.' Grant's sudden grin caught her off balance as it had done every time he had surprised her with it. 'What is the first place you want to explore with me?'

'The water garden.'

'We do not have a water garden,' Grant pointed out.

'I know. I think we should, don't you?' *He need never find out.* She forced herself to smile and found it was real. Tomorrow might never come, Christmas was a long way off and, for now, they were happy.

Chapter Twelve

Grant came with her to visit Anna, who delighted him by smiling and gurgling and gripping his fingers. He picked her up, despite the nursemaid's warnings about babies who had recently been fed, and tossed her up to make her laugh.

'Never mind, my lord,' Jeannie said consolingly, ten seconds later. 'I'm sure it will sponge off.'

By the time Kate had found her bonnet and cloak, Grant had surrendered his milky coat to a silently disapproving valet and changed to a battered old shooting jacket and well-worn boots. 'I have a suspicion that water gardens mean bogs,' he said as he joined her on the steps down to the rear garden. 'At least the sun is shining.'

Kate led the way across the formal parterre to the lower level where a lawn, uneven and rank despite the gardeners' best efforts with scythe and roller, sloped away from the woods.

'The view from the parterre in this direction is dull and this lawn leads nowhere except to that boggy patch just inside the woodland. See, where all the alders are, and those rushes, beyond the bank?'

'There's a spring there. I remember that it used to be a good place to find frogs. I think Grandfather had the bank thrown up to keep the water from the lawn.' Grant strode towards the woodland, then stopped as his foot sank into mud. 'And not very effectively, by the looks of it!'

'We can skirt round.' Kate was already leading the way and scrambled up the bank. 'I thought if the bank was breached and the spring water channelled, then it would come out here. We could excavate a chain of ponds across this lawned area and puddle the bottoms.'

Grant had walked further along the top of the bank, but he turned to look back at her. 'And what do you know about puddling bottoms, Lady Allundale?'

'I read about it in a book I ordered on making artificial water features. You need a great deal of stiff clay, then it is spread across the bottom of the hollow and trampled down by lots of men in stout boots.'

'Lots of men?' Grant was frowning now.

'I thought it would be valuable employment for the local people. But if you think it would be too costly, of course I understand.' How foolish to allow her imagination to run away with her when she had no idea how far Grant's resources would stretch. He had this estate and a London house to maintain, a son to educate and now a wife and daughter.

'It sounds like an excellent idea. I was simply disappointed that when you said *we*, you meant a gang of hefty labourers. I had assumed you and I would be puddling in the mud.'

'Us?'

'Mmm.' Grant seemed oblivious to her gasp of scandalised laughter as he looked around the boggy patch and then further into the woods to where a shaft of sunlight lit up one of Kate's favourite places, a glade of soft grass spangled with wild flowers. 'I like the idea of getting very wet and very muddy with you. I appreciate your eye for landscape as well, my dear. What do you make of that sunlit patch through there?'

'It is lovely and usually quite dry underfoot because it is on a slight slope. I would not like to damage it if we do make the water garden.'

'It merits further inspection.' Grant held out his right hand. 'Let me help you around the edge of the mire.' Intrigued, Kate followed. 'How very wise of you to bring a cloak,' he observed as he turned to face her and she caught her breath at the wicked intent in his expression.

'Why?' Although she could already guess and his fingers were at the ties at her neck.

'Because we do not want grass stains on the back of that charming walking dress, do we?'

'Grant! In the open? What if someone sees us?'

'Who?' He looked up from spreading the cloak on the grass. 'No one can see this spot from the house—I used to hide here often enough as a boy.'

'I don't know! Gardeners, gamekeepers. Poachers,' she added wildly as her husband tossed aside his coat and began to untie his neckcloth.

'The gardeners are scything the front lawns. The gamekeepers are chasing the poachers over there.' Grant knelt down and gestured vaguely to the east. 'I am tired of being serious and sensible. I am tired of duty. I want to be utterly frivolous with my wife.' He held out his hand. 'Do you want to be frivolous with your husband?' he asked as his fingers went to the fastenings of his falls.

* * *

An hour later Kate flopped back on to her crumpled cloak beside the long, naked body of her husband as he sprawled face down, half on and half off the cloak.

'That,' he observed without moving, 'was excellently frivolous.'

'I would never have thought it.' Kate snuggled against Grant's flank, glad of the heat of his skin. The breeze was cool through the trees, despite the sun almost reaching its height. 'If I had been asked to describe you, *frivolous* would be one of the last words I would have thought of.'

'I used to be wild, a rakehell in training, my grandfather always said.' Grant rolled over on to his back. 'When I was at university with Gabe and Alex and Cris they called us the Four Disgraces. That's why he did not oppose my attending medical school. He said a few years in cold, dour Edinburgh delving into cadavers would sober me up better than anything short of a spell in the army and with less chance of him losing his heir.'

'Did it sober you?' Kate buried the chilly tip of her nose in the angle of his neck and shoulder and smiled as he muttered in protest. He stopped complaining when she slid her hand, palm down, across the flat planes of his chest and began to play with the curls of hair.

'Coming home and finding my grandfather recovering from a heart seizure did that. I was needed here and I couldn't expect him to carry the burden of the estate and all its business while I pursued an interest that could only ever be that—an interest.'

She sat up, but stayed close to his warmth as she admired the lean, masculine beauty of the body lying beside her. The only flaws were the raking scars from his right shoulder, disappearing down to his shoulder blade. That was what she had felt the first time they had lain together.

Kate leaned over and touched them. 'You said you were in the army for a while. When was that?' She could feel him bracing himself against the desire to shrug her hand away.

'I volunteered in '15, when Bonaparte escaped from Elba. I was at Waterloo and escaped with my life and a healthy horror of warfare.'

'So you were wounded and these are battle scars?'

'No.'

She stared at them. There was something familiar about them, the way the flesh had been damaged, the way the weapon had raked through the flesh. Then she remembered Jason Smith, who had been Henry's groom years ago. He would get drunk and pick fights and he was, from all the rumours, a nasty dirty fighter when he'd taken drink. Then one evening he had come staggering into the kitchen, pouring blood, and Kate had helped the housekeeper dress the wounds. Long, raking parallel cuts like these, the result of a slashing blow from a broken bottle. Surely Grant was not the kind of man who got involved in barroom brawls? But that flat negative had been a clear warning, and if he had wanted to explain the scars, then he would.

'And then you married?' she asked as though her questions had not interrupted the story of his life.

'Yes.' There was no change in Grant's tone, but he sat up and reached for his clothes. The affirmative had been as flat as the negative and just as clear a warning. *No trespassing.* 'You are getting chilled, best to get dressed before the gardeners decide to scythe the back lawns, as well.'

He helped Kate with laces and pins, exhibiting the facility with feminine garments that she had noticed back in the bothy. If she had felt a little more confident, she might have twitted him gently on the subject, but she had strayed far enough into dangerous waters with that question about his first marriage.

'We need a summer house, you know.' Grant sat on a tree stump to pull on his boots. He pointed at a flat area in the centre of the clearing. 'If we built one there, it would have a view down to your new water gardens.' He stood and stamped his feet firmly into the battered old boots. 'Then we can be frivolous whatever the weather and with less chance of scandalising our innocent staff and the not-so-innocent poachers.'

'Classical or rustic?' Kate laced her half-boots, determined to be as sophisticated about the prospect of future al fresco lovemaking as Grant was. The prospect was delicious in itself, but most of all she treasured the fact that he was becoming so relaxed with her. Surely, soon, the scars from his unhappy first marriage would fade?

'Classical,' Grant said. 'A little temple in the woods. It will have a fireplace and an inner chamber we can lock and a room for picnics on warm rainy days.'

They strolled back up to the parterre, hand in hand, bickering gently about how a chimney could be incorporated into a classical temple, and were met by Charlie, his tutor at his heels.

'There you are, Papa! Have you fallen off your horse? Your hair is on end and your hat has gone. And, Maman, did you know your cloak is inside out?'

'Lord Brooke, we have discussed the fact that a gentleman does not pass personal comments on the appearance of others, have we not?' Mr Gough was so straight-faced that Kate was certain he had a very good idea of just what his employers had been doing.

Charlie grimaced at the formal address, the signal that he was in the wrong. 'I am sorry, Maman, Papa. Only, I was looking for you. The post has come and there are letters with Uncle Alex's seal on, and Uncle Cris's and a very splodgy one that must be from Uncle Gabriel, I think, because he told me he had lost his signet ring whilst dicing with a German count and—'

Mr Gough cast up his gaze as though in search of heavenly assistance. 'Lord Brooke, we will return to the schoolroom and you will translate *I must not speculate on other people's business* into Latin and then write it out twenty times in a fair hand.'

'Ouch,' Grant remarked when his son had departed with the air of a condemned man heading for the gallows. 'I am not certain I could translate that with any elegance these days.' He ran a hand through his tousled hair, twitched off Kate's cloak, shook it out, draped it over his arm and opened the door for her. 'Those letters, I hope, are the replies to my invitations to our first house party.'

Kate was conscious that he was watching her for a reaction. Did he fear she would be unable to manage a small, informal gathering, or was it his guests' reactions to her that gave him more concern? No man would want his closest friends to think he had made a poor marriage, that his wife was not good enough for him.

I am *good enough,* she told herself. *Good enough for him and for his friends. And I can manage a country house party more easily than he thinks.* The thought of confounding Grant with her ability gave her an inner glow of unworthy satisfaction, even if it was only a small thing. Henry liked to entertain his friends and his wife,

Jane, uncomfortable with country gentlemen and their hearty manners and unsophisticated pleasures, had been more than happy to unload the burden of organisation on to Kate.

If truth be told, it was the thought of female guests that gave her the most apprehension. Men, if they were comfortable, well fed and provided with plenty of sport, tended to be uncritical of their hostess. Ladies, on the other hand, were not. Polite, charming—and if they sensed a weakness, as relentless as a flock of pigeons pecking away at a pile of wheat grains until there was nothing left but the husks.

'Let's hurry and open them,' she said and was through the doorway into the shadowed hall with, surely, enough enthusiasm to convince Grant that she was not nervous in the slightest.

'Alex and his wife can come,' he said, studying the first letter. He opened the others. 'So can Cris and Gabriel. But they both say they will not be accompanied by their sisters. Gabe, in language I will not use to my respectable wife, assures me he will inflict neither his latest *chère amie* upon us, nor a respectable fiancée—which it is unimaginable that he will ever have, by the way—and certainly not his unmarried sister.' Grant folded the sheet with its sprawling black handwriting and grimaced. 'Now I come to think about my last encounter with her, that is probably a good thing. She can talk the hind leg off a donkey and needs diluting with a very large pool of other guests. Cris merely thanks me most properly for the suggestion, but tells me that he will be unaccompanied, as his sister is newly betrothed and will be staying with her future in-laws.'

Grant handed her that letter and Kate scanned the

elegantly written page. 'He sounds somewhat cool,' she ventured. 'Is it the prospect of meeting me?'

'He always sounds cool, although this does seem more detached than usual.' Grant took the letter back and read it again. 'It isn't us, it is him. Something's wrong, I think. He's been in Russia or Denmark or somewhere in that direction, doing a vaguely diplomatic job for the Foreign Office.'

'Not as an ambassador?'

'No, far more undefined than that.' Grant looked thoughtful and Kate did not probe. If his friend was engaged in espionage, he certainly would not want to speak of it. The poor man probably needed some peace and quiet and homely comforts after the stress of a foreign court.

'I suggested May 20 and they all say they can make that. Is it convenient for you?'

Two weeks? 'Certainly,' Kate said with a sense of fizzing excitement. Her first house party as mistress of Abbeywell and the chance to understand Grant much better through his friends. She could hardly wait. 'That will be no problem at all.'

The house was quiet, finally. Grant leaned back against the door of his bedroom and yawned. Charlie, still overexcited from the day before at the prospect of all his favourite honorary uncles arriving at the same time, had been difficult to get to bed. Anna, with the knack of small children for knowing when adults were tired and distracted, decided to wail endlessly and Kate had been absent-minded throughout dinner. And, to put the cap on a wearisome evening, she had indicated in an embarrassed murmur that it would not be a good time for him to visit her bedchamber.

So now he was feeling selfish for feeling disappointed when she was obviously self-conscious and uncomfortable. The decanters had been set out and he went to pour himself out a finger of brandy, shifting his shoulders under the heavy silk of his robe in an effort to ease the ache in the right one, which always complained when the weather turned cold and damp.

He'd been short with Kate yesterday when she had asked a perfectly reasonable question about the scars. On an impulse he tossed back the brandy and strode to the door, stopping only to remove the key from its hiding place in the indented base of a Japanese bronze figure and to pick up a three-branch candlestick.

It was over a year since he had been in the empty suite. The door swung open with a faint creak and the cold, stale air hardly moved the candle flames. He could still smell burning, he was convinced, even though all the fabrics and carpets had been torn out and destroyed, the walls and floor scrubbed. The seat of the fire was obvious from the heavy charring of the floorboards in front of the hearth and near the door where the edge of the rug had been was a dark patch. His blood.

He made himself walk further into the room, telling himself that he could not hear the crackle of the fire, the screams, the child's wailing cries. He could not smell the smoke, the burning brandy... But they were there, in his head, the memories mixed with the sounds and stench of the battlefield, the screams of the dying, and afterwards, those hideous pyres...

Then he was through into the bedchamber. It was still furnished, for the door had been closed that night and the smoke and flame had not penetrated here. It smelt of dust and old polish and faintly, unmistakably, there was the scent of jasmine in the air.

There were sounds here, too. A woman crying. Screaming. Sobs and reproaches. Pain and grief. To pull himself back into the present left him sick, but he made himself walk around the room checking coldly, methodically, for damage, signs of damp, of mice or mould. These chambers were spaces, that was all. They had no memory, no life of their own. The phantom sounds and smells were all in his head and he could overcome them, drive them out with the laughter of a son who was healthy and happy, the scent of a woman who found joy in his lovemaking, the smiles of a baby who reached out when she saw him. He had experienced no nightmares since he had returned to Abbeywell—he was healing, even if his lacerated shoulder never would.

He walked back, locked the door behind him, returned to his room. Yes, he could sleep now.

Chapter Thirteen

Kate woke, blinking at the darkness. Something had roused her. A shout? All was quiet, but instinct made her get up and tiptoe to the dressing room door, which stood ajar. Anna was fast asleep and there was no sound from Jeannie, who slept in a small room just along the corridor.

It must have been an owl, or a vixen's strange cry. Then she heard it again, distinctly now, unmistakably a human voice.

'Charlie!' It was Grant and she ran to the connecting door, threw it open expecting to find some emergency—a sick child, sleepwalking, an accident—her mind ran through the possibilities. But the room was dark and still, except for the sound of muttering and movement from the bed.

'Grant?' There was no reply. A cold finger of unease moved down her spine. Kate backed away into her own chamber, found by touch the candle and tinderbox by the bed and, hands shaking, struck a light. 'Grant?' This time she could see him naked on the bed, the sheets a tangle around his legs, trapping him. He seemed to be trying to drag himself towards the edge of the bed.

'Charlie. I'm coming. Charlie…' He was deep in the throes of a nightmare.

Kate bent over him, put her arms around his shoulders and tried to make him lie down, but he was too strong for her. 'We have Charlie. He is safe, quite safe,' she murmured, then repeated it loudly, but it did nothing to calm him.

Then something in the tension of Grant's body changed. 'Dream,' he muttered. 'No.'

He knew he was in a nightmare, Kate realised, and he was fighting against it, forcing it back with the strength of his mind as much as his body. She held on tightly, pulling the rigid body against hers, stroking down his back. When she touched the scarred shoulder she felt him flinch as though the wounds were raw.

With a heave Grant threw off her restraining hands, fell back against the pillows. 'Couldn't help her,' he muttered. 'Charlie…'

'He is here. You saved him. Charlie is safe.'

'I know,' he answered her rationally, irritably, even though he was asleep. 'Damned dreams…' And then he was still, relaxed, deeply asleep.

Shaken, Kate backed away from the bed, the candle flame wavering. She put up a hand to shield it and realised it was her own panting breath that made it move. Grant had been dreaming about the fire that killed his wife, she was certain. Dr Meldreth had said something about Grant being injured during the fire, but the only scars she could see on his body were the slashes on his shoulder and they were not burns. How could a fire cause those? But a weapon could, a broken bottle could.

None of it made sense. Kate stood watching her sleeping husband, then, once she was certain he was deeply unconscious, she pulled the covers up over him. Should she stay? No, she decided, staring down at his profile, stark against the white of the pillows. He had dragged himself out of that nightmare by sheer willpower, as far as she could tell. He would hate to know she had been watching his struggles against it.

But what had triggered it? she wondered as she turned away. She had seen no sign of bad dreams when they had slept together. The candlelight caught a glint of something metallic on the little table by the door and, curious, she went to see what it was. A key. A door key very much in the style of those for all of the bedchambers on this floor. It was in her hand before she realised that she had moved to pick it up. It was not the key to this room, that was protruding from the lock right in front of her, Charlie's room was never locked, in case of accidents. Hers, too, was unlocked.

Madeleine's suite. It had to be. Kate hesitated for perhaps ten seconds. Grant did not want her, or anyone, in those rooms. But whatever had happened there had scarred him, mentally and perhaps physically. It was giving him nightmares and the experience had been so bad he could not tolerate any mention of it. How could she help him if she did not understand?

The door opened with a faint creak like the protest of her conscience, but Kate kept going. This was the lesser of two evils and Grant need never know she had been in the rooms, she told herself.

The forbidden door opened easily and she stepped on to bare boards. The air was cold and dry and, stripped of its furniture, the room seemed enormous and overscale, like something from a fairy tale. *Bluebeard's chamber.* The light of the single candle that she held created deep pools of shadow in the corners, the edges swaying as her hand trembled. Something dark spilled like a puddle in front of the hearth and for a moment Kate thought it was a body fallen there, draped in a black velvet cloak.

'Nonsense,' she muttered and shook off the superstitious dread. 'Too many Gothic novels, you will be seeing ghosts next.' Even so, it took resolution to walk towards the pool of blackness. She stopped, her toes at the edge, and saw that the boards at her feet were charred by the heat of an intense fire. Instinctively she stepped back, repelled by the thought of her bare skin touching the blackness. There was another patch of darkness by the door and she made herself walk to that. There was no charring here, the boards were intact, although scrubbed until the grain showed. She had the cold certainty that this was blood, but there was no way of telling in the dim light.

The bedchamber door was closed. It yielded to her cautious push and Kate stepped into Madeleine Rivers's most intimate world. The room was feminine, exquisite in every detail, decorated in shades of blue with touches of silver, tarnished now, but still catching the light from the candle flame.

The dressing table held its array of bottles and jars, a silver-backed hairbrush and hand mirror. There was just the lightest film of dust, so whatever Grimswade said, one of the servants was coming in to keep the rooms clean. Then Kate saw a single line, fresh-traced through the dust. She held the candle flame close. It looked like the mark of a fingertip that had come close to one perfume flask. *Essence de Jasmine.*

There was a large mirror on a stand and Kate looked up to see herself reflected in it—pale-faced, pretty enough, dressed for warmth and comfort in a sensible nightgown, bare feet showing beneath the hem. The woman whose room this was would have scorned to look like this, she sensed. She glanced at the dressing room door, but did not try to open it. The thought of prying into the other woman's clothes was abhorrent.

Slowly, forcing herself not to run, Kate closed the door, crossed the sitting room and let herself out into the familiar world again. She turned the key in the lock and tiptoed back to Grant's bedchamber, laid the key down where she had found it and retreated to her own room.

What had that taught her? *Nothing,* she concluded as she climbed into bed and pulled the covers up tight to her chin, although the room was not cold. There were marks of a fire, possibly of blood. But she had known that already. She had intruded into Grant's private nightmare, against his wishes, and she had discovered nothing that might help.

Let that be a lesson to you, she would have said to Charlie if she had caught him prying. Now she had a guilty conscience, a definite case of the shivers and another secret to keep from Grant.

May 20—Abbeywell Grange

Grant strolled through the rooms of his home and shook his head with bemused pleasure. Kate had seemed understandably nervous when he had first come home, not just of him, but at the thought of making any changes to the house. With the confirmation of the house party all that reserve seemed to have been swept away, although he worried that she was overdoing things. It was almost as though she had flung herself into the preparations as a way of burying her nerves.

After he had visited Madeleine's rooms the nightmare had resulted in the inevitable headache and bad dreams every night afterwards. He fought both nightmares and the pain as he always had, but the relief when Kate shyly asked him back to her bed was acute. Somehow making love to his wife kept the demons at bay and he had not dreamed again.

But Kate was working too hard and he worried about that. When he waylaid her in the corridor and swept her into either his or her bedchamber, lists and note tablets would scatter along with her stockings and petticoats as he undressed her. Whichever room he walked into appeared to have a member of staff—some of them unfamiliar to him—working away. The billiard table was brushed to a perfect nap, while new blocks of chalk stood aligned under the racks of cues. His study acquired three more comfortable leather armchairs.

Grimswade was found in solemn consultation with his mistress on the correct number of packs of cards to order and brand-new umbrellas were set in stands by all the outer doors, along with every walking stick the house could muster. When Grant caught his wife emerging from the backstairs and kissed her, she tasted of sugar and cinnamon, but when he began to kiss with more enthusiasm, and the intention of licking it all off, she batted him away and scurried off muttering, 'New recipes!'

Charlie entertained them before his bedtime every evening with an entire repertoire of poems and recitations, Anna acquired at least half a dozen new dresses and the small drawing room was declared out of bounds to men as it was transformed into a ladies' boudoir.

'Grant! Oh, there you are.' Kate hurried in, seized his

hand and began to pull him towards the door. 'I need you to come upstairs immediately.'

'An admirable idea,' he agreed, allowing himself to be steered towards the stairs. 'But have we time? I expect they will begin arriving in about an hour or so, and your hair looks dashed complicated to fix if it comes down.' As it would, if what he had in mind—

'*Grant.* I want you to look at the guest bedchambers, not to…well, not to do anything else.'

He loved the way he could make her blush, while at the same time she threw herself into whatever amorous idea he had in the most enthusiastic way. And she was beginning to have ideas of her own. Grant paused on the landing, happily recalling the uses to which a set of library steps could be put, and was ruthlessly tugged to the first set of rooms.

'Is this all right for Lord Avenmore? He is the one I am most worried about. Lord and Lady Weybourn are newlyweds, so I thought what we would like and arranged their suite accordingly.' That produced an intriguing pink glow over her cheeks. Grant thought again how satisfying it was that he could make Kate blush. It made him think about making love to her…

'Grant, are you attending?'

'Yes, my dear.' It was his best husbandly voice and it usually worked whenever he had lost track of the conversation in erotic daydreams.

Kate gave him a decidedly old-fashioned look. 'And by the sound of it, Lord Edenbridge values comfort and informality, so his rooms were easy. But Lord Avenmore…'

Grant surveyed the room. It had always been an elegant chamber, but now it was decidedly masculine, with the landscapes replaced with large architectural engravings and all the Dresden china swept away to be replaced by Chinese blue-and-white export porcelain. It would suit Cris de Feaux's austere tastes very well and he said so.

'I didn't know what to do about books, so I have selected a mixture for all of the rooms. But I think we should consider redecorating some more suites very soon, because the rooms I have allocated to Lord Edenbridge are really almost shabby, and if you want to entertain larger parties in the future, it will be difficult. There are your grandfather's rooms, of course—but I hardly like to suggest making changes there if you would find that upsetting.'

'No, you are quite right. They would turn into three respectable guest rooms. I'll have the personal items moved to my rooms and the study. The study and the library are the places that remind me most of him anyway. I have no sentimental attachments to the bedroom suite.'

He was rewarded by a warm smile and glanced at the clock on the overmantel. Perhaps there was just time.

'And then there is the suite next to yours,' Kate said with the air of a woman steeling herself. 'The one with the locked door.'

'No!' He swung round away from her, his vision blurred by the smoke, his ears full of the obscene crackling laughter of the fire, the screams…the screams and the air full of the smell of brandy and burning and the pain in his shoulder and head so bad he could not focus, could not make that hellish decision…

'I realise there are sentimental reasons why it would be difficult, but it is a large suite, and if we were thoughtful with the decoration and furnishing, there need be nothing to remind you,' Kate continued. The sensible, slightly nervous voice flowed on, the remarks perfectly reasonable. Grant hauled himself back from the edge of his waking nightmare and made himself stand still, listen to her.

'How do you know it is a large suite? Have you been in there? I told the servants that the door was never to be opened except for a monthly cleaning.'

'I know.' He realised that Kate was standing her ground with an effort of will, that he was probably frightening her. He made himself step back, widening the space between them, and saw her make the effort to relax her hands from their tight grip on her skirts. 'But…I assumed, from the space I have been given for my suite. And it is obvious the areas that those rooms occupy, one only has to look at the adjoining rooms.'

'No,' Grant said. 'No, it is not obvious.' The angle of the external walls was deceptive at that point, the arrangement of the inner rooms, confusing.

Kate was not blushing now. She was pale and stammering, the picture of guilt. She made no attempt to deny that she had entered the suite. 'But…sooner or later Charlie is going to wonder why that door is locked. What will you tell him? Do you want to make it into some s-secret chamber of horrors to give him nightmares?' Kate was regaining her confidence now, he saw, driven by the force of her argument. She took two rapid steps forward, caught his hands in hers. 'Grant—'

'That room *is* a chamber of horrors,' he said between lips that seemed frozen. 'And it gives *me* nightmares. You've been in there, I don't know how, but you have been, against my expressed wishes. Now, do you want to probe any more? Do you want to dig out secrets that don't concern you, pry into my feelings and thoughts? Because the answer will be *no*, I tell you now.' He flung his hands apart, dislodging hers. 'You had no right, *have*—'

Grant broke off at the sound of a very heavy footstep outside the door. As he turned, Grimswade appeared in the opening. Somehow he bit back the demand that the butler go to the devil. 'Yes?'

'A carriage is approaching, my lord. I believe it is Lord Weybourn's conveyance.'

'Thank you. We will be down directly.' He followed Grimswade along the corridor without turning to see if Kate was following him, without a word to her. He was dimly aware, through the crashing headache that had descended as he lost his temper, that he should go back, apologise to her. Try to forgive her, if he could, for that intrusion. He kept going, down the curves of the front stairs, across the marble floor, the percussion of his boot heels on the stone like daggers stabbing behind his eyes.

Footmen flung back the double doors as he approached and sunlight streamed in, blinding him. Instinct took him out on to the top step, the swirling lights that distorted his vision revealing the shape of the approaching carriage like an image that had been torn across and reassembled out of true.

He was conscious of a presence at his side, of Kate's delicate scent. She made no move to touch him. Then the shape that was the carriage stopped. Footmen hurried down the steps, Grant fixed a smile of welcome on his lips. His vision was failing as the circle of broken, dancing lights enclosing nothing but blackness moved inexorably outwards. In a moment he would be blind.

'Grant! Are we the first?' It was Alex.

'Yes, you are. Welcome.' A figure in green wavered beside Alex and he broadened the smile, painfully. 'Tess, you are more than welcome to Abbeywell. Come and meet my wife.'

Then they were up the steps and beside them. He managed not to retch at the waft of rose scent as Tess stood on tiptoe to kiss his cheek. Alex gripped his hand and, turning, tucked it through his own. 'Migraine?' he murmured. Then he raised his voice. 'And this must be Lady Allundale, you clever devil, Grant. Ma'am, I am Alex Tempest and this is my wife, Tess. I am delighted to meet you at last.'

Alex swung round, taking Grant with him to stroll into the hall. 'Ladies, you will excuse us, but I must be off to consult Grant's valet this minute—I have a hideously uncomfortable nail working through the sole of these new boots.'

Grant found himself climbing the stairs and managed to get out, 'What the blazes—'

'You are blind with a migraine, Lady Allundale is as white as a sheet and Grimswade looks as though he has sat on a poker. What's wrong? No, don't try to talk. Same room as usual?'

Alex steered Grant into his bedchamber, pushed him on to the bed, pulled off his boots. 'Lie down, I'll send your valet in.'

Grant tried to sit up and was ruthlessly shoved back. 'I can't… You are guests, Cris and Gabe will be arriving…'

'We're friends, not guests. Leave it to me.' There was a rattle of curtain rings, the light against his eyelids was reduced. Then silence, broken only by the soft-footed entrance of Griffin, who pressed a glass into Grant's hand.

'Willow-bark powder, my lord.'

He gulped it down, wincing at the bitter taste, lay back

and tried to make his mind blank, relax his tense muscles. As soon as he could see, he would have to go downstairs and, somehow, come to terms with Kate.

Chapter Fourteen

'Here they are.' Lady Weybourn turned to the door. 'Or, rather, here is mine. Where is Grant, Alex? I didn't think he looked well.'

'Migraine.' Alex Tempest strolled in to the drawing room and smiled reassuringly at Kate. 'Haven't seen him blind with one for a while. I've sent his valet to him,' he added as Kate jumped to her feet with a murmur of distress. 'He'll be fine as long as he's quiet. There's nothing to be done.'

With him on his feet the only courteous thing to do was sit down. Griffin would send for her if she was needed and probably the last thing Grant wanted was his unsatisfactory wife fussing over him. She sat and Alex dropped his elegant length into a chair. 'He is subject to migraines? I did not know.' It was his anger at discovering her trespass into the forbidden rooms that had triggered it. And Lord Weybourn said he was *blind* with it.

'Only occasionally. It is very stressful situations when he can't act to resolve things, that's what usually sets them off. If he can act and *do* something, then Grant copes with anything.' Alex Tempest smiled his lazy, reassuring smile

again. 'And he's a stubborn so-and-so. He'll be on his feet
the minute he can see clearly, even if his head still hurts.
I don't expect that blow he got in New Town helped any.'

'No, probably not.' She wrenched her thoughts away
from guilt and worry and focused on her guests. 'Now,
would you like to take some refreshment, or shall I show
you to your rooms first?'

'Some tea would be very welcome.' Lady Weybourn
unpinned her hat and set it aside, then peeled off her
gloves as Kate rang for Grimswade.

'Tea and some food, Grimswade. Do you know where
Lord Brooke has got to?'

'I do not, I regret to say, my lady. However, I venture
to suggest that the production of cake will cause him to
appear.'

'Uncle Alex!' Charlie erupted into the room and leapt
at Lord Weybourn, who caught him, stood up and held
him upside down by his heels.

'Good afternoon, Lord Brooke.'

His wife rolled her eyes at Kate. 'Do put him down,
darling. He'll be sick.'

Eventually order was restored, Charlie was silenced
by the threat of the withdrawal of cake and Kate once
more embarked on making polite conversation with these
two very informal strangers.

'You have known Grant for a long time, Lord Weybourn?'

'Alex, please. Yes, since university, along with Cris
de Feaux and Gabriel Stone. We were known as the Four
Disgraces, but I assure you we are sober and responsible now.'

Lady Weybourn snorted inelegantly. 'Nonsense, darling. You are merely better at hiding the insobriety and

irresponsibility these days.' She turned to Kate. 'I think we are very brave, taking on two of them. We must see what we can do about finding nice civilising wives for the others, don't you think, Lady Allundale?'

'Oh, Kate, please. I don't know the others, so I really can't say.' The thought of Grant being a Disgrace would be funny if she wasn't feeling so apprehensive and guilty.

'These days we think of ourselves more as the Four Elementals, because of our names,' Alex continued, ignoring a whisper of, *And because that's the name of the inn in Ghent they meet up in*, from Tess. 'Tempest—wind, de Feaux—fire, Stone—earth, and Rivers—'

'Water,' Kate finished, relaxing a little. It was almost impossible not to, around these two. They would be good for Grant, she knew it.

'Two more carriages are approaching, my lady.'

'Thank you, Grimswade. We had better have more tea and cake brought in.'

'I'll come out with you,' Alex offered as she stood up with a murmur of apology. 'You can't be expected to greet those two by yourself.'

'They are quite safe really.' Tess walked beside her to the front door. 'At least, *mostly* safe. Gabriel is unsettling and Cris is terrifying, but just pretend you don't notice.' She waved enthusiastically as the two coaches, both driving at breakneck speed, came to a crashing halt.

Pretend I don't notice? How? Kate waited with butterflies somersaulting below her diaphragm as a footman opened one door and the other was thrown wide. The man who climbed languidly down with a nod to the footman was, Kate realised, probably the most handsome man she had ever seen. He was also glacially blond, blue-eyed and dangerously composed. Why dangerous?

'That's Crispin de Feaux?' she whispered to Tess.

'Indeed it is,' the other woman whispered back. 'I always think of archangels and flaming swords.'

He strode up the steps and bowed over the hand that Kate, expecting to shake hands, had extended. 'Lady Allundale, I am delighted to meet you at last.'

'Kate, allow me to introduce the Marquess of Avenmore,' Alex drawled. 'Cris, Lady Allundale. Grant's flat on his back with a migraine.'

'The prospect of losing to me at cards again, I assume.' The dark, loose-limbed man one step below the marquess needed a shave, a haircut, and had obviously chosen his expensive clothing for comfort. He smiled at Kate, a wolfish baring of his teeth that had her stiffening her spine before she offered her hand.

'Edenbridge, at your service.' He took her hand and neither kissed nor shook it. 'Clever, clever, Grant,' he remarked, closing his long fingers possessively around hers.

Oh, yes, this is definitely the unsettling one. 'Do come in.' Kate tried to look sophisticated, as though dark-eyed men with feral smiles murmured ambiguous compliments to her every day. He released her hand and she even managed not to snatch it back and hide it behind her back. 'There are refreshments in the drawing room, unless either of you would like to be shown to your rooms first?'

They all voted for refreshments, trooping after her into the drawing room, as much at home as she was. *More so,* she thought, nerves jangling as she worried about Grant, fretted about her marriage, restrained Charlie from causing havoc and somehow made conversation. She was certain it was thoroughly banal and that four people who obviously knew each other well would much prefer to be talking amongst themselves rather than answering her polite enquiries about their journeys.

And upstairs her husband, whom she had tried to deceive, was lying blinded by pain and she could do nothing to help him.

'Do have another ginger biscuit, Lord Avenmore. Such fortunate weather for your journey, was it not?'

Grant lay with hard-learned patience and watched the plaster details of the ceiling over his bed gradually come into focus. His head still felt as though it was gripped in a vice and pain stabbed behind his eyes, but the worst was over. The attacks were always short and savage and it took a while before bright light and loud noises were tolerable.

Normally he would sleep for several hours until the sickness and nausea were gone, but somewhere downstairs Kate was greeting his three best friends and he understood her well enough now to guess that she was doing so with poise and grace despite the ordeal. Because it would be an ordeal, meeting people who knew him better than anyone and far better than she did.

And then there was her unfamiliarity with high society. Cris, simply by standing around, had been known to make dukes run a nervous finger around their neckcloths. Gabe was enough to make any relatively unsophisticated lady flustered and Alex and Tess were so head over heels in love that they could only serve to point up the deficiencies in his own marriage.

And Alex had seen at once that something was wrong. Grant shifted cautiously and, ignoring the way it made the room move about, sat up. He had to get down to Kate. The acid anger still churned in his stomach as he forced himself to his feet and he stopped his unsteady progress across the room to his boots to analyse it.

His wife had disobeyed him, deceived him, so why did he feel guilty about being angry with her? He stared into the mirror at his narrow-pupilled eyes and rigid mouth. The sight made him feel considerably worse. He needed to think, but it was hard enough staying on his feet. Yet instinct told him to move. He reached for his boots, winced as he bent his head and made the effort to pull them on. Grant got to his feet and made his way downstairs, steeling himself against the tide of talk and laughter, punctuated by Charlie's whoops, that rose to meet him.

'Grant.' There was anxiety on Kate's face, as well as relief in her voice. She half rose from the chair, then sat down again, and he realised that, thankfully, she was not going to make a fuss over him.

Neither Cris nor Gabe stood. They knew too well that getting up, slapping him on the back or shaking his hand just now would make his head feel as though it had fallen off. Cris waved a greeting with a stylish turn of his wrist, Gabe merely smiled his pirate's smile. Charlie opened his mouth and was promptly scooped up by Alex, who wagged a finger at him until he subsided.

'My apologies for not receiving you. One of those confounded migraines.' They had left his usual chair for him, so he sat down and tried to focus.

'Charlie, take your father his tea, please.' Kate handed the boy a cup and turned back to her interrupted conversation with Gabe, which, to Grant's amazement, appeared to be about *vingt-et-un* and the calculation of odds. Perhaps he was hearing things.

Ten minutes later Mr Gough came down to remove a

reluctant Charlie and give the adults some peace. Then his guests decided that they should retire and wash off the dust of the road. They left, waving him back into his chair when he would have risen. 'We're family, remember,' Alex said airily. 'We'll find our way, Kate, never fear.'

It left him, head still pounding, sitting opposite his wife. She looked decidedly pale now the animation of talking had left her. 'Kate.' He realised he had no idea how he felt about her.

'Please don't. You could not reproach me half as much as I am reproaching myself. We were building trust between us, weren't we? And I destroyed it.' Bravely, she kept her gaze on his face and he remembered that it was her courage that had first impressed him.

'No, we were not.' It came out more harshly than he had intended, a snarl at himself as much as at her. Kate bit her lip and Grant closed his mouth before he said anything else unconsidered.

'I am not going to apologise any more.' She levelled a steady look at him across the teacups. Grant looked down and saw her hands were shaking. When Kate saw the direction of his gaze she curled them loosely in her lap as though willing them to stillness. 'I have said I am sorry, and I am, but my motives were good. Mostly. I cannot acquit myself of some curiosity.'

She admitted inquisitiveness and he knew she wanted to remodel that part of the house, but neither of those could be described as a *good* motive. Grant almost said as much, and then he saw the anxiety in her eyes, stopped thinking about his own feelings and saw hers. *Because if the positions were reversed, I'd have done the same thing.* Of course he would.

If Kate had been hiding some secret that gave her

nightmares, made her short-tempered and laid her low with migraines, he would have done anything that he could to discover what it was and try to set it right, whether she said she wanted him to or not. She was too important to him now—he would not have shrugged and ignored her pain, left her to carry the burden alone. Which meant that he was important to her. He knew himself well enough to recognise that when he was angry it took nerve to stand up to him. Kate had risked his anger and so he must forgive what she had done.

Forgive. And that meant telling her the truth, because otherwise she was going to fret herself to flinders over him. *Hell.* The thought made him nauseous all over again, his shoulder seemed to flare with remembered pain. What would she think of him? That he was as good as a murderer? It was, after all, what he thought of himself often enough as he lay awake long into the night, because that was better than sleeping and the dreams that came with sleep.

With another woman he would never have the confidence in her discretion and her understanding, but he could trust Kate, he realised.

'Yes, I can see that your motives were good.'

Kate's expression changed subtly. Relief, possibly. Anxiety about what he would reveal? Or regret that she had pushed things this far? He had always known her to be self-contained, now he could not read her thoughts, interpret her emotions, and he knew he should be able to. This was his *wife*, he should be able to understand her because that was what happened in real marriages and he wanted this one to be real.

Grant forced his reluctant tongue to form the words. 'I would not let you in to my secrets. Where's the trust in that? And you were not idly curious, I know that. You wanted to help, despite my best efforts to keep you out.'

'Most husbands would maintain that a wife must obey them,' Kate ventured. He thought of someone edging out on to thin ice, testing each step, listening for the ominous cracking. He had failed her by not trusting her before. Now she was wary of how far this tolerance went.

'Even if they are wrong. Yes, I know. I do not want to be a husband like that. Will you come here, Kate?'

She stood up, looking demure, except for the hint of a smile, and he realised with a flash of insight that she was relieved and something more positive than that. Happy? The relief at being able to understand her made his own lips curve in response.

'You have a headache,' she said.

'So don't bounce.' Grant opened his arms and Kate curled up on his lap, her head on his shoulder, and he gathered her in tight, tucked her head under his chin and thought how right she felt there, how perfect her weight on him was.

'Have you had these headaches all the time we have been married?'

'No. When we first got here I was so busy that I was too tired to dream. I had them in London, now and again, but they are always worse here.' He felt the familiar guilt at his own weakness, even as the rational part of his brain, the part that had studied medicine, told him that it was not something he could control by willpower.

He could almost hear Kate working it out. 'You have slept with me every night since you returned from London and you have not had nightmares, not ones that disturbed your sleep and woke me.'

'I suspect that sex helps,' Grant said, hoping he had

not shocked her. It had occurred to him, these past few days when he woke refreshed after a solid night's sleep.

'Of course!' Kate sat up, bumped his chin with her head, murmured an apology. 'The night you woke me up because you were dreaming and I went into your bedchamber and found the key was the first time since we had been sleeping together that we…haven't…' She seemed to find it difficult to select the right word. 'Made love.'

'Well, there's the answer,' he said, feeling, for the first time since that confrontation upstairs, like smiling. 'Lovemaking as often as possible.'

'It will cure the symptoms,' Kate said seriously, apparently not ready to joke about it. 'But not the cause. Have you talked to anyone about what happened when Madeleine died?'

'My grandfather, when it first happened. The other three.' He gestured at the ceiling, but she knew what he meant. The other three of the close band of four friends.

'Did you tell them what happened or how you feel?' Kate asked.

'How I feel? No, of course not. I told them the facts.'

Kate pushed at his chest until she was sitting upright, her expression wry. 'Men! Tonight, when we go to bed, tell me what happened and tell me how you felt, how you still feel.'

'I realise I owe you an explanation, that I can't make a mystery of this any longer, but what the devil do my feelings have to do with it?'

'I want to understand,' she said as she slid off his knee and stood up. 'How is your migraine now?'

'Better.' He rolled his head and flexed his shoulders. 'My neck's stiff, but that's usual afterwards.'

'You should take a hot bath.' He almost smiled again at the confident tone. Planning and making decisions seemed to cheer Kate up as much as it did him. 'And we'll take our time changing for dinner. Let's look in on Anna and Charlie on our way up,' she suggested. 'With our guests and our plans for later, I think this should be an evening for adults, don't you?'

'Oh, yes,' Grant agreed. 'Most definitely.'

Chapter Fifteen

Kate accepted a shelled walnut from Cris de Feaux, who was cracking them with one hand while moving the cruets around the table to demonstrate some obscure point about the Schleswig-Holstein question that her husband and Gabriel were arguing about.

'Thank you,' she murmured, too engaged with the argument to feel shy with him any more. He was beginning to intrigue her, with his sharp intelligence and sardonic observations. But he was unhappy, she sensed. It was hard to tell with such a controlled, contained man, but she thought he was acting, putting on a false front of normality for his friends. She wondered whether he resented the fact that two of them had married and there was certainly something in his eyes when he looked at Alex and Tess, but she thought it was pain rather than resentment or jealousy.

'The convolutions in a walnut are as nothing compared to Gabriel's mental processes,' Cris observed, breaking into her musings. 'Of course the Danes have a good claim to the territory,' he added as Alex joined in the argument. 'But the German states...'

Kate met Tess's eyes and smiled. She had been pleased with herself for remembering to rise and nod to Tess when everyone had finished dessert and she had been taken aback when the other woman said airily, 'Must we? It is only us after all.'

'Why, no, I would be happy to stay if the gentlemen are not inhibited by our presence.' They certainly would not be removing a chamber pot from the sideboard to relieve themselves, as she knew Henry and his male guests did as soon as the ladies were out of the way, because her wary inspection had revealed that was not done in this household. On the other hand she had always assumed that the men liked the freedom to discuss sport, politics and women.

'I would wager that you and I know quite enough about politics to keep our end up in a discussion,' Tess had announced. 'And if they want to talk about bare-knuckle boxing or duels, then I am all agog to hear about them, too.'

'But that means we won't be able to discuss opera dancers or our latest flirts,' Alex Tempest said plaintively and was punished with a well-aimed walnut thrown by his wife.

But, despite the teasing, the arguments were anything but frivolous. From her hours of lonely reading Kate realised that they were all travellers who knew the Continent well—and that included Grant, although she knew he had not been abroad since their marriage and she had no idea why he would be travelling across the Channel in any case.

'After the way we treated Denmark during the war, I am surprised they are a friendly nation now,' she remarked, making herself join in the discussion and not spend the evening silently puzzling over her husband.

'The fact that we bombarded Copenhagen twice?' Grant asked. 'Things in that part of the world are so complicated, even after the Treaty of Vienna, that they are probably grateful for a friendly trading partner who doesn't want to realign their boundaries.'

'You've never had any problem buying horses in Holstein, have you?' Gabriel Stone reached for the decanter and refilled all the glasses within reach.

'None. You'll have to come down to the stables and look at my latest crosses with Yorkshire coach horses. They are going to be the carriage horse of choice if I have anything to do with it.'

So that was what the handsome bay horses down at the stables were. They were not riding horses, she knew that, but not being a good horsewoman herself, she had never been curious enough to ask about them. Now it seemed that Grant was enthusiastic about horse breeding and she'd had no idea. Another side of her husband that was unknown.

The men got up, lost in an intense argument about something new that had escaped Kate's notice whilst she was brooding. 'Come and look at the atlas,' Grant was suggesting as he headed towards the door. 'It should be clear on a large-scale map.'

She and Tess were alone, one at each end of the table. 'That's done it,' Lady Weybourn remarked. 'They are off on the subject of Waterloo and we probably won't see them until breakfast time now. I shudder with relief every time I remember they were all four in that hell and none of them was wounded.'

'Shall we go into the drawing room?' Kate suggested and was surprised, and pleased, when the other woman took her arm in a companionable manner.

'Is Grant better now? He looks it.' Tess kicked off her shoes and curled up in an armchair in a scandalously casual manner.

Kate remembered something that Grant had said about Alex's wife being born on the wrong side of the blanket and never having a come-out. Despite that, she seemed relaxed enough about her place in society, which was encouraging. If she could do it, so could Kate. And then she remembered that she would have to negotiate London society while avoiding one particular aristocrat and it all seemed impossibly difficult again.

'Grant is much better, I think.'

'Had you had a row?' Tess asked with a cheerful lack of restraint. 'I thought you both looked positively stony with each other when we arrived, but of course that might have been his headache and your nerves at the thought of us all descending on you.'

'A row?' Kate temporised. She was not going to be indiscreet about Grant, but she did wish she had someone to confide in, at least about her husband.

'He's not like Alex. We have rows at least once a week and no one's any the worse for it and we usually end up laughing our heads off, or in bed. Or both,' she added with a wicked smile, apparently not noticing Kate's flushed cheeks. 'But Grant is so self-contained. Alex says he virtually never loses his temper—not to show, in any case. But you are obviously doing him good.'

'I am?' Kate murmured, lost in the face of so much frankness.

'When I first met him I had sprained my ankle and he was very kind to me, but his eyes held so much sadness, even when he was smiling. That's gone now.'

There was the fleeting memory of that look in his eyes

when they were in the bothy and, afterwards, when they reached Abbeywell. She had thought that the haunting sadness had gone because he was home again, and with Charlie, but Tess implied that it had been there for longer than just that difficult journey from Scotland. 'I know the look you mean. And you are right, it isn't there now.'

'That's love for you,' Tess said, her smile tender and secret.

'But it isn't,' Kate protested. 'We're not in love. Surely Grant told you all in London about how we met, why he married me? This is not a romance, this is a marriage of practicality.'

'Well, yes.' Tess sat up straighter, the smile gone. 'But he did not have to *marry* you to get you out of the fix you were in. There were all sorts of things he could have done to help you. He must have been attracted to you right from the beginning. And the way you look at him…'

'He needed a stepmother for Charlie,' Kate said stiffly. 'I needed a father for Anna and there was no time to discuss all the options, she was about to be born. And I don't love him.' *Do I?* Tess arched one dark brow. 'And Grant does not love me,' she added with rather more certainty.

'I am sure you know better than I,' Tess said, but the smile was back.

'Knows better than you about what, my darling?' The men were back in the room before Kate could answer that sly remark. 'Surely no one knows better than you about anything,' Alex Tempest added.

'Wretch.' Tess tilted her head back to look up at her husband. 'Have you men finished fighting the battle again to your own satisfaction? Because if Kate will excuse me, I am for my bed. It has been a long day.' She paused as she passed Kate. 'But I am right, you know, about at least one of you.'

Tess's departure broke the party up. Alex, it seemed, was not prepared to let her go up to bed without him, Gabriel suggested that Lord Avenmore come up with him so he could lend him a book he had just finished and, with the departure of her guests, Kate wanted nothing more than to get Grant alone upstairs.

'My chamber or yours?' he asked as they climbed the stairs.

'Yours.' He would be more relaxed there, she sensed. *I don't love him, I am not in love. I like him, I desire him, I am so very grateful to him, but…love? I still hardly know him and, anyway, I am not very good at recognising love.*

'I like your friends,' Kate said and went to help him out of his coat when he dismissed the waiting valet. 'Let me untie your neckcloth.' She enjoyed the closeness of standing toe to toe, unwinding the body-warmed muslin from around his neck, exposing a glimpse of skin beneath.

'Good.' Grant bent to nuzzle her temple as she stood folding the cloth. 'They like you, but then I knew they would, all being men of taste and discrimination.'

They undressed slowly, helping each other, pausing between garments for a lingering caress, a kiss. But without any spoken agreement Grant reached for his heavy silk robe when they were naked, while Kate retrieved her own robe from her room. She sat down facing him across the width of the hearth, studying the austere profile, the straight nose and firm mouth. He was a handsome man, her husband, and, yes, she looked at him and enjoyed doing so, just as Tess had observed. That did not mean she was in love with him.

'I married very suitably and far too young,' Grant said without preamble. 'We were *both* too young and I had very little experience of well-bred young ladies beyond the ballroom. I was disappointed that Madeleine seemed so cool, but she had seemed willing enough to marry me, and neither of us had been brought up to expect some passionate love match. We rubbed along well enough until Charlie was born and, naturally, I would not have dreamed of returning to the bedchamber for quite a while after that.'

'It sounds like a very lonely marriage,' Kate ventured.

Grant's shoulders moved in the ghost of a shrug. 'It is what we both expected, what I had grown up with. Then I visited her room one night and was told that she had done her duty by bearing me an heir and surely, if I wanted to *indulge my male lusts*, I could set up a mistress. I pointed out that sex within marriage was not a question of lust, and besides, I wanted more children and surely she did, too.'

He turned his head against the back of the chair until he was staring into the cold grate. 'I asked myself if I had been clumsy or insensitive in bed, I thought about Charlie's birth. I wondered, even, if there was another man she loved, had loved all the time we had been married. But she denied there was anything. Sex, she thought, was squalid and *animal*. Childbirth was *horrid*, especially as she really had little interest in children. Of course there was no one else—she had been reared to do her duty and she thought she was doing it. But if I felt she was not, then, naturally, she would resign herself.'

'Not very encouraging,' Kate murmured, secretly appalled. She could understand Madeleine's fears about childbirth, but why hadn't she confided in Grant, talked about it, rather than erected that wall of icy rejection between them? And her husband might have acquired a little more experience since his first marriage, but surely his lovemaking could not have changed *that* much? Perhaps, she mused, some women simply did not enjoy the physical side of marriage.

'No, and in retrospect I can understand her. She had been raised with no expectations of marriage beyond status—that was how she measured a successful match. A good wife gave her husband an heir, and, she reluctantly accepted, a spare. Her mother had instilled in her the belief that men were essentially bestial in their desires and that a lady endured their attentions out of duty. From the beginning she was expecting it to be a painful, distasteful, messy business. But the rest of her duty came easily to her. She knew how to behave impeccably in public, she enjoyed enhancing my standing, and with it her own. She loved to spend my money to make herself a decorative and fitting accessory at my side. But I failed to see all that. I thought another child would kindle warmer feelings, both for it and for me. Madeleine became pregnant within months and the birth was complicated. She lost the baby.'

'I am so sorry.' And he had lost a child, too, although she doubted anyone had comforted him about that.

'After that she became…difficult. She began to drink, to behave wildly. In public she was as impeccable as always, but in private it was a nightmare. The staff tried to keep drink from her, but she would find it. I never left her alone with Charlie and I certainly did not go to her bedchamber again. Grandfather would lecture her on her duty and she consigned duty to the devil.'

'You must have been tempted to have her committed to some form of care.'

'She was my wife so I did my best to look after her. I blame myself for getting her with child too soon, for not being able to save the baby.' He closed his eyes as though trying to block a vivid memory. 'I worked with Meldreth, did what I could, but he had to try to turn the baby and they were both so exhausted, mother and child. It was a miracle Madeleine lived. She was so angry with me for getting her pregnant again, it was as though she was fighting me. Every time she cried out it felt as though I had just, that moment, inflicted the pain on her. I still do not know whether it would have been better to have left the room, got out of her sight. Was I there because of my conscience, flagellating myself, or was I doing the right thing? I still do not know.'

His expression was so bleak it was hard to speak. Kate reached for the right words. 'Of course it was the right thing to do. You had some medical training, Dr Meldreth needed your help, your strength. But how could you be expected to have succeeded when an experienced practitioner could not?' She remembered the strain on his face, the shadows in his eyes as he worked to save Anna through that long night in the bothy. 'It must have been so hard for you to help me as you did.'

'No. That was a blessing, something I could do. There was no one else, I could hardly make things worse and I might make things better. And once she was born and I knew it would be all right, then it felt so good, as though I had been given a second chance. Up to that point, I admit, it was difficult to push the fears away.'

'But you kept on trying, you kept my spirits up and never let me see you were afraid of the outcome.' He smiled at that and she sensed it was a comfort. 'In the end, what happened?' she prompted when Grant fell silent.

'Come to her rooms.' Grant stood, took a key she recognised from his pocket and led the way the short distance along the passage. Kate saw his hands were steady as the key turned and the door swung open. They both carried branches of candles and she set hers on the hearth, while Grant placed his near the door.

'My wife died in this room,' he said, his face stark, his voice harsh. 'She died in front of my eyes and I did nothing to save her.'

'And that is only half the story,' Kate said when she could speak again. 'I know there is more to it than that, there has to be. Tell me.'

'I came home one night from dinner at a neighbour's house. Grandfather was beginning to fret because it was late and Madeleine had Charlie with her and when the nursemaid went to take him to bed she wouldn't let the girl in. I knew then there was something very wrong, because she hardly ever kept him with her or spent any time playing with him. The door was locked. I could hear him crying, so I broke it open.'

Grant walked into the room, towards the cold, empty hearth, where Kate waited, silent. 'It was hot, the fire was roaring in the chimney. Charlie was crying on the sofa that was over there, but it was angled away from me so I couldn't see him.' He gestured towards the side of the room away from the chimney. 'He sounded fretful and hungry, but not frightened.

'Madeleine was standing there, just where you are. The tray with the spirits was turned over at her feet, the liquid soaking the carpet. She had a cut-glass decanter in her hand.' He closed his eyes again and spoke without opening them. 'I think she had been drinking directly from it. She was certainly drunk. I walked across.' He moved as he spoke, blind, lost in the memory. 'I tried to take the decanter from her and she swung it at me. It hit the side of my head and smashed.' His left hand, fingers spread, speared into his hair. 'And then she must have panicked, I think. I tried not to hurt her, to take it from her gently, but I was half stunned. She swung it again and it hit my shoulder, cut down through my coat to the skin, and I fell.'

Kate glanced at the dark patch on the boards that endless scrubbing had not removed. She had been right. It was blood. Grant was still speaking, eyes still closed.

'I think I was knocked out for a moment. When I came to there was blood everywhere and there was screaming and Charlie crying. For a moment I was back on the battlefield with the noise and the smoke and the dreadful smells…' He stopped and opened his eyes. 'You do not need to hear it all. The brandy had splashed all down Madeleine's muslin gown, the carpet was already soaked. She must have staggered back towards the fire and her skirts caught. The carpet was ablaze. I crawled across, got Charlie and dragged him back. The door burst open and help was there, but it was too late for her.'

What to say? *How terrible. How tragic. Poor woman.* All so obvious and so meaningless. She would say what she thought, what concerned her, even if it was not the comforting platitudes that convention expected. 'You know you did the right thing, don't you? To go to Charlie and not to try to save Madeleine?'

'Yes.' Grant almost smiled at her. 'Yes, I know. I only had so much strength, I was bleeding like a stuck pig and she was probably beyond saving, even if I had gone directly to her. I had to get the child to safety.'

'Then, if you know that, accept it—'

'What is the problem? The problem, my dear, is that while my rational brain accepts it while I'm awake, my dreaming mind does not, it seems. A policy of *out of sight, out of mind* has worked to an extent so far, but you are right, I cannot continue like that, ignoring the existence of this room, ignoring that night.'

He stood up and held out his hand to her. 'Come, sweetheart. Let us go to bed, lock this door on the horrors of this room for another night.'

Chapter Sixteen

Grant kissed her, gently, sweetly, when they reached his bedchamber again. They shed their night robes and Kate climbed into bed beside him and lay on her stomach, her chin propped on her hands as she frowned at the harmless stack of pillows. 'So, what do you want to do? Leave the door locked for ever?'

'No. You are right, I cannot risk Charlie becoming curious.' He began to play with the ends of her hair as it spilled across the sheets. 'He is growing up and I need to deal with this for all our sakes.'

'Let us be practical, then,' Kate said, lifting her chin to look at him. He was stretched out, hands behind his head, the muscles of his upper arms and shoulders in strong relief. A wave of desire washed over her and she suppressed it. They could make love when this was decided. 'Pull the house down?' she suggested to shock him into suggesting a counter-solution.

'Demolish it? Rather an extreme solution—besides, I am fond of all the rest of the old place, so is Charlie.'

'Rip out those rooms, tear up the floorboards, get rid of the fireplace and everything in the bedchamber, put new dividing walls in to change the space completely.'

'That would work,' Grant said thoughtfully. 'And what do I tell Charlie?'

'Woodworm?'

'That's a lie.'

And Grant hates lies. 'Tell him that the floor is dangerous. And it is. Dangerous to your peace of mind, dangerous to his if he ever sees it and asks what the marks of fire are, what that dark stain is.'

'Clever.'

'Of course.' Kate said it smugly to make him laugh and, to her great relief, he did.

'Come here.' He hauled her up unceremoniously to lie on top of him. 'Thank you. I was beginning to think I was losing my mind. A man ought to be able to cope with such things.'

'Not everything, not horrors, not unless he is an unfeeling brute.' She laid her cheek against his chest and blew gently into the dark hair, smiling as his nipples contracted tightly. 'I think you feel more guilty because you did not love her.' It was dangerous to talk of love. As soon as she used the word, she had a horrid feeling that Grant might think she was fishing for him to say that he loved *her*. Which of course he didn't. Nor did she expect it. It was not as though…

'Is that some feminine logic that escapes me?'

'You cannot mourn her, only her unhappiness and the unhappiness she caused you. You dare not think too much about her in case you find you are relieved at her death.'

Beneath her the long, hard body had become very still. Kate could feel the thud of his heart, the slight rise and fall of his breathing. Then Grant said, 'You hit hard, do you not, honest Kate? You drag out thoughts that I had not even acknowledged.'

'I like you,' she said and raised her head to look deep into the troubled green eyes, half shielded by dark lashes. 'I hope I am your friend as well as your wife and your lover. Who can be honest if not your friends?'

'My closest male friends do not suggest such things.'

'Because they are male. Does Alex confide how much he loves Tess? Does Cris admit that he is in love?'

'Is he?' Surprise seemed to jerk Grant out of his inward-looking thoughts.

'I think so. He is certainly not happy, although he hides it well. I cannot be certain, of course, but there is something in his expression when he looks at Alex and Tess, and I saw it once, reflected in a mirror, when he was looking at us. Happy marriages. I cannot believe that he would be unhappy over not being married, because he could remedy that soon enough, he is so very eligible after all. Which makes me think he loves someone and it is not returned. Will he tell you about it?'

'Poor devil. I never thought to say that about Cris, and as for confiding, at knife point, possibly, otherwise, not,' he admitted with a faint smile that vanished as he frowned, back searching into his memory. 'I was not relieved she died. No, never that. If I could have gone back in time, never married Madeleine, then perhaps I would have done—but then I would not have Charlie, would I?'

Kate felt him relax as he thought of his son, then he smiled properly and she sensed the loosening of his taut body. 'We'll turn that space into rooms for the children. A bedroom each, a schoolroom, a nursery. That will chase the ghosts away better than any exorcism.'

'Grant, that's a brilliant idea.' Kate wriggled up to kiss him and realised that he had relaxed enough to be thinking of his new wife, not his old—or perhaps it was just his body that was doing so. She slid her tongue between his lips and snuggled her hips closer against his and smiled as her husband rolled her over with a possessive growl. He would not have nightmares tonight.

But, as she went down into the whirlpool of sensation with him, the thought flickered through her mind that they were making love without restraint and without care for the consequences. Strange that she had never given it a thought before tonight. The children's suite might need more rooms one day…

'You are happy.' Tess linked her arm through Kate's as they strolled across the parterre.

'Yes,' she admitted. 'We…confronted our problem. Look, you see that rough lawn down there? We are going to turn that into a water garden.'

'I'm so glad—about both the problem and the water garden.' Tess was not easily diverted from her theme. 'And I am happy for both of you. I only met Grant fleetingly before I married Alex, but I liked him very much. I am so glad he has found someone to love, someone who loves him.'

'I…' *Oh, why deny it? You are head over heels in love with the man.* 'Grant does not love me. I told you the truth, that it was a marriage of convenience. We hardly know each other yet.'

'Alex and I did not know each other very long before I knew that I loved him. Mind you, it took an awful lot to make him realise that he loved me, even when I set about seducing him,' Tess admitted with a candour that made Kate smile despite everything. 'Men are not very bright about emotions of that sort.'

'Nor am I. I don't want to have my heart broken. I

thought I was in love before, with Anna's father, but I was not. Now I feel like this about Grant and it can be wonderful in… I mean, it is wonderful being with him.' She must be the colour of a peony.

'Wonderful in bed?' Tess teased. 'For me, too. Aren't we lucky? Such *talented* men.'

'Yes. But Grant doesn't expect love in marriage. He certainly didn't find it with his first wife and that was a disaster that's haunting him still. He really did not want to marry again, not for himself. He did it because he wanted to rescue me, and because Charlie needed a step-mother and because he had promised his grandfather.' She watched a rabbit hop across the grass, stop to eat something, then, suddenly alarmed, make for the woods. That was how she felt—calm and content, then frightened by fears she could not quite name, doubts she could not express.

'I should be happy with what I have—a good man, two lovely children, security, physical bliss. And yet…'

'And yet you want it all and it will hurt all the more if he does not love you, because you can see so clearly how it could be.'

'And Grant says that *I* hit hard,' Kate said with a rueful smile.

'I was brought up by nuns to be painfully honest and it is difficult to remember tact sometimes. Are you sure he does not love you?'

'Quite sure. I believe he thinks he did the right thing in marrying me, which is something. But if I vanished off the face of the earth tomorrow?' She shrugged. 'He would be truly sorry, but his heart would not be broken.'

'What will you do?' Tess took off her bonnet and

began to swing it from its ribbons, turning her face up to the sky.

'You will get freckles,' Kate warned. 'Do? Why, nothing. I can't imagine ever having the courage to tell him. He would be so kind about it.' She shivered.

'Yes. Horrible,' Tess agreed. 'He would pussyfoot around being nice to you and you would never know what he really felt.'

'I think we should go through the things in Madeleine's bedchamber,' Kate suggested as she and Grant found themselves alone in the dining room waiting for their guests to join them for luncheon. 'Do you think there might be items you could give to Charlie as a memento of his mother? He would treasure that.'

'You wouldn't be jealous?' Grant seemed puzzled. 'He's never known her, he can't really remember her and he loves you. Why do you risk that by making her more real for him?'

'What he feels for me cannot be diluted by what he feels for anyone else. He loves you, he loves me, he loves his grandfather's memory and he can love his mother—that makes more love, not less.' *Tess was right,* she thought, *men really are confused about love.*

'I suppose that is true.' Grant caught Kate around the waist and pulled her into his embrace, to the imminent danger of the nearest place setting. 'He won't love you less—you are here and you are easy to love, Kate.' He said it with a smile as he dipped his head to kiss her and Kate lurched back clumsily, sending a knife clattering to the floor.

There was the sound of someone clearing their throat and Cris de Feaux remarked, 'My dear Grant, we are more than happy to take luncheon on the terrace—you only had to drop a hint, you know. But I'm sure a fully laid table is a most uncomfortable place to...er...bill and coo.'

Grant released her, scooped up the knife and waved the others into the room. 'If a man cannot kiss his own wife in his own dining room without being accused of disgusting practices, things have come to a sorry pass,' he remarked as he held a chair for Kate, then walked around to take his own place. 'Billing and cooing indeed. Where on earth did you pick up such a bourgeois expression?'

Gabriel Stone sat down next to Kate and gave a snort of laughter. 'I would pay good money to see the Marquess of Avenmore billing and cooing.'

Kate kicked him sharply on the ankle.

'Ouch,' he murmured. 'My dear Lady Allundale, if you wish to flirt, might I suggest that firstly you *caress* with your delightful foot and secondly that we do it away from your husband's jealous eye? I have no desire to face him at dawn. The man is too good with a firearm.'

'Oh, stop it,' Kate whispered back. 'I do not want to flirt with you, Lord Edenbridge, and you know it. Kindly do not tease the marquess.'

'Why ever not?' He turned his wicked smile on her. 'Teasing Cris keeps him human. He'd be too perfect to be true if we didn't.'

'He has feelings,' she said vehemently. 'Even if you do not.'

'Ah, Lady Allundale, just because you are in love, you do not need to wish the affliction on everyone.'

'It is not an affliction,' Kate snapped.

'No?' The dark, knowing gaze moved from her to Grant, who was engaged in an energetic argument with

Alex Tempest at the other end of the table. 'If you say so, sweet Kate, I must believe you.'

Infuriating man. Kate passed Gabriel the bread and butter with more force than elegance. *He knows I love Grant. Which means if both Tess and he can see it, then Grant must be able to see how I feel, as well. On the other hand,* she mused, pushing a slice of cold chicken around her plate, *perhaps Grant doesn't see, any more than he and Lord Edenbridge can perceive that Lord Avenmore is suffering.*

She was making herself dizzy, going in circles. Kate made a superhuman effort, pushed all thoughts of her marriage to the back of her mind and enquired about Lord Edenbridge's family home in repressive tones that managed to curtail even *his* tendency to tease.

'We need a builder,' Grant said a week later as they stood and waved goodbye to the three carriages.

'Not an architect?' Kate shifted Anna into a more comfortable position and kept an eye on Charlie, racing down the drive for a last wave to his favourite 'uncles'.

'No, the sketches we did will be enough for a good joiner to work from.' Grant turned back to the house. 'I thought to ask Wilson to sort all the personal items from the bedroom. The gowns, perfume bottles, the curtains, all of that kind of thing will go anonymously to charities in Newcastle for them to sell.' He hesitated. 'There's a miniature of Madeleine. Should I give it to Charlie now, do you think, or wait until he is older?'

'Now, I think.' Kate moved close to his side. 'You remember that tomorrow I have a number of ladies visiting for tea? I met them at Mrs Lowndes's charity sewing circle. Some of them are bringing children with them, which will keep Charlie occupied. That will give Wilson the opportunity to tackle the room.'

She stopped in the doorway and called to Charlie, who came racing back with Rambler, the elderly pointer, at his heels. The secrets and ghosts would soon be gone from this house and from Grant's heart, driven out by sawdust and hammering, plasterers and cheerful, noisy builders. Summer was coming, the valley was blossoming and her children were, too. Her husband seemed happy and she was learning to live with loving him in secret.

Christmas, and London, were a very long way away, Kate thought as she turned back to the hallway and her waiting husband. A long way. Grant would see how happy they all were here and it could only get better. When autumn came he would not want to leave this place for the dirt and noise and artificiality of London.

She held out her hand and he took it and, as he bent to kiss her, there was nothing but warmth in the green eyes that smiled into hers.

November 23—Abbeywell

'Lady Mortenson is holding a party and we are invited.' Kate waved the letter in Grant's direction.

'What date is it?' Grant looked up from the copy of the *Times* that was folded beside his plate.

'The eighteenth of December.' Kate spread damson preserve on her toast and passed her wardrobe in mental review. She would definitely need a new gown and probably some evening slippers, as well.

'That's a pity, we'll miss it.' Grant was still intent on the Parliamentary news.

'Why?'

'We will be in London by then, of course.' He looked up as if surprised she even had to ask.

'*London?* But you never said anything about London.'

'I most certainly did.' Grant tossed the newssheet aside. 'When I came back in May I said we would have the summer here, then go back to London.'

'After Christmas.' Somehow she stopped her voice rising to a shriek. 'You said *after* Christmas.'

'Yes, but the building work is proving far more disruptive than we thought with all the work they are doing on the chimney flues.' He was using what Kate thought of as his *husband being reasonable* voice. It usually amused her, especially as she won half of the battles that necessitated the use of it. Now she dropped the toast, jam-side down, on to the plate and stared at him as he continued, just as reasonably. 'We can't use half the downstairs rooms because we can't light fires there and the house is getting colder and colder. And you said yourself only the other day that it is making a lot of work for the staff, trying to keep all the dust under control. If we weren't here, they could shut up all the rooms, put dust covers on the furniture, retreat into the warm part and let the builders get on with it. I thought we could go down next week.'

'Next week?' Kate echoed faintly. Over Christmas week London would be quiet and starved of fashionable company because most of the *ton* would be at their country estates. But at the beginning of December she was sure the capital would seem as busy as always. It might not be the Season, but society would still be there in force.

'I'm sure I said something.' Grant shrugged. 'Perhaps I just remarked about it to Grimswade and Bolton. And

Wilkinson.' He picked up the paper again. 'I'm sure I mentioned it to Wilkinson.'

'My lord.' Kate kept her voice level because it would not do to shout in front of the footmen. 'You may have told your butler, your secretary and your bailiff, but you did not tell your *wife*.'

'There is no need to worry, my dear.' Grant seemed blissfully unaware that he was within an inch of having the jam pot thrown at him. 'The staff are well practised in getting packed up for London. We'll take the chaise for ourselves and the travelling coach for the children and Jeannie and Gough, and then another coach for the luggage. This fine dry weather seems set to hold.'

'Thank you, Giles, that will be all.' Kate waited until the footmen had gone out and the door had closed. 'My lord, I do not want to go to London.'

'Why ever not?' Finally she had his full attention. Probably the repeated use of his title gave him an inkling that all was not well.

'Because—' *My lover will be there. Anna's father. The man who ruined me and who has every cause to wish to see me in prison. My brother might be there and will try his damnedest to ensnare you in his schemes. Because you'll find out that I told you a pack of lies. Because I am terrified that everything we have built is going to fall apart.* And she could say none of that.

The six months that Grant had been at Abbeywell had been months of contentment. They had grown closer and had fallen into a domestic routine that appeared to please both of them. Their nights were filled with passionate lovemaking and Grant showed no sign of tiring of her, even though he had not declared any feeling for her beyond affection. The children were flourishing.

We have become a family, Kate thought, *but it is all founded on lies. My lies.* They were companionable, but sometimes that companionship felt merely polite and distant and Kate knew there was an invisible barrier between them that stopped them achieving the closeness that might lead to a mutual love. She suspected it was her own guilty conscience that had raised that sheet of glass. She dared not break it and the more time went past, the harder it became to even contemplate telling him the truth. It was as though the right moment had slipped through her fingers and was now vanishing, too far gone to catch.

The marriage was like a house built of cards. If Grant discovered the truth, then it would all come tumbling down—their family life, the children's security, Grant's reputation if, as she suspected he would, he insisted on confronting the criminality of what Henry had done. At some level Grant must sense that she was holding something back from him, but he was too much the gentleman to force the issue.

Or perhaps he does not care enough, she thought in her darker moments. He must have had enough drama and emotion with Madeleine not to want to demand a confrontation with her. Surely now he wanted only a quiet life with a wife who satisfied him in bed and loved his children. *But it is so lonely sometimes.*

'Why are you so reluctant to go to London?' Grant asked.

'Charlie will miss Christmas at home.'

'The town house is familiar to him now—besides, this house at Christmastide can only hold bad memories for him. Let him have this year somewhere entirely different and then the following year the recollections will be dimmer, the house will be much changed and we can enjoy the festive season here.'

That was perfectly, unarguably, reasonable. Kate tried another tack. 'I'm shy of London. I won't know how to go on there.'

'Of course you will.' Grant was beginning to look impatient now. 'You are quite at ease with company in the neighbourhood, you are well informed on the issues of the day, you make excellent conversation and you dance very well and you'll have fashionable gowns—there is nothing at all to be alarmed about.'

'I can't help it,' she said. 'I am.'

He was puzzled now, she could tell, and in a moment he was going to move from puzzlement to suspicion. 'Where is the courageous woman I found in that bothy?'

There was nothing for it. Unless she developed a disfiguring rash or broke a leg, she was going to have to face London society. 'Facing critical leaders of fashion is far more alarming than giving birth, believe me,' Kate said with a laugh that she hoped rang true.

Grant visibly relaxed. 'I will be there by your side.'

That is what I am afraid of. 'Of course.'

Chapter Seventeen

Something was wrong with Kate. Grant paced along the terrace, welcoming the cold, rolling his shoulders to relax them after two hours of solid work in the study with his bailiff and secretary, sorting estate matters out so that he could safely go away for a few months. Was whatever had made her so wary of London related to the reserve that was always present just below the surface, however cheerful she seemed, however lost in the passion of their lovemaking?

He wanted to trust her totally and yet, somehow, he could not. Was it the ghost of his first marriage haunting him, holding him back from that complete act of faith? He only wished she would tell him what it was that put the shadow in her eyes, those moments of constraint when he sensed she was holding back from telling him… something. It was hard not to think, *Confess something.* He told himself it was not jealousy that he felt, that she was not still pining for Anna's father. After all, she had told him she had not loved the man, and besides, what did it matter if she had? Theirs was a practical, companionable marriage, not a love match. Kate was passionate and responsive in bed, and that was what a man needed, not some foolish romantic fantasy with moonlight and roses. And heartbreak.

'My lord?'

He turned to find Jeannie standing outside the long window to the drawing room, Anna in her arms. 'Yes?' He strolled across to tickle the baby under her chin and she laughed at him and held out her arms.

'Could I leave Lady Anna with you a moment, my lord? I brought her down for an airing, but there's much more of a nip in the air than I realised and I want another shawl for her.'

'Of course. I'll wait with her in the drawing room.' He took Anna, who immediately fastened both chubby hands on his neckcloth and proceeded to demolish it as he carried her into the warmth.

'You, madam, are a menace to any gentleman with pretentions to elegance,' he chided and held her away while he went to examine the damage in the mirror. Not so bad, at least she hadn't chewed it this time. Anna laughed up at him and he smiled back, then sobered as a thought struck him. What if Kate's reluctance to go to London was a fear that a lack of resemblance between her husband and the child might be noticed? After all, Anna had reached the age when a proud mama might be expected to produce the child for a few minutes for morning callers to admire.

Their local acquaintance had known Anna as she grew up and, presumably, were used to her and accepted her as Grant's child without question. Now he shifted Anna until he could hold her up facing the mirror beside his own face and compared their features—straight brown hair in a shade nearer his dark tones than Kate's lighter tresses. A face that would, he was sure, echo her mother's as she grew out of babyhood and the promise of height that would fit well with both her assumed parents.

And green eyes. He shifted her round again so he could study them more carefully. Several doting matrons had remarked on those eyes—'Green, just like her papa's!' That was useful.

Anna was watching him now, eyes wide, and he realised that her eyes were not like his after all. They were a paler, clearer green with gold flecks and a dark rim around the iris. The effect was beautiful and unusual and when she grew up he imagined they would give her a unique charm. He checked his own eyes in the mirror— a darker green that verged towards hazel when he was tired or angry, so he'd been told. No gold flecks, no dark ring. But that was not a problem, Anna was like enough in various characteristics to both of them not to raise the slightest suspicions. It might be a different matter if she was a redhead or a pale blonde. He was conscious of disappointment that he had not found the reason for Kate's anxiety.

'Here we are, my lord, her warmest shawl. I'll take her now, shall I?'

Jeannie bore Anna away to the terrace, leaving Grant frowning at his own reflection in the mirror. Kate was perfectly competent socially, she was intelligent enough to learn and adapt quickly and she was usually confident enough to be aware of that. Could it be that she feared encountering her brother? He knew he should have insisted on making contact with the shadowy Mr Harding of somewhere in Suffolk, but he had managed to forget all about Kate's brother and she had done nothing to remind him. He should confront her about all of these things, but he sensed that if he did he would destroy the happiness they now had, perhaps simply for a phantom of his own imagination. He would watch and think and see how she took to London, see what clues he could discover.

He strode out of the drawing room and along to the little room Kate had claimed as her writing room, tapped and went in. 'Kate.'

She jumped, blotted her page and tutted irritably at him. Sometimes he made her cross simply because it was so rare to see her lose her self-control and he wanted to see the real woman that she kept so carefully hidden behind the facade of the good wife and mother. She revealed that face in bed, when she lost all inhibition with him, and she had shown it when she had helped him fight his demons over Madeleine, but there were times when he thought she was moving further and further away from him.

'I'm sorry.' He moved to stand behind her and ran the back of one finger down the exposed nape of her neck, enjoying the sensual little shiver she gave. 'Were you writing poetry? I am sorry if I have made you blot the final stanza.'

Kate gave a little snort of laughter, the irritation vanishing as fast as it always seemed to. 'No, I am not writing poetry. This is a shopping list for the linen warehouse. There hardly seems to be a decent sheet left in the house.' She twisted round to look up at him and he kept his hand where it was so that his fingers trailed round her neck as she moved. 'Do you think I should be writing odes to my husband's eyelashes?'

'Are they so worthy of praise?' He felt absurdly anxious that she should say so.

'They are indecently long and thick.'

'Are they indeed? Indecent, eh? All the better to tickle you with.' The confrontation he had come for was less interesting than the possibilities presented by a flustered wife, a comfortable chaise longue and the thought of how his eyelashes might be employed.

'Grant!' It was accompanied by a most encouraging blush. He turned the key in the lock, twitched the nearest curtain across the window and advanced on the desk.

'Grant—only half the window is covered.'

'If anyone is standing in the middle of the flower bed, on a box, contorting their neck in an effort to see in through the uncovered area of the window, all I can say is that we have more flexible staff than I imagined.' He stripped off his coat and waistcoat as he advanced. 'Am I going to have to chase you round the desk?'

'Do you want to?' Kate slipped off the chair and retreated to the far side. 'I warn you, I have a quill and I know how to use it.'

Grant hopped on one foot, then the other as he tugged off his boots. Kate was not making much of an effort to escape, which was interesting. He had never tried to make love to her downstairs and he had expected her to be shy of doing so in broad daylight. When he emerged from the folds of his shirt and prowled towards her clad only in his breeches she edged away around the desk, then, when he was within arm's reach, extended the quill like a rapier and flicked his right nipple with the point of the feather.

'*Touché,*' Grant conceded, moved his right hand and, when her eyes flickered to follow the movement, lunged, caught Kate around the waist and bore her off to the chaise. She tried to bounce up. He flipped her skirts up over her head and, as she struggled to extricate herself, pressed a kiss into the exposed triangle of curls at the junction of her thighs.

Kate went very still, but did not resist as he eased her knees apart, settled his shoulders between them, bent his head and brushed his lashes up the inside of her thigh, over the white, soft skin. There was a sudden heave and the skirts settled over his head plunging him into semi-darkness as he shifted the subtle caress to her other thigh.

That convulsive movement was all the resistance she gave as he worked his way up, fraction by fraction, towards his goal. She was aroused, there was no mistaking that. Grant parted the delicate folds, touched once with his tongue, and Kate came apart in his hands. He used his lips and mouth in a long, demanding kiss that had her writhing on the couch before he shook off the folds of her gown, pulled down his breeches and sheathed himself in her pulsing, hot body in one hard movement.

'Grant.' Her face was buried in the angle of his neck, her arms locked around his shoulders as he thrust. 'Grant, I—'

'Come again,' he demanded, controlling, somehow, his own need. 'Come for me again. *Now.'*

And she did, pulling him with her into the maelstrom.

I almost told him I loved him, Kate thought as she cradled her husband in her arms in blissful discomfort. The sofa cushion, a hard, cylindrical bolster, dug into the base of her spine, her corset was doing its best to stop her breathing and Grant, though without any spare flesh on him, was a significant dead weight on top of her. *Thank goodness I didn't.*

'Kate.' Grant's voice was muffled and he heaved

himself up until he was sitting on the end of the chaise. 'You were trying to say something just then.'

'Probably *more*, or *again*,' she temporised. 'Goodness, after that, how do you expect me to recall my own name?'

He grinned. 'Flatterer. Kate…' That change of tone from teasing to serious within the space of two words was ominous. She braced herself. 'Is the problem about going to London because you fear coming across your brother? I know you haven't written to him. Perhaps we should make contact now, before we go.'

'No.' She pushed down her skirts and scrambled to sit upright at the end of the chaise. 'Please, Grant. It will be too awkward. I cannot forgive him for how he behaved and he will not forgive me. Let sleeping dogs lie.' He still looked unconvinced as he refastened his breeches. 'It isn't as though my parents are alive, or that I have other siblings.' Which was true. She had cousins, but they were even more country mice than she was.

'If it upsets you so much, I will not insist.' Grant pushed his fingers through his hair, the habitual giveaway that he was frustrated. He would circle round, come back to this, she knew.

'And Henry would be a most unsuitable uncle for Charlie, a really bad influence.' That went home, she saw. 'May I have the carriage tomorrow? I need to go into Newcastle to have my hair done.'

'Surely the coiffeur will come here, or it can wait until you get to London?'

'Oh, did I not tell you?' She had not, quite deliberately. 'I saw an advertisement in the *Newcastle Courier* that Monsieur Ducasse, late of Monsieur Maurice's establishment in Bond Street, has set up in Newcastle. And Monsieur Maurice advertises in all the best journals—*La*

Belle Assemblée and so on. I would feel so much more comfortable with a fashionable style. I wrote to reserve a private parlour at the King's Head and he will attend me there.' Grant opened his mouth and she said hastily, 'Wilson will accompany me, of course.'

'Then of course you may have the carriage.' Grant got to his feet and lifted her hand to kiss the tips of her fingers. 'Not that you need any changes to make you look quite delightful, my dear.'

'Flatterer.' She laughed up at him and pulled his hand back to rest fleetingly against her own lips. *I love you and now I will lie and deceive and do whatever it takes to get through this ordeal without you ever discovering who the woman you married really is.*

'Kate?' Grant stopped dead in the hallway, then advanced slowly, like a cat who has seen something that may be prey, or may be something alien and dangerous. 'What have you done?' he demanded as he completed the circle.

Grimswade, who had appeared the moment the carriage drew up, effaced himself, closely followed by Wilson clutching Kate's bonnet, pelisse and reticule.

'Monsieur Ducasse gave me a new style.' She smiled brightly at him and fluffed the soft curls that framed her face. 'I think it's very dashing.'

'He's cut it.' Grant's green eyes were narrowed as he studied the effect.

'Just the front. I knew it would curl if he did that. The back is still long, so it can be put up. You see?' Kate turned right round, skirts belling out.

'It changes the shape of your face.'

She still couldn't work out whether he liked it or not,

or whether he realised that she had plucked her eyebrows into a finer arch. 'I think it shows off my cheekbones. I didn't know I had any before.'

'And the colour...' Grant was prowling again.

'Just a shade darker. Monsieur Ducasse said it would make my eyes look bigger.' He came to a halt in front of her and she widened her eyes at him. 'And bluer.' And he had stained her eyebrows to match. Wilson had the little brush and bottle safely tucked away.

'You look more sophisticated,' Grant said at last, when she thought she would go dizzy from holding her breath.

'Is that code for *older*?' She hoped it was. She wanted to look as different as possible from that wide-eyed, unsophisticated girl who had been the bait to catch a lord in a blackmailer's snare.

'Just a trifle.' Grant seemed to have relaxed, lids heavy over his green eyes. 'It certainly makes you look more... experienced.' There was a wealth of hidden meaning in the one, drawled, word.

He likes it. That was a relief.

'Maman!' Charlie appeared, at the run as usual, skidded to a halt and stared. Then he circled her, just as his father had done, but with his mouth open.

Grant laughed. 'Your *maman* has had a haircut. Fancy, isn't it?'

'It's prime!' Charlie approved. 'Is it for London?'

'It is.' Grant's gaze met hers over the boy's head. 'I'm glad you are getting into the spirit of the London expedition, Kate. It is past your bedtime, Charlie, off you go.'

'I'm doing my best.' She bent to kiss the boy before he ran off to the stairs, then slid her hand through the crook of her husband's elbow and leaned in a little, enjoying the smell of leather and the hint of coffee and the familiar, beloved scent that was simply *Grant*. She had been away all day and she had missed him, even for those few hours.

He turned his head from watching Charlie's retreating form, looked down at her and became very still. His eyes, which were usually green, darkened to hazel, as they did when he was tired, or angry or aroused. And this was definitely arousal, reacting to something he saw in her expression. 'Kate.'

Her chest was so tight that her lungs felt hollow. He was going to kiss her, here and now in the hallway, and she was going to say it, tell him she loved him, and she could not, must not. Not when she was lying to him, deceiving him. 'Of course, it will mean a great strain on my dress allowance and my pin money.' She fluttered her eyelashes outrageously. 'Will you increase it, or will you be mean and beat me if I overspend?'

'I might do both,' Grant said, low-voiced. 'I might increase it so you may buy outrageous garments and then spank you just for the hell of it.' His expression promised considerably more pleasure than pain and she knew he was not a man who would raise a hand to a woman in anger. Was spanking another of those erotic games he was beginning to show her?

'That sounds interesting,' Kate murmured. 'But you'd have to chase me first.'

'That can be arranged.' Grant looked up. 'Yes, Grimswade, what is it?'

'Should I tell the kitchen to put dinner back, my lady, seeing as you have only just got in?'

'Goodness, is that the time?' For a moment she had thought the butler had overheard Grant and was suggesting delaying dinner while she was pursued around the bedchamber by a playful husband. Really, she must get a grip on her imagination! 'I'll go straight up now. Don't inconvenience Cook, thank you, Grimswade.'

'Thank you, my lady.'

'Coward,' Grant whispered in her ear as she passed him.

If only you knew, my love. Pray heaven that you never do.

Chapter Eighteen

December 15—Grosvenor Street, London

'More treasures?'

Kate nodded to Wilson and waited until the maid closed the bedchamber door behind her before she answered. Grant was standing at the foot of the bed and eyeing the heap of packets and bandboxes that the footmen had just brought up. She rather thought he was on the verge of smiling, but she could not be certain—after all, she had spent almost a week doing nothing else but shop.

'Yes. And you have bought a stack of neckcloths and at least two waistcoats, and a new evening suit and three pairs of boots.'

'I have.' Yes, his mouth was just twitching at the corner.

'One has to dress,' Kate drawled, risking it. 'At least that was what I heard one lady say to another while I was in the fitting room at Mrs Bell's.'

'That is absolutely true. Think what a spectacle Bond Street would be if one did not.'

'Especially if Prinny was on the strut.'

Grant shuddered. 'I did not need that image being put into my mind, thank you!' He picked up a large flat box from the floor. 'And what does this contain?'

'Um…I was hoping it was something you wouldn't see in broad daylight,' Kate confessed.

Grant weighed the box on the upturned palm of one hand and looked at the shop stamp on the lid. 'Ah, the cost of this, I imagine, is in inverse proportion to the amount of fabric it contains.'

'It was a *trifle* expensive. I was hoping it might be the sort of thing that would get me chased around the bedchamber.'

'But not spanked?' Grant had a speculative gleam in his eye. 'Try it on for me, and we'll see.'

'At four o'clock in the afternoon?' Her pulse was racing along with her imagination.

'I really cannot persuade you out of the idea that there are *respectable* times and places for lovemaking, can I?' Grant piled the parcels on the bed on to the floor, then sat down and pulled off his boots.

'I can be persuaded.' Kate picked up the box and whisked into the dressing room. 'Close your eyes.'

He was quite correct about the cost. If looked at dispassionately, the negligee consisted of nothing but floating panels of pale blue silk gauze, a large number of silver ribbons and dark blue silk flowers appliquéd in various strategic positions. Crushed up it would fit in a soup bowl and, as a garment, it was utterly impractical for anything except tormenting one's husband. She had thought it delicious the moment she saw it.

When she looked around the edge of the door Grant was leaning against a bedpost, arms crossed, eyes closed. He was wearing nothing but a severe expression. Once,

Kate would have been alarmed, now she could read him well enough to know she was being teased, especially as there was nothing to disguise the fact that he was finding this arousing.

She tiptoed up, swirled round so her gossamer skirts whispered across his legs and ran to the other side of the bed. Grant's reflexes were fast and he was on her heels, reaching for her as she scrambled across the bed, silk panels flying. Kate made it to the other side just as Grant somersaulted across the bed and landed on his feet in front of her.

'That is the most outrageously provoking garment I have even seen.' He was breathing far harder than the amount of activity justified.

'And you have seen many?'

Kate could have sworn he had actually growled, although as she found herself seized, upended and face down over Grant's knees, she could not be certain.

'Now, then, let's check the workmanship.' One large hand at the small of her back was more than enough to hold her down, even if she had wanted to struggle, which she did not. A wriggle or two, though…

There was a flurry of fabric, a whisper of silk, and then there was nothing over her buttocks but air. 'Quite impractical,' Grant observed. 'I cannot imagine how this would keep you warm on a chilly evening.' There was a tantalising pause, then one palm moved slowly over her right buttock. 'This would, though.'

It was only a light smack, more noise than anything. Kate squeaked, then gasped as he did the same to the other buttock.

'Warmer? Certainly pinker.'

What was warm was the thrust of his erection against

her stomach. Kate decided she liked this game. 'Beast! Savage!' She wriggled against him and was rewarded by a flurry of light open-handed slaps. She realised the wicked sensation of being powerless while Grant did what he liked was making her excited, breathless and very, very needy. 'Grant?'

'Hmm?' She felt the pressure of his lips on one sensitive buttock. 'Shall I stop? Perhaps you are right and this isn't the thing to be doing in the afternoon. We could get dressed and discuss the Parliamentary report in the *Times*.'

'You haven't checked the design of the front of the negligee. What if they stinted on ribbons?'

'What an appalling thought. I would have to wrap you in a cloak and take you straight back to the shop to demand a refund.' He turned her so she was sitting on his thighs and tipped up her chin. 'A very becoming shade of rose. Are you flushed because you enjoyed being spanked, or at the thought of being carried through the streets in nothing but this flimsy thing and a cloak?'

'Both,' she admitted as he began to untie the ribbons, counting as he went.

'…nine, ten…' His voice was not quite steady as he gave up on the little bows and lifted her, then brought her down so she was straddling him as he sat. 'I need to see it in motion,' he said, his voice husky as he lowered her with aching slowness until he was sheathed inside her. 'Like that.' She held him, burrowed close against him so the friction of the fine gauze fretted her nipples, and his, and felt the control he had been tantalising her with snap. *'Kate.'* He broke in six powerful strokes, took her with him into the whirlwind and then stayed, deep inside her, his arms around her, his forehead on her shoulder.

Just as she was sliding into sleep Grant murmured, 'I didn't hurt you, did I?'

'Of course not. I knew you would never hurt me.' She sat back, ran one finger down the straight line of his nose and smiled when, eyes still closed, he put out his tongue to catch the tip. 'And you aren't cross about all my shopping?'

'Of course not.' Grant opened his eyes and fell back on to the bed, bringing her with him. 'I've kept you locked up in Northumberland away from all the shops for months.'

'I've been extravagant, though.' He shook his head, but she persisted with her confession. 'I'm…nervous. It took my mind off things. It's quite dangerous really, spending all that money. It must be like gambling or drink.'

To her surprise he didn't laugh at the notion. 'You are probably right. But don't worry, if you can see the danger, then I doubt you are in it. But don't be nervous, Kate. I'll look after you. I won't let the society sharks near you.'

'I know.' *But you can't protect me from the monsters I've unleashed myself, my love.*

Grant climbed to the next step on the grand staircase leading to the ballroom of the Marquess of Larminster's ballroom, the setting for the marchioness's 'surprise' birthday reception for her husband. The event was a surprise for no one, least of all the long-suffering and newly sixty-year-old marquess, but he enjoyed indulging his wife and she enjoyed parties, the larger the better.

It was not the event that Grant would have chosen for Kate's introduction to London society, for the place was full to bursting and the noise level indescribable. It was also packed with the important people Kate needed to make a good impression upon if she were to obtain the entrée to the right circles and the friendship and approval of the ladies who made society go round. And they were married to the men Grant mixed with socially at his clubs and would be forming alliances with, and against, in the House of Lords.

As he stood with as much patience as he could muster in the receiving line, he looked down at his wife again, still coming to terms with how sophisticated and elegant she looked. It occurred to him that the height of his hopes had been that she would 'do', pass muster, not be a disaster. How little faith he'd had. Somewhere, always in the back of his mind, was the image of the bedraggled, exhausted, desperate woman in that bothy, the knowledge that she was not trained up for this world, that she carried scandal with her.

Despite coming to know her—her courage, her humour, her intelligence, her breathtaking natural eroticism—he had still taken it for granted that she could not cope with this world with its dagger-sharp criticism, its rivalries and sophisticated pleasures.

'Grant,' Kate murmured. 'We're moving again.'

Up another step, almost at the top now. She was still nervous, he could see the almost imperceptible tremor of the beading around the bodice of her gown, but she looked magnificent. Not a traditional beauty, she would never be that, but somehow something better. *Elegant, charming, warm,* he thought. *And sophisticated with her new hairstyle. And the minx has been colouring her lashes with lampblack and, if I'm not very much mistaken, she's using lip stain.*

Like a soldier she'd put on her armour to go into battle for him. *She makes me so happy.*

The realisation hit him as though someone behind him had punched him between the shoulder blades. Happy. He was actually, positively happy. Not just now and again, like when he was playing with Charlie, or feeling the wind in his hair when he galloped unchecked across the moor, or won a hand of cards against Gabriel, but bone-deep happy. That had come with this marriage. Somehow he had moved, without him realising it, from simply coping with life and snatching what pleasure he could, to a feeling of inner contentment. But he had not been conscious of feeling happy. *When did that happen? Just now? Yesterday? Weeks ago?*

A sharp elbow nudged him in the ribs. *'Grant, it's us.'*

'Sorry, air-dreaming.' Hell, in a minute he'd be shouting with laughter, capering like a fool for a fascinated audience. Grant found a social smile from somewhere, plastered it on and advanced on the marchioness. 'Lady Larminster, may I introduce my wife, Catherine?'

'Lady Allundale.' The marchioness raised artfully curved eyebrows as she studied Kate. 'Delightful,' she pronounced.

'Lady Larminster.' Kate's curtsy was perfectly modulated.

'Larminster, here's Allundale's wife at long last.' The marquess inclined his head and beamed at Kate, who curtsied again. 'You've taken long enough bringing her to town, Allundale.'

Grant had no trouble interpreting that as, *So what is wrong with her?* 'All due to my sins, ma'am. I'm greedy, jealous and possessive and don't want to share her.' As he spoke, he realised that was all quite true. He wanted to scoop Kate up in his arms and sweep her off back home. He wanted to do something about this strange fizzing joy inside him.

'Well, now, there's a declaration of the kind one doesn't hear enough of in these cynical days. Do you hear that, Larminster?'

Beside him he could almost feel the warmth of Kate's blushes, but when he walked her away from the receiving line and could look at her face he saw the light dusting of rice powder had subdued the colour, or else she was pale through nerves.

'She's a bossy old besom,' he said as he steered her into the reception room. 'But she means well.'

'I'm sure she does.' Kate's chin was up. 'That was very gallant of you, to say those things.'

'I meant them.' *You make me so happy. You have transformed my life.* How the blazes did one say these things to one's wife in the middle of this scrum? Surely there was a withdrawing room somewhere? Gabriel would have slipped a coin to a footman and would know the location of hidden nooks before he had even sized up the ladies at any social event. Alex, in the old days, wouldn't have been much slower. But Grant had never enjoyed dicing with scandal under the very noses of chaperons and sharp-eyed husbands and had always conducted his affaires with considerably more discretion.

'What is amusing you?' Kate obviously didn't find anything at all amusing about the hot, noisy throng and was eyeing them with a social smile on her lips and eyes as wary as any gladiator thrust into the arena, wondering where the lions hid and just how hungry they were.

'I'm regretting not bribing a footman, that's all,' he said vaguely. 'Come, let's circulate and I'll introduce you to some people you'll like.'

And, by a miracle, he managed to locate many of the acquaintances he had hoped to introduce to Kate. The pleasanter young matrons with small children of their own, the cheerful chaperons whose gossip was friendly, not vicious, and several gentlemen he could trust to treat her to polite and harmless flirtation or intelligent conversation.

After half an hour he felt she had relaxed enough to leave her with a group of his friends while he went to find her a glass of ratafia. When he got back she had Mr Whittaker choking with laughter over her description of their vicar confronted by the flock of sheep that wandered into the church during his sermon, pursued by a very amorous ram. By her side the Reverend Herbert, one of the Bishop of London's more irreverent curates, was extemporising a sermon of his own on the subject of lost lambs while making eyes at two young ladies who appeared very willing to stray in his direction.

Grant had never realised that Kate was a natural raconteur before, but she was holding her small audience gripped while, with perfect poise, she spun the tale in such a way that the poor vicar was described kindly and yet the scene was irresistibly funny.

'Do let me introduce you to my sister, Lady Allundale. She pines for witty conversation.' Whittaker took her arm, removed the ratafia glass from Grant's hand and steered Kate off into the crowd. She seemed more than happy to go with him.

'You look as nervous as a hopeful mama whose chick has just been launched into the stormy seas of the Season,' a familiar voice remarked.

'Alex.' Grant relaxed a trifle. If Alex was there, then Tess was as well, so that was two more allies. 'I don't know about looking like a hopeful matron, but I'm certainly nervous—Kate is painfully shy about all this.'

'She looks stunning. Very chic. I like the hair.' His friend was watching Kate with the eye of a connoisseur.

Grant narrowed his eyes at him, then told himself not to be ridiculous. This possessiveness played havoc with the common sense. 'She does, but she doesn't look like my Kate any more when she's dressed up like this.'

'Ah. *Your* Kate. I wondered how long it was going to take you to notice.' Alex's mouth twitched into its lazy smile as Grant frowned at him.

'Of course I notice. She's my wife.' He did his best to sound offhand. This new awareness of his feelings was too sensitive to discuss, even with Alex.

'No *of course* about it. Tess says we men have to be hit over the head with it before we realise it isn't lust or liking. When did you get hit with the brick?'

'An hour ago,' Grant admitted. 'At the top of the staircase, two couples from the head of the receiving line.'

Alex's hoot of laughter had heads turning, including Kate's. She raised her hand in a little wave, then turned back to her new acquaintances. 'No wonder you are looking vaguely concussed. Love does that. I assume Kate is aware of your feelings?'

'*What?* Don't be an idiot. Of course I'm not—' Grant managed to get his snarl down to a whisper. 'She makes me happy, that's all. I realised just now that I hadn't felt like this…for ever. And it is due to her. But that's contentment and liking and lus—er, compatibility in bed. It is not love. Ours is a marriage of convenience, you know that. And stop mopping your eyes, it isn't that funny.'

'No?'

'No, it is not.'

Alex rolled his eyes and returned his handkerchief to its pocket in the tails of his coat. 'There have been times when I've been deluded enough to think you quite intelligent, Rivers. I will leave you to stew and go and see who Tess is making eyes at and rescue them.'

'Don't say anything.'

'About what? The fact that you are *happy*? Or the fact that you're an idiot?' Alex strolled off, leaving Grant to practice deep breathing in the middle of the crowded floor in the intervals between greeting acquaintances, bowing to ladies and attempting to get his emotions and his brain into some kind of alignment.

He was an adult male with considerable experience of life and women. He had faced his man in a duel, he had fought at Waterloo and somehow got out of that intact, he had dealt with hysterical mistresses throwing the porcelain from under the bed before now. He wasn't a romantic youth desperate to transform simple liking, affection and desire into some hearts-and-flowers nonsense that could only end in disillusion and anticlimax. He was happy. His marriage made him happy. That was a wonderful realisation and now he could just get on with his life.

Chapter Nineteen

Kate was beginning to relax. In fact, she thought with a small start of surprise, she was actually beginning to enjoy herself. No one had pointed a finger at her, crying *Fallen woman!* or *Blackmailer's accomplice!* as they did in her worst dreams. She could see no one who looked even faintly familiar, except for Alex and Tess, and her new acquaintances were all pleasant and even positively friendly.

Grant had seemed a little strange for a moment while they had been waiting on the stairs, but perhaps he had been nervous for her, which was understandable. She had no idea how her shaky legs had got her up those stairs, but now she was happily answering questions about which days she was at home to visitors and promising to take Anna to call on Mrs Whiting, who had a baby girl almost the same age.

She sensed Grant with a prickling awareness that had her glancing back over her shoulder with a smile, even before he arrived at her side. Was he proud of her? She hoped so, because she thought she was doing very well indeed.

'My dear.' He rested his right hand at the small of her back, a possessive gesture that made her shiver pleasurably. 'I am afraid I must tear you away. If you will excuse us?' He nodded and smiled and was perfectly polite as he detached her from the group and began to walk her back towards the entrance.

'Grant, is something wrong? You haven't had a message about one of the children, have you?'

'No, nothing is wrong. I need to talk with you, that's all.'

So I must be doing something wrong... No, that can't be it. I know I have not put a finger out of line. Was he unwell? She looked up at his face as he took her arm as they descended the stairs, then sent a footman for their things. He looked tense, keyed up. It must be one of his wretched migraines, although it had been weeks since he had suffered one. Perhaps anxiety about her had triggered it.

Kate stayed silent and did not fuss, even when they were seated in their carriage. She was finally rewarded for her patience when Grant threw his hat on to the seat opposite, ran both hands through his hair and said, 'I am sorry to have dragged you away. You seemed to be enjoying yourself.'

'I was, very much. I have made some new acquaintances and that will make the next engagement even better. But it is no matter, there will be many other opportunities to talk with them.'

'There is something I need to speak to you about. Something important.'

Not a headache, then. Nor did he seem displeased. 'What is wrong?'

Grant had not put on his gloves and she peeled off her

own so she could slide her hand into his. It was warm and steady and closed around her fingers in a reassuring grip.

'Absolutely nothing is wrong, quite the opposite, in fact, but I think I will wait until we are home before I tell you.'

'Very well.' Comforted, she settled back and did her best to contain her curiosity.

In her bedchamber Kate handed over her evening cloak and gloves to Wilson and then dismissed the maid and waited with what patience she could muster.

Grant was normally reserved, she knew that from experience, but this seemed to be a secret out of the ordinary. Perhaps Prinny had offered him a diplomatic post and he was doubtful whether she was prepared to sail to Brazil. Or he had decided to take Holy Orders. Or buy a very large and expensive yacht. Or…

'Kate. I have never told you this… In fact, I have only just realised it, but this marriage makes me very happy. You make me very happy. I cannot recall ever feeling like this. Not all the time.'

She hadn't heard the door open and, lost in fantasies about sea voyages and cathedral closes, she could only stare at him. For a second she thought she heard him say *I love you*, then her brain made sense of what he had actually said and her pulse seemed to stutter. 'You… Grant, did you just say that I make you happy?'

'Yes.' He raised a quizzical eyebrow, seemingly expecting more of a reaction. 'I realise it is rather a sudden declaration, but is it so surprising?'

'When?' Her voice was strangely croaky. 'When did you realise it? I had no idea you had been feeling *un*happy.'

'I haven't.' He shrugged. 'Well, about Madeleine, of

course. But I had become used to thinking happiness was a matter of fleeting pleasures, of the absence of pain. This evening, at the top of the stairs just before we reached the receiving line, I realised that it is a positive thing, something that can fill me—and all because of you. Not the most convenient location for a revelation of that kind, you must admit.'

No wonder he had seemed so strange. Kate realised she was simply staring at Grant, unable to articulate a sensible response. Like, *I love you. And perhaps you are in love with me and don't realise it.*

'I'm sorry to be so dramatic about it.' He came further into the room and the door closed behind him with a click that made her jump. 'But I never speak to you about how I feel for you, how much I treasure what you have done at Abbeywell to make it into a home, how good you are with Charlie. I feel as though you have lifted a weight off my soul that I never realised was there. If that makes me sound ridiculous, I can't help it. I thought I ought to be open about how I felt.'

That was heaping coals of fire on her smarting conscience. Grant was offering her an honest declaration of his feelings when she did not deserve it, when she had lied to him in fact and by omission. But there was one thing she could be honest with him about, something she could give him, a response to his declaration. Not the full truth, of course, not that she loved him. She had been waiting too long for him to say it first, now she suspected he never would and her own love would be a burden to him.

Kate stood up and went to stand in front of him, linked her hands behind his neck and looked up into the steady green eyes. 'You make me happy, too. More than happy. With all my heart I am glad that you married me.'

He closed his eyes and rested his forehead against hers and sighed, a long, slow, difficult breath. 'Kate. Kate, I am sorry I never said these things before. I am not very good at emotions, I don't know how to be.'

'I understand.' She thought she did. He had grown up without his parents' marriage as a model. He had been raised by an elderly widower and married to a woman who had rejected and hurt him. Somewhere, deep inside, in a place he probably didn't even know existed, he had raised barriers to ever making himself as vulnerable as love would render him.

'You don't have to say things, to pretend to feelings you do not have. It is enough to know I make you happy. I just need you to know you make me happy, too,' Kate said, picking her way through, wary of saying anything that would make him suspect she loved him, force him to say the words that would be a lie. 'You were my Christmas miracle when you found me in that bothy and saved us. I am so glad I am your wife.' She stood on tiptoe and kissed him, and after the faintest hesitation he kissed her back, slowly, tenderly.

I must confess, tell him about Jonathan and Henry now. I can't deceive him any longer. It will hurt him that I have left it so long, but to leave it even longer can only make things worse.

He lifted one hand and began to pull the pins from her hair, drawing his fingers through it until it fell free on her shoulders. 'I am going to carry you off to bed and show you just how happy you make me, but before I do, I must tell you how proud I was of you tonight. I know you were nervous and unsure, but you did your best in spite of that and your best was magnificent.'

There was so much warmth and pride in his voice. If she did not know better, she might have added *love*. She didn't deserve any of those feelings, and if she told him the truth about Anna, the truth about her brother, then that pride would vanish, he would despise her.

'Thank you,' she murmured. 'It was far less daunting than I feared.' It had been—once she had assured herself that there was no sign of Viscount Baybrook, or of Sir Henry Harding, blackmailing baronet, either. Surely if Jonathan was in London he would have been invited to such a magnificent event as the Larminsters' reception? It was less likely that Henry would be there, but he might be in town if he had been both emboldened and enriched by extorting money from Jonathan, and it would be just like him to extract an invitation somehow.

Grant was working his way into the elaborate fastenings and folds of her gown and she arched her back to help him. *I will tell him tomorrow,* she resolved. *I cannot shatter this moment. I cannot, it is too precious.*

Grant used no erotic tricks, no titillating little games, only the magic of his mouth and his hands and his long, hard body, and Kate realised that she had learned to give with as much passion as she received. When he eased into her, slowly, achingly slowly, she realised that it was the exchange about their feelings that had given them this extra awareness of each other, of what they could be together.

There was no hurry, no rush to climax. Grant would stop moving and simply lie there, his heart beating over hers, his gaze locked with hers, his body filling and completing her. Then he would dip his head to take her lips and move again until Kate was lost in a spell of sensual, swirling pleasure. They were close, so close.

I love you, she thought and it was as though it was enough to tip them over into bliss, into a place where they were no longer two people, but one whole being, just as she had dreamed.

They made love again in the morning when they woke, a passionate tussle of urgency and need that left them panting and laughing. Grant ducked a flying pillow and pounced on Kate, tickling mercilessly, then subsided, pulling her against his side.

'I needed to laugh with you, Kate.'

Yes, I needed to laugh, too. I'll talk to him after breakfast, she thought as they subsided, breathless. 'Grant—'

'Hell, is that the time?' He rolled off the bed and made for the door to his room. 'I'm due at a meeting at the Lords at ten. Ungodly hour, I know, but I promised Pilkington. I think I will be supporting his group over several important pieces of legislation and we must discuss tactics.' He turned back, looked at her, shook his head. 'Incredible, I don't deserve to be so happy.' Then he was gone.

Kate was left staring at the door. It gave her no comfort, nor any inspiration. Finally she tugged the bell pull for Wilson. She couldn't sit in bed all day, her mind a blank. Perhaps a complete confession was not the answer. What if telling Grant about the blackmail made him an accessory unless he reported it to the magistrates immediately? He was loyal and she could imagine he would struggle with his conscience before incriminating her in such a shameful scandal, but he was also honourable.

He could not connive at extortion, so he would have to take action.

Perhaps she could establish Lord Baybrook's situation first. If he was safely married, that was one thing—he would probably go to great lengths to avoid her. But if he were not, he would probably still be smarting from Henry's demands, leaving aside the question of whether he would think her a loose woman on whom he could take revenge of a non-legal kind.

Once she knew the facts, then she could truthfully tell Grant that she had fallen foolishly for Jonathan Arnold, Lord Baybrook, but that, when Henry had approached him to tell him he must do the decent thing and marry her, Baybrook had revealed that he was already betrothed.

But then could she admit to Grant that Henry had known all along about Baybrook's impending betrothal, had set up a trap from the start? That he had demanded money, not as a settlement on the child, but as hush money so that its existence was never revealed to Baybrook's future father-in-law, the famously puritanical, and staggeringly wealthy, Lord Harlington?

Henry had sent her away to Scotland, not to hide her pregnancy, but to hide her from Baybrook and, when the child was born, to keep her out of his reach, to hold as a future threat against payments. When she had protested, told Henry that he should wait, not press demands beyond a decent competence to raise the child once Baybrook was safely married and in funds, he had threatened to take the baby as soon as it was born to make certain he had control and that Kate could not do anything *foolish*, as he put it. *Or honest,* she had thrown at him and he had laughed in her face.

She realised that she did not know what Jonathan's

reaction had been to Henry's demands for money. He was a rake, but not a fundamentally wicked man, she was certain. Surely he would have made a reasonable settlement on his love child, as soon as he could afford it. But Henry had no intention of settling for *reasonable*, not with Lord Harlington's fortune shimmering before his eyes. Jonathan might be paying up, being bled, or he might have told Henry to go to the devil.

And if he was paying, then she could not, in all conscience, let the blackmail continue.

Wilson came in, followed by Jeannie, Anna in her arms. 'She's fretting over her little tooth, my lady. Such a grizzle, she is, aren't you, my pet?' Jeannie handed her to Kate, who tried to soothe her and think clearly at the same time. One thing was certain, she thought as she gently massaged the sore gums, it was a recipe for disaster to sit passively waiting for disaster to strike, or to confess all to Grant when she did not know the facts.

After breakfast she checked the *Peerage* and a London directory in Grant's study, then rang for Jeannie. 'I would like you to go to this address in Hill Street and see if it is occupied.' She handed over the direction of what had been Baybrook's town house before his marriage. 'I need to know the name of the owner, whether he is in residence and whether he is married. And I need you to find this out without revealing why you are asking.'

Jeannie knew, she was certain, that Anna was not Grant's child, although it had never been spoken of between them. She met Kate's gaze and bit her lip. 'You'll be looking for a…relative, my lady?'

'Yes, that's it. A discreet enquiry.' She knew she could be putting a strain on Jeannie's loyalty. 'It is something about which I need to have all the facts clear before I speak to his lordship.'

The unease faded from the nursemaid's face. 'Aye, I can see that. Can I leave Lady Anna with you directly after breakfast, then, my lady? I could be walking past on an errand, sprain my ankle and have to hobble down to the area door to beg help from their cook. All kitchen staff gossip if they get half a chance.'

Jeannie came back mid-morning, rather pink in the face and inclined to giggle. 'I've made a conquest, I think, my lady. A Scottish footman at the Hill Street house. I managed to trip on a paving stone outside, right into his arms, and when he heard my accent he carried me down to the kitchen and then back up again after I sat awhile. And he insisted on calling me a hackney.' She sobered instantly when she saw Kate's face. 'I'm sorry, my lady, I'm blathering on. It is Lord Baybrook's house and he's in residence with his wife and they've just come back to London after their honeymoon tour.'

'Thank you, Jeannie. That will be all. I appreciate your assistance.'

So now what? The bad news was that Jonathan was in London, but the very good news was that Henry had not managed to do something so dreadful that the marriage had been called off. Although it still might mean that he was extorting money from the viscount, and if that was the case, then she had to stop it. It seemed, more and more, that she was going to have to approach Jonathan directly, assure him of her good intentions and discover just what her brother had done. The thought of Grant getting in the middle of this unholy mess didn't bear thinking about. He would be furious, he would call Jonathan out—and then someone might end up a widow.

It was a plan of sorts, but it did not make her feel any better. Hiding the truth from Grant had been bad enough, but now she knew the extent of his affection and trust, it felt like the worst of betrayals. But there was Anna, an innocent child to consider. And the equally innocent Lady Baybrook, and her own sister-in-law, unwittingly married to a blackmailer.

Now all she had to do was engineer a meeting with Jonathan and trust to his good nature and discretion. It seemed an awfully big risk.

Chapter Twenty

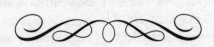

Grant did not come home for luncheon, which was not unusual. What was out of the ordinary was the note that arrived from him on Brooks's Club notepaper.

> Today, of all days, when I want to be with you, they ask me to meet the Home Secretary! Goodness knows when I'll get away, but I'll tell you all about it at dinner, I promise.
> Yours,
> G.

Kate rang for Jeannie and for Grimswade. 'I feel like taking the air with Anna. Lord Brooke is going for a walk with his tutor, I believe. Have the carriage sent round, Grimswade, if you please.'

When the butler had gone she turned to the nurse-maid. 'I hardly know what I hope to achieve by this, but if I see Lord Baybrook, I will try to snatch the opportunity to speak with him. But I do not want him to see Anna, so you must stay in the carriage.' Jeannie seemed about to say something, but Kate forestalled her. 'I can't go out without a maid or a footman, his lordship would be furious. And there is no one else I can trust. But I probably won't encounter Lord Baybrook.'

'It's a nice afternoon,' Jeannie observed. 'A gentleman might take a stroll to his club.'

'Yes.' *And at least it will get me out of the house. I feel like a turnspit dog on a treadmill.*

Kate gave the coachman a circuitous route that took in a number of shops that she might plausibly want to visit and which brought them via Hill Street to Grosvenor Street. There was no sign of Jonathan's tall and elegant figure sauntering along, nor when they turned down Berkeley Street towards Piccadilly. 'It was ridiculous to think I would see him,' she observed to Jeannie. 'The number of places a gentleman can be in even the small compass of Mayfair must be countless.'

And then, as the carriage slowed to a crawl in the Piccadilly traffic, she glanced up Dover Street and saw him. 'He's there!'

Jeannie tugged on the check string, the carriage pulled over to the kerb and they stared at each other. 'I cannot accost him in the street.' Kate watched as he reached the road junction, a polished wooden box under his arm. 'He's been to Manton's, the gunsmiths, I think. Jeannie, look, he's crossing over to Green Park.'

'Hurry, my lady.' Jeannie opened the door and kicked down the step. 'You can speak to him in the park, there aren't many people around. I'll follow along behind, as if I'm not with you.'

Jonathan was held up by a brewer's dray while Kate, catching the attention of a crossing sweeper, was over the road before him. He went through the gate and into the park, not apparently in any hurry, for he strolled past the reservoir and cut across the grass towards the Queen's Walk. Kate walked briskly, came alongside him when there was no one close and realised she had no idea what to say.

He must have seen her out of the corner of his eye, for he stopped and raised his hat slightly. And then stared. 'Madam, do I know you?' The dawning recognition on his face would have been comical if things were not so serious. *'Catherine?'*

'Yes. Jonathan—Lord Baybrook, I need to speak with you.'

He had his composure back. His voice was icy, but perfectly controlled. 'I am sure you do.' His eyes ran up and down the fashionable outfit she wore. 'I see you have acquired some expensive tastes on my money.'

'No, I have not. Is Henry demanding payments from you? It is not with my agreement, believe me.'

'Believe you? My dear Miss Harding, why should I believe a word you say? The last true thing you told me was that you were innocent of a man and *that* I did not need telling, for you were a most uninteresting tumble,' he drawled. 'Your rat of a brother informed me you were with child. My child. Is that true or have I been paying out every month for nothing?' The mask of unconcern was slipping to reveal the fury beneath.

Anna. I can't let him find Anna. 'Yes, I was pregnant. I thought Henry was going to insist that you marry me.' She felt the heat rise in her face as Baybrook gave a bark of laughter. 'I did not think you would. But I thought you would make me a small allowance so I could bring the child up decently. That was all I wanted, all I expected. I had no idea that Henry was…'

'A blackmailer? Oh, really, my dear. Doing it rather too brown if you expect me to believe you knew nothing of this.' His anger was beginning to ride him now, overcome his habitual elegant indifference. 'Well, make your demands, and then I will tell you how I intend to deal with you.'

'I have no demands. I needed to know what Henry was doing—I haven't seen him for a year. I'll stop him, I swear. I'll do everything I can to stop him.'

'Do you take me for a fool, my dear?' He turned to face her fully, his voice a snarl of frustrated fury now. 'Do you think because I sampled your very rustic charms that I can be cock-led into another compromising situation? Have you any idea what life is like lived at the toleration of a Bible-thumping old bigot who doles out his money like drops of his own blood, always alert for any moral lapse that can be the excuse for a sermon or for withholding funds?'

'No, but—'

He caught her wrist, jerked her towards him. 'There are many reasons why I do not drag you down to the nearest magistrate's office this minute, but there are equally many, many reasons why you should be very afraid of me, my dear. Very afraid indeed.'

Over his shoulder she could see Jeannie, her face a picture of anxiety and indecision. *Stay there, do not try to help. Stay there,* she tried to signal.

Then he was jerked away from her. The wooden box fell to the ground and burst open, two duelling pistols fell out on to the grass, exquisite death glinting in the winter sunshine.

'Take your hands off my wife before I break all your fingers,' Grant said pleasantly, his own hands fisted in the lapels of Lord Baybrook's elegant coat. 'You'll need them to fire one of those pretty toys you've just dropped.'

For a long moment they stared into each other's eyes, almost nose to nose, two male stags in their prime locking antlers over a female. Then, when Kate thought she would burst with the tension, Jonathan stepped back, hands raised in the fencer's signal of yielding.

'Your *wife*? Allundale, is it not? I am Baybrook. My apologies, I had no idea. In fact, I had misread the situation totally. The lady asked me something and I thought—forgive me, madam—that she was...well, not to beat about the bush, I completely misunderstood her status. I could see no one with her. I was deep in thought and most unfortunately leapt to the conclusion that she was...er...importuning me.'

'Lady Allundale?' Grant's rigid formality failed utterly to veil the fury in his eyes.

He'll kill him, Kate thought. *If he has the slightest idea what is happening...* Jeannie, thank heavens, was keeping her distance, had turned away from the three of them so the child in her arms was not visible.

'It was, as the gentleman says, a misunderstanding. I was cutting across to the path, stumbled and caught at his arm and must have blurted out some words of apology. When he spoke to me I was confused, I did not realise what he thought and then when I did I was agitated, which made things worse... Jeannie had fallen behind, so I appeared to be unescorted.' She managed a tight social smile for Jonathan. 'Sir, it was entirely my fault. I am quite unused to London.'

He was a quick thinker, she had to hand it to him. And a brilliant actor. He was all contrition, all elegant apologies, and Grant was left with no option but to accept them.

He bowed, the merest inclination of his head, and offered Kate his arm. Jonathan bowed in his turn, picked up the pistols and strode off towards the Queen's Walk.

'Did he hurt you?' Grant demanded the moment they were alone. She shook her head and saw him relax a little. 'And what the devil was Jeannie playing at? Well?' he demanded as the maid hurried up to them. 'When you escort your mistress your duty is to stay with her, not stroll about like a moonling.'

'Anna has been very fretful,' Kate said hastily. 'I expect that is what held you up, Jeannie.'

'Yes, my lady, and then when I saw the gentleman, I didn't know what to do. Not when I had Lady Anna, because I thought he would frighten her.'

'Very well. Where is the carriage?'

'Waiting near the palace, my lord, at the end of the Queen's Walk.' Jeannie gave Kate the tiniest of nods.

'I'll go back with you in that case. I was walking back from the Palace of Westminster across the parks. Fortunately.'

'Yes, wasn't it.' Kate clung to his arm and hoped he would attribute her shakiness to the after-effects of the encounter with Jonathan and not shock at his own appearance combined with a hideously guilty conscience. 'That gentleman was not a friend of yours, then?'

'The Viscount of Baybrook? No. I've hardly ever seen him that close to. The man was a gazetted rake, and a wild one at that, before his marriage. I never ran in those circles, even when I was sowing my own wild oats— the gambling was too deep for me, for one thing, and I dislike being sodden with drink half the time. Now his father-in-law holds the purse strings so tight that Baybrook hardly dares sneeze without permission, by all accounts.' They walked on in silence until they were almost at the gravelled walk bordering the high walls of the fine houses that overlooked Green Park. Grant's fingers stroked reassuringly over hers and gradually her breathing calmed.

'It is strange, though, there was something so familiar about him.' Grant shrugged. 'Perhaps I've come across one of his relatives. Society is so interbred, I may know a cousin of his and not even realise it. Now, where is the carriage?'

It was waiting at the end of Milkmaid's Passage, where a footpath led from the park to the front of St James's Palace. 'Why did you not take the groom with you?' Grant demanded as they settled themselves inside.

'Um…idiocy?' Kate ventured and was rewarded with a smile.

'I shouldn't be cross with you. I forget what an innocent you are in London. This is not the moorlands where you may stretch your legs accosted by nothing worse than a flock of sheep.'

'No, my lord,' Kate said meekly and saw, from the smile in Grant's eyes, that she was forgiven. 'Sheep can be very dangerous, you know.' *I don't deserve him. How am I going to get out of this mire without someone getting hurt?* 'How did your meeting go, my lord? It was satisfactory, I hope?'

'Most. I suspect I have landed myself with a great deal of work, but I am interested in social issues.'

She would get the details out of him when they were alone and, perhaps, convince him that she read the newspapers, too, that she had views on social policy and could discuss the problems he was going to be tackling. *If he is still prepared to talk to me.*

Kate stared blankly out at the passing clubs and shops as the carriage climbed the slope of St James's Street. *What am I going to do about Jonathan and Henry now?*

Grant stood in front of his dressing mirror, tying his neckcloth and attempting to pin down the niggling sense of unease at the back of his mind. He had swept Kate upstairs and made love to her so thoroughly that she seemed to be entirely satisfied that he was not blaming her for the Green Park incident. It also served to satisfy his own primitive male feelings of ownership. He grimaced at himself as he acknowledged the response. Still, it could have turned nasty if he had not come across them. The behaviour was typical of Baybrook, by all accounts. The man might no longer be able to carry on his dissolute lifestyle, but he obviously could not resist accosting an attractive woman when one crossed his path.

What was unsettling was that the strange incident had reawakened all his niggling doubts about Kate. He had been trying to suppress them, tell himself that they were simply leftovers from his experiences with Madeleine, and that now he was so happy in his marriage they would vanish. But they had not. Perhaps the lack was in him and he had lost the ability to trust completely.

'Move the candles up, would you, Griffin?' The valet shifted a branch of candles to the left-hand side of Grant to balance those on the right, and he leaned close to the glass to slide in his tiepin. *Just so.* He met his own gaze in the mirror and grimaced. He was turning into a damn dandy, peacocking about for his Kate.

The thought lifted his spirits. Amused green eyes smiled back and he went still. *That* was what had been nagging away—Baybrook's eyes. For a few tense seconds they had stared at each other, almost nose to nose. And Baybrook's eyes were green, an unusual clear colour with golden flecks and a black rim to the pupil. The colour he had seen when he had compared Anna's eyes to his own. It was too much of a coincidence, that bizarre encounter between the earl and Kate and the colour of the man's eyes. *He is Anna's father.*

'My lord?' Griffin murmured, the equivalent from him of a nudge in the ribs.

'What?'

'Are you quite well, my lord? A migraine, perhaps?'

'No, I'm fine, just distracted by business.' He had to think about this, try to work out just what the other man knew. It was interesting that, although Jeannie had been with her, Kate had obviously not shown Anna to her lover. *Her ex-lover,* he told himself, exerting all his willpower to steady his breathing, his instinctive reactions. *Don't get into a jealous rage over this. There is no way he and Kate have been together since we married. Although what she was plotting now with apparently chance meetings in the park...*

The thought of Kate getting up to something underhand was like a stab. Was this what he had sensed was wrong all along?

He turned away and stood while Griffin eased him into his evening coat. A sliver of doubt seemed to have slid into his heart. She had lied, he realised, told him Anna's father was dead. So what else had she not told him? The cold fist closing around his gut was all too familiar from years of dealing with Madeleine's lies and evasions. *But not Kate. I need to trust her!*

Hell, he would be whimpering next that it wasn't fair, that she had told him she was happy with him. He was a man and he'd show some backbone over this, but he was not going to confront Kate with it, not yet. He examined that decision for cowardly motives and decided it was only right, and fair, to investigate first. If he was wrong about her, then a direct accusation would shatter that miraculous happiness between them for ever.

The place to start was her family. He should have insisted on contacting her brother before now. 'Griffin, fetch Mr Bolton to me at once. He is in, I assume?'

'Yes, my lord. He remarked he had some notes to transcribe. I believe he is in his room.'

When his secretary entered, tugging his sleeves down with one hand and running the other ink-stained hand through his hair, he looked harassed. 'My lord, I'm still working on your notes for this morning. I should have them finished—'

Grant waved a dismissive hand. 'My handwriting is execrable, I know. Some time tomorrow evening will be fine, for goodness' sake. Have your dinner in peace. Thank you, Griffin, that will be all for now.' As the door closed behind the valet, he added, 'In the morning I need to speak to a discreet enquiry agent.'

Bolton's eyebrows shot up. 'My lord? What sort of enquires, might I ask? I will enquire at your solicitor's office, but such men may come with, er, different specialisms.'

'I wish to trace someone, a connection of Lady Allundale's with whom she has lost touch.' He made himself smile. 'A bit of a black sheep, if you get my meaning. I would like to reunite them, but I will need to be satisfied of his character before I do so.'

'Of course, my lord. One cannot be too careful. I assume this will be a surprise for her ladyship?'

'Precisely,' Grant agreed. If she had deceived him

about her lover, then had she told him the truth about her brother—the man she was so very reluctant to get in touch with, despite her new position? If Kate was in trouble, he would do whatever it took to get her out of it, but the deceit wrenched at him. And now he was deceiving her and telling himself it was for her own good. Somehow he was going to have to go downstairs, face his wife over the dinner table and put on a mask, pretend nothing at all was wrong.

Caring is the very devil, Grant thought as he walked downstairs, schooling his face to reveal nothing whatsoever. Certainly not fear.

Chapter Twenty-One

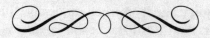

'Allow me to summarise and make certain I have this correct, sir.' Mr Martin, the highly respectable and discreet enquiry agent Grant's solicitors had recommended, glanced down at his notes.

Grant, or Mr Whyte as he had introduced himself, sat in the comfortable client's chair in Mr Martin's elegantly simple office off Ludgate Hill and made himself sit still and apparently relaxed as Martin recapped.

'There is a gentleman, probably by the name of Henry Harding, resident, possibly in Suffolk, who entertained Lord Baybrook in the spring of last year. The gentleman is married, has a sister named, probably, Catherine, and is of a somewhat profligate nature. You wish to identify him.'

'That is correct.' Grant was fairly certain that Catherine had given him her correct name, because she surely would not risk the marriage being invalidated by her using a false one. 'How long will it take you?'

'If he is in Suffolk, and he is a gentleman, then not long. But if the information you have been given is incorrect, then I will need to attack this from the direction of

Lord Baybrook's movements and that may require some, shall we say, excavation.'

Grant remembered Kate's hesitation in answering his questions. At the time he had attributed that to exhaustion. Now he wondered. 'I would not be surprised if the county is incorrect.'

'Let us say a week, Mr Whyte.'

'So fast?'

The enquiry agent smirked modestly. 'I have many sources, sir. And Lord Baybrook is, or was, a colourful character. I will send to your solicitor as soon as I have news.'

Grant took his leave and hailed a hackney carriage to take him to Brooks's Club. He was avoiding going home, he knew that. He knew he could not make love to Kate and hide from her that something was wrong and so he pretended to have far more work with his Parliamentary colleagues than he was actually undertaking and retired to his study every night after dinner until he thought she would be asleep.

If this went on for more than a week, he was going to be desperate with the need to hold her, he knew that. Kate had shown him happiness, taught him how to trust his heart to someone else. Now he struggled not to flinch back from that trust, like a man who has already been grievously burned and who expects the same pain again when he reaches out. Something was wrong and he would make it right for her, trust that her reasons for pretending that Baybrook had not been her lover were good.

Grant had expected Kate to comment on his absence from her bed, perhaps to fuss that he was overworking, but she did neither. It was as though she was holding herself back from him, but he could not decide whether it was because she was frightened, or ashamed or simply could not trust him with her secret. In the small hours of the night he had lain awake, alone in his big bed, and fought back the suspicion that she did not care for him after all, that seeing Baybrook had rekindled her feelings for the other man.

Now he looked down the length of the breakfast table and felt all his affection for her welling up, forcing back the suspicion and the anger. She was not Madeleine. He should try to trust her and he would not question her, let her see his doubts and how his faith had been shaken.

'My lord.'

He looked up from the sirloin that he was mangling and could not help but smile at the dignified way she addressed him whenever the staff were present. She did not call him *my lord* when she was screaming his name in the throes of passion, her limbs tangled with his, her nails raking his back.

'My lady?'

'I think I would like to take a small trip, have a day or two away from London. I am not feeling quite myself and the weather is so fine, I thought the sea air would do me good.'

'Brighton?' Grant suggested. 'It should not be difficult to get good lodgings at this time of year, but it will be devilishly cold.'

'I really wanted to go now. To Southend-on-Sea, I thought. So much closer.'

'Southend? It is certainly respectable, but isn't it a trifle...dull?'

'I only want the fresh air and it will do the children good, don't you think? We could go on the steamer easily in the day.'

'I doubt I can get away immediately.'

'If Charlie comes, then Mr Gough can provide a male escort and I'll have Jeannie and Wilson. I could even take one of the footmen.' Kate looked anxious, not like someone planning a short holiday.

'Very well, if that would please you.' He looked directly at her. 'I'll miss you. I know I haven't been very good company these past few days, but even so, the house will seem empty without you.'

Kate was colouring up. Where had this sudden urge to go into Essex come from? Did she just want to get away from him, or was there some more sinister reason? He felt suspicion flare.

'Thank you.' She managed a very creditable impression of pleasure tinged with concern. 'If you are sure? Well, then, I'll speak to everyone and organise it. If I write to the Ship Inn for rooms, I should hear tomorrow and we can set out the day after. We had accepted very few invitations for the next few days. London is becoming very quiet now.'

The Ship Inn? Did she know the town or had she been doing some research? he wondered. 'Certainly, and do use Bolton to book the steamer tickets and so forth. He can send your regrets for the various engagements and I'll see which I want to go to by myself.'

'The first post, my lord.' Grimswade proffered a salver.

'If you'll excuse me, I'll take these off to the study and deal with them.' He stood as he spoke, the letters in one hand, one with the distinctive handwriting of his solicitor's head clerk on the top.

He broke the seal as soon as the door was closed behind him and drew out the letter from Martin enclosed in the wrapper.

Lord Baybrook spent a week as the guest of Sir Henry Harding, baronet, at his estate, Belchamps Hall, in the parish of Hawkwell, Essex, in the period specified. I am unable, as yet, to provide you with details of Sir Henry's character and means, but I am able to confirm that he is a married man with a sister named Catherine Jane Penelope.

I have sent my assistant by this evening's mail coach to Rayleigh, the nearest town, with instructions to discover as much as possible of Sir Henry's situation within the day.

Grant reached for Cary's road book from the shelves beside the desk and opened it on the map of southern England. Hawkwell was apparently too small to be shown, but if it was close to Rayleigh, it was also close to Southend. Not more than five or so miles, he estimated by eye. If Kate was going to Southend, then he was going to Rayleigh.

The steamer was an adventure, at least for Charlie, who was so thrilled that he was rendered speechless, although not still. Mr Gough got Kate, Jeannie, Wilson and the baby settled in the warm shelter of the first-class saloon with Giles the footman to watch over them and was then towed from one end of the vessel to the other by his charge. Kate knew this because, with great regularity, Charlie would erupt into the saloon, compose himself with an effort and inform her of some riveting fact concerning the engines or the weight of coal consumed or the potential speed of the ship, then rush out again to interrogate some unfortunate seaman.

'It is very comfortable compared to a coach,' Kate

remarked to Wilson, who was sitting bolt upright clutching her mistress's dressing case on her knees and eyeing their fellow travellers with suspicion.

'Indeed, my lady, although what it would be like on the open sea may be another matter.'

'Yes, I am not sure about venturing to Margate,' Kate admitted. 'I have no idea whether I would be seasick or not.'

But the saloon was comfortable, the company, if rather varied, was respectable enough and the speed was astonishing. Kate looked out of the nearest porthole at the passing river scene and told herself that everything was going to be all right. Henry would be at home and he would see reason about stopping his extortion. He might even be persuaded to pay the money back, although Kate was far less confident about that. But the main thing was to make him stop his criminal activity and write assuring Jonathan that he would hear no more from him.

Then, when there was no longer a crime involved, she could confess everything to Grant and just hope and pray that he would understand. In broad daylight when she was feeling strong, she was confident, but in the small hours, as she lay awake fretting about everything from him working too hard to the loss of his faith in her, she could not help but recall his words.

I am just saying, for the record, that I will call out any man who lays a finger on you—and do my damnedest to kill him. And if your Jonathan had abandoned you and not drowned, then I would go after him and kill him, too. What if he called Jonathan out for failing to marry her? But, heartbroken as she had been at the time, if he *had* married her they would surely be in an unhappy marriage now, she would never have met Grant—and it was Grant she loved. And Grant who, one day, might love her.

It was only when the hired chaise was bowling across the flat farmlands around Hawkwell that Kate began to think uneasily about Henry's reaction. What, exactly, would her brother do with a sister who turned up, exceedingly inconveniently, and threatened to crack the golden egg he was relying on? She had nothing to threaten him with to make him do the right thing and she would not put it past him to lock her in the attic while he thought out his tactics. It was not as though he had ever expressed any affection for her after all.

She had left Charlie and Anna with Jeannie and Mr Gough at the Ship Inn, but she had not told either of them where she was going, which, in retrospect, was not sensible. She had said nothing last night as they settled into the accommodation—now she knew she should at least have taken Jeannie into her confidence. The low-lying pastureland looked sodden and depressing as she stared out of the window, biting her lower lip as she thought.

'Giles, when I go into the house I am visiting, I will take Wilson with me, of course. I would like you to remain in the carriage. Let the window down a crack and then you will hear the church clock. It strikes the quarters. If I am not out within an hour, or if I do not send you a note with my name underlined, then I want you to go to Mr Gough with all speed and ask him to come here and demand to see me. He is to take no excuses, do you understand?'

Giles looked appalled. 'My lady, my lord would have my hide if he thought I had let you walk into somewhere dangerous!'

'It is not dangerous, exactly. I certainly would not take Wilson with me if it were, but the owner may want me to stay against my will.'

'I've got a hatpin,' the maid said darkly. 'And I'll use it. No one will hurt my lady if I have anything to do with it. You do as you're told, Giles.'

'Yes, Miss Wilson.' The personal maid to the lady of the house easily outranked a mere footman. It seemed that Giles was more in awe of her than he was of his mistress. 'I'll listen, like you say, my lady, never fear.'

Kate felt easier with some precautions in place, even though she was probably being completely melodramatic and the worst that might happen was that Henry would laugh in her face and throw her out. *And if that happens,* she resolved as the chaise drew into the courtyard in front of Belchamps Hall, *then I am telling Grant everything.*

Leaving Giles anxiously listening for the clock, Kate marched up to the front door and beat a tattoo with the knocker. The heavy oak door creaked open and she found herself face-to-face with Claridge, the butler.

He said stolidly. 'Yes, ma'am?'

'Claridge, do you not recognise me? Miss Catherine.' She took a step forward as he gaped at her. 'Where is Sir Henry?'

The butler gave way before her, but he still looked utterly taken aback. 'In…in his study, Miss Catherine. But—'

'You were not expecting me, quite. And it is Lady Allundale now, Claridge. There is no need to announce me, I know my way.' Strangely she felt confidence flooding back as she smiled at the butler. She was here to fight dragons, defeat them for the sake of her love and her happiness. She lifted her chin, set back her shoulders, lifted her imaginary sword.

'Yes, miss. I mean, my lady.'

He stepped aside, jaw working as though he was searching for words, and went along the familiar panelled hallway, past the foot of the stairs and the great carved banister rail she used to slide down on her tummy when she was a child. They passed the door into the sunny front parlour, where she would sit and sew with her sister-in-law, and up to the door to Henry's study, not a place in which the women of the household were welcome.

'Make Miss Wilson comfortable if you please, Claridge.'

She entered on her knock and almost stopped dead in surprise. The old gloomy study Henry had inherited from their father had been swept away. Now it was freshly painted and boasted a handsome mahogany desk and chairs in the latest style, new bookcases and an array of books in fine leather bindings. The window had been converted into French doors leading out on to the rear terrace, and as she came in, she saw Henry standing there, the door ajar, apparently letting some chill fresh air into the stuffy room.

'Madam?' He blinked at her and she realised that for a moment he did not recognise her with her smart clothes and the gemstones winking in her earlobes. *'Catherine?'*

'Good afternoon, Henry.' She sat down in the chair opposite the desk, laid her reticule and tightly rolled umbrella on the glossy new leather surface and smiled warmly at him. 'What a handsome study, it must have cost you a pretty penny.'

'What are you doing here?' He stalked from the window

and stood clutching the back of his chair. 'Where in Hades have you been?'

'Oh, living my life.' Kate pulled off her gloves, slowly, finger by finger, as she looked around. 'While you have been accumulating the pretty pennies, it seems. What else have you been spending the money on, Henry? Oh, and I would love a cup of tea. And perhaps one of those delicious scones Mrs Hobhouse always used to make.'

He was so taken aback that he yanked the bell pull without arguing. Claridge must have been standing right outside the door. 'Sir?'

'Tea. Scones.' Henry flapped a hand at him and sat down. 'What are you doing here? And where did you get those clothes and those jewels?' He flung himself back in the chair and laughed. 'Oh, I see. You've found yourself a cosy little niche as some man's ladybird, have you? You're cleverer than I thought if you've fallen on your feet that way. Or should I say, on your back?'

'Don't be coarse, Henry.' Kate took the little silver case from her reticule and tossed a card across the desk to him. 'My husband would not appreciate it.'

He picked up the card and stared at it, the pasteboard creasing in his grip. 'Lady Allundale? *Lady Allundale?* How the devil? He knows about the brat?'

'What brat would that be, Henry? My husband's daughter?'

He stared at her. 'You couldn't have convinced him it was his, you were too far gone when you ran off.'

Claridge came in, placed a tray on the desk in front of Kate. 'Thank you, Claridge, that will be all. Tea, Henry?' she asked sweetly as the door closed.

'Damn the tea.' He watched, drumming his fingers on the arm of his chair, while she poured herself a cup, taking her time. She pretended to hesitate over a choice of scones until he demanded, 'What do you want?'

'I've come about the blackmail, Henry. It has to stop.'

'What blackmail?' He tried to look haughty and affronted.

'Don't pretend, Henry. You have been extorting money from Lord Baybrook. It is immoral, illegal and probably dangerous. His father-in-law won't live for ever and when he dies Baybrook is going to be a very rich man.' She took a sip of tea and was proud that her hand was rock-steady. 'Rich enough to take revenge on you in any way he chooses. Legal or illegal.' Was it her imagination, or had Henry gone pale?

'What do you want?'

His immediate move to negotiation made her wary. She had expected counter-threats, or, at the least, bluster. 'For you to stop demanding money. Write to Baybrook, tell him that no more will be asked.'

'Is that all?'

Of course it was not *all*. He was still being too accommodating, too calm. 'And you will return all the money you extorted.' Henry's jaw dropped. 'Just how much did you receive, Henry? How much did you demand from Baybrook every month?'

'Two hundred,' he snapped.

'Two hundred pounds? Two thousand four hundred a year. My goodness, that was ambitious, Henry.'

'He can afford it. And it is guineas, not pounds.' He smirked, obviously counting the golden treasure in his mind.

'Two thousand five hundred and twenty pounds,' she amended. 'A mistake to gloat about the guineas. That's an additional one hundred and twenty you are going to give me.' Could she convince him his only hope was to give her the money, or would he call her bluff?

'Give you the money? Are you insane? Why should I do a damn fool thing like that?'

'Because I'll see you in gaol if you don't, brother dear. My child, my fear and danger, my near disgrace. I think I have earned it, don't you?'

Chapter Twenty-Two

Grant held the hired hack to a controlled canter as he entered the village of Hawkwell. He had made good time, leaving London by post-chaise for Rayleigh as soon as Martin's assistant returned. Kate might have had a fast passage by the steamer, but he would be close on her heels.

'I couldn't do as much as I'd like, sir,' the man had explained, passing the notes across. 'But there's the address. In Rayleigh he's run up a fair amount of debt and they say he's a spendthrift on his own pleasures. His wife doesn't spend much at the local dressmaker or milliner, though. They think he keeps her on a pretty tight string and there are rumours he's not above knocking her around when he's in his cups. He also has a bit of a reputation for gambling—cock fights, the local card school, that sort of thing. The merchants I spoke to didn't have much of an opinion of him as a landowner. They say he leaves it all to his bailiff and he doesn't pay enough to get a man of the right calibre to do that wisely. I've made a note of the major debtors, sir.'

Now Grant drew rein in front of the church lychgate

as a thin man in a clerical collar and bands came out and closed it with care behind him.

'Good day, Reverend.'

'Good day, sir.' He smiled up at Grant. 'Have to take care or we get straying sheep in the churchyard and the silly creatures poison themselves on the yew. One could wish the Good Lord had given such useful animals more intelligence, but one cannot question His ways. May I assist you in any way, sir?'

'I am looking for Sir Henry Harding's house. Belchamps Hall, I believe.'

'Yes, indeed.' Was it his imagination or did the vicar's smile become less genuine? 'You have the right road. Just continue through past the green, take the second on the left and it is rather under a mile.'

'Thank you.' Grant touched his whip to his hat brim and urged the hack into a trot. So, debts, a reputation for gambling and not the vicar's favourite member of his flock. If Sir Henry was a churchgoer at all.

The clergyman's directions were accurate. Grant came alongside a high brick wall at about three-quarters of a mile from the village and then slowed as he saw a hired vehicle standing on the driveway. A postilion was perched on a low wall smoking a clay pipe and, clearly visible through the window of the vehicle, was the face of his own footman.

'Giles.'

'My lord!' The footman threw the carriage door open.

'Is her ladyship inside?'

'Yes, my lord. She went in three-quarters of an hour ago. My lord—'

Grant swung down from the horse, tossed Giles the

reins and strode up to the front door, leaving the footman mid-sentence. He had his hand raised to the knocker when instinct stopped him. Better to scout the ground before blundering in. Something strange was going on with Kate and her brother and he would rather discover what it was without it being filtered through whatever barriers they chose to erect.

The house was very quiet. Grant glanced into windows as he trod softly around the moss-covered path that skirted the walls. In one room a lady sat, head bent over some sewing, but she was no one he recognised. He rounded the corner to find himself on a flagstone terrace overlooking a bleak, level garden. Halfway along a glazed door stood ajar and, feeling a touch melodramatic, he walked cautiously up to it. Voices came clearly from the room inside.

'Just how much did you receive, Henry?' That was Kate's voice. Grant edged closer. She sounded very calm, very cool and strangely dangerous. He was grappling with that when she added, 'How much did you demand from Baybrook every month?'

Blackmail? That had to be what they were discussing.

'Two hundred,' a man snapped. And that must be her brother, Henry.

'Two hundred pounds? Two thousand four hundred a year. My goodness, that was ambitious, Henry.'

Kate sounded not at all shocked. In fact, from her question, she had obviously expected to hear that money was being extorted. A faint hope that she was talking about money for the support of her child faded. That sum was way in excess of what might be expected to provide for a by-blow. Not that he'd ever had to do the sums himself... Grant jerked his attention back to the voices in the room.

'And it is guineas, not pounds.'

'Two thousand five hundred and twenty pounds. A mistake to gloat about the guineas. That's an additional one hundred and twenty you are going to give me.'

Nausea gripped his gut. Kate wanted the blackmail money, was demanding it in a hard, cold voice that belonged to another woman, not the one he'd married. Not his Kate.

'Give you the money?' her brother protested. 'Are you insane? Why should I do a damn fool thing like that?'

'Because I'll see you in gaol if you don't, brother dear. My child, my fear and danger, my near disgrace. I think I have earned it, don't you?'

Grant reached for the door handle, his vision blurred by a haze of anger and betrayal. Kate, his Kate. He would never have believed that the woman he trusted with his life and his honour would turn into this hard-voiced, grasping witch.

Never have believed it. He jerked his hand back so hard his knuckles hit the rough surface of the brick, the pain like a dash of icy water in the face. *Trust.* If he abandoned her at this first test of his feelings, what did that make of their marriage but a hollow sham? This was Kate. Yes, she had not told him that Baybrook was Anna's father. Yes, she had not told him why she had come to Essex. But there could well be reasons as painful and as difficult to talk about as his feelings about Madeleine had been. He owed Kate his faith and, if things really were bad, his understanding and forgiveness. He had to get her to trust him to give her that and he could begin by not leaving her to fight this dragon alone.

* * *

Henry was spluttering now. 'Where the devil do you think I am going to get that money from? I have spent most of it.'

'Well, unspend it, Henry. Sell things, borrow, pawn. I want a banker's draft for every shilling.'

'Or what? All right, I agree that I'll write to Baybrook, tell him his debt's paid. But you can't get the money out of me, and if you utter any more threats, I'll just have to keep you here until you see reason.'

So, she had been right to leave Giles with instructions. 'My man is outside in the carriage. He knows what to do if I do not come out, or if I send him a note without a certain code word in it. I really am not as foolish as you always thought me, Henry. And as for how I intend to extract that money from you, why, I will simply confess all to my husband. Grant Rivers is a law-abiding, honest man and—'

The door behind her opened. 'I am flattered that you think so, my dear,' said a deep, calm voice.

'Grant.' Kate found she was on her feet, facing the door where her husband stood surveying the room with a chilly hauteur that sent a dangerous wave of sheer desire through her. Behind the broad shoulders in the caped greatcoat she could glimpse the butler, bobbing about in agitation.

'Sir? My lord?'

Grant half turned and handed Claridge his hat and gloves. He kept hold of his riding crop. 'Thank you. That will be all.' He shut the door in the butler's face. 'Sir Henry Harding, I assume? My brother-in-law.' He stayed on his feet, looming over the seated man at the desk. 'I wish I could say it is a pleasure, but I doubt it will be, for either of us.'

'Grant, please sit down.' He might be intimidating Henry, which was a good thing, but he was terrifying her.

'If you wish, my dear.' He picked up one of the heavy carved chairs that sat against the wall and spun it across, one-handed, to thud in front of the desk next to Kate, then he sat down, crossed one booted leg across the other and began, very softly, to tap the riding crop against the polished leather. 'So, allow me to summarise the situation as I see it, Harding. Your sister is with child by Baybrook. You send her away where he cannot marry her even if he wishes to, and then you extort money from him under threat of informing his immensely wealthy and very, very moral prospective father-in-law. Am I correct so far?'

Henry stared like a mesmerised rabbit in front of a stoat until Grant slapped the crop harder against his boot and Henry twitched. 'Yes, well...'

'And you put her in the way of a confirmed rake in the first place? Yes, I assume so. And not content with ensuring that he pays a suitable sum to your sister to raise her child decently you decide to keep it all yourself—and to ask for as much money as you think you can possibly extract. Yes?' There was another slap of whip on leather.

'Yes. But now she wants it all! She threatened me!'

'With me. Very wisely. I am trying to recall what the judicial penalty for blackmail is.' Grant rocked the heavy chair back and studied the ceiling, deep in thought. 'So few people come forward with a complaint, that is the problem. Most seem to deal with it by other methods. Direct methods.' He brought all four chair legs back to the floor with a thud and Henry cringed back in his own seat.

'You mean *murder*? Catherine said you were an honourable man!'

'And she is correct, I hope. Let me think now. The navy is always short of men. That would give you a healthy outdoor life with plenty of fresh air and exercise, and we are not at war at the moment, so there are only falls from the mainmast, shipwreck and over-amorous shipmates to worry about. Oh, and the food, of course. Or there's the East India Company—always on the lookout for men, I understand. A pity India is such an unhealthy country, but we can't have everything. I am making new acquaintances all the time these days. Men of influence in the navy and the East India Company for example.'

'You wouldn't.' Henry was pale now—in fact, Kate thought he might vomit on his shiny new desk. 'I'm a married man.'

'From what I hear Lady Harding would be quite relieved by your absence. Of course, your loving sister would support her in remaining here, make sure she had a good bailiff and not the useless one you inflict on your tenants now.'

'I'll pay! I'll find the money somehow, although I don't know how...'

'We'll work it out, never fear, Harding.' Grant stood up and nodded to Kate. 'Ready, Lady Allundale? I'll be back tomorrow, Harding. Oh, and don't try to make a run for it. I know far too much about you.'

Kate was confused, anxious and deeply relieved to have Grant there, all at the same time. The mixed emotions might be uncomfortable, but at least he now knew the truth about her. But how did he feel? There was no way of telling, not when she could not ask him, could not take his hand and look into his eyes. He was in control of himself, of Henry and of the situation, but whether he was furiously angry, disgusted or merely resigned to her betrayal she had no idea, and a chaise containing a lady's maid and a footman was not the place to find out.

She thanked Giles for his attentiveness and Wilson for her patience and then sat, hands folded in her lap, her mind utterly blank of any kind of meaningless small talk while Grant surveyed the flat farmland on either side of the road back to Southend. He had tied the hired hack on behind the carriage, so she had not even had the time to sit and think without looking at him and having that steady green gaze look straight back at her.

Perhaps this was how a prisoner in the dock felt as she watched the faces of the jurors. Guilty or not guilty? Condemned or pardoned?

Somehow she kept control of herself on the interminable drive back. Kept her chin up, her back straight, her expression composed. One did not show weakness in front of the servants. Besides, pride would not let her give way.

When they reached the Ship Inn and Grant issued orders for the hired horse's return she dismissed Wilson and Giles and climbed the stairs to the large suite of rooms she had taken. Jeannie and Anna were bright-eyed and pink-faced from a chilly walk along the beach. Charlie and Mr Gough were still out there, swathed in scarves, skimming pebbles, prodding driftwood and doing whatever men and boys did by the seaside.

'His lordship has returned with me. Please let everyone know that we are not to be disturbed until dinner time. His lordship has a great deal of business to attend to.' *Such as dealing with his deceitful wife.*

'Which is our room, my lady?' Grant had come up the stairs while she stood on the landing, steeling herself.

'Through here. I took virtually the entire floor.' He was addressing her formally and the chill of it was like the touch of a cold finger on the nape of her neck, unpleasant yet bracing. She walked in through the door he opened for her and took the chair by the window, let the light fall on her face. There was no hiding anything now.

Grant sat down facing her and leaned forward, his forearms on his knees. 'Are you all right, Kate?'

It was the last thing she expected him to say, this expression of concern for her, and it almost undid her.

'Don't cry,' he said, firmly and without reaching for her. *The prosecuting counsel*...

'I am not and I will not.' Easier to promise than to keep, she suspected. 'You seem to know a great deal, but I expect you would like me to tell you myself why I have lied to you.'

Grant moved, an involuntary gesture that she read as acknowledgment of her betrayal. So be it. 'Henry likes to gamble and he met Jonathan in some hell or another and invited him to stay. I think he had made up a plan on the spur of the moment when he realised that Baybrook needed to escape his creditors and get out of London for a while before news of his debts reached Lord Harlington, his future father-in-law. I did wonder whether it was some deep-laid plot or whether Henry simply had a flash of inspiration, but it was probably the latter. He brought him home, made much of him, invited all his cronies round for card play, let him shoot our coverts. And did nothing when Jonathan began to flirt with me. I thought Jonathan was serious, that Henry's unconcern meant approval. I was inexperienced, lonely—ripe for the plucking, I suppose.

'I told myself I was in love, that he was an honourable man who intended marriage. I was not the first naive girl to fall for it and I will not be the last. When Jonathan had gone, his pockets lined with enough winnings from the local squirearchy to keep his tailors happy, I realised he had made me no promises, not even to write. And then I found I was expecting and Jane told Henry and he went off to London.'

'To tell Baybrook he must marry you.' Grant leaned back in his chair and steepled his fingers. *The judge listening to the evidence, weighing it up...*

'That's what he told me, but I realise now he knew perfectly well that Jonathan was in no position to do that. He was contracted to the daughter of a powerful and wealthy man and he could not afford to risk that alliance. Henry told me about it when he got home. *He'll pay,* he promised. And like an idiot I asked if that meant there would be enough for me to have a little cottage somewhere, raise the child in modest respectability. He laughed and said that we did not need money for that, he would find a home for the baby easily enough. And then he explained it all, how he could extort money from Baybrook for years, how he needed to get me out of the way so Jonathan could not find me, how a foundlings' home would take my baby.'

'I think I would like to see your brother through the sights of a duelling pistol on the nearest common at dawn,' Grant remarked. 'What did you do then?'

'I did as I was told and I went up to the lodge in Scotland.' Now they were coming to it. The story so far had been one of her own foolish innocence in allowing Jonathan to seduce her. But what followed was not innocent. 'I should have written to Jonathan, told him that I was not in league with Henry, promised him I would support a statement to a magistrate. But I didn't. I allowed myself to be used. And then it was too late, I was on my way north and all I could think about was how to get away, how to keep my baby.'

'You left it very late.' Grant's voice was dispassionate. She found she could not look at him, so she watched Charlie running along the road towards the inn, laughing and calling back to Mr Gough. *My son. I could lose him, too.*

'I wasn't well at first, and then I had no money. It took me a long time to get it together, stealing the odd shilling from the housekeeper's purse over weeks so no one would notice and suspect. They were all paid by Henry. I had nothing to offer them to win their loyalty.' Charlie had vanished, but she could hear his voice faintly from the hallway below, happy, laughing. She shrugged. 'You know the rest.'

'Why did you tell me that Anna's father was dead?'

'At first, just instinct to hide, to cover up. That was why I told you I came from Suffolk and didn't tell you about Henry's baronetcy. And then, later, you were so protective, so possessive. I was afraid you would confront Baybrook, call him out. If I told you about the blackmail, then that made you an accessory after the fact, didn't it? So you would have no option but to expose Henry, and I know he deserves it, but it could have ruined Jonathan if his father-in-law found out and cut him off financially.'

'You have a high opinion of my sense of honour and of how law-abiding I am,' Grant said drily. 'It did not occur to you to tell me this whole story and let me set it right?'

'Of course not. I had deceived you, allowed you to marry me, save Anna and myself, embroiled you in this. How could I turn around and dump the whole mess at your feet?'

'It was why you were so reluctant to come to London, I suppose. Kate—' He broke off. His lower lip caught between his teeth, then, as though he was making himself ask, he said, 'Did you meet Baybrook in Green Park by appointment?'

'No! When you told me how you felt about me, saw for myself that you were happy in our marriage, saw how much you trusted me, I knew I had to stop pretending everything was all right. I went looking for Jonathan to find out exactly what Henry had been demanding, promised him I would put it right somehow. I saw him in the park that day and followed him.'

'Anna has his eyes, that unusual clear green with gold flecks.'

'She got that from him?' Kate shook her head, bemused by the detail. 'I can't remember what colour his eyes are. Anyway, I knew I had to go to Henry, make him stop, get the money and pay it back.'

'All two thousand five hundred and twenty pounds,' Grant said.

'How did you know it was that much?'

'I arrived outside the window just as you were discussing it, demanding that he give it to you.'

Kate thought back on what she had said, when she had said it, when Grant had walked in the door. So that was how he knew so much. 'You must think I am as bad as he was, that I wanted the money for myself?'

Chapter Twenty-Three

'I had a bad moment.' Grant held up his hand and she saw the raw graze across his knuckles. 'I hit the wall, which was foolish. But you are my wife, Kate. I owe you my loyalty. I owe you my trust.'

He meant it, she could tell. For a moment the happiness bubbled up, almost painful in its intensity. Then she realised that he was making himself trust by an effort of will, against the evidence. The happiness wavered and went out like a candle flame in the wind.

He has to trust me because he is loyal to me. Not because he knows I wouldn't do such a thing, not because he loves me. Grant is honourable and Madeleine rejected him and Charlie. Now he has the courage to risk his heart and his happiness all over again on a woman who has been deceiving him since the moment we met. What if I let him down, slip up, fail to have the nerve to always be truthful?

Grant needed to believe in her, she realised. He needed that faith that she would be true to him.

I am on a shaky pedestal where I have no right to be.

'Thank you.' She could feel the pedestal rock beneath her feet as she groped for balance, the right words. 'I was optimistic in thinking Henry would actually give me the money, but I had to try. I would have given it all back to Jonathan somehow.'

'Will you let me deal with this if I promise not to call Baybrook out? I will repay him, assure him of our silence, of the end of Henry's extortion, provided he forgets he ever met you.' When she opened her mouth to protest he smiled thinly. 'And Henry can repay me.'

'It may take some time.' It seemed she could breathe again. Grant believed her.

'I will put some of my own people in. That will sort him out. He may come to think longingly of a nice sea voyage to India after all, by the time I have finished with him.'

'I am glad you are on my side and not against me,' Kate ventured, daring a feeble joke. Grant's smile was still tight. 'I should not speak lightly. And I should not expect you to deal with Baybrook. It was my fault. I will—'

'You will do no such thing.' With the suddenness of a pistol firing Grant lost his temper. He was on his feet, his fist thudding into the wall, his voice a barely contained shout. Kate stared horrified at the smear of blood from his unhealed knuckles, the mark of violence across the neatly papered wall. Grant never lost his temper, never shouted. He swung round, towering over her. 'I deal with threats to my family, my wife, my daughter. Is that clear?'

Kate nodded, unable to drag her gaze from his face. 'I am so sorry.'

He swore, crudely, harshly. 'And don't apologise!' It was a shout now. Grant slammed away across the room, turned and glared at her from ten feet away, six feet of infuriated male pride and muscle. 'Your brother, who should protect you with his life, uses you, an innocent, to bait a honey trap, makes you party to a criminal act, puts you in fear for your child. You could have died in that hovel. You probably would have done if I had not come past by the merest chance. You have the guts to fight for your daughter, take risks for her. You have given my son the mother he deserves, made my house a home, driven away my demons.'

Grant lifted his hands, scrubbed them across his face. 'Don't you dare apologise to me, Kate.' He stared at her as though he had forgotten who she was, what they were doing there. Stared as if he was having a revelation and not a very happy one at that. Then he moved. Ten long strides took him past her to the door. 'Get back to London first thing tomorrow, let me sort this out. I don't know when I will be back.'

He stopped, turned on the threshold and came back to her, pulled her into his arms and took her mouth. The kiss was hard, possessive, almost punitive. Through her confusion she could taste his anger and his desire and, beneath it all, a sort of desperation.

And then he was gone, booted heels clattering down the steps.

'Lady Allundale?'

Kate blinked and the room came back into focus. Mr Gough was standing in the doorway, regarding her warily. 'Yes?'

'His lordship has…er…left?'

'Yes,' she repeated and somehow managed to think of something other than Grant's mouth on hers, kissing with the sort of desperation a condemned man might use if he were to be hanged the next day. 'We are going back to London tomorrow morning, first thing. Please can you arrange that, Mr Gough?'

'Certainly, Lady Allundale.'

'Was that Papa? I didn't know he was coming here. I heard him shouting.' Charlie appeared from his bed-chamber door, a clean shirt half on. 'Papa never shouts like that.'

'He has had a very trying day, dear.' *Possibly almost as trying as I have had.* Kate forced back the hysterical laughter that was threatening. 'We will be going back to Grosvenor Street tomorrow, first thing.'

'Oh, good.' Charlie's anxious expression turned to a broad grin. 'It is interesting here. I like the sea. But it's not long until Christmas and we've got to get ready.'

'Yes, of course.' Kate hoped she looked less fraught than she felt. Christmas had completely slipped her mind. There was the anniversary of the old earl's death to deal with and the challenge of creating a perfect new set of Christmas memories for Charlie and presents to buy and... *And a husband who I thought I understood and now...*

'Run along and finish getting changed, Charlie. And try not to bother Mr Gough. He has lots of things to do.'

She went back and sank down into the chair, considered indulging in hysterics and concluded, rather wildly, that they would have to wait. 'Wilson!'

'Yes, my lady?' The maid had a pile of folded underwear in her hands. Gough must have lost no time in telling her the news.

'What is the date?'

'The fifteenth, my lady.'

The old earl had died on Christmas Eve. They would travel back to London tomorrow and she must decide the best way to handle the anniversary for Charlie. Then there was Christmas to prepare for, which was also Anna's birthday. When would Grant be back—and in what mood? No, this was definitely no time to have the vapours. Kate blew her nose briskly and found some paper and a pen. Lists were what she needed now. *And my husband.*

The clock struck midnight as Kate reached for the last sheet of paper and began to wrap up the pretty dress length and ribbons she had bought for Jeannie. All the presents had been bought in exhausting expeditions around the shops in the days after they got back from Southend.

All that was left was to worry about Grant. The note had arrived this morning from, of all places, Newport Pagnell. What he was doing there she could not imagine, nor could she gauge his mood, for it had simply read:

I will be there on the twenty-fourth. G.

Something had been written beneath that scrawled initial, then crossed out. She had squinted at it, held it up to the light, to a candle flame, and all she could make out was a small circle. Or perhaps a heart.

Now it was Christmas Eve. She had not dared hope, had hardly dared think about Grant and instead had plunged into planning, shopping and endless decision-making. The staff were not used to the family spending Christmas in London and seemed incapable of making the slightest decision without her. So footmen had been dispatched to enquire when evergreens would be available in Shepherd's Market, Cook had been given guidance on two weeks' worth of menus, decisions had been made on when the staff would have their Christmas meal, which carriages would be required for what church services and when a holly wreath should be hung on the front door.

Now Kate just wanted to sleep and not be plagued by dreams about Grant vanishing into the mist. She gathered up the scissors and ribbon, brushed paper scraps off the bed and took off her robe. As she reached for the snuffer, there was a noise from Grant's bedchamber, then another. Muffled, cautious sounds. Sounds of someone who did not want to be heard.

When she snuffed the candle a thin line of light showed beneath his door. He was home.

Kate reached for the wisp of negligee that lay at the end of the bed, then, with a shake of her head, fetched the old flannel wrapper. This was no time for seduction. Either this marriage would hold because of what was in their hearts and in their minds, or it would not.

She made no effort to be quiet as she opened the connecting door. Grant was sitting on the side of the bed in the position she knew meant that he was contemplating pulling off his boots and was really too tired to bother, or to ring for Griffin. He looked up as she entered and she stopped, thinking wryly that when she had been rejecting thoughts of seduction she had not counted on the physical effect that her husband had on her. He looked saddle-weary, travel-stained and beyond tired. And he also looked magnificently male, strong and determined.

'I am so glad you are home,' she said simply. 'Let me.' And as she had once done before, when she had first come to Abbeywell, she straddled first one leg, then the other, and pulled off his boots.

'Thank you.' He waited until she turned and then reached out, put one hand on either side of her waist and drew her in to stand between his spread thighs. 'I went to see Charlie first, woke him up. I wanted him to know I kept my promise to be back.' He looked up at her, serious, watchful.

'Of course.' She resisted the urge to smooth his wind-tangled hair. Goodness knew what had happened to his hat. 'Has he gone back to sleep or did he tell you the plans for tomorrow?'

'He told me and went back to sleep. I had to promise to inspect all the decorations, right down to the very miniature yule log in the drawing room. You've done a magnificent job between the pair of you.' He put his head slightly to one side as he studied her face. 'Don't you want to know where I've been?'

'I don't care, so long as you are back here.' It was the truth. She trusted him to deal fairly with Henry and she knew he had not called Baybrook out. He would not risk killing Anna's father. She gave in to the urge then and lifted her hands to cup his face. 'I missed you.'

'I lost my temper back there in the inn.'

'I noticed.' Was that the faintest curve of his lips? 'You lose it so rarely that it is most impressive when you do.'

'I swore.' *Yes, that is most definitely the beginning of a smile.*

'But not at me.' He had her tight against him now and the old flannel wrapper seemed to be having no effect on his body's responses.

'No. At me.' The ghost of the smile flickered and was gone. 'Kate, you have a very short-sighted husband who could not see what was under his nose, nor read what his heart was telling him.'

It was suddenly very hard to breathe, let alone speak, so she leaned forward and kissed him lightly on the lips until the gentle returning pressure gave her courage. 'You can read it now?'

'Yes. And I love you, Kate. I think I have loved you for a long time and had no idea what it was. I should have realised in that moment in the receiving line at the Larminster reception that what I was feeling was something far more than happiness.' His voice was harsh, but the green eyes locked with hers were tender and vulnerable and full of promises. 'I puzzled over why I trusted you despite your deceptions, despite what I heard with my own ears, and then it hit me in the Ship Inn. And I had been cold and grudging. I made you tell me your secrets as though I was forcing a confession out of you, when I should have taken you in my arms and held you and protected you and trusted you without reservation, without you having to explain a thing.'

'Oh, my love. You aren't a saint.' She tugged at his arms and he came to his feet, held her by the shoulders as he stared down into her face. 'We could both have trusted more, risked more—if we were perfect, but we aren't. We are human and we had both learned the pain of love betrayed.'

'You called me... Kate, you can't...' How could the fact that this strong, articulate man was having trouble getting a simple question out make her so happy?

'I can. And I do. I love you, Grant. I have loved you for months and I did not dare tell you.'

'Did not dare?'

'You would have been kind to me, wouldn't you? You would have felt sorry for me. I could live with loving you without hope of that being returned, but I could not bear your pity.'

'Oh, Kate. That must be the only thing you would not

dare.' Grant pulled her in close so that she was against the hard strength of him, safe and surrounded by love. By impossible, wonderful love. It didn't matter that Grant smelt of leather and sweat and horse. It simply made this moment more real, more certain that it was not a dream. 'I love you so very much.'

'Come to bed,' she said into the crumpled folds of his neckcloth. 'Show me.'

'I'm filthy,' he protested half-heartedly, his fingers already on the buttons of his waistcoat.

'Most of it is your clothes.' Her fingers were as urgent, pushing the coat back from his shoulders, tearing a ribbon on her old robe as she threw it aside. 'I don't care. I just want you. Now, always.'

There was no finesse left in either of them. They fell on to the bed in a tangle of limbs, of kisses, of desperate fingers, all impeded by Grant's breeches, which he kicked off with a final heave before he rolled Kate over, covered her with his body and slid into her in one movement.

Then he stilled, propped on his elbows, his hips cradled by her thighs, his forehead resting against her brow. 'Home. Home at last.'

His heart thudded over hers, his breathing was ragged, his fingers, always so sure, so controlled, shook as they sifted through her hair. The lack of control touched her as no skilled caresses could ever have done and she tipped her head to capture his lips, curled her legs around the slim hips and rocked him deeper.

It became a blur, a mixture of passion and love, of relief and joy and urgent need. Kate knew she was talking, broken phrases, words, his name. 'I love you. I love you. Grant...'

He stretched up above her on his hands, tightening

the junction between their bodies so she could no longer tell where his pleasure ended and hers began. She looked up and saw he was watching her, even as he lost control and let the wave crash over him. 'I love you. Kate. Now. Always. *Kate*.'

Chapter Twenty-Four

They went to church in the morning with Charlie and sat and thought about the old earl and then came home and spent the day talking about him. Grant told them tales about his own childhood and had Charlie alternately gasping and giggling about the tricks he used to play and the trouble he would get into.

'Truly? You let all the hounds into the house while Great-Grandmama was having the Ladies' Church Social and they ate all the cakes and peed on the Chinese rug? And you climbed all the way to the top of the great oak on the front lawn?'

Kate rolled her eyes at Grant, who grinned and shrugged. 'And fell out and broke my arm and spent a month learning to write left-handed so I could do all the lines my tutor set me as punishment.'

'Tell me again about Great-Grandpapa and the bishop and the bull at the church fête.'

Kate curled up in her armchair and indulged herself by watching Grant, relaxed and happy, sprawled on the hearthrug with his son. The day that could have been so sad, the anniversary of a loss where they could not be together, was turning into a happy time and, she suspected, the beginning of a family tradition. She and Charlie had planned it together, both of them, she was certain, convinced that this time Grant would be home in time.

After luncheon Charlie announced that he was going to write down the stories in case he forgot any. 'And I'll add my stories, too,' he added, marching off to the desk by the window.

Grant put his arm around Kate and pulled her down beside him on the sofa at the other end of the room. 'I must tell you where I have been these past days.'

'I confess I am consumed with curiosity about Newport Pagnell.' She curled into the crook of his arm and played with the curling ends of hair around his ears. It was bliss to be able to touch Grant without wariness, without being afraid that her gestures would be read, quite correctly, as signs of love.

'I took your sister-in-law there. When I left you I went back to Belchamps Hall, riding a positive tidal wave of anger with your brother. She overheard our discussion and delivered a bombshell to dear Henry by announcing that if he was paying off his debt to Baybrook, he could pay her an allowance and she was going to live with her sister.'

'So Henry is going to repay the money? I would have thought that was like wringing blood out of a stone.'

'Apparently I look forbidding enough for him to believe my threats about the navy or India. One of the brightest clerks in my banker's office is going down there to do a complete audit and Henry's about to acquire a new bailiff in the form of Grimswade's nephew, who is as tough as his uncle and has been cutting his teeth as my farm manager.'

'You are brilliant, Grant.' She kissed his ear.

He broke off in an attempt to capture her lips. 'Temptress.'

'Grant! Not in front of the children.'

'Anna's fast asleep and Charlie's lost in composition. Oh, very well, I'll behave, but that gown is devilishly provoking.' When she escaped to the other end of the sofa he growled, but carried on with his story. 'I made arrangements with Henry, sent off all the necessary letters, conveyed Lady Harding, bag and baggage, to Newport Pagnell and got back to town late yesterday afternoon. Then I tracked Baybrook down—'

'You didn't hit him or call him out or anything dreadful?'

'No. I managed to convince him that I intended to give him money, not demand it, and we ended up having a very civilised dinner at his club. He's not the scoundrel I thought him to be. Or perhaps I should say that he isn't now. He seems to be genuinely fond of his little heiress and he doesn't want to hurt her, at least as much as he doesn't want her father finding out about his sins. He's more than grateful about the return of the money and he accepts that it was not your doing.' He looked at her quizzically. 'What is it?'

'Men are so strange. You were breathing fire and brimstone, you were ready to call him out just for insulting me in the park and now there you are dining with him.'

Grant shrugged. 'He gave us Anna, didn't he?'

'Yes, so he did. And Madeleine gave us Charlie.'

He pulled her close again and they sat in silence,

watching the children as the winter daylight ebbed into darkness and the candlelight glowed off holly berries and swags of evergreens and the fire burned bright in the grate.

Kate had thought of the same night one year before as she'd carried Anna up to her cot and Grant and Charlie went to change for the grown-up dinner they had promised the boy so that he could make the toast to his great-grandfather's memory. A year ago she had been cold, desperate and in pain with no hope for the future, only a desperate will to make it through somehow.

I wonder if I can be any happier than this? she thought, watching Grant bend to kiss Anna goodnight. *Perhaps, when I tell Grant the final secret I am keeping.*

Christmas morning dawned bright and, to Charlie's huge delight, snowy. 'May we make a snowman?' he asked at breakfast. 'There's all that snow in the back garden. Or...' His eyes grew wide. 'The park! We could build dozens of snowmen, an army of snowmen!'

'This afternoon,' Grant promised. 'Presents first. Anna's birthday, then the staff, then our Christmas presents.'

Anna was predictably more enchanted by the silver paper, the flicker of candlelight and the trailing scarlet ribbons than she was by her presents, but, as Kate pointed out to Grant, he was going to get far more fun out of her presents than she was.

'I know. I want to spoil her, to make up for that first birthday, that first Christmas,' he said, smiling at the dolls, the pretty dresses, the stuffed rabbit and the little horse on wheels.

'You gave her that first Christmas,' Kate whispered

in his ear and then found she had to blow her nose very inelegantly.

They lit the yule log together, played with Anna, listened to the sounds of fiddle music, singing and laughter wafting up from below stairs. It seemed the staff were having a good time getting ready for their Christmas meal. Charlie, bursting with pride, led Kate and Grant, with Anna fast asleep in Grant's arms, downstairs to deliver the family's Christmas good wishes and thanks for all their hard work during the year.

'He is growing up so fast,' Kate whispered as Cook gathered Charlie to her capacious bosom and gave him a hug that turned his ears scarlet. Then they trooped back upstairs, collecting Mr Gough as they went, and shared out Christmas presents.

My family, Kate thought as she watched them, the love filling her heart as softly as the snowflakes swirling down outside the window. Charlie was thrilled with a new saddle and a pair of ice skates. Grant peacocked around the room in the heavy silk robe Kate had found for him and winked at her to show he knew exactly how she imagined him wearing it, with nothing underneath. The tutor was delighted with a subscription to a circulating library and Charlie presented his parents with two pairs of handsome, and only slightly lopsided, bookends that, he confided, he had made with the assistance of the estate carpenter.

Kate was trying not to crane her neck and see if there was anything left in the litter of paper for her when Grant announced, 'We are going out for a walk.'

'We are?' Kate almost protested that it was too cold, too snowy, and that she wanted to spend as much time as possible with Anna on her first birthday. But there was something about Grant's expression that was both serious and yet happy. He had a surprise for her and she was not going to spoil it for him.

'Yes, and I have a new bonnet for you to wear.' He lifted a hatbox, white with bright red ribbons, from beside his chair.

Kate took the box and opened it. The bonnet nestled in tissue paper, a confection of white velvet with a wide brim to frame her face and a delicate pale blue gauze veil with deeper blue silk ribbons, the colour of her eyes. 'Grant, it is lovely. It is almost—' *Bridal.*

'You did not have anything pretty a year ago,' he said. 'Shall we go out now? We'll be back in time to build a small snowman, Charlie.'

Kate took Grant's arm and allowed herself to be led through the snowy streets, along narrow ways she had not known existed, up to the door of one of the little chapels of ease that had been built to serve the expanding neighbourhood north of Oxford Street. It was not one they had ever used and, when they entered, it was obvious from its plain furnishings and lack of memorials that it was not a fashionable church.

Grant had been carrying something in a straw basket, the kind that a goose would be brought home from market in, and Kate had been vastly curious to see what it held. He set it down on the porch and took out a posy. Trailing ivy, the red of holly berries, the pearl glow of mistletoe, crimson ribbons.

'It was rather a plain wedding, was it not?' Grant said and handed her the bouquet. 'One sprig of holly, if I remember rightly. I think we should do it again, don't you?'

'It made me very happy, that first ceremony,' Kate said, wondering how it was possible to want to cry, even as she smiled. 'But I would like very much to marry the man I love, all over again.'

'Shall we?' He crooked his arm for her and together they walked down the aisle. She saw a clergyman waiting in a side chapel, two chairs set before him.

'Welcome.' He came forward, shook hands, ushered them to the seats. 'I have never blessed a marriage on Christmas morning before,' he confessed. 'Weddings, yes. So many working people take advantage of the holiday. But this is rather special, is it not?'

So special. 'Grant, thank you,' she whispered and did not realise she was crying until he took off his gloves and gently wiped away the tears with his thumb. He was giving her the one thing their marriage lacked, the one thing she had not thought important until that moment—a romantic wedding day.

The clergyman handed them a battered prayer book to share. 'I thought we would read it through,' he said. 'And then I will do the blessing.'

They sat, following the familiar words read in the old man's steady, gentle voice. Grant slipped the ring he had given her from her finger and then, as he made his vows, slid it gently back.

'With this ring I thee wed, with my body I thee worship...'

Kate knew she was crying again, happy tears that slid down her cheeks and moistened her smiling lips and, when they rose from their knees, made their kiss salty and sweet.

She thanked the clergyman with Grant, linked her arm through his again and went out into the brilliant sunshine of the snowy noonday. 'That was the most perfect Christmas gift, thank you.' He simply squeezed her hand against his side, but she could tell from his face that he had been deeply moved by the little ceremony. 'When you came, that Christmas Eve, I thought you were my Christmas miracle. And now we have another, our love.'

'We have two very different Christmases we will never forget.' Grant's voice was husky. Neither of them spoke for a while as they crunched through the snow.

'I have a gift for you that might make this one even more memorable,' Kate confessed as they came into Berkeley Square. 'I did think I ought to wait another few weeks, just to be certain, but I can't bear to keep the secret.'

'Oh, my love.' Grant stopped dead, right outside Gunter's tea shop. 'I did wonder whether you were simply blooming because you were happy or whether there was another reason.'

'Both,' Kate said. 'I'm in love, I'm blissfully happy and I think we are going to be a family of five for next Christmas!'

* * * * *

MILLS & BOON®

Why shop at millsandboon.co.uk?

Each year, thousands of romance readers find their perfect read at millsandboon.co.uk. That's because we're passionate about bringing you the very best romantic fiction. Here are some of the advantages of shopping at www.millsandboon.co.uk:

* **Get new books first**—you'll be able to buy your favourite books one month before they hit the shops

* **Get exclusive discounts**—you'll also be able to buy our specially created monthly collections, with up to 50% off the RRP

* **Find your favourite authors**—latest news, interviews and new releases for all your favourite authors and series on our website, plus ideas for what to try next

* **Join in**—once you've bought your favourite books, don't forget to register with us to rate, review and join in the discussions

Visit **www.millsandboon.co.uk**
for all this and more today!